Kooper

Hounds of the Reaper MC

S.J. Rowe

S.J. Rowe

Copyright © 2025 S.J. Rowe

All rights reserved. This book or any portion thereof may not be reproduced or used in any manner whatsoever without the publisher's express written permission except for the use of brief quotations in a book review.

Cover Design: Frauke Spanuth
Editor: Hot Tree Editing

First printing: November 2025

www.sjrowe.com

This is a work of fiction. All characters, names, events, incidents, and places are of the author's imagination and not to be confused with fact. Any resemblance to living persons or events is merely a coincidence.

Kooper

For anyone who needed a little more time to fall in love. Sometimes it's instant. Other times it takes a little arguing, good food, and a few very naughty thoughts.

To Rodeo, for still loving me after all the crazy I put you through.

And as always: Cin-Cin-ohh-La-La!

Hounds and Their Old Ladies 9
Chapter 1—Kooper 10
Chapter 2—Ruby 20
Chapter 3—Kooper 30
Chapter 4—Ruby 41
Chapter 5—Kooper 52
Chapter 6—Ruby 62
Chapter 7—Kooper 74
Chapter 8—Ruby 85
Chapter 9—Kooper 96
Chapter 10—Ruby 108
Chapter 11—Kooper 120
Chapter 12—Ruby 131
Chapter 13—Kooper 141
Chapter 14—Ruby 151
Chapter 15—Kooper 163
Chapter 16—Ruby 174
Chapter 17—Kooper 186
Chapter 18—Ruby 198
Chapter 20—Ruby 221
Chapter 21—Kooper 231
Chapter 22—Ruby 241
Chapter 23—Kooper 252

Chapter 24—Ruby 262
Chapter 25—Kooper 272
Chapter 26—Ruby 284
Chapter 27—Kooper 293
Chapter 28—Ruby 303
Chapter 29—Kooper 313
Chapter 30—Ruby 325
Chapter 31—Kooper 334
Chapter 32—Ruby 343
Chapter 33—Kooper 351
Chapter 34—Ruby 361
Chapter 35—Kooper 370
Chapter 36—Ruby 382
Chapter 37—Kooper 392
Chapter 39—Ruby 412
Chapter 40—Kooper 422
Chapter 41—Ruby 431
Chapter 42—Kooper 441
Chapter 43—Ruby 449
Chapter 44—Natalie 458
Chapter 45—Psy 464
Get a Free Book 466
Thanks for Reading 467

Also by S.J. Rowe 468
About the Author...469
Connect with the Author 470
Chapter 1 - Maddy 472

RUBY—

I'm the club princess. I'm Daddy's little girl. I'm not scared of anything. Or I wasn't. I used to be those things. Now I'm just here. Waiting. Not sure for what or who, but I don't even care enough to go find whatever it is I'm supposed to be looking for. My dad was my whole life, till he wasn't. And now that he's awake, it's worse than when he was dead. Who am I if I don't even know myself?

KOOPER—

I see her. I didn't want to at first. She was a job. A means to get something I wanted. But things change, as they often do. I expected aspects of this. I understood there were risks involved when I took the job and signed up for this. But the reward outweighs it all. Till the goal line wasn't what I wanted anymore. Till I realized that not only did the rules change, but I did too.

I told her dad I would protect her. And I have. She's still breathing, even if she's just a shell of herself. I should be okay with that. I *was* okay with it. But that was before. Before she got under my skin and showed me what waking up with her in my arms could be like. What fighting with her can do to my heart compared to the silence of her never talking to me. She might not like it. I don't think *I* like it. But one thing is clear: Ruby is my girl, and I'll make her see that even if she comes at me kicking and screaming.

TRIGGER WARNING:

This book contains swearing and scenes that some readers may find uncomfortable, to include the mention of rape, physical and emotional violence, and abuse. If you have any issues regarding this book, please reach out to the author using one of the links on the Connect with the Author page.

Hounds and Their Old Ladies

- Law (Karter) and Special K (Katrina)
- Chains (James) and Mama Bear (Maddy)
- Bulldog (Jax) and Lady (Izzy)
- Flint (Tyler) and Kitten (Jules)
- Mad Max (Max) and Fairy (Cheyanne)
- Gator (Reese) and Troublemaker (Bailey)
- Bass (Logan) and Brooklyn (Milly)
- Casper (Ford) and Billy (Krista)
- Domino (John) and Menace (Viv)

Chapter 1—Kooper

"What a *fucking* night," I mumble as I push open the clubhouse door. I'm loud enough for a few brothers to agree with a grunt as they head to the bar and I go to the pool tables, picking up where I left off.

A few hours ago, we were all bullshitting over cards and complaining about losing to Flint. Fucker has always been good at cards. I half suspect he counts them, but whatever. I only ever stay for a few hands, and then I'm at the pool tables. I was here playing a round with Domino when Flint rang the alarm that Chains' woman and kids were under attack. Then shit really went south when we learned a few things, mostly about her, and got a ton of questions as to why the Devils Damned are after her.

That woman has to have balls of steel to have lived in hiding under her house most of her life and still seem normal. Not sure I or any brother would have turned out right in the head after who knows what she went through.

"Want me to rack them?" Flint calls as he meets me at the tables, and I nod. Ten seconds later, a prospect gives me a beer, and all is right in the world. Chains has a mess to deal with, and as a Hound brother, I'll deal with it when he asks me to. But till then, I've got no place to be but here drinking and shooting the shit. We all know shit is about to go down. You don't get a few dead Devils Damned and not have more crap to come, but right now ain't that time. So I do what all Hounds do—live my life till I've got to defend it. And right now, life is fucking grand.

Till it ain't.

I'm not pissed about Chains' old lady waking up from whatever General gave her to sleep it off. Don't even care that she's yelling and throwing a fit about needing to see the kids. A yelling woman ain't new in this place. Usually a vamp or some wannabe girlfriend is making a ruckus that most of us tune out.

What drives a nail into my good mood is when I see a certain pain in the ass sneak behind the bar. One who's shit at hiding, since Bulldog also sees and calls her out, skimpy outfit and all. I might find her annoying, but that doesn't mean I'm blind. No makeup, but she can still pull the eye. She's young, maybe younger than some of the girls who hang around here. But her eyes? If you look closely enough, you can tell she's seen some shit and knows more than those twice her age. She's wearing close to a vamp-style outfit, even if she thinks it's suitable pajamas for the night. If she were anyone but the boss's kid, she'd be kicked out right about now.

Now *she's* the one making a scene. I swear to Christ, we can't have one normal night without someone bitching, and usually it comes from the fairer sex.

"Might learn a few things while you're down there," I chirp when she complains about the floor being sticky. I don't know why I spoke up, but I've got no reason to shy away from her. She's an annoying brat who always gets her way and needs to start learning things.

"Fuck off, Kooper. I ain't about to get on my knees to blow your fucking ugly ass."

I roll my eyes at her stupid comment. It's so not happening.

"Never fucking wanted you to. Just thought you could learn how to clean up after yourself for once instead of getting us to do it." I turn my back on her and go back to the game.

Ruby ain't my problem, just a nuisance I don't understand. I get families being in the club, even if I've got none of my own here. And sure, she's the president's only kid and the only thing he has left to live for. But still. Ruby's in college. She needs to stop hanging around the clubhouse and running to Daddy anytime she needs something. She has to grow the fuck up like the rest of us.

"Why do you always got to put her down like that?" Flint asks with a slight eyebrow raise sent my way over the pool table.

I ignore the look as I line up my next shot. "Girl's got to learn one of these days that she can't just expect her dad, or any of us, to pick up after her." I sink the two ball and walk around to take another shot, glancing up at him briefly before I look back at the table. "Maybe she ain't the only one who needs reminding."

Flint shakes his head. "Ruby's special."

His words make me miss my shot wide, and he snorts at the look of shock on my face, I'm sure.

"Not like that," he says. "She's Law's daughter. The president's daughter is always treated like glass, no matter what club you're with."

Now it's my turn to snort. "Glass ain't even a word that should be used within a ten-mile radius of describing

Kooper

that one. I'll give you that she gets special treatment, but at the end of the day, she's still outside the club. Women come and go. Even if she becomes someone's old lady one day, she's going to need to be a bit tougher at taking care of her own shit. I feel sorry for whoever claims her ass. He'll either have balls of steel, or she'll have them around her neck."

"I think the saying is 'She'll carry them in her purse.'" Flint aims for his shot, and I shrug as I grab my beer and take a swig.

"Never seen Ruby carry a purse. And if she had a man, she'd take his balls, stab them with a needle, and just wear them around her neck to show not only him but God and country as well who he belongs to."

"Kooper." My name is bellowed across the bar, and I look toward the voice, but I already know who it is. Only one man can get away with yelling at me like a child and not get a fist to the face.

"What did you do now?" Flint asks as he eyes the president, who's waiting for me to come over.

"No clue," I sigh as I set the pool cue down, grab my beer, and head toward the boss. Some might think his bark is worse than his bite since he's got a look that some say is the silver fox incarnate. At least that's how the vamps around here describe him. They're always trying to get on his dick, but the guy has zero time for club pussy. He had an old lady once and never wanted a replacement.

I knew of Special K, but other than knowing a name, it never went beyond that. From the way the boys who were close to her talk about her, she seems like one helluva woman. If I had that as my old lady, I wouldn't want to taint any memory with a girl half the damn club's been with either.

"You need something?" I look right into his dark almond eyes, giving him the respect he's earned. Not just from his position in the club; being the president doesn't come with instant approval from everyone. It's earned. Good bosses know how to get everyone on board. Even if they disagree with a situation, they trust the man making it. Like we all do with Law.

"My office." He leaves the *"now"* part out as he turns and heads up the stairs, knowing I'll follow.

I don't drag it out. When he crosses into his office, I'm shutting the door the moment he takes his seat, and then I take the one across from him in front of his desk.

"What did you want to see me about?"

"It's about Ruby."

I don't even hide my sigh or my eye roll. "She complaining or some shit because I spoke the truth down there?"

He shakes his head. "Ain't about that, but I'm not keen on how you talk to her, even if she needs someone to call her on her bull most days."

I'm a bit taken aback that the prez agrees with me. But not enough to express it other than to keep listening to what he has to say.

"What happened tonight with Chains' soon-to-be woman has me thinking. Club's got enemies. Some we know; others we don't. And as the president, more than one is going to think that a club issue should be dealt against me. Got no issue with that. I took the chair knowing the risk and ain't stepping down unless it's pried out of my cold, dead hands.

Kooper

But despite that, and despite what we Hounds think, there will be a point where it could slip through my fingers."

I adjust in my seat, not liking where this conversation is going. I'm not a lifer to the club. Did some time in the military as a cop, then moved to diplomatic security for a bit. It was a Hail Mary career choice someone in Uncle Sam's pocket threw my way in hopes that I'd stick around longer. It worked for a bit, but not as long as I'm sure they'd hoped for. Guarding diplomats has you seeing a different part of life. Not only in the bodyguard world on how to keep things operational, but some of the shadier shit people do that others trust. It made me physically sick one too many times, and I hung up my badge before going out drinking one night. Which led me to a bar, and then another bar, and then I stumbled into Law, literally. A couple of hours later, and after a hell of a lot of coffee, I agreed to prospect and have been here ever since.

"Spit it out, boss. Ain't one for reading between the lines." I can do it if I have to, but why guess when you can get it directly from the horse's mouth?

"Got one weakness in this world. And it ain't a secret. If something happens to Ruby, I'm not sure which way I'd go. I can claim all I want that I'd choose the club or a brother, but I don't know, and I ain't willing to find out. I know your past. Know what you're capable of. And I want you to be permanently assigned to Ruby."

"Say what?"

"Don't need you tailing her all the time, but if she needs someone to call, I want it to be you. I want you to check her place and make the security safe. To look into guys who fuck with her, and you fuck back. It ain't the perfect plan, but I'd feel better knowing it's more than just me looking after her."

"And if I fail and she still gets nabbed or worse?"

Law lets out a deep breath. "We'll cross that bridge when we get there. All I want to know is I've got someone on the inside who sees something I might not."

"Why me?" Some might see this as a punishment, others as a promotion. I'm holding back on what I think till I get the full story.

"You ain't been around like everyone else. She's got no ties to you. No way to twist you off what I want."

At least he's smart enough to get that Ruby has a pull around here with the brothers, even if it's a little sister pull. I don't think any brother is dumb enough to want to try something with her. It's not that Law won't allow it, but I don't see anyone stupid enough to deal with her type of crazy. And she is. Crazy, that is. There's all types of crazy. Some are cuckoo in the head, and then others are like Ruby—a loose cannon that you don't know when it'll go off. And when it does, the destruction can be massive or minimal. It's all unknown till it happens.

I rub my index finger just under my lip and think through his words. I might not be the smartest man alive, but I've learned to consider multiple scenarios before ever agreeing to anything. And I only do it when I can see more than a 60 percent chance of this going in my favor.

Like how I ended up with the Hounds. They showed up when some might say I had no other choice but to join them. They'd be wrong. I always have a Plan B, C, and D when Plan A goes to shit. Joining a club was Plan L if I really think about it. But they spoke pretty words, and the more I thought on it, the more I saw possibilities I couldn't get on my own.

I was coming off diplomatic duty. Most of my connections were still tied up in red tape, and if I wanted to venture out on something alone, I would be. Sure, I had a few favors to call in to help set shit up, but other than that, it was just me. Having a club gave me more than one door to go into. The odds were overly in favor of club life then, and still are. Even if I'm not so sure about the latest door presented to me.

"What do I get out of this babysitting gig?"

He shrugs as he leans back in his chair. "What do you want?"

I lean forward and rest my clasped hands together on the desk. "The club. I protect your daughter, and I get your chair when you're ready to step down."

Silence.

To his credit, Law doesn't protest outright or shoot me. Both would be understandable reactions. But there's a reason he's the boss. Like me, he takes the time to think everything through. To weigh it all before reacting.

He keeps his face neutral, like I do. I've got no read on him other than knowing he's considering it.

"Ruby doesn't come with the chair."

I shake my head. "Never said I wanted her."

His eyes narrow at my words before they even out again. "Can't promise the club's vote."

"You can make a recommendation," I say with a tilt of my head.

He takes a deep breath. "What if I had someone else in mind?"

I don't fault him for already thinking ahead. That's what he does, sees the problem seven paces down the line. And I've got a feeling I know who he's thinking, but that doesn't mean I can't be just as good. When I became a Hound, I saw possibilities for more. More opportunities, more resources. Sure, the "power" is cool too. But if I lead the Hounds, the mother chapter, my resources would be endless. I could take this club further than what others might do. I want more than just monitoring our area. And I'm not alone in that. Not sure how this will pan out, but I've got to at least get my hat in the ring first before I start making changes.

"Who says you can't take two under your wing till the time comes? No one needs to know what you really want, just what you say when it comes to it."

"And if I don't get to make the call? If I go out before I can pass it on?"

I lean back and raise my shoulders once. "Like you said about Ruby and the possibility of her getting taken or worse. We'll cross that bridge when we get there."

"What if I say no? That I'm not interested in this trade of services or whatever you want to call it? I could kick your ass out right now. Hell, one yell to the brothers and every single one would gun you down if I wanted it."

I nod at his words and then shake my head. "Do what you've got to do. You're the one who called me in. You have your pick of the brothers. You know me, and you know them. I don't do things for shits and giggles, which you also know. You expected me to ask for something. Maybe not this, but be honest with yourself. It was on the table. Half the reason you said Ruby doesn't come with the deal is because you already thought I would ask that, and it was your line in the sand." I wait a beat and square off with him as I hold his stare. "For now. Depending on how deep this shit goes, she might also be on the table. You willing to risk that?"

One beat before he nods. "For her safety, I'd risk almost anything. Even death."

I stand and hold out my hand. "Then we have a deal."

He looks at me, then at my hand before offering his up, but not standing to match my height. When we lock hands, he pulls me down just a bit so the power dynamic is clear. I might have come up with this, but he has everything *in* this. I'm just one man. He's *the* Hound. He made this club what it is today. I can't overlook that. I respect the man too much not to.

But I've also got to think about me. And my end goal. Dad always said, "The only person looking out for you is yourself." Something I've lived by every day. Still do. Law could have told me to stuff it and fuck off. Or hell, he could have told me I was babysitting his little girl and there was nothing in it for me at all. But he didn't. And now the cards have been dealt. Who the fuck knows where they'll land once life starts dealing too.

"Keep her alive and I'll do my part to get you the chair. That's my guarantee."

Another thing my dad taught me: There are no guarantees in life.

Chapter 2—Ruby

"You free after class to do some more apartment hunting?" I ask Natalie as I take the seat next to her. We rarely have classes together, but we were both either dumb or smart and signed up for summer classes. I still say dumb because we chose more school over going to the beach. Of course, the beach is like a zillion miles away from us since we live in mid-central USA, but we could have done the drive in a day or two. Then we could have lived on the beach as tent bums for a month.

Okay, that sounds worse than summer school. Maybe smart *is* the better term.

"Yeah. I was just planning on going to the Coffee Shack to study. Probably better if we find a place to live rather than eat my weight in pastries."

I snort at that. Nat weighs less than a buck fifty on a day after binge eating. She's one of those types that has a crazy metabolism. If she were into bulking up and going into weightlifting competitions, I think it would be the only way she'd actually gain some weight. But while she has no issues eating—or not eating, depending on her mood—working out is almost against her religion. Or that's what I assume. Anytime I offer her the chance to be my running buddy, she turns me down. Her loss. I'm a fantastic workout friend. Sure, I yell the whole time that it's stupid we're doing it, sort of like school in the summer, but we get through it. And I fully

Kooper

believe that if you yell, you burn more calories than if you just silently do the workouts.

Nat got stuck with me—and I do mean stuck—in freshman year. We were both slotted to live on campus, and while my dad footed the bill to get me a nice dorm, I still had to share it. Part of the campus rules. And there were only four options available. One had no AC, two were coed, and the last was girls only. Want to guess what my dad made sure I had?

Yeah, all girls. Scary Stary is what we called Stary Hall. That much PMS in one building is never a good idea. Nat opted for the cheapest and chose the no-AC unit. We would have never met if it weren't for the dean deciding no-AC buildings were from the 1700s and shut them down. And they did it one week before school started. They've only got half a brain, in my opinion. Saw the lack of air-conditioning as wrong but couldn't figure out what to do till the last minute. So they just moved everyone into rooms that were already booked, changing occupancies from two to three. Not sure how that passed the building codes, but someone approved it.

That's how Nat and I became roommates on day one. We had another girl—I don't even remember her name—who came in, saw us, and walked out. I heard later that her parents just bought her a condo so she wouldn't have to live with "strangers." Which totally defeats the whole "get to know people" aspect of college, but whatever.

Oh, and I'm sure me saying, "Hi, bitch," when she showed up was also another point against me. Nat didn't seem to have an issue with it, but that's why she's still around and the other one isn't.

We quickly found out that we had no connection in classes, other than a few basic courses, but what we did have was the need not to pry. I had a few of the brothers drop things off, and other than a smile here and a wave there, she didn't even look at them twice. Which gave her major points in my eyes. Back in high school, I had to run off more wannabe friends than not just because they wanted to be close to one of the guys and thought I was their meal ticket to get there.

Nat has never been like that. She's quiet. Not shy, but not one to fill the space. Sometimes I feel like she's hiding parts of herself, but then again, so am I. Dad wasn't keen on my going to college so far away, but he was better knowing I was living on campus, with everything within walking distance and a no-boys-after-ten dormitory rule. Now that we're both about to be juniors, our time is up. School rules. And Dad is taking it the hardest.

Whatever. Dads are weird. Nat just gives me a smile every time I complain about it. I try not to do much of it around her. She has no one. She was in foster care till she aged out. Lucky for her, her grades were good enough that she got a full ride here from Florida. Not sure why you would want to leave the beaches for this place, but she always says it's peaceful around here.

I think she's nuts. But I still like her. Which is why I love college so much. The two of us? Never would our worlds have crossed if it weren't for college. We come from completely different backgrounds. I have a giant family, even if it's not all by blood, and she's all alone. I'm going into physical therapy, and she's undecided. Hell, we don't even dress the same.

Kooper

Her style is conservative to modest on a good day. Jeans are a key aspect of her wardrobe, plus a knitted sweater most of the time or just a plain T-shirt with some saying on it. Her most unique feature is her hair. Midnight black and down to her ass. If she were on the back of a bike, I wonder if it would get wrapped up in the exhaust or tire. Hell, it could whip around and blind the biker, and they'd end up bloody and in a ditch.

As for me? I might look like a badass biker bitch with the leather, tight clothes, and even my hair gets looks sometimes, but I'm nice-ish. Well, I'm nice when they're nice back. But I know why I get the looks and lip curls from those who don't know me. Black hair mixed with pink-and-red braids ain't a look for everyone, but I like it. And fuck you to whoever thinks they can tell me what I do and don't like.

Night and day is what we are, and about to be homeless as well. I open the school paper and take a gander through it just as the professor shuts the door. And from the stack of papers he's holding, I know today is going to be a long-ass class.

I don't even control my groan when he pulls up the PowerPoint and I see he's slotted seventy-eight slides for today's lecture. Looks like I won't be secretly checking out homes in the back row like I planned. I could slump it and take Nat's notes, but I swore I would never do that. I'm not the cheating kind. And yeah, I think taking notes from someone else in class is cheating. If you're there, your notes are on you. You ain't there? Well, you only get the notes if you're sick or for family emergencies. Having a hangover from the night before doesn't count either.

Something I was mad about a few months back when I was very tempted to break my rule. But I didn't. Despite what people think, I've got my rules. Dad instilled some, but mostly it's me. And rule number one is don't flunk out of college. One, because I'm not the repeat type of girl when I flunk a class. Don't want to do that. And two, I owe it to Mom in heaven to give it my all. She might not be here to see me graduate, but I will damn well make her proud as she watches over me. And I know she is. Who else is telling me I need to buy more shoes? She always had a closet shoe addiction. And if it's not her, that means I've got a problem, and I refuse to admit it.

"That place should come with a hazmat suit if you sign a lease with them," Nat says with a shudder, and I agree.

"I think we might have to opt for a place that comes with a kitchen. I know it's more than we want to spend, but I don't think I can take seeing another microwave and hot plate combo." We're trying to keep the rent low. Mostly for Nat's sake. Sure, I've got a number I want to stay under, too, because despite what some think, I don't enjoy taking money from Dad. He earned his money, and I want to as well. Of course, I wasn't against his philosophy that he'll cover room and board if I keep my grades up.

Nat has a job at the school library. Part of her scholarship deal—room and board stipend with a full ride if she works on campus. So far, she hasn't had any issues with it, but I know she isn't willing to up the budget. It either means I take on more of the rent or she gets another job. And

I really don't want her to do that just because I can't live with rat poop on my hot plate.

I chance a glance at her as we walk back to my car parked down the street. This place is in town and has zero parking close. Another drawback.

"At the very least, a decent parking spot." Her mumbled response has me tripping over my feet for a second, laughing in surprise.

"Exactly. So, you in? I take on more of the rent, and we look for nicer places?" No reason to beat around the bush. I want her to know that while we might not be close, that doesn't mean I don't want to be. It's easier to keep her out of the know sometimes, but I still want her around. Plus, breaking in a new friend takes too much work.

She shrugs.

"How about I buy you a coffee and we talk it over?"

She turns her head and raises a single eyebrow. "Throw in a muffin and you're on."

I grin with a nod and turn toward my car, only to groan when I see the truck that was blocking my view of it parallel parked up the street pull away, revealing a motorcycle parked right behind me.

"Shit."

"Problem?" Nat asks as she looks around.

I tip my chin toward what's about to be a headache. "Just an asshole." Sometimes keeping Nat away from the club is a problem. She doesn't know when someone is a giant jerk compared to the others.

"Ex of yours? Want me to get rid of him?"

Seriously? This girl is shyness personified till she isn't, and then something like that slips out of her mouth. Color me pink with shock when she even quickens her pace a bit and steps in front of me, either to block the guy's view of me or to protect me. Whatever it is, it ain't normal. And especially not from a girl. Women rarely do that kind of thing unless they're family. Boys? Well, men—boys don't do shit but play with their joysticks. But men step up sometimes. If one does for me, it's because something serious is going on in the club, or the guy thinks it will score him points with my dad. Usually it just pisses me off, but right now, I'm too confused by Nat's actions to do more than just walk in her shadow till we get to my car.

"What do you want, Koop?" I ask as we get close to where he's leaning against his bike.

"Who says I want anything?"

"You wouldn't be here if you didn't. So spit it out and be on your way. Don't got time to deal with your sorry ass today."

"Mouthy one, aren't you?"

I roll my eyes. "You just now getting that? Figured you were smarter than that. Been here over four years now. You should do better at learning shit. Maybe my old man is going lax in the recruiting bit. I'll be sure to tell him to get someone who can spell IQ next time."

I unlock the doors to my car and open the passenger door to let Nat in, but she doesn't budge. She doesn't look scared, just assessing everything. Just like Kooper. He's eyeing her like she's a puzzle he's about to solve. Once he's figured out whatever he wants, his attention turns back to me.

Kooper

"Your dad put me on babysitting duty."

"Seriously?" My hand holding the car door open falls to my side. Can we just stop with all the shocking shit today? I've never been off my game so much in my life. It's one thing after another.

He pulls a cigarette from his vest pocket and lights it before nodding. "Yup."

I cross my arms. "Next you going to tell me you're moving in with me and I have a curfew or some shit?"

He shakes his head as he blows out some smoke. "Nah, don't got time for all that. I'll do the job, but I don't believe in playing games. Your dad wants me to watch you, so I will. Do me a favor and don't try to avoid me and shit. You see me, you acknowledge it. You stick to the rules, and we can all get through this with minimal issues."

"And the rules are?" It's Nat who speaks. All I do is glare.

Kooper shrugs and takes another drag of his cigarette. "Shared location on her phone. Gives me a rundown on her normal routine. No sleepovers or trips without approval first."

"Seriously?" I wave my hands. "I'm not five fucking years old."

"Could have fooled me."

My mouth drops open. I've never been talked to like this before. Ever.

He stands upright before straddling his bike and starting it up. "If you could do shit on your own, you think I'd be here? Think about it. Text me when you find a place, and I'll check it out." And then the asshole drives away, and I'm left there with the door still wide open and my mouth on the fucking ground.

I slam the door and then go to my side, dropping into the driver's seat with a huff. I hit the steering wheel five times and then shake out my frustration as Nat gets into the car and watches me work through a tantrum. *Just like a five-year-old.*

I glare at my reflection in the mirror, but it doesn't do much more than stare right back at me.

"Is your dad in a gang?"

I deflate at her words and grab the steering wheel with both hands before I close my eyes and put my head against it. "It's a club. They call it a motorcycle *club*. He's the president and overprotective, but I love him." I take a deep breath and turn my head just enough to see her without moving it from resting against the fabric-covered wheel. "That going to be a problem?"

We've never talked about this before. For two years, she's seen a few brothers come and go, but we never spoke about the details.

"They going to be living with us?"

I shake my head.

She grabs the seat belt and buckles up, then looks straight ahead. "Good. Because if they did, we'd need a bigger place."

She side-eyes me and gives me a small smile. One that has me breathing steadier and sitting up straight too. I start the car and pull into traffic, heading to my favorite coffee shop near campus. I have no clue what I'd do without

Kooper

Nat. I like her. And that she can deal with the club is a win in my book.

Chapter 3—Kooper

Six months later

"Look, just take the damn sandwiches." Ruby tries to push the tray into my hands, but I don't take it.

I don't even take a step back, just keep my hands at my side. Should have known that taking gate duty was going to suck today. I woke up to a hole in my sock. Nothing good ever comes when you get holes in your footwear. It's an omen for a bad day if I ever heard of one. Some say it's nuts to think like that. Those are the same people who say, "Just put one foot in front of the other and see where the world carries you." To that, I question them on what goes out in the world first. If it's a sock with a hole and your big toe is exposed to the elements, well, that shit is liable to get frozen or cut off. That doesn't make for a good day. Might be an extreme, but so is thinking that your feet just carry you places without a thought in your mind as to where you're headed.

"Don't want them."

"They ain't for you, asshole."

Kind of seems like they are with the way she's pushing them on me.

"Then why ask me to take them?" I smirk at her and watch the red rise from under her shirt.

She growls low, and I don't even hide how big my smile is at her annoyance. "They're for the club, not you."

Kooper

I look down at my vest and then back at her. She might not like it, but I *am* club. But if she wants to be petty and exclude me, then I can be more blunt about it so she gets the point.

"Still no. Club ain't interested."

"Never known any male to turn down free food." She pops her hip as if she caught me in a lie or some shit.

"Those finger sandwiches?"

She eyes the plate in her hand that's covered with tinfoil.

"Maybe. Why?" Her eyes narrow at me.

I shrug as I cross my arms. "Bikers don't do finger sandwiches. Besides, you're coming from Mama Bear's bachelorette party. Pretty sure they're shaped like dicks—another thing bikers don't eat."

Her glare might work on some of the brothers, but I'm immune. Been doing babysitting duty for months now. We might not get along, but the job has been fairly easy so far. She's kept to the rules. Doesn't even try to push them. Either she has no life or is just better at hiding shit from me than I care to look into. Whatever. I'm doing my job. She's breathing. It's a win in my book.

"Whatever." She turns and huffs away.

"Nice chatting with you as always, Ruby," I call out to her as she goes back to her car and puts the tray in the back seat.

She doesn't even look up, just flips me off as she tosses out her words. "Eat shit, Koop."

Chuckling, I turn back to my phone as I watch her drive off out of the corner of my eye, followed by Izzy.

Princess is in the back seat, and I lift my head enough to give her a nod as she waves. Ruby might be the club's princess, but Bulldog's kid owns the name. And the attitude. Thank Christ she and Ruby aren't the same age. Those two would be more than a handful if they ever got together. They would take over the world, and not a single brother could stop them. I feel bad for any poor fucker who gets stuck with one or the other.

A while later, my phone rings, and I see it's Law calling.

"Yo," I answer. "What's up?"

"You with Ruby?"

"Nah, she left here about twenty minutes ago." I'm used to this question. Get it a lot, actually. Usually ends with me driving to wherever she is, which is why I'm making my way to my bike as I talk. Her dad might have put me on babysitting duty, but that doesn't mean I'm watching her location all the time. I have it set to notify me if her phone falls or if she's in a place for over thirty minutes. From what I've seen in the past, a fallen phone could mean just that, or that it was tossed from a person's hand or was still in their hand when they fell. Getting that notification has saved the lives of three people I was protecting in the service. I was able to either get them medical attention after being pushed out a third-story window or chase after the kidnappers who thought dropping the phone would be all they needed. The length of time a phone is idle has also saved lives. However, with Ruby, it just notifies me about how boring her life is. Girl's more stagnant than hair gel.

"She's on I-80. Heading to campus. She says someone's trying to run Izzy off the road."

Kooper

"On it." I end the call as I start up my bike. Don't need more than that to get me started.

As I pull out of the gate, I turn the app on that lets me track Ruby, then put the phone in my holder at the front of my bike and gun it. I hear other bikes in the distance, so I know I'm not the only one who got the call. A ping on my phone shows Flint's getting the word out to everyone he hadn't already called. Not sure if I was the first call the boss made or the last, but I know I was the only one he was calling to look after his girl and not anyone else's.

I get the notification of a phone drop and watch as her location doesn't change at all. Wouldn't make sense if she were still driving. Could mean a million things, but I ain't one to speculate till I see what's really going on. I plan and prep for all scenarios but never guess the outcome.

As I get close to her location, I see an SUV pull away from the side of the road and race down the highway. I don't chase. Not my job. But I get a description and note that the license plate is missing. Not sure what Flint's going to do with the details I give him, but it's better than nothing.

I slow and look at the right side, where another car is already parked with doors ajar. I look over the bank and see Izzy and Princess getting out of the car with two other women I don't recognize as I hear sirens not far out. I don't get off my bike to check them out. All I know is they aren't who I'm looking for. I glance back and see nothing behind me, then look left. A bit of dust in the air, but nothing I can see from the angle I'm at. But the road has deep embankments on each side, and what some might see as just dust in the air, I see as a clue.

Turning my wheel, I cross to the other side of the street and ride the edge back the way I came till I see Ruby's car nose-end deep to the ground. No sign of life at all, as all the doors are closed, and I can only see airbags through the windows.

I've trained in many terrains, prepped for missions in the Army, in the Diplomatic Security Service, and with the Hounds' mercenary gig we're starting up. I'm prepared for anything. And yet I still trip over my damn feet to get to Ruby's side as quickly as possible.

I hold my breath as I rip the driver's door open, finding her slumped over the wheel.

"Oh, please don't do this to me." I barely touch her, just enough to check her pulse, and my head drops in relief.

She's alive.

Standing, I roll till I'm leaning all my weight on the side of her car and pull out a cigarette. I need one after this shit. My heart is still beating faster than I would like. I should be used to this by now. For every life I've saved, it's always felt like I've lost that many as well. I thought I was over this gut-wrenching fear. Thought I'd moved past this.

But seeing Ruby not moving? I rub my chest to ease the ache as I puff on my cigarette. I've only got a few moments to pull my shit together before another brother sees me. Everyone knows I watch her. It isn't a secret. Don't want it to be. It's easier if everyone knows what my job is. That way, no one is pissed when I pick her over another. Like I just did with Princess. Bulldog might skin me alive for not going to his daughter's aid if it wasn't already known that I'm on Law's payroll to protect his own kin. Not that I get paid any extra; I just don't have to deal with other shit jobs over this one.

I pull out my phone and text the boss, letting him know his girl is alive. That's all he'll care about. We won't know if she got more than a bump on the head till the paramedics come over. All the job requires is that she's breathing, not what condition she's in.

Might be easier if she were in a coma.

I laugh at my thought. Even if Ruby were bedridden, she'd still be a menace to society. Her dad would just have me chained to her hospital bed. At least with her out, I can breathe fresh air and ride my bike.

"Sir, do you need assistance?"

Looking up, I see an EMT on the roadside and shake my head.

"I don't, but those in the car do." No clue if Abigail is alive or not. I saw her in the passenger seat when Ruby was trying to have me take the penis sandwiches. I know she's still close to her, despite that her brother died before joining the club. If we did honorary memberships, she'd have one. But unless a woman wants to be a vamp or an old lady, the club has no room for them.

Ruby, like all the kids, is somewhere in the mix. They get the protection but still aren't in the know on most shit. We keep them safe, more than we do with vamps who hang at the club, but still try to keep them out of most of our shit, unlike old ladies.

Old ladies know the rules. They keep their mouths shut. We don't outright tell them what's going on, but I've never met an old lady who wasn't worth her weight in gold.

Each one is a badass in her own right. Club doesn't have many right now, but those who are earned the title and the respect that goes along with it. So if they hear something, we know they're good with it.

Kids? Never met one who knew when to shut up. Princess talks more than she should about things that no little girl should know. Teddy and Grace are still learning the club life, so no clue on them. And Ruby is just a handful enough to be an issue. Her dad has the president patch, but she walks around like she owns the place. It's a look for sure. One most can't pull off. She does, though. I'm just not sure if it's a look or an attitude and expectation all at once.

So far, she gives me the most sass, usually when I tell her no—something she doesn't hear a lot from the rest of the brothers. Not that I've ever seen her ask for something beyond the normal bullshit. I just like telling her no to see her get all riled up. Her angry face is funny to me. She tries to look all mean and pissed off, but it just reminds me of the model looks you see on billboards selling perfume or some shit, all pouty lips and sharp cheekbones—something she hates being compared to. She doesn't want to be just another pretty face. She wants people to think she's as fearless and badass as her dad. Girl doesn't realize that her dad's image is all a front. He looks like that just to keep her, and the rest of the club, out of shit that could get someone killed.

Can he be a dick? A badass? Sure. We all can. But to keep the look on every second of the day? It's an act. Get the old man drunk a bit and ask him about his late wife. Or hell, just ask about Ruby and you'll get a bumbling fool of a man who's proud as fuck at what his daughter has done with all

Kooper

the judgment of the entire town and sometimes the state breathing down her neck. Guy is all bark.

I climb back up to my bike when I'm sure the EMT has it all handled and walk over to the line of brothers. We don't give a fuck that we're taking up prime real estate in the middle of a major road and blocking traffic on all sides.

I notice a few prospects walking to cars that are lined up on either side, either to answer questions or tell someone who's complaining to shut the fuck up. What helps, I'm sure, is that not even the cops who've arrived on the scene are yelling at us to move along. Granted, we make a huge donation to their causes every quarter. Money goes a long way in all directions.

"Domino, keep an eye on Ruby and Abs, will you? They're just down the hill."

He nods and heads in the direction I came from as Casper raises an eyebrow.

"Thought that was your job?" he asks.

I shake my head. "Only to make sure she's alive. We're going to need to call it in to get a tow truck out here. Her car is wrecked from what I can tell. Probably not going to be able to drive it out."

"Already on the way. Figured it would be easier to have both her and Izzy's cars towed since we all took our bikes," Casper says, nodding toward where Izzy is getting into an ambulance with Princess as two other ambulances are let through by our guys.

I raise an eyebrow in question at the multiple EMS vehicles.

Casper nods as if he gets it. "Ruby's roommate was in the car with Izzy and got hit or something. Blood everywhere. They're taking her in a separate vehicle to keep Princess from seeing more blood."

"And the third?" I ask.

Casper shrugs. "Must have gotten the call from the one looking in on your charge. She or Abigail must need it. Just hope whoever is driving has brass balls, 'cause the boss is going to lose it if he sees his little girl pulling up to the hospital in an ambulance."

"He won't be the only one," I mutter, already knowing that Bulldog is going to rip the place to shreds. Hound men don't do well when one of their own is hurt. Even worse when they ain't here to see what's going on when it happens.

"Get your fucking hands off me!"

"Ahh, Sleeping Beauty is awake at last," I say, looking toward the wailing banshee that is Ruby as she emerges onto the road ahead of a distressed EMT attempting to offer aid.

She pulls out of his grasp once more and marches toward me and the rest of the boys.

"Well?" she demands.

"Well what?" Casper turns and spits on the ground, away from the rest of us.

"Did you get who it was?"

She's a far cry from what she looked like when I first saw her today. Her outfit is rumpled, there's a knot on her head, and her skin is darkening from the black eye she got from the airbag. A bit of blood is running down her chin from a split lip, but other than that, she seems fine. But she's fucking crazy if she thinks we're going to talk club business right now. Not because of who she is, but where we are.

"No clue what you're talking about," I say and raise an eyebrow at her. From the steam rising off her, she gets it but hates it all at once.

"Whatever. Where's my dad?"

"On his way to the hospital. He was across town when you called him. Said he'll meet us there," Casper supplies.

"Fine. Whose bike am I riding on?"

I snort at her.

"Ah, miss?" The paramedic is still close. He never did turn back to Abigail. I hope they have someone else working on her or something. I would hate to think Ruby's rant pulled medical attention away from someone who needs it so she didn't run into traffic or something. "Protocol requires that you ride with us. You were unconscious when we found you, and we need to make sure you don't go under again. If you get on the back of a bike, you risk falling. If someone has a car, they could take you, but unless they do, you must ride with us."

She keeps glaring at me as if it's my fault. But I'm not the idiot who ran off the road. Not sure how it happened, but I'll get the details on it soon. Just not here.

"Fine. But I'm not riding alone." Ruby turns and stomps back to her car.

At least she has the sense to get back to Abigail. I was half afraid she'd force me to ride with her. And I'm not getting in a cage unless I'm the one driving. I learned a long time ago that they really don't let just anyone drive ambulances. And they especially throw a fit when you do it anyway.

Chapter 4—Ruby

"Can I go home yet?" I complain to the nurse, who just gives me one of those sad, pitiful smiles before leaving me behind the curtain.

I'm in the emergency room, but at least not a solo one. There are a ton of people in here, from the noise I can hear, but they've got me blocked off with the curtain like a contagious person. Can't catch what I have. Well, they can catch my hands if anyone tries to poke me again with a damn needle, but other than getting bitch-slapped, I'm not going to contaminate anyone.

I huff and cross my arms, ignoring the pain it puts on the bruise my seat belt left across my sternum. Pain I can live with—means I'm alive. What I can't live with is the waiting. Waiting on someone to release me. Waiting on my dad to find me. Waiting on anyone to tell me anything. They keep treating me like a victim. Sure, I got run off the road. Sure, I was the one driving and got a bump on my head. That doesn't mean I can't also walk and talk like a normal person.

The curtain gets pushed back, and Dad walks in, flanked by Casper and Kooper. I glare at the latter and ignore the other. One pisses me off because he's breathing; the other just makes me mad at how he pretended like I was crazy at the crash site. Fine, okay, I get it. I went wild. I spoke out loud about things that are only discussed behind closed doors. But can you blame me? I was attacked! I demand answers.

"Ruby girl, are you okay?"

"I'm fine, Dad. Airbag did most of the damage. Nothing's broken on me, but I don't know about the car."

"The boys took your car to the shop. We'll get it fixed up, and you'll be back on the road soon."

"Thanks, Dad." I won't say it out loud, but having a car is the closest I get to real freedom. I want a bike, but my dad will never go for it, so I settle for riding bitch with him or any of the brothers ballsy enough to give me a lift. But even then, it comes with an end in mind. With a car, I get to decide when I stop. I make the decision on how far I go. It's all on me. No one else.

"Tell me what happened." It's a request from the president, not from my dad. There's a difference in him. I get it. Grew up with it. I understand it better than most. He was Dad when he saw me, but now he's the president of the Hounds of the Reaper MC. He needs to know the details to end threats against his people and their properties.

"We were going back to our apartment. Abigail was going to spend the night with me and Nat before she went home. We came from Chains' place, drove by the clubhouse, then headed out. I watched all the streets and saw nothing out of the ordinary till a car cut me off and gunned it for Izzy's. I tried to push their car off the road, but we got caught up, and I was the one who went spiraling off the side like a damn rookie." I look away with a glare. All that talk about being capable, and I can't even get on top of one little car race. Pathetic.

Kooper

I might hate myself more than I do everyone else right now. They might treat me as fragile, which I see as worse than death, but I'm the one who got us into this mess. If I had swerved instead of going in for the kill, I might have been able to get a different outcome, one that would have put them in the hospital with me watching my dad ream their ass. Instead, I get Tweedledee and Tweedledum watching on as my dad treats me like a fucking prospect who knows nothing about anything. At least that's how it feels. Sure, all he did was ask. But I swear I hear it in the tone. See it in the look. I've disappointed him somehow. He won't say it, will maybe even deny it, but I feel it. I know I did.

"You get a description of the vehicle?"

I sigh and look back at him with a shake of my head. "Black SUV with the plates removed. Tinted windows, too, so no clue if it was a man or woman."

He looks at Kooper. "Matches your description."

My unofficial stalker nods in agreement. Glad I was able to corroborate what he said. Not.

"Boss." Domino pokes his head into the curtained-off area. Guy's decent enough to give me a nod. "Looking good, Ruby."

I snort. "Thanks."

He grins, and his boyish charm has me giving him a small smile in return before rolling my eyes and resting my head back on the pillow to stare at the ceiling. For a hospital that screams "cleanliness in all things," there sure are a lot of stains up there. I guess some things are harder to clean than others.

"You got something to say, Domino, or you just checking in on my girl?" Dad asks, and I can hear the slight warning in his clipped words. He might never say it out loud, but me dating a club member is off the table. And them being interested isn't even a possibility in my dad's eyes.

"Both. Bulldog is pulling up."

"Shit," I say at the same time as Kooper. I stare at him for a second before turning back to my dad, who's nodding at our assessment.

"I'll get General to release you. Have a brother drive you and your friends home. I'll get the car to you tomorrow or some type of wheels if it needs more work than that. Charge your phone, 'cause I'll be calling once I know you're home safe." Dad comes around the bed, leans down, and kisses my forehead like he has ever since I can remember. It makes me feel special, even more so knowing that after Mom died, I'm the only one in his life he shows an ounce of affection toward. Even if those moments seem few and far between sometimes.

Dad leaves, following Domino, and Casper trails behind them, squeezing my leg as he goes. I guess it's his way of checking in on me. I give him a small smile, already over my anger issues. They come and go pretty quickly. I can get riled up real fast, but then I also come off it just as quick. I like to think I'm special like that, but apparently it's a typical woman thing. Or at least that's what my doctor and every man who's ever tried to date me has said.

"Why are you still here, Koop?" I don't know if he hates that I shorten his club name or not, but no other woman does it, and I like to think it annoys him. A little jab I get away with—at least for now. I know his brothers call him that, too, but for them, it's out of respect. There is zero respect when I do it.

He tilts his head and studies me. I don't like having this much attention from him or anyone else. It's like I'm under a freaking microscope, and he's learning shit about me that *I* don't even know yet.

"What?" I squawk just to get a reaction from him, but he gives me nothing other than more head tilting.

"Whatever," I mutter and look away as I rest my head back once again. I stare at the off-white curtain that's blocking my view to whoever or whatever is on the other side of it. Could be a wall for all I know. What I do know is it's more interesting than having a man who you despise on most days because of the lack of freedom he represents staring at you.

I've got nothing against Kooper. Well, he's an asshole. Always has been ever since he joined the club. At least to me, anyway. I don't know much about him. Maybe I could have gotten along with him. Found common ground or some shit. But that was before he took the babysitting job my dad gave him. Before he started tracking me and making me feel like the cage I pretend isn't there is clear to be seen.

"He ain't disappointed."

"What?"

He says it again, just as normal as can be, but his words hit closer to what I'm feeling than I'll admit. No one has ever called me out on my own issues before. No one has seen them. It feels strange that he would.

"Law doesn't care if you didn't get the description of the vehicle or the driver. Doesn't even care about the damage to your car or what happened to Izzy and Princess. He only cares that you're still here."

I force myself to swallow and then nod. I know he can see my chest rise and fall from the deep breaths I'm taking in through my nose, but I refuse to open my mouth to pant out my small panic that Kooper, out of everyone else, is seeing me. The real me and not some image I put on. I doubt even my dad knows who I am. How can he when *I* barely know? I'm an act. That's all I've ever been since I learned how. Be what others want to see. Be the person they expect. Hide your own thoughts and feelings because no one gives a damn about them but you. Well, Mom did. But she's gone. And I swore not to be soft again after her death. I have to be hard. I have to show everyone that I'm unbreakable. I'm not about to let what happened then happen again. When I fell completely apart and let anyone say or do anything to me if it made them feel big. I was too lost in my head with grief to stand up for myself. Dad wasn't any better back then. We finally both got better with time. It just sucked while we went through it.

"I know." I want it to come out harsh, like I don't care. But it sounds weak, even to my own ears.

"You don't have to be strong all the time." There's no sass or smirk behind his words, no hidden jab I can find, but I still feel it. He might think he knows me, but he has no clue.

"Yeah, and who's going to put me back together when I fall? You?" I narrow my eyes at him before snorting and shaking my head as I look down and pick at my nails.

It's a cheap shot. We both know I'm on the outside of most things. Not in the club because I'm female, but still close enough because I was born into it. Not a civilian

Kooper

because of who my parents are, but still have to play as if I am, since I've got no place else to make a name for myself. I'm outside and inside in both areas. Stuck in the in-between. Sounds like a bad horror movie.

"I'll make sure your roommate knows where you are."

I hear him push the curtain open, then close it and walk away. Only when I can't make out the distant sound of his boots on the hospital floor do I look up and stare at the spot where he was standing.

I don't know why I don't like the guy. Since he became a prospect, I've never liked him. He pisses me off all the time, and mostly it's just because he's there. He's annoying. Pigheaded. Arrogant.

Sure, his ass is nice in jeans, and the tattoos on his arms are brilliant, but looks only get you so far in life. Just ask any vamp. Every woman who decides they want to be a fuck buddy at the club is gorgeous. No doubt about it. But not a single one is someone I want to get personable with. And the same is to be said for them wanting to get to know me. Some people just don't click. You know it the second you meet. That's Kooper and me. We aren't meant to click. Which makes him the ideal candidate to be my babysitter in my dad's eyes, I'm sure.

The curtain is pushed back, and I react as much as I can, sitting upright in my bed. They still have me hooked up to a machine for who knows what. When I see who it is, I gasp.

"What the hell, Nat? What happened to you?"

When I asked if she could ride with Abigail and me in the ambulance, I was told she'd already left. I never even asked why she was in an ambulance of her own. Figured it was the same as us, just a precaution or some shit. But no. My girl has full-on bandages all over her nose and looks like a serial killer with half a mask on.

"Broken nose. Princess's mom hit me when I was trying to help keep her in the car and not get kidnapped."

"Shit. Princess's mom did this? Why didn't they tell me? Is Princess all right? Are *you* all right?" I feel betrayed on a whole other level right now.

"Not sure if they knew. I just told your dad when I passed him in the hall. He said he was on his way to get Bulldog and take him to Princess's room. And other than looking like a freak for a few days, I'll live. It's just a broken nose. I've had worse."

I raise a brow. "Really?"

She laughs kind of awkwardly and then shakes her head. "No, but I'm trying to stay positive about it."

I nod but don't believe her. Every now and then, Nat says things that make me think there's more than she's letting on. She claims to be an orphan who got a scholarship for school and works on campus to pay for rent and stuff. She's wicked smart, so some of it might be true, but I'm not sure about all of it. But I don't push her. Never have, and don't think I ever will. Sometimes we have to have secrets, not only to save ourselves but others. God knows I do. If she doesn't pry into my life, I've got no reason to pry into hers.

For now, at least.

"Come on." I pull the stuff off me, ignoring the beeps. I'm done with this hospital. "Let's find Abigail and get home."

Kooper

"Think I saw her talking to some of your dad's friends in one of the waiting rooms."

Nat keeps in line with me, both of us ignoring everyone as we make our way out of the emergency room. Surprisingly, not a single person stops us. Either they want me out just as much as I want to be gone, they don't care about their patients, or my dad already fixed things for me to leave. Might also help that General, a club brother, is one of the resident doctors here and has enough pull to make things happen.

"You can call them brothers, you know."

"But they *are* your dad's friends. Or I guess the guys who work for him. Besides, none of them are *my* brother, so it feels strange to call them that."

I just shrug. It's never felt weird for me. It's just who they are. I call them a brother, and they call me Law's kid. Not all of them get along with me, and some are more of a brotherly love than others. But I know how clubs work, and I like the Hounds. Not just because I was born into it. I've been around long enough to have seen a few other clubs come in or met some on the road. Not every club out there treats its family the same as the Hounds. I've got a good thing here, I know that. I also like the fact that not every single Hound is a dick. Can they be? Oh hell yeah. They have one, so it comes with the territory. But I know my dad would never let anyone in the club who's a complete jackass. If my dad approves of them, then I show my respect. Not only because they're Hounds, but because I respect my dad's judgment. If I didn't, we would have a shit relationship.

My dad is one of my best friends. Sometimes I feel like I can't talk to him, but he tries. He really does. He wants me close not only to keep me safe but because he likes that we hang out. We connect. I'm not a daddy's girl or a tomboy type. I'm just Ruby. I know the rules of all sports worth watching. I can shoot and throw a knife at a target with general accuracy. I can rotate my tires and change my oil. But I can also put makeup on and not look like I'm trying too hard. I can walk *and* run in six-inch heels. I'm a badass pretty girl. My mom and dad taught me so much. They gave me everything.

All I ever want to do is make them proud. Even if it's all built up in my head.

At least that's what the school shrink says. I got a free session once and tried it out. You know, give everything in college a try at least once. Except drugs. That's a hard no. I've seen too many people strung out on that shit to know better.

The shrink said I put my dad on a pedestal, one too large for me to climb up and be on his same level. That it's all in my head about never being good enough to be his daughter or something. I said he was shit, told him to fuck off, and left fifteen minutes before the session was supposed to end.

I know how badass I am. I know I'm a fucking awesome girl. I've got a minor flaw, though. A part of me thinks I need to prove to my old man and, by association, the entire club that I'm just as good as them. I get that it's my issue. The whole "only men in the club, no women" rule was never something I could wrap my mind around as a child. I always told my dad I was going to run the club with him when I was small. Each time, he told me I couldn't. That just further cemented that I should. Or prove that I was just as good despite my girly parts.

"You ready?" Prospect asks as he sees me emerge from behind the emergency doors into the waiting room. Abigail is already standing there talking to him.

"Yup. Think we can stop at a drive-through on the way? I'm in need of some seriously greasy food, and fries are right up my alley."

The guy smirks and nods before giving a chin lift to the rest of the brothers standing about. I don't see Dad or Kooper, but I know my whereabouts will be reported to both.

Guess that's a point in the club's favor. You never have to go hunt down someone to tell them bye or anything. Someone is always there to do it for you.

Chapter 5—Kooper

Three months later

I eye the girl Flint brought up to the officer level. She ain't much but a pile of mud. Another night of bullshitting around the club and another random issue coming about. This one's a perimeter breach that turned into a mud-crusted woman who looks about three seconds away from trying to run down the stairs on one leg. I noticed her limping up the flight, refusing to take Flint's offer of help. The idiot just smirked at her response, but I'm smart enough to know that piqued his interest. Piqued mine as well. A woman who comes into the wolves' den with her head held high, even if she's shaking like a leaf, ain't the normal type. And Hounds don't deal in normal anything.

If I were ever to have a woman longer than just a night, I'd take a strongheaded one. Even a bit crazy in the head. Need that in a woman who's willing to stick it out around here. And to deal with me. I ain't the easiest to get along with. Or so I've been told. I've never had a girlfriend. I fuck them and then leave. Or they do, and there ain't no hard feelings about it. It's just the way it's always been. If I were to have one who stayed, I'd need her to be interesting for more than a night. You can usually figure out a person in one night. I'd need someone with a bit of a crazy personality to keep me guessing *and* interested for more than a few hours if she plans to rope me into a relationship.

Kooper

First it was Chains and his Mama Bear. Tonight, Bulldog claimed his Lady. Who's going to go next is anyone's guess. Maybe it'll be me and this country bumpkin who just rolled onto our property. She's intriguing for sure. But before I can even start thinking about getting her washed up, I hear the boss yelling from the other side of his office door.

"I fucking told you I would take care of that shit. Don't you for one fucking second think I won't skin your hide, girl." I wait a beat, like all the other brothers up here, as we look at one another. Could be anyone he's talking to on the phone. Anyone in the world. But it isn't. We all know that. And I'm holding my breath for him not to call me in.

"Kooper! Get your ass in here."

"Fuck," I grumble, then sneer at my brothers when they snicker at me as I stomp by them. When I agreed to the babysitting gig, I didn't expect this much of an issue. I have her place all wired. Not a peep of anyone looking into Ruby for any other reason than her being her: annoying as shit and not a mouth guard on her at all. If I wanted to spend money on her, I'd buy a muzzle. But it would be a waste, as the girl can't take a hint to save her life.

"Close the fucking door," the boss says, and I do what Ruby never does. I listen.

"What did the princess do now?" I drawl. Getting tired of all the issues I have to deal with. First, it was getting her and her roommate into a place that was safe enough for the boss to approve of. Had to pull a few strings to get it done right. Ruby still says it was her doing, that her super awesome negotiations got the price to something she and Nat could afford, even though I told her it wasn't. It took me and some *stronger* words with the landlord to make it so the girls weren't getting ripped off. Ruby denies I did that, that the club was involved. Sure, fine, whatever. If she wants to pretend that she's all big and bad and can do things in the world alone, I've got no issue with it. It's just part of the job. Securing the assets. That's all it is. Who gives a fuck about where the credit goes in her mind? I've got my own mind, too, and I know the truth.

Then it was the car. Hers was totaled according to the insurance company when she got run off the road a few months back. Getting her one that she approved of—again, a fucking nightmare. Boss had his own specifications as well. I did, too, but mine were for the job. It had to have certain safety features so if she was in a wreck again, police, EMS, and I would all be notified at once. She only cared about how many chargers and cupholders it had. And the color. Can't forget the fucking color. Ruby red. Of fucking course. She calls it her signature color but only wears it on her lips and a bit in her hair. Otherwise, she's in black leather or dark colors.

Hell, just last week, it was her goal in life to find a job. Can we say nightmare much? I'm all for her earning money and getting experiences, but not at the cost of my social life. If she has a job, I'll have to be vetting people on the regular. Now, I only do it when each semester starts and I see who's in her classes. A job has randoms coming in from all directions. No way can I do a scan of them in less time than it would be for them to take her out. I would have to be stationed closer, and I refuse to live on campus or be that far from the club. I could hire someone to watch her, and I might still, but not yet. I was able to convince Law to talk her out of it, claiming her need to study shouldn't take a back seat to putting a few extra dollars in her wallet. It worked. Well, they fought and shit, but it saved me from looking at a second place to rest my head at night.

"Her landlord keeps upcharging her, claiming damages inside the apartment. But that would mean he's getting inside her place without her permission. You've got cameras in there. You see anyone coming in or out who shouldn't be in there?"

"Other than the slew of boy toys?" I dangle that in front of him, and he closes his eyes and runs his hands down his face.

"Don't want to hear that shit."

I let him freak out a second longer before I shake my head. "Nah. No one but her and the roommate. I'll take another look, though. What do you want me to do when I'm done wasting an hour of my time?"

He opens his eyes and levels me with a glare. "Take care of it."

I nod once, and then I'm out the door. Back to more bullshit.

The brothers know the drill, and not a single one stands in my way as I walk to my bike. I don't need to check the feed; I already know I'll find nothing. Instead, I head to the problem itself. And in less than two hours, 'cause I'm pissed I have to do this at all, I'm banging down the door of the landlord.

Yeah, I know where he lives. Ran his background the second the girls wanted the place he put up for rent online. I keep notes on most things in a file I can access on my computer and phone, so pulling up his address was easier than switching lanes on a busy highway.

"Yeah, yeah, I'm coming." The growling on the other side of the door might intimidate others. Hell, anyone but me or any Hound, really.

As the guy opens the door, I note that he looks the same as the last time we had a chat. Except that was at his "leasing office." It was a damn coffee shop, but whatever gets the guy off. He played football in college, and luckily for him, he still has the bulk thirty years later. Too bad he never had the brains. The comb-over look isn't working for him much, especially with the handful of hairs left to use to cover up his bald-ass head. The second his faded blue eyes catch a look at my face and then the patches on my vest, he pales, and I smile.

"Shit," he says and then turns and runs, trying to slam the door in my face.

I keep it from shutting with my boot in the door, pissed at the small bit of pain it causes. My shitkickers are heavy-duty as shit and weigh a ton since they're supposed to protect my toes and foot in general from an accident on the bike. Doesn't mean that I don't feel things when the instep gets smashed.

I slam the door open and absently note that I ripped a part of it off the hinges as I hunt down my prey. I don't do the talking-taunting thing that most Hounds do when they go hunting. Why? You just tell your prey where you're at with your voice. I prefer the silent, deadly approach.

The guy, Gerry Wallace, is truly an idiot. His home, unlike the girls', is two stories. It's a long floor plan with a straight shot from the front door to the back, but instead of going out, he heads up the stairs. I give chase and round the top steps, moving to the left just in time to prevent getting shot.

I look at the hole in the wall behind me, as does Gerry.

"Did you just try to shoot me?" It's a dumber question than the man in front of me, but I'm flabbergasted that I was the idiot who almost let that happen. I was annoyed at having to do this before. Now I'm raging out and barely hanging on.

I take four steps and grab the shotgun barrel just as he loads it and gets another shot off, but this time, I'm pushing the barrel up in the air, and it hits the roof. Debris falls on me, and I feel my mood get darker a second before I push the barrel back into his face and bust his nose open. Then I rip the gun out of his grasp and hold it in my left hand as I punch him with my right.

"Big fucking mistake, Gerry." I punch him again, and he stumbles and falls. Breaking open the gun, I see one is still in the chamber as I hold the barrel at the guy's cheek. He hisses from the hot metal pressing into him, but other than that does nothing.

"I just wanted to talk, Gerry. To see if you and I could come to an understanding about Ruby's apartment. But no, Gerry had to grow some balls and think he knew what was right. Didn't you, Gerry?" I always like using their name over and over when shit like this goes down. I want them to grow to hate their own name. To fear that one day it will be me saying it again to them. And the fear of hearing it said out loud will cause them to pee themselves. Like Gerry is doing now.

I don't even acknowledge that he pissed himself. It happens a lot. You don't get used to it, but you just deal with the expected.

"Now, about Ruby's damages."

"None. There are none," he backtracks.

"But the pain you caused her, and me for coming out here, is damage in itself. Isn't that right, Gerry?"

"I'll take a hundred bucks off the rent." I push the barrel into his nose, and he cries out in pain. "Two! Two hundred off a month."

"Make it four for each of them, and we call the damages paid off."

"Come on, man, that cuts me off at the balls. I'll barely make a profit from that."

I move the gun to his junk. "We could always remove them permanently."

"No, no." He's quick to shake the idea off. "Four hundred each. Promise."

I back off, taking two steps back and lowering the barrel from his groin. I watch him take a deep sigh of relief and close his eyes.

Only when he thinks it's over do I pull the trigger.

He screams as he grabs his knee. "What the fuck, man?"

"That was for taking a shot at me. You missed, so you only get that. If it were a direct hit, I'd make mine count too. Get your shit together, and don't pull this crap again. I might have come alone, but don't think that means the Hounds won't drag you to hell. If you think revenge is going to be your next bet, let me remind you that I know where you live, where your parents live, and where that little girl you have lives. I know everything about you. If you take me out, a file gets sent to my boss and his friends. I might not be alive to end you, but they will be, and they will take out your entire damn line while they're at it."

I watch him take that in. They say reading a person is easier if you've known them for years. I say it depends on what you're trying to see. When I watch the shock fade to fear and then recognition that I'm not bullshitting, only then do I head out, taking the shotgun with me. He might have other weapons in his house, but I don't hear him move as I leave his place, so I know I'm good to turn my back as I ride away.

It takes me another fifteen minutes to get to my next stop. I carry the shotgun up to the second story and bang on the door once. I could use the key, but I don't want her to know I have one.

"You're not pizza," Ruby says as she opens the door dressed in an oversized tee with biker shorts underneath. When she crosses her arms, I see she's not wearing a bra. The curve of her breasts gives away her age—young. Too damn young to know what a pair like hers can do for men.

Not me. I never was a boob guy.

"And you're not what I ordered either."

She rolls those eyes so perfectly some days, but at least she leaves the door open when she turns to go back inside.

I follow and make a note that Nat's bag is gone. She keeps it on the hook by the door when she's home, so she must still be at the library.

"Dad sent you?"

I nod when she looks over at me before plopping down onto the couch and grabbing the remote.

She sighs. "I told him I'd take care of it."

Her place is relatively clean. A small kitchen with only a few dishes in the sink. The round dining table is covered with textbooks and notebooks, letting me know Ruby's keeping up on her studies. If she ever slacked off, her dad would have her hide. Not because he'd be pissed if she spent his money on college for nothing, but because she was wasting her potential. But Ruby ain't the type to just sit and be lazy. She's always doing more and putting her all into everything. Might not have grown up here, but I've done the research and saw that she was the valedictorian of her high school but chose not to do the speech. Instead, she opted to have the next two best in the school do it as a duo. Most had no idea Ruby had that much power, but her elders realized she was clever and smart and had a pull that drew people in to do what she asked. Just like her father.

"He said it had been going on for a bit. How much did you lose to him while you were 'handling' it?"

She glares at the TV, and if she were a dragon, smoke would be coming out of her nostrils. "A grand. Dad only got onto it when I slipped up and made the mistake of saying too much when I applied for a job and some asshole called him."

Fuck. I missed it. Not sure why the boss didn't tell me, but that only means I'm getting lax in my duties. I might not like the job or the person, but it's a job. I've got to give it my all if I expect to get what I want out of it in the end.

I've been giving this the bare minimum. Just enough to keep her breathing. But if I want to keep her breathing *and* prevent me from taking these day trips more often, I've got to dive in deeper and watch closer. Might add more time in my day, but in the end, it'll save me hours on the road. Not that riding my bike ain't awesome. I just wish it were on a road I wanted to be on and not one that leads me back to her.

"I'll get you your money back."

She turns toward me. I know she sees the shotgun in my hand, but like the club kid she is, she doesn't even blink as to why I have it.

"Thought you'd want me to learn from my mistakes." She tilts her head just a smidge, allowing some of her hair to fall off her shoulder.

I shrug. "Did you learn something?"

She snorts as she goes back to flipping through the channels. "Yeah, not to trust a man."

"There you go. No need to be out of cash while you're at it."

Her head whirls toward me at my words, her face laced with confusion. Can I be a dick? Yes. Have I been one to her? Yes. But money doesn't seem like a reason to be one.

Before she can question me on it, I turn and open the door just as the pizza guy raises his hand to knock. A pimply-faced kid with glasses gives me wide eyes as he takes in my vest and then the shotgun still in my hands.

"$16.50," he squeaks out.

I pull a twenty from my wallet and put it on the box before walking away. I need to get back to Gerry. He owes me a grand twenty now. If he's lucky, he'll get it before I grow impatient and blow out his other kneecap.

Chapter 6—Ruby

"You want to talk about it?" I give Natalie the side-eye as I pull out of the parking lot of the coffee shop we just left.

Today was meant to just be a chill day. Just take out the new girl, Jules, for a coffee with a few of the others involved with the club since she's in and yet still on the outside till Flint claims her ass. It's coming; I don't need to see it to know it. Also helps that the boys don't really keep their mouths shut about gossip at the club. Maybe about club business, but not about who's making out with who. And the fact that the amnesia chick had her tongue down Flint's throat before he left on some uber-secret mission is just juicy enough to get the brothers talking. Even heard a few were taking bets on how long it would take him to put the old lady title on her.

I've got to admit, there are worse options out there for a guy like Flint. I like him. Always have. He can fuck up like the rest of us, but at least he's good at groveling. Or, in club standards, dealing with bitch duty till he's in the clear to go back to the way things were.

Nat continues to ignore my question. She ignored it in the shop when the old ladies asked about why she went crazy on some Asian woman who came in for a snack. She played it off well, though. Had me almost questioning if I had hallucinated her chasing the woman off and yelling at her from the door.

Kooper

I kept my mouth shut then. I don't want to scare her off. She might not know it, but I cherish our friendship. She's the only person I know who became my friend because of who I am and not who my dad is or because I'm part of the club.

Nat's never been inside. She might have come to town for a meal here or a bachelorette party there, but never to the clubhouse. That's people's homes, and I would never invade a person's home like that by inviting guests to it. Now, if brothers do it, it's whatever, but I've still got kid access. Which is no access to anything other than getting myself through the gate, unless something's going down. Either I'm kicked out to keep it closed-door or brought in for my own protection. It's the president's call, and I'm just the president's kid. Fewer rights than a tourist on a visa some days.

"I'm just going to keep asking. Might as well tell me," I say in a sweet voice. Well, the sweetest I can manage. Some might say it's cringy, but I'm not really known for being sweet.

"It was nothing. Can we just drop it?"

I feel my face pull back at her words. Natalie's the quiet, shy one between the two of us. Well, frankly, everyone is shy next to my loud-ass attitude. But the sass she just threw at me is so out of character for her.

"Sure, we can drop it." I glance at her out of the corner of my eye. "If it really is nothing." My words are hard, letting her know I'm not about to drop shit.

Taking a deep breath, she shakes her head, then rests it against the side window and watches the trees as we pass.

"Just someone from my past who I thought I was free of."

I keep glancing at her, but also keep my eyes on the road. Neither of us wants to be in a car accident ever again. The bruising lasted way longer for both of us than we were told by the doctors after our last visit.

"Want me to get the club involved? They can take this problem out if you want that. Just got to ask."

She's shaking her head even before I finish talking. "No, it's not their fight." She looks over at me and reaches out to grab my hand on the steering wheel. With a small smile, she says, "Thanks, though." She pulls away but continues. "This is something I have to deal with alone. I didn't expect to see them again, and that's on me. But now I know they might be around, and I'll have my guard up."

"Is this someone I should be worried might be of the 'shoot first' type?"

Now I get a full-on grin out of her. "Nah. They just talk. They're all words, no substance. Just a headache, really. I promise, no issues you need to worry about or for your dad's club to get involved in. Consider it family drama."

"Except you don't have a family," I point out.

"Exactly." She rests her head on the back of her seat. "That's what makes it so complicated."

I let her sit in her own head for the rest of the drive home while I try a breathing technique I read about. I'm all for finding sensible ways to let my anger out. Sometimes it doesn't work and I end up hitting someone or something, but I just got this car, and despite Nat obviously hiding shit from

Kooper

me, I don't want to hurt her. And if I push too hard, I could do more than hurt her—I could hurt myself.

Right now, Nat is my safe haven. I'm not some girl who can't do things on her own. Who can never leave the nest or something like that. I have friends here—well, acquaintances, really. I can't trust people outside the club most of the time. Those I keep close are inside the club. My whole damn life is wrapped up in it, and I don't even fight it. But I know I need to be connected to those outside it as well.

I've got plans. Big ones. I'm going to start a physical therapy practice after college. It'll take a few years, but you've got to have goals if you plan to go anywhere in life. And if I want to bring in clients from outside the club, I need to make nice with the civilians.

Natalie is my trial period. Sorry to say, but I'm using her. I still like her, but I'm testing myself out on her, seeing if I can be reasonable long enough when people piss me off to keep going without breaking things. 'Cause I just know that the first *Karen* type to come into my place of business will not be leaving smiling. And that's going to cost me a ton in lawyers' fees, I bet. That's why I already started saving. Not for the place to set up shop, but for the attorney who'll take my case. We all know it'll happen; I'm just preparing for the inevitable. If I were smart, I'd get myself caught by one of the prelaw kids around here. Might save me financially, and if I can ease them into who my family is, maybe they won't be such a punk-ass bitch around them after a while.

But so far, despite me forcing myself into situations to meet said students, I walk out with shivers of regret and disgust. I can barely last three minutes talking to any of them before I'm leaving. I can't even imagine being intimate with one. Yuck.

I'm sure the "good old boy" type does it for some. Most, according to the girly magazines in the checkout stands, but I've never liked clean-cut. I've tried. A few times, actually. Each one left a bad taste in my mouth, and only one of them got close to actually trying to kiss me. Emphasis on *trying*. He missed me and hit my fist. Several times.

When we make it back to our place, we dump our bags at the small half table closest to the front door that we jokingly call the foyer. I grab us each a drink, her a water and me a Red Bull. I don't need the caffeine, but I like the taste. It's crap for my teeth and liver, but it's better than cocaine, and that's how I rationalize most things. If cocaine is bad, then the other things that are bad for me are on that level. But so far, nothing has been that harsh, so I like to think I've never had anything terrible in my life.

After parking my ass next to Nat on the couch, we put on a rerun of *Friends* we've both seen and just veg. It's a routine of sorts. No one really talks when we both get home. It's like a detox for having to go out and socialize or something. I swear I got the best roommate, because she gets me on so many levels. I need my quiet time, just like I need my ass-kicking time. It's all about balance in my book.

"How did Tits—I mean Jules get two prospects kicked out of the club? You never told me that."

Nice of her to remember some of the things we talked about at the coffee shop before she went apeshit on that customer. Which we're meant to pretend didn't happen.

I shrug but don't look over at her. "It was a few days back. Dad asked me to come and do some work on her

Kooper

shoulder, and she was sitting at a table coloring. We started talking, and then some assholes used my *favorite* word, and shit went down."

"Oh."

I glance at her and notice her wide eyes as I nod. I've got a problem with one word, and one word only: cunt. I'll use it myself, hypocritical bitch that I am, but I refuse to be called that or for another person I know, and like, to be called that either. I knew instantly that Jules was one of the girls I could get along with. So when a punk-ass wannabe biker opened his mouth, I shut it for him. His and his friend's.

"Exactly. Koop was pissed when he saw what I did." I smile as I lift the can to my lips and take a long drink. Seeing him mad makes me all tingly on the inside. I bet it's how the devil feels when he pisses off God.

"Koop? You mean Kooper? The guy who's like your babysitter or something? Why was he pissed at you?"

"Civilians ain't meant to touch a brother, even if it's a brother in training."

"Civilian? Aren't you club?"

Sometimes I forget that, like Natalie, I keep a lot of stuff about me and my past out of our conversations. She gets a few things, but not everything.

"Civilian can apply to many people. I'm part of the club because of my dad, but I'm not *club*. I shouldn't have touched them at all. Rules say if someone not club has a problem with a brother, they're to report it to the person they're connected to. Like an old man, or in this case, my dad. I should be kicked out, or my dad should be punished for what I did."

"But he isn't because he's the president of the club, right?"

I shake my head. "More like because of what they said to me. I might not have been in the right for what I did, but I was justified enough to have it overlooked. Especially when one of them came to and started talking to Kooper as if it was fine to call the president's little girl a free piece of ass. Well, that and they had no clue who I was, which is idiotic. I mean, if you're applying for a job, which prospecting basically is, you learn everything you can about the company and who works for what. The guys were kicked out for pissing off Kooper and showing they were only there for the free ass that comes with the patch and not the honor to wear it."

I finish my drink, crush the can, and set it on the coffee table. I would throw it across the open floor plan we have to the trash can, but it's full, so it would just fall to the ground. Like the other three pieces of trash I threw on it already before we left this morning.

"What's the difference in age?" she asks.

"Between who?"

"You and Kooper."

"Twelve years."

"Wow."

"Right? Guy acts like my dad most days." I shake my head at the thought, but her small smile catches my attention. "What?"

"That's oddly specific for someone who doesn't like the guy."

My mouth drops a bit, but I close it before I have a full-on jaw drop.

Kooper

"What? Boys talk. They mentioned his age once, and I did the math. I'm good at remembering things. That's all."

She pulls her lips into her mouth as she hums at my words and nods as if that explains everything. Which it does. It's nothing more than me just remembering a simple fact.

I turn back to the show and ignore my roomie... for all of ten seconds before she opens her mouth again.

"So, what did he do before all this?"

"Four years Army, then six in DSS, the Diplomatic Security Service. Would have kept up with it, too, but he got tired of the bullshit and the Hounds found him first." I say it as if the teacher asked me how many bones are in the body.

"And his real name?"

"Dixon Hobbs. I overheard one of the brothers call him that when they went over taxes or something a while back." Just more facts that mean nothing. But when I look at her again, I roll my eyes as she tries to hold in another smile. "What now?"

"Just that you know a lot about him."

I cross my arms and look forward. "I told you—boys talk. I listen. That's all there is. Ask me about any other brother and I'd know the same."

"Right."

I turn on her quickly and fling my arms out. "Seriously. The guy's friends with my dad. And I have a good relationship with my pops. So don't go thinking I've got a daddy kink or some shit."

She holds up her hands to ward off any attack I might send her way. "Whoa—never said all that."

I nod at her and sit back in my seat, crossing my arms once more as I glare at whatever Ross is saying to Rachel. I know this episode but have no clue what's being said right now.

"But *you* did." I can hear the smirk in her voice, but I refuse to look and confirm it.

"Whatever." I stand and march to the trash can. Her chuckle follows me as I pick up the trash, stuffing it into the overflowing bag before tying it off. I would love to yank the door open, but I don't want to put a hole in the wall. The landlord will try to claim more damages, this one true, and I don't want to give him any more money.

Surprisingly, he lowered our rent and even gave us a month free because we "overpaid" when he was harassing us about issues with the place. I know Kooper had something to do with it. And I would fight him on it, but it worked in my favor. Why push it?

I stomp down the stairs and walk down three units to toss our trash away. I could just set it outside the door— we pay for "trash services," as they call it—but I need the walk. Actually, I need more than that right now.

The thought of me and Kooper in any capacity beyond hating each other makes my skin crawl. He's an asshole. Overbearing. Cocky. Not my type in the slightest. In a certain light, sure, he could be considered hot. But then he opens his mouth and ruins everything.

When I get back to my place, the TV is off and Natalie's door is shut. She's studying or napping. Either way, I'm free to do what I want. I change quickly, pick out my favorite playlist, write her a note, and head back out.

Kooper

I don't have a routine for when I work out or anything. I'm not training for a marathon like Jules, so I can eat my weight in nachos. Despite what people think, I have a very healthy relationship with my body and my look. My mom taught me the value of loving yourself in all shapes and sizes from the day I was born. If I put on a few pounds? Awesome. If I lose some? Awesome too. I've been a size four to a size twelve. I go up and down depending on whatever's going on in life. I don't have an eating disorder, and I'm not anorexic. I eat when I'm hungry, and sometimes I overeat. Other times, I live off Red Bull and gummy bears. There's no rhyme or reason for what I do, at least not one I've ever found.

I also work out because I get bored, and with all the sugary treats I eat and drink, I need to release the energy. If I were a painter or a writer or something, I'd use that as my outlet, but I'm not that creative. I can color between the lines and do a retelling of *Cinderella* for bedtime, but that's about it.

Some days, I lift; others, I join a spin class. Today, I've got no plans to stay inside and just want out. So I'm running. I'm sure Kooper is tracking me, the asshole.

I don't know why Nat's words bugged me so much. I've never seen Kooper as anything but annoying. He seems to be everywhere and nowhere all at once lately. Before I went to college, he was just the bad lighting near the pool tables at the club. Now, he seems to have his own blue light special overhead that pops up more than I expect him to.

When he first told me he was my babysitter, I was pissed. I thought I would have a tail everywhere. But true to his word, he's kept it to the minimum since I follow the rules.

Which, while annoying, are not the worst I've dealt with. And the longer it goes on, the more I actually give him some credit for being ballsy enough to just tell me what's going on and not sneak about. He might be the first person to ever just call a spade a spade around me. Everyone else plays games and keeps secrets. Even my dad.

To this day, Dad has never acknowledged that he put Kooper on babysitting duty. I've tried to give him ample opportunities from the smooth wording I drop, but nada. He either knows I know or doesn't. The entire club knows Kooper is my solo bodyguard, but I've really got no clue if anyone knows that I'm in on the details.

I won't say it out loud, and I sure as hell won't tell him to his face, but a part of me is impressed by the way Kooper handles me and my shit. It's not with kid gloves. He doesn't give me the princess treatment. He doesn't treat me as anything, really. I'm just a job. One who isn't left in the dark on the big things. Small things like how my landlord went from a prick to a nice guy aren't my concern. But the big things, like knowing he can see the route I run today and get involved if needed, it's… nice.

Dad takes care of me, but I know he has a lot going on. He literally carries the weight of the Hounds on his shoulders. I tried on his vest as a kid, and it weighs a fucking ton from what I remember. Of course, I was four and have never been allowed to try it on again after he saw me wearing it that one time. He smiled, took a picture, and then told me it wasn't for me. Just like being in the club.

I push myself harder, needing my lungs to burn a bit more to push out any attempt at my body wanting me to feel emotions. I have them, but I don't like to feel them. I sure as hell don't like to show them. Except anger. I can never let that one go.

And truthfully, I never try *that* hard to hide it.

Chapter 7—Kooper

Three months later

"This is such a bad idea," Flint says, but I don't see him walking away from the table we've set up to listen in on the girls talking a few feet away.

I grunt in agreement but say nothing. I already spoke up in Church and got shot down. Law wants to know how much Cheyanne knows. I get it. She's an outsider who's tied to a former spy whose own country turned on him. She might be smarter than most of us combined, but we don't know if she's smart enough to be working for the right side. So far we've caught her with our enemy, talking only, but about buying a person. Mad Max has a thing for her, so that makes it harder to do a full interrogation. That guy is stacked and bigger than a damn mammoth. We're not about to lock up his girl and expect him to be okay with it.

So they decided we would listen in on Cheyanne getting to know the old ladies, to see if they talk shop and shit and whether she tries to get some information from our people. Oh, and Ruby is the damn ringleader.

Girl's barely old enough to drink legally, but somehow she's capable of sniffing out a traitor? Can she do it? Probably. It's Ruby, for fuck's sake. But should she?

She's been through a lot. I've looked deeper into her past lately. She was close to her mom and dad all her life. Made a few friends here and there, but mostly got in fights at school for defending her pops. When her mom died a few years ago, it hit her hard. She went with her to every chemo appointment. Took a leave of absence from school to do it. It put her a year behind, but she made up for it when she went back. Before she left high school, she was the youngest in the class. Then she became the oldest. She could have just gotten her GED and been done with it, but apparently she promised her mom she'd walk the stage. So she stuck with it at her high school, got top grades, and no one knew a goddamn thing about her other than her mom died and her dad's in a motorcycle club.

Every fight she had, she won. She got a reputation at school, not about sleeping around but that she wasn't someone to fuck with. Something she clings to still with the way she holds herself. Well, to those who don't look closer. But I'm beginning to look. Maybe not as close as I should, but I've got a job to do.

I see the pressure she puts on herself. She might think it's just her normal mantra, but she doubled her class load this last semester. She's not working at a job, but she's working harder than any student. And I know she signed up for summer classes again, for all three programs they're offering. Girl doesn't have an off switch. Some might see that as good; I just see it as one hell of a burnout when it comes.

She lets off some steam, at least. She works out twice a day sometimes. Other times, it's nothing at all. Just randomly when the thought pops into her head from what I can tell. But every night, like clockwork, she hops on her computer for some online gaming. And she's good. Really good.

Again, it's random *what* she plays each night. But it's all live action, and all with other players around the world. Her gamer tag? *Owner of Cerberus.* She even has a profile picture of her holding the leash of a three-headed dog. I was shocked when I found that out about her. The irony of her claiming to be Hades and leading around his hounds isn't lost on me.

"Quiet," Bulldog hisses.

"Well, that's easy. Just take your clothes off in front of him. Never seems to be a problem for me when I do that. Or hell, just get on your knees and give him a blow job. Never known a man to turn one of those down," Ruby chimes in, and I swallow my damn tongue as Law drops his head to the table with a groan.

"So didn't need to hear that. This *is* a bad idea."

Law might be grossed out by his daughter's words, but I'm sickened by the mental image.

And why in the hell is my mind picturing her before *me* on her knees? I think I might puke.

I tune everyone else out, including whatever is being said by the girls. I know Flint's recording this so we can play it back later if needed. I can get that play-by-play or just ask one of the many brothers pretending to have a poker game at our table instead of listening in on the girls' table across the bar.

It's just because you're getting close to her. My mind is scrambling for a reason that makes this better. It's still in shock from the image as well. Never, and I mean never, have I ever seen Ruby in any way but as a job that was annoying. Not a single thing about her turns me on.

Okay, fine, she has a snatch body, but I never noticed.

Well, I didn't think I did.

But there's that damn image again in my head. Her on her knees, in one of those black corsets she loves to wear so much. But instead of the leather pants, she has a thong on and no shoes. Mouth open and waiting, hair free of braids and ponytails, just dangling down her back. Her piercing eyes staring at me, and only me, waiting for me to take it a step further.

I shake myself out of it as I push my palm into my dick to prevent it from inflating any more. The roar from my brother and seeing Bulldog and Chains trying to restrain Flint gets me back on task.

"Let him go," Law says a second too late, as Flint is already across the bar and laying into his woman, denying her fears. He ain't quiet about it at all, so we can all hear him say how much he loves her.

I take a seat at the table beside Law. I was meant to just be a fly on the wall, watching over the game but not playing it. They figured if more people seemed interested in the game, it would be believable that we didn't care what the old ladies were talking about.

Obviously that cat's out of the bag since Flint heard something he didn't like his old lady saying. But from the way they're making out and heading to his room, I guess they made up.

"What're your thoughts?" I ask the boss.

"That I need to douse my ears in bleach after hearing half of that shit. Especially the parts Ruby said."

I grunt in agreement.

"But do I think Cheyanne is a bad seed? Nah. She could have asked questions left and right after the girls started complaining about their men. Or even put in a few snide comments about their fears. Girl's clean from what I can tell. She might be smart, but I'm not sure she knows what she's doing. We'll keep on it, at least to keep her safe till Mad Max decides what he wants to do."

I nod. Law makes the rulings around here, but it's clear that Mad Max isn't playing with this one. He's looking at her like a brother looks at an old lady. Hounds rarely interfere with that shit, unless we have to. And Law is pro-old lady. He had the best and wants us all to have that too. He never pushes anyone into it, but if he needs to, I think he'd push a brother out of it if the guy is too lovesick to see the cancer that she would bring to the club.

"Make sure Ruby gets home all right, will ya?" He stands and pats me on the shoulder, then leaves. Doesn't even wait on me to nod. Guess he doesn't have to. I gave him my consent a long time ago when I took this gig.

Standing, I stretch out my neck, feeling the pop over hearing it as I watch Chains smooth-talk his woman into going to his bunk room. Most of the brothers have cleared out with their old ladies already, leaving Ruby still seated with Cheyanne.

I see Ruby check her watch before she says, "Looks like luck is on my side. If I leave now, I can make it to the kegger being thrown in the dorm across the street from my building. Might even get real lucky, if you catch my drift. Later, new girl."

Kooper

"Ruby!" I yell after her as I take another step in her direction. "You still got babysitting duty tonight."

That's half the reason she's here tonight. Ruby comes in once a week and watches the brothers' kids so they can get some time with their old ladies and she can get some side cash. It was the only job her dad agreed to her doing. And it's usually only on the weekends so as not to interfere with her school schedule.

"Fuck off, Koop. I'm getting laid. You watch the brats." She doesn't look back as she flips me off and goes out the front door.

"Shit," I say a second before I hurry after her. I wouldn't put it past her to go and do what she wants. She knew this was just a ploy to get Cheyanne to talk. Her cover was that she had to babysit starting after nine. She was meant to be here in the club till then, then go on babysitting duty. But it seems I'm the only one still following the plan.

Of course, the kids aren't here tonight. Bulldog had his ma get Princess, and Chains has a few brothers at his house watching his kids because they've got some kind of sickness you get from school and needed to be in bed early.

"Ruby!" I call out again as I get outside and the clubhouse door closes behind me. A few brothers on the far side of the lot give me a nod. Domino points to my left, and I see Ruby trying to get into her car.

I run over and catch the door before it swings shut.

"Fuck," she mutters when she notices I'm blocking her escape.

"Exactly what you aren't going to do."

She looks up at me from her seated position, and I force myself not to stumble backward, gripping the door harder to stay upright. That damn image from before pops into my head again. She's at the right height to be on her knees before me, and the narrowed look she's throwing at me has me thinking it would be just like this. Her challenging me. She wouldn't be waiting with her mouth open like I'd pictured before. She'd fight me every step of the way, but want it all the same.

Jesus, I need to get a fucking grip.

"Actually, that's *exactly* what I'm going to do. And unless history changes in the next ten seconds and somehow we go back to the Stone Age or some shit, you don't get to tell me what the fuck I'm going to do or who I'm going to do it with. So fuck off. Or, better yet, go get yourself laid. Free country and all that. Find a vamp to suck you off so you can forget about what I'm doing for one night. It won't kill you."

"But it might kill *you*," I growl.

Her words are both pissing me off and turning me on. I'm sick. Fucking sick is what I am. But she might be right. I might just need a fuck. It has been a while.

"Is that a threat?" she asks me point-blank. No fear in her voice, no worry. Just holding my stare as she challenges me.

I grind my teeth in response, and she raises an eyebrow, no doubt seeing my jaw clench.

"Didn't think so. So stop cockblocking me and get the fuck out of my way. I did my job. Now do yours."

She pulls hard on the door, and I let it go so it slams shut. She doesn't even flinch before starting the engine and

Kooper

pulling out of the parking spot. I don't move, even when some gravel hits my legs from the force of her wheels spinning.

I count to ten. Twice. Then once more backward. It doesn't work. I'm still pissed off. Grumbling to myself, I get on my bike and head after her. I don't want to do it. But I have to.

Not because her dad told me to get her home safe. But if asked, that's what I'm going to tell everyone was the driving force. I refuse to say that the thought of her getting some punk-ass kid's dick wet makes me want to go on a killing spree.

In some cultures, I'm old enough to be her dad. Others, a big brother. In this one, it's just a work thing. I ignore everything as I zoom down the road and then ride her ass all the way back to her place. I make it known that it's me. I let her see that I'm not going away.

And to my amusement, she goes home. Doesn't stop at any place but her own. I park a few spots down from her and watch her go up the stairs and inside her apartment. She doesn't even spare me a glance, but I smile anyway. I ruined her night. Who the fuck knows if she had a date or not. She sure as hell doesn't now.

I check her feeds and see that she's alone with Natalie, then put my phone back into my pocket and get comfortable. It's going to be a long night.

I wasn't planning on spending it on my bike. But if it keeps her from going out and doing something stupid, then I'll do it. And that's the territory we're in with Ruby right now. She's mad at me. When she gets mad, dumb shit happens. It happens to everyone when they go looking for trouble. It finds them.

Lucky for her, I'm here to make sure I take out the problem before she even realizes it. Not that she seems to appreciate it, but fuck it. I've got nothing else to do tonight. Might as well do something I'm starting to enjoy—annoying the hell out of Ruby and ruining her fun.

"Bring my daughter back home. Kicking and screaming if you have to."

Law's words repeat in my head as I speed down the highway, not caring what the legal limit is. Boss gave me a job, and I'm not about to fail. I swear I was just here, but that was two days ago. Lots of shit's happened since then.

We should have seen this coming. *I* should have. The Devils Damned aren't idiots. Well, not all of them. Especially their VP, Duke. He must have known we were coming. Not sure how or if he actually planned for this shit to happen tonight.

Going after a Hound's family is the definition of starting a war. Going after the president's daughter? This won't end till Duke's in the ground and most of his brothers are too. I don't give a shit if he has his club's backing or not. In my eyes, all of the Devils Damned just signed their death warrant when Duke made the comment that he's taking out the club's heart. Our weakness, he thinks.

I growl to myself at that thought. A heart isn't a weakness but a strength. Having a heart isn't a flaw; it has

Kooper

you seeing things clearly. Sure, sometimes you need to make a call that costs a person's life. Being emotionless isn't good. It's lonely. It gets you nothing in life. I've done it. Act it every day. I hide that my heart leads most of my moves. I'd rather let people think what they want. It leaves them more vulnerable than what they think leading with a bleeding heart does.

Boss made a call. He went after Duke instead of waiting to make sure his kid is safe. It's the smart move, but I'm only one man. I can take out a lot, but I might not get to Ruby in time. Even if I do, I'm still only one man.

I feel my phone buzz and push the Call button to talk through my helmet. "Yeah?"

"I got her still at the school, in one of the auditoriums. Looks like a speaker or some shit," Mike says quickly.

"You got eyes on her?"

I called in a favor, knowing Flint was too busy with his own stuff to waste a second on tracking Ruby. Domino was manning the comms back home when Flint went to get his old lady. After Flint confirmed he took out two of Duke's men to keep them from getting Kitten, the call was put in to secure the rest of the property, to include Ruby. Domino needs to keep his focus on the rest of the old ladies and what's going on with Mad Max and his girl. A single favor called in from a former DSS operative won't wipe out the debt he owes me, and it saves everyone time when I do it my way.

"Yeah, third row from the back."

I take a deep breath, but I know it isn't over. Just because she's there doesn't mean that a threat isn't.

"I'm fifteen out still. Keep me posted." I end the call and pull back the throttle even more. A lifetime can pass in fifteen minutes, and I refuse to allow it to be Ruby's. Not on my watch.

As I pull up to the front of the campus, I get a ping that Ruby's event ended, and she's headed out. The next ping is a location drop. I drive across campus, ignoring the wannabe cops and people yelling at me to not drive on the grass. I don't give a fuck. Till I get Ruby in my sights and secured in a location that I feel is safe, I will do as I damn well please.

Chapter 8—Ruby

I still don't understand why the college requires us to attend these seminar things. It would make sense if it were a play or something and I was getting credit for writing a synopsis. But no. This is for University Seminar, a required credit that I have to take that's meant to help me adjust to college life and explore the resources the school offers. You're supposed to take it in your first year, but I pushed it off, hoping it would just go away. Like parking tickets. But sadly, I still have to take it. And I still have to pay those tickets. I have to attend three of these damn things and turn in the ticket stub or pamphlet they pass out.

Well, joke's on them because, like the last two, I brought my Organic Chem book and was reading it while sitting in the back row. If I'm going to be forced to attend this when I've already gone to the weekly hour-long class, I don't see a need to waste more time.

I'm sure if I'd taken this course freshman year or even in the fall, the seminars might have been better. As it is, I'm a month shy of the end of spring semester, and I've got very little left to choose from. It was either this discussion on Jane Austen in regard to today's society or the benefits of snails to beauty products and face creams. At least with Jane Austen, I read her book *Pride and Prejudice*. Well, I saw the movie. It counts. The movie was awesome, and I'm told it's just like the book. As for snails, to my knowledge, I don't put them on me or wear them. Maybe I should have gone to that seminar instead, just to confirm it, but whatever. The credit has been acquired, and I have the pamphlet in hand to prove it.

I walk with the rest of the students down the steps and out of the auditorium hall. Mostly women came to this one—surprise, surprise—and it was pretty packed. I was able to hide easily as I read my class assignment.

The night heat is a breath of fresh air as I pull off my leather jacket and set it over my crossbody bag. There are a few groups milling around, talking about everything from the seminar to what they're doing after this, and even my boots. I've got on killer heels with spikes down the back like a spine. They're tricky to wear but look awesome. I wear them when I'm feeling feisty, like a dinosaur. Nat calls them my Spinosaurus heels, and she ain't wrong.

The revving of a motorcycle gets my blood pumping like nothing else does, and I look in the direction I hear it.

"What the hell?" I mutter as I see Kooper flying across campus at me. I'd recognize him and his bike anywhere. Especially since I glared at it half the night two nights ago from my window, wishing it would go away.

There was a party I knew about. I was thinking about going. But I wouldn't if Kooper was going to be at my side. There was a glint about him that night that said he was in a mood to be squirrelly like that and ruin my fun.

Which he did. Sort of. I also kind of didn't want to go. So I looked out the window half the night and played *Fortnite* the rest of it. And I got to do it in comfy clothes, so it was actually a delightful night for me. Again, not something I'm going to thank *him* for. So if that's what he's here for, he can go right to hell.

Kooper

I haven't been able to get a decent workout in over the last few days, and my temper is at a boiling point. If he's looking for a fight, I'll give him one that he won't soon forget.

"Koop, what the fu—" The sight of his gun pointed at me has me going stock-still. I know I piss him off, but I really never thought it would go this far.

I duck when I hear the shot, my mind already telling me I would have felt it before I heard it if I was hit. But I still take a second to look at my body to see if any parts are oozing blood. Another shot goes off, this one from behind me. I turn and see some guy coming across campus, sprinting with a gun raised.

People all around me are screaming and running around like they have no idea where to go.

"Get inside," I yell, but I don't know if anyone can hear me. "Go back inside and lock yourselves in." I keep low to the ground as I try to see what's close to me for cover.

The campus is landscaped like most are, kept pristine with nicely trimmed grass and small round bushes. They do shit for cover.

Somewhere, Kooper lost his bike, and now he's right in front of me, pulling me up by the arm and pushing me back behind him. I don't know where we're going, but I'm not about to stop and ask. I go where he's pushing me and duck when he pulls me down.

"What the hell is going on, Koop?"

He reloads as we hunker behind a tree.

"The Devils Damned VP, Duke, put a hit out on every piece of property the club has."

I don't think I've ever been so scared in my life. Not for me, but for my family. "Mama Bear? Princess? Grace?" The idea of anyone getting hurt is like a tsunami of emotions I don't want crashing into me.

"Fine. Hounds took out the threat before anyone was hit. Everyone is going back to home base to check in. You're the last one still out." He fires off two more rounds.

"We can't stay here."

He nods at my assessment as we both look behind us to see what cover we have to work with. People are still scattered across the yard in small groups, huddling together, hoping no bullet will find them.

"Where's your car?"

"Around the building, a block down."

"It's too far. If we make it to my bike, we might have a chance to get out of here. I'll give you cover fire. You start her up, and I'll be right behind you."

Back the fuck up. I must have missed something. No way in hell did Kooper just tell me to drive his bike. Do I know how to ride? Of course. Despite my dad's protests, Mom made sure I knew how to handle anything between my legs— another thing Dad hated hearing. But she and I both knew I was only interested in learning about the motorcycle and not a man's third leg.

"Stop gawking at me and get moving. On the count of three, run your ass off, and don't make me regret it. The keys are still in her. One, two—"

I start running before he says *three*, and he starts shooting. I see his bike—big, black, and the sweetest thing

Kooper

I've ever seen in my life right now. I chance a glance back and miss a step, going down with a twist of the ankle.

I let out a small cry like a stupid girl, cursing to myself as I look down and see I tripped over a damn sprinkler that popped up. A dozen others around us start going off at the same time.

I look at Kooper and see he's still pinned behind the tree, but thankfully, he isn't paying attention to me. I don't think my ego can take him laughing at me falling on my ass after we get out of this.

I move to stand, but I can tell my ankle won't take my weight. I don't think it's broken, but I'm going to need some ice on it. So I do the next best thing: I crawl to the bike.

"Ruby, get your ass up!" Kooper yells at me, and there goes my pride.

"Ankle," I shout over my shoulder and continue to crawl. I'm close. Just a few more feet and I can get on the bike. I know once I get there I can get it started. I will break my damn leg if I have to for us to get out of this.

A bullet hits the dirt right in front of me, and I halt my progress as I look back and see Kooper watching me. His eyes narrow, and I shake my head. I already know he's going to play hero, and I so don't need his death on my conscience.

As he stands, I scream, "No!" But he doesn't listen. He fires twice across the yard and then races to me. He grabs me by the waist and runs us both to his bike. Another shot rings out, and we both go flying, me from being dropped by Kooper and him from getting shot in the back.

I can barely brace before my head hits the tail of his bike, and then I land on the ground. My ears ring and my vision blurs as I lie there. My head hurts like a fucking bull ran a horn through it. I touch it, wincing, and pull my hand back. I see multiple sets of fingers, but that doesn't concern me as much as the blood running down my hand.

Pushing up, I look over and see Kooper fighting with someone. I think it's the guy who was firing at him, or maybe someone else. I don't know. Kooper's getting his ass beat from what I can see. Or at least the three versions I see are. I close my eyes tight and shake my head to line myself up, but it's a bigger mistake than when I decided that orange looks good on me.

I turn to the side and puke up everything I ate before coming out tonight. It doesn't clear my vision, but it's all I can do to hold myself upright and not fall into it. I feel dizzy and think the ground is spinning. Maybe the earth started spinning at a crazy speed and I'm feeling it, or I just have one helluva concussion.

"Come on, Ruby girl, we've got to go," I hear Kooper say. Then his hands are pulling me up, and I almost crumple on him. "Easy. I got you." He helps me onto his bike with one arm and then holds me up a bit before getting on himself. "Just hang on."

I squeeze my arms tight around him and hear him grunt in pain before he adjusts his arm. Then the engine purrs between our legs, and we are out of here. I close my eyes and just pray that I don't get sick again. Throwing up doesn't freak out a biker. Doing it on his bike? It's a good way to never get invited back again. Unless it's your dad's bike and you got sick because you ate too much cake on your eighth birthday and begged him to take you out on his bike as a gift. When that's the case, you get an ice cream for crying about it, but you still have to wash the bike the next day. Dad was nothing but fair, even if he did it with a smile and a sweet treat.

I must have dozed off somewhere between leaving campus and landing here, wherever here is.

"Going to need you to hold still while I get off the bike, and then I'll get you."

I nod at his words and fall forward when he eases off, but he steadies me with his hands as I go to grab the seat he just vacated.

"Easy."

"That's what the vamp said," I slur, blinking a few times to focus enough to see we're outside a hospital.

"Pretty sure it's 'that's what she said.'"

"But vamps *are* easy."

He wraps a hand over my shoulder and pulls me toward him before helping me all the way off his bike.

"Wouldn't that mean a Hound would have said it and not a 'she'?"

We stumble toward the emergency room doors. Good boy that Kooper is, he parked in a regular parking spot, ignoring the fact that we're the ones who need the emergency spot.

"Why are we walking? We're injured."

He looks down at me, and I see him roll his eyes before he looks forward again. "You got a scratch on your head and that's it."

"And what about you?"

"What about me?" he grunts.

I give a deep sigh and shake my head. "I might be seeing double or triple depending on what's in front of me, but I still see that your arm is limp as shit next to you."

He just glares straight ahead.

"Like your dick," I snicker, then end up coughing and slowing us down further.

"Thought the vamps were supposed to say that?"

My eyes go wide at his teasing words a second before we stumble into the not-so-busy waiting room. Either Kooper drove us farther away from the shooting, or no one else was hurt and needed aid. I'm praying for the second. I might not like everyone I meet, but I don't want to be the reason a person is injured. If that guy was there to take me out because I'm the kid of someone in the club, then I should be the only one hurt. Well, *they* should be way more hurt than me. Dead. They should be dead.

I should ask Kooper if he took care of that guy or just got us out of there. I'm not looking for club details, just need to know if I should watch our backs as Kooper tells the nurses at the station that we need help.

"Always protect your six." Dad's voice echoes in my head, and I take a deep breath and look behind us, closing one eye to limit the double vision.

"Don't worry, we weren't followed." Warm breath fills my ear, and I blink and slowly turn my head to look into his intense eyes.

Kooper

"Miss, please take a seat." The small moment we shared breaks at the nurse's clipped words, and I turn to see a wheelchair. I snarl at it.

"Rather walk."

"Sit down before you fall down," Kooper says as he forces my ass into the chair.

I get off a glare at him before I'm turned and wheeled back. I know he's following me. No way would he let me go into a hospital alone after what just happened. If we were back home and this were General's hospital, a brother's place of business, I might be alone. But from the looks of things, this ain't it. For one thing, the hospital walls are lime green. The ones back home are beige. I prefer that to the puke color, but I'm not the one who has to look at them all day. Hopefully, we'll only be here a few hours.

"Let's get you up on the table, and we'll get that wound clean and checked before the doctor comes in and has a look."

I always did like nurses more than doctors. They seem to be the ones who do most of the stuff anyway. Doctors get the credit, but the nurses are the ones who patch you up and put cute color Band-Aids over your boo-boos.

In typical Hound behavior, Kooper stands guard at the open curtained-off area. He watches everything going on, and I watch him.

"You talk to my dad?" I ask.

"Phone's broken."

"Want to use mine?"

He raises one eyebrow. "You got it on you?"

Shit. It's back there. If I'm lucky, campus police will find it and just assume I lost it when I was running for cover like everyone else. I don't need to get kicked out of school over this. I doubt they would blame a victim, but who knows how people will see this.

Fuck. That also means I lost my damn pamphlet. I'll have to go to another stupid seminar to get full credit for that intro class.

I shake my head. "Dad's going to be pissed if he has to buy me a new one." Phones are fucking expensive, and this is the third one he's bought me this year. I'm not exactly graceful. I can walk in eight-inch heels, but ask me to hold a phone and not drop it or knock it off a counter or desk and you're just asking for trouble.

"Here's a concept: Get one that isn't so expensive and maybe *you* could afford it yourself."

I narrow my eyes at him, but then the nurse tells me not to so she can start stitching up the cut I got from his damn license plate. I know he's just pushing my buttons because that's what he does, but I'm mad about everything. And while I have no money, thanks to Dad saying I shouldn't get a job except for babysitting, relying on my pops is just part of my life. I would love to support myself. It would be a dream come true. But I know my dad also enjoys having a part of me that still needs him.

Which I'm sure Kooper gets, but he's still a prick about it.

"You might want to check him out, too, once you're done with me. I think he has a dislocated shoulder."

I smirk as I see the fury flare in his eyes. Kooper's like every other biker—big, bad, and a fucking pussy when it comes to asking for help. Bet he'd rather be the one to knock his shoulder back into place, but if he's going to play his role of asshole, I'll play mine too: pain in the ass.

Or in this case, the shoulder.

Chapter 9—Kooper

"So, want to tell me how all this happened?" The doctor checking over the stitchwork the nurse did on Ruby looks over at me. And the damn sling on my arm.

Considering everything, I say we got off lucky. A dislocated shoulder for me, a concussion, a gash on the head, and a twisted ankle for Ruby. I made them look at her leg after she mentioned my minor shoulder issue. Did it hurt? Yeah. Did it mean I couldn't drive home and have my brother, someone I trusted, look at it? Hell no. But the nurses here wouldn't hear of it, and since my goal is to keep our heads down, I relented and let them do it.

When I saw Ruby open her mouth to call out the shot on my back, I gave her one shake of the head, and that had her shutting up. Just because she's looking to one-up me doesn't mean she gets to draw attention to us being in a shooting that's probably all over the news right about now.

Thankfully, there was no penetration where I got hit, and it only looked like a bruise when the nurses took my shirt and jacket off to examine my arm. I was able to convince them it was nothing. An added benefit of the special lining the club invested in for all Hounds to have in their biker jackets. We don't always wear them, but I put it on more times than not. It's meant to help with road rash if I ever fall off my bike because of some fucker who can't drive, but it also keeps me alive if some idiot thinks it's wise to shoot a Hound in the back.

"Just picking up my girl for a ride, and some asshole sideswiped us into a ditch."

"We can have the police here soon to take your statements to file the report." He doesn't even look back at me as he gives Ruby another concussion test. It's pissing me off. No way does he need to keep looking at her so much. The nurse already did the job; he just needs to sign the damn paperwork to let us out of here.

I shake my head at him. "No good, Doc. Didn't see what the car was. It was too dark for any description."

My words have him stopping long enough to turn and give me his full attention. "I see. And what about you?" he asks, turning back to Ruby. "You see who it was?"

She shakes her head. "My eyes were closed. I was just enjoying being on the back of my man's bike without a care in the world."

I smirk. Her response is part of the job to make this believable. But it also does something else. It makes the doc take a second to really see my vest and understand that touching her might not be the wisest thing to do if he wants to keep his hands in working condition. Not that he knows we aren't together, but it's my job to keep Ruby safe. And that means keeping creeps away from her.

"Right. Let me get those discharge papers, and I'll have the nurse go over the medications I recommended. It's best if she doesn't fall asleep for the next twenty-four hours to make sure nothing happens."

"Oh, trust me, sleeping is the last thing on my mind. Isn't that right, big guy?" She gives me a dramatic wink, and I don't hold back the eye roll. That's over the top, but whatever it takes to get the guy out of the room and us on the road back home is fine by me.

Five seconds after the doctor leaves, Ruby's smirking, and I just know I'm going to get an earful.

"Just picking up your girl, huh? Why, Kooper, I've never been so flattered."

I shake my head as I look down at my feet.

"Keep saying such sweet things and Dad might have to kick you off my detail."

Her words trigger something in me. Something deep and dark that I never thought was an issue till two days ago when that image got into my head. It was only once and never again, but I have this sick fear that somehow Law will know I thought that about his daughter. Someone I should only see as an assignment and never, ever as anything beyond that.

She stands, her ankle wrapped and her feet in slippers to keep her toes from freezing. She looks like a temptress with the way her hair is blown out and her normal badass updo isn't there. But there's also a softness about her that anyone would be a fool to think was her real self. She's a tigress waiting to pounce on anyone not strong enough for a woman like Ruby.

"So, you going to carry me to our chariot so we can have our long night together, lover?" The sass that comes out of her mouth makes me want to find a way to shut it. And not just with my hand over it.

Kooper

Her words have my blood boiling. And not all of it is because I'm mad. No. A deep, dark, depraved, sick part of me likes what she says.

"I ain't here because I want to be, I'm here because I *have to be*. Your dad gave me a job, one I don't intend to fail. And the only reason I got stuck with you is because everyone else worth their salt turned it down, and I've got a background in asset protection. Trust me, if I had a choice, it wouldn't be me. So pack up your shit and let's go. Your dad wants you home, and I've got a vamp waiting on me to give me something good for all the shit I had to do today."

She keeps the stupid bright smile on her face, but I see a bit of light fade from her eyes. I watch that spark that's all her go out, and that same depraved part of me that shouldn't like her words feels bad that I caused that hurt.

I shake my head and walk out of the room as soon as the nurse comes in. She tries to stop me, but I ain't having it. A single look has her backing off and talking to Ruby as I walk down the hall. Not enough for full privacy, but this way I can still keep an eye on my pain-in-the-ass charge.

I dial a number and wait for someone to pick up.

"Wrong number."

"It's Kooper," I say quickly before Domino hangs up. I'm calling from an outside line to the one directly inside the tech room, something none of us ever do unless we don't have a choice.

"Shit, Kooper. What the hell, man? Reports are coming in about a shooting. You and Ruby okay? Why aren't you calling from your phone? Is this thing secure?"

"Not sure, so keep it light. Ruby and I are fine. At the hospital doing a look-over."

"She okay?"

"Hit her head. We'll be back soon once we get the all-clear from here."

"Got it. And the phone issues?"

"Ran into some problems. Need you to clean and clear the primary phone. I'll bring this one in. It's a new one I picked up real quick." I know he's catching what I'm not saying. My phone was lost or destroyed during what went down. I didn't even know I didn't have my phone when I saw this one on the ground and picked it up before I grabbed Ruby and got us out of there as the sirens closed in. There was a shootout on campus, so no doubt the cops would show. I'll admit that their response time sucks, but I'm not about to complain too much. We were able to get out and weren't stopped by anyone. "Need you to do some scrubbing too."

"Got it," Domino says. He might not be as good as Flint, but if he finds footage of us on any security cameras on campus or of us leaving, I'm sure it'll be erased soon. It'll also give him some idea of what went down if he hadn't already been looking into it. Like I said, he isn't as good as Flint, so he might not have gotten that far into it yet.

"Talk soon." I hang up and turn off the phone before popping out the battery and SIM card and putting them in separate pockets. I should toss the whole thing, but I want whatever intel Flint can get off it once we're back at the clubhouse.

Kooper

I walk back to the room just as Ruby takes the paperwork, and I hear the nurse comment that her *husband's* paperwork about aftercare is in there too.

Jesus fucking Christ.

"Let's go," I bark, and Ruby doesn't jump like the other woman. She just gives the nurse a smile and limps out, not asking for a hand and not waiting for a wheelchair. It's a slow gait, and that's the only reason I do what I do.

"Don't got all day." I scoop her up and stride out the front doors. I'd like to think the glare on my face keeps Ruby from popping off some ridiculous snark, but one look down at the princess's smile of expectations has me growling under my breath.

"Now, now, that's no way to act as you carry me to the chariot we spoke about earlier."

I so want to drop her on her ass, but I promised the boss I'd keep her alive. And while a fall to the floor won't kill her, it might cause issues if she complains to Daddy and he asks what she said that made me decide that leaving her behind was a wise idea.

One thing I learned early in life is that any bit of denial about something has at least 1 percent of truth in it. And that's 1 percent too much for Law to know about.

The drive is quick. I break every damn speed limit and run every red light I see. Don't give a fuck. I need her off my bike. Her arms no longer wrapped around me. Her heat gone. Every part of her at least ten feet or more away from me right now.

The compound is a mess with everyone coming in, which is perfect. I get her off my bike, and then I'm gone.

Another brother can deal with her. Hell, she has a dad. She's his problem now. I just need space. A minute, an hour, a few days—I'll take anything.

As I get to my room, I close the door, not slamming it like I want. I'm in control; no need to show I'm not. I walk to the attached bath and turn the shower on, then get under the spray and just breathe. Till I hear a noise I recognize as my door clicking open and someone coming closer. I close my eyes, already knowing who it is.

"Hey, handsome, need some help washing?" It's a vamp. Probably has a name, and I probably know it, but right now she's just a faceless club girl looking for dick.

Her words should make my cock jump. It should spring to attention for a bit of release. Even my mind should be on board with the possible endorphin high.

But my mouth opens before I can think. "Not now."

Two words that have the girl walking away easily enough. But those two words let me know I'm fucked. Completely and utterly fucked.

Women screaming ain't new around here, but it does draw a crowd. It's been quiet since Duke, the Devils Damned VP, went missing after the club's raid on his sex trafficking ring and his attempt to take out those close to the club a few days before today. A screaming woman should seem like things are back to basics, if the scream were in glee or ecstasy. But it draws the ear, and the eye, when it's clear that

Kooper

it isn't either of those things. Especially when it's Flint's old lady, Kitten, and she's yelling into her phone.

"He did what? That motherfucker! I'm going to kill him. You stay right there. I'm on the way."

I think her stomping toward the cars is what drives Flint into action more than her words.

"Kitten, what's going on? Who we killing, and how many body bags we bringing?" Flint asks as he catches his girl and grabs her arm to spin her around and face him.

"You ain't killing anyone. That asshole is all mine. Goddamn bastard left my girl on the side of the road 'cause she wouldn't put out. Fuck that shit. Only reason why I'm the one killing him and not Bailey is 'cause I got a yard to bury the fucker in."

"Wait, that was Bailey?"

Of course Ruby would stick her nose into this shit. She might not be an old lady, but she runs this place like she's head bitch some days.

"Yeah. That asshole she was seeing just proved that he really *is* an asshole, and not just because I didn't like how he saw the club."

"Well, you ain't doing it alone, girl. That bitch of yours is my kind of woman. You go, I go." Ruby nods.

I roll my eyes at her. At them all, really. No one is thinking clearly. Especially Ruby.

"Might want to check the head wound. I doubt you'd do much damage even if you were given a shot," I say as I rub my forehead with my middle finger. The crazy woman is mad at me for it. Doesn't make sense. I save her life, she falls and bumps her head in the process, and it's my fault? What-the-fuck-ever.

"Fuck you very much. I've been putting men in their place since I was fourteen and grew boobs. Didn't need Daddy and the club to fuck them up when they got too handsy, and I sure as shit don't need either now. Believe it or not, I know how to cut a man's dick off and get away with it. It ain't my first rodeo."

"What?" Law growls as he pushes past me and the rest of the boys.

I don't move. I can't. My body is locked down on her words.

She rolls her eyes. "We'll talk about it later. I handled it. Mom knew, even helped, so don't get all protective over shit that's in the past. Just know I ain't as weak as you like to assume I am 'cause I only show you the side you want to see. The doting daughter and all that shit. But remember, I came from you and Mom. Special K had a special way she did shit, and she taught me well."

"Fucking hell." Prez grabs his daughter and pulls her in tight.

If she hid that from her old man, what else is she hiding?

I turn and walk away. Don't need to hear anything else; I got enough. I know the boss would expect me to deal with it. Even if Ruby thinks she took care of it, it ain't over. I just didn't expect the amount of rage that went through me at hearing her talk. I knew that despite everything, I got close to her. I ain't nonfeeling like so many think. I can't just shut it off. I shut it down, so no one sees, but I get attached like anyone does on a job. And that's what Ruby is—a job. One

Kooper

I've been on for what feels like decades. I've learned things about her that I doubt others know. That she likes pickled chips and not salt and vinegar ones. That she likes olives in her margaritas thanks to Mama Bear teaching her that. She rags on nerds but is a closet Star Wars nut with a Lego collection that rivals some men's baseball card collections. And she's a gamer with some serious skills on the keyboard. She has layers.

And despite her saying she handled it, she's still feeling what happened to her when she was a child. A fucking child. If her mom helped, that means she was well. Meaning all this shit went down before Ruby was fifteen. I don't care how old the guy was. He could have been her same age, older, younger, doesn't matter. I plan to find him and fuck him up so that he ain't breathing when I'm done.

You might think it's impossible to find a guy like that after so long. That shit happens, and it's possible. For most people who don't have a name, sure, it would be downright impossible. And I don't have a name. Got nothing but what she said. She cut off his dick. Not many of those show up at a hospital. Fewer properly reported. So that's my starting point. I already know where Ruby was when she was a kid. It's my job to know about her past life so I can protect her future.

I slide onto my bike, back her out, and head to my place. It's not much. To those who pass by, it looks like a storage room off the side of a strip mall. But once you enter the code to unlock the door, you're greeted with a set of stairs that go down. Nothing big, but it's loaded with some food, a bed, and a TV to keep life from being too boring, along with a small arsenal and my security system. I have eight monitors running. Law doesn't ask me how I keep track of his girl, and I don't tell him. But I know my way around computers enough to do what I do. Not enough to cover the ground Gator and Flint do, but I hold my own. They don't even know what I've got down here. I built this system for myself. I have a small third-party team that I use to track things further if I need to go that deep. It's a group of guys I knew from back in the service. We all left for greener pastures—I went biker, they went dark web. We stay out of each other's way, but we've all got enough favors to call in on one another to keep things professional between us.

I go to the only screen that I keep off and power it on. While it takes a second, I grab a beer from the fridge, twist the cap off, and throw it across the room into the trash can I keep in the corner. Taking a long pull, I sit and wait. This system is linked only to my group of people. I don't keep it online or active for a reason. But when it's on, I know it's only a matter of time before someone notices and reaches out.

And just as expected, Brantly types first.

What's the job?

No job. Just information.

But I want a job.

Of course he does. No one wants to just be a paper pusher. A job means getting your hands dirty. But for this one, I plan to be the one to experience that joy.

Next time. Not sure if I even believe that, but I said it, and now I've got to stick with it.

Another thing that we make sure happens in this group: Once it's said, it's a done deal. No backing out. Ever.

What do you need?

Kooper

I don't question how any of the boys get information, just like they don't question me. I could do it, but I already know my time is limited in my space. The beeping of a text coming in from Law confirms that.

I tell Brantly what I want and then power off. I'll be back in a day or so and get it from him then.

I check the feeds on Ruby's place, making sure no unwanted guests or landlords have stopped by while she's out. Nothing but the damn roommate who seems to do nothing but read. Boring.

I never got people who find the fun in reading. Especially when they make a movie out of it. Just save the time and sit through the two-hour-long movie rather than read about it for twelve. Sure, some things are left out, but you get the big parts. There was an adventure, someone died, someone fell in love, the end.

Whatever.

Locking up, I toss the trash I collect from my place and then get back on my bike to do what I do best—babysit a pain in the ass.

Chapter 10—Ruby

Hearing I'm just a problem is a hard pill to swallow. Sure, I know I can be. I know this isn't a job Kooper wanted. But actually hearing him say it when we were at the hospital a few weeks back? It sucked. Still sucks. Which is probably why I can't get his words out of my head.

Well, that and Dad's fussing. I can fight my own battles. I have, and I won them. Some things don't need to be spoken about. But I get a damn bump on the head, and I seem to have vomit of the mouth and just tell him everything. Well, not everything. Just one thing that Dad is still freaking out about. I'm not sure if he's mad about me never telling him or that Mom and I handled it without him. If he had his way, the guy would be six feet under. And I'm sure he's looking. Dad's like a dog with a bone. Even if the bone is used up and across state lines and has nothing to do with the dog anymore, he wants it. He wants to ruin and destroy it. Even though I already did. I think that's what pisses me off most. He can't just let it go. He has to put his final stamp on it.

Poor little Ruby just can't do shit without her dad coming in to finalize it.

I throw my pen across the room and growl to myself. I'm so wrapped up in my head that I can't study properly. I need a break. Or ten.

Kooper

I would go for a run, but it's pouring out. And as much as I don't mind the rain, wet socks are the worst. It's like a type of torture. I can handle wet shoes, but there's just something about wet cloth on my feet that irks me.

Thankfully, I'm back home for the weekend, and I know a perfect gym that has an indoor track. I can't handle a stationary system of any kind right now. I need to go fast and slow and just pound out everything that feels like a ball in my chest.

I change quickly, grab my keys, and I'm out the door before I think beyond the need for freedom that a run can give me. The gym is packed. Typical. Misfits, appropriately named for the group of friends Troublemaker and Kitten belong to, is one of the best gyms in the state. They have everything and more. Even a spa section, which might be a good idea for after the run. A little treat for myself.

With an extra pep in my step for the possible massage I'll be getting later, I speed-walk to the doors. I don't want to fall on my ass from the rain. Been there, done that. Like I said before—wet socks are a no-go.

"Well, if it isn't the queen bitch herself."

I turn at Jordan's words and smile wide, going over and giving him the biggest hug I can. He wasn't my friend before Kitten and Troublemaker found their guys in the club, but I claim him as my own now. And his husband, Meekail, but that's just because he's superhot with the whole Shemar Moore doppelgänger thing going for him.

"How's business?" I ask as I pull back and move to the desk to sign in.

"Same," Jordan says with an easy smile. "Better, actually. Especially with the eye candy we've got going on around here." He wiggles his eyebrows, and I just roll my eyes. The guy is a complete nut for his man, but he does like to tease, and especially me. He says he never sees me with a man and therefore needs to find one for me. I've tried to tell him I've got a few back at college, but to him, if he doesn't lay eyes on a man, then I'm single.

I guess he's right. If I were serious about anyone I was dating, I'd bring them around the club. I just haven't found the right guy yet. You know, one who won't take off running the second dear old dad threatens him within an inch of his life if he makes his baby girl cry. Well, Dad or any of the twenty-odd brothers who would gladly tell him too.

"Well, keep them out of my way."

"Why? You afraid one might snag your attention?"

"Nope." I grab a towel and the locker key I checked out. "Just worried that they won't keep their eyes off me, and then you'll be liable for them hurting themselves when they trip over their tongues and land on a barbell."

He chuckles as I head to the lockers, stashing my stuff before going upstairs. The track they have goes around the entire upper floor. It's not exactly the scenic route I wanted, but I can watch those working out on my level and those below if I get bored enough.

I give myself a good five-minute stretch, and then I'm off at a steady pace. Not many use the indoor track, opting for stationary systems instead. Within seven minutes, I'm bored, but my head's still all over the place. I need to run a few laps to get me out of whatever this is.

Which seems to be happening more lately. I'm not sure what's going on with me. I can't be having a midlife

Kooper

crisis; I'm too young for that. I still like the career path I'm on, so it's not that. I love my family, no matter how chaotic it is.

Maybe you just need a man.

Of fucking course Jordan's voice pops into my head. Typical.

And talk about timing issues. Especially when I glance down and see a certain pair of eyes watching me from below.

Eyes that pull me in, and for a second, I feel like I'm floating. Till I hit the ground and realize I freaking fell over my damn feet. I look over the side of the glass partition and see that he's gone. Which is exactly what I wanted. No way was I going to live it down if Kooper found out I fell head over heels, literally. It's something Kitten would do, and has done, for her man, Flint. Hell, any of the old ladies fall into that category. But not me. I'm too coordinated for that shit.

"You good, Ruby?"

My eyes bug out of my head at his voice behind me. I shake myself a bit before I lean back on my hands and look at him with my head thrown back so he's upside down in my view.

"Just peachy. Why do you ask?"

He looks at me, then the ground, then goes far enough to gesture that I'm sprawled out on the track like a freaking exercising noob.

"Just getting in a few extra warm-up stretches."

"But you already did your normal prep work."

Now it's my turn to give him a look that has him looking away as I stand up.

Just how long was he watching me? And did he run up here to check on me? Is Kooper being... sweet?

S.J. Rowe

"Stalker much?"

"It's what I get paid for."

"And you running up here to see if I was okay after falling? That in the job description too?" I take a step forward and bat my eyelashes at him.

He rolls his head back and around till his eyes land on my hand that I put on his arm. I smirk as I give his bicep a small squeeze. Not sure if it's a reaction or he did it on purpose, but it flexes, and I squeeze it again just for fun.

"You seem to have a habit of falling down when I'm around. Not sure your daddy wants you to hurt yourself every five seconds. It only increases his insurance bill. And if you're going to fall for a guy, make it one who's interested in you and not paid to watch. Unless you're on a stage, that is."

I drop my hand and turn around. "Joke's on you. I'm clumsy, not interested."

"Says the woman who can run up six flights of stairs in hooker heels."

I shake my head and get back to my lap. I get ten steps in and feel a shadow.

"What are you doing?" I ask.

"Some call this running."

"You can't do it somewhere else?"

"All the treadmills are taken, and I don't know if you noticed, but it's raining outside."

"Whatever. Don't let me keep you." I move to the outside lane and slow my pace, hoping he passes. But the asshole doesn't.

"*Now* what are you doing?"

Kooper

"I find it easier to keep you from falling and hurting yourself if I'm close enough to catch you."

"Push me down is more like it," I grumble.

He shrugs. "Only time will tell."

And then the jerk shuts up and just runs. Right. Beside. Me. The entire time. I go fast; he keeps pace. I slow; again, he's right there. I try to push myself into a solid ten-mile run, and the guy doesn't even get sweaty. It's a freaking joke.

I don't take the time to stretch after my run, just limp down the stairs, get my stuff from the lockers, and then huff and puff to the front desk to drop off the locker key.

"Damn, sweets, you look horrible." Jordan's lip rises as if he smells something foul. And a quick sniff of my shirt lets me know I'm the issue. "Well"—he grins—"no more than usual."

"Skank." I swallow and feel sandpaper at the back of my throat. "Got any water?"

"Yup." He grabs a bottle from below the desk and sets it on the counter. I go to reach for it, but he pulls it back. "Three bucks."

"Seriously?"

He shrugs. "Hubby says I've got to stop giving the cow away for free."

"It's milk that you give for free. And why are you charging? You never charged before."

He winces. "Technically, we always charge for bottled water. Hence the big sign behind me that says water bottles are *sold* here. I just never charged you before. But Meekail is all in a snit about my latest Amazon purchases. He won't let me buy anything else from them till I pay off the latest credit card bill. And since I love Amazon more than you, you get charged. Three bucks, buttercup. Pay up."

And in typical fashion, I ran out of the apartment with just my driver's license and my keys. That's it. No wallet, no cash. I don't even keep spare change in my car.

"Forget it," I grumble as I turn and head for the door. I can survive the fifteen-minute drive home. Will I feel like death in the Sahara when I get there? Sure. But what else am I going to do? Spend thirty minutes at the water fountain till I quench my thirst? Those things go so slow, and I feel like a damn dog lapping up the water.

"Two coconut waters." Kooper's voice, once again behind me, makes me glare. Damn bastard has to be greedy and get two? He shouldn't even need them. He barely broke a sweat, so there's no need to replenish electrolytes. The guy really needs to go die under a rock somewhere.

"Ruby."

"What?" I don't even look back as I respond to Kooper.

"Here."

I turn, and a freaking water bottle hits me dead center in the chest. My arms fly up to catch it, and that's when I see it's coconut water.

"Try not to die on the way home," he says before turning and heading back to who the fuck knows where. When I left the track upstairs, he was still stretching. He never said I should, too, but the look he gave me pushed me to run down the stairs faster just to spite him.

Kooper

I glance at Jordan, whose bugged-out eyes likely mirror my own. Kooper is an ass. A complete and utter ass.

But I'm not about to turn down a free drink. I'm on a college paycheck, after all. Meaning I have nothing, and anything free is amazing. I've never drunk coconut water before. It's not good. Like at all. But I keep it and drink it on the way home. Not the wasteful type, despite how much of a smile it brings to my lips to think I can just throw this out the window as a screw you to Kooper. Not that he would know, or care.

But if he didn't care, why did he buy it for you in the first place?

My inner beast has a point. One I refuse to think about any longer as I pull up just as Dad does, and everything else is forgotten as I soak in some much-needed solo time with my pops.

"Hey, Nat, you home? I brought pizza," I singsong as I walk into the apartment.

"And guests," Abigail chirps from behind me as she shuts the door.

"You're not a guest. You're family," I say as I put the pizza down and open it up to grab a slice. I burn my mouth on the first bite and have to breathe through my mouth as I pant, but I refuse to let the piece in my hand go.

"More like another roommate." Natalie smiles as she comes to the living area after shutting her door behind her. She always keeps it closed. I never say anything because I know she isn't dealing or something crazy like that. Trust me, I'd know. And she doesn't give me shit when I don't speak up on things that I'm sure seem odd about me. Like sometimes leaving at a moment's notice to help with the club or something and not filling her in. When I got the head injury, I just said I fell. Nothing more. She knew I was at the seminar where the shooting happened. She was meant to come, too, just for support, but ended up not going. She never asked if I was there. Never questions anything I do, or who I bring home. Which isn't that often, but it usually happens once or twice a month. And it's always Abigail.

"That's true. Hey, you think we can start charging her rent?" I say.

Nat shrugs. "Only if she springs for the electric bill."

"Ugh, again? I swear we just paid it," I groan.

"That's the thing about bills, honey. It's a monthly issue."

"We really should start stripping," I mumble around another bite.

"I've seen you dance, Ruby. You ain't got the moves." Abigail grins as she picks up her own slice, blowing on it enough to take a bite and not swat at her melting tongue.

"Kitten's dance group offered to give me lessons." I pout.

"Which one is Kitten again?" Natalie asks as she picks off the black olives. Which is fine, since I put them on my pizza. She likes pepperoni, and I like black olives. So, naturally, we get both, and she deals with it. We could do half and half, but I end up bingeing on pizza during gaming nights. Like I plan to tonight with a new gaming friend—whose username is Bowser, so it won't last long. And why should we have to have a slice without olives?

Okay, I sound like a bitch even to my own ears, but Nat's cool about it.

Plus, I'm the one who splurges on the pizza every time. A rule we made freshman year. The person who buys gets to decide, and the other can eat it and not complain or go without. It's not perfect, but it's never been an issue for us. There's a reason Nat's my roommate. We get along better than anyone else I know, even if I don't know everything about her. That might be the reason it works so well. We're close and yet still complete strangers in other ways.

"Kitten is the one with amnesia and goes by Jules. She's with Flint. And her best friend Bailey—who's now Troublemaker, it seems—is with Gator."

"When did that happen?" Abigail asks.

I shake my head at both of them. "If you guys didn't keep ditching me for the vet internship and whatever coffee thing you had going on, you'd know this shit."

Abigail shrugs. "Need the money."

Natalie just puts more pizza into her mouth. She was meant to come with me the other night to watch M perform and then to hang out at the club. M is a pop-up dance group that Kitten, Troublemaker, and the rest of the original Misfits are in that does dance numbers while a movie plays. A mix between Broadway and *Rocky Horror Picture Show*, but in a random location, and they never do the same show more than once. The other night was another epic performance, but everyone was all coupled up. I was madder about being the only single lady to talk to than Natalie ghosting me.

"Oh, that reminds me. Troublemaker has a lingerie store. Check this out." I pull out my phone and go to her website. "It's called A Little Spice. Aren't they just to die for?" I show them the clothing line that I earmarked. I have about ten lingerie sets in my cart ready to go, but then I saw she had a clothing line too. It's small, but I know she can grow with it. I already have a few ideas to ask her to make. And then give me a discount on. This shit's not cheap, and Daddy Dearest, while he loves me, doesn't treat me like the spoiled princess *some* biker brothers think I am. I get an allowance for bills and a small "fun money" fund. I've been saving up that fun section for a while, waiting to splurge on a new game or Lego set, but nothing's grabbing my attention. Well, not till now anyway.

"Ooh, that's cute. Think Troublemaker would extend the friends and family discount?" Abigail wags her eyebrows as she takes the phone and starts looking through the website.

I shrug. "You've got to show up to be considered family."

"Touché, my friend, touché. I'll be there at the next gathering. Just tell me when."

I smile and look at Natalie. She takes a second, but then she nods. She's in too. Good. 'Cause I really can't have the old ladies getting any ideas. As it is, they keep harassing me about not having a guy. If I don't get some backup, the next time I show, I might get set up on a blind date. They're just crazy enough to think it's a good idea. Despite that my dad's the president of the club and will skin any man alive for looking at me in any way other than friendship.

Kooper

Unless it's Kooper. Then Dad allows any looks he gives me since he's paid to do so.

I've really got to ask how much he's charging. Because whatever it is, I'm worth more. I'm a real peach. A bright shiny one that's full of sugary sweetness and a pit that's hard to the core.

Chapter 11—Kooper

"Fireball old-fashioned, please."

I breathe into my whiskey before taking a healthy gulp. Ruby has no freaking clue about alcohol, much less what makes a good whiskey.

"That for you or someone else?" I know she heard me. Of all the damn places she could have ordered a drink at the Flying Monkey, she came to my side and ordered next to me. Well, two seats down. Still my area.

The Hounds might have spread out a bit when we came in for Troublemaker's claiming of Gator, but most are still toward the stage on the opposite side of where I am.

Claiming ceremony. What a joke. Women don't claim Hounds. That's what *we* do. Hounds of the Reaper can claim the soul of another person through death or in partnership. There's no way to reverse it and take a Hound's soul. We're already damned, and we like it that way.

But in typical fashion, Ruby's at the center of everything and just riling things up. The brothers were told to come tonight to a place that isn't club but still owned by us. At least Ruby knew not to pull this stunt on holy ground, or what we consider holy to us Reapers. A little dance, a little show, and some fancy words are all this was tonight. If Ruby thinks she changed anything, despite her claim that things were going to be different going forward, she's dead wrong.

"What if it were for me?"

Kooper

"I'd tell you to have fun."

"And if it's for someone else?"

"That it's a shit drink, and you should get them something better."

She scoffs. "So, you'd save someone you don't know over me?"

I give her a narrow look. "It's whiskey, not hemlock. It won't kill you."

"Too much of it will."

I grab my drink and take another sip. "Well, too much of anything will kill you."

"What a way to go, huh?"

Her words surprise me, and I glance at her out of the corner of my eye to see a small smile on her lips as she looks over the glass. Not sure if she's talking about the drink anymore or something else.

She looks… well, she looks good enough to fuck. A fucking wet dream if I were still a prepubescent boy and had those kinds of dreams. Now they're filled with death, if I dream at all. Not my own, but me killing. Destroying anything in my way as I fight to get to something. No clue what I'm looking for. It's been the same damn dream for the last five years. Just fighting and fighting, searching for something or someone. I bet a psychologist would just love to get a hold of me for a session.

"Ruby!"

I look over her shoulder and see Abigail waving her over. She's already surrounded by some guys, none of them ours.

"Got to go. Looks like my girl found us some dates for the night."

I barely hold back the scowl I want to throw them. They look young. Could be college kids or townies. All I know is they ain't club. And from the way they're looking at Ruby as she bounces over to them, they aren't planning to talk about school. Or hell, anything at all, based on the way their tongues are practically on the floor and their eyes are glued to her cleavage. Girl really needs to start wearing turtlenecks or something. Not the normal corset push-up thing she has on. It's like a damn plate under her chin with how high her tits are. I bet I could rest my whiskey on them.

"She giving you trouble again?" I spill my drink as I jerk my hand, and my head, turning around to look at Law. I hope to God he thinks I was looking at his little girl out of anger and nothing else.

Because why would I see her as anything but a job? I surely wasn't looking at her tits. Or any other part of her. And no unholy thoughts were running through my head. Not a one.

"Something like that." I adjust in my seat, just enough to find a way to bring pain to my cock to keep it down more than ever.

"You ever get any information on that little problem?"

I know exactly what he's asking. He's never told me to search for the guy who hurt his girl. He never had to ask. We were both on the same page: No one hurts Ruby. For him, it's a fatherly thing. For me, well, I'm not sure when I got on board, but the idea of someone other than me making her frown pisses me off more and more with each passing day.

Kooper

When I do it, I'm a sick sonofabitch who likes that kind of pain. But when others do it? Yeah, not going to let it happen.

"Already took care of it."

He leans back as if I offended him. "You did."

I nod once, watching his reaction. I see anger on his face and a bit of hurt there too. "That a problem?"

"Was hoping to take care of it myself." There's an edge to his words. I try not to read too much into things. Hurts me more times than not, especially when I'm wrong. But I know I'm not wrong on this. My gut tells me all I need to know. Boss man is jealous that I took out the threat to his daughter. He's feeling like he should have been the one to do it and not have another, especially another man, do it instead.

"It was a small matter." I grab my drink and finish it. "Your girl did a number on him. He was just waiting for the Reaper. Bastard welcomed him in and everything," I say, trying to take the sting out by telling him that his little girl was able to handle the matter, and I just did the cleanup.

It's mostly true. The guy was living a life. Not a grand one, but living is more than most do. He drank a bit too much but was still holding down a job at a fast-food restaurant as a drive-through operator. He ran at first when I busted his door down, but then he saw my cut. Only word he said to me was "Finally." He was too much of a chickenshit to take his own life like he should have, so he waited till I did it for him. Which took just a single blow to his head, and I didn't even blink doing it. Guy deserved worse, but he wasn't worth the time. Ruby moved on, so I was going to as well. I also wasn't going to tell her what I did.

For her, it's in the past. Something she dealt with and lived through. Molestation, not rape. Probably the only reason Law hadn't known about it before. She got her own retribution for it. I still don't know all that went down, but I got enough to know there wasn't penetration. I have to live with my imagination, which is far darker than any Grimm Brothers fairy tale.

I might not know everything about Ruby, but one thing is clear: She wants to deal with her problems alone. She needs help most of the time, which she hates asking for. And I'll give her hell each time we have to step in to help. But the girl really tries to take on the world by herself.

Too bad for her. She's still too coddled by her old man to know what it's like to have it spit it back out at her. She needs to have a little bit of the world crumble around her to learn to enjoy the good. At least, that's how I see it. If she thinks that asshole is still out there, she might think twice about letting someone close. Someone who shouldn't be standing by her side in the first place.

Someone like the fucking blond meathead who's staring at her right now.

"Good. Good." Boss nods and walks away. Who the fuck knows where. I'm not about to follow and ask.

I flag down the bartender and order another round for myself.

"Make it two," Atom says as he sits on my left.

"Three," King chimes in as he takes up my right.

"Boys." I give them each a chin lift. Got no problem with a brother sitting beside me. I'm not antisocial, like some of the others. I don't go all out and make myself the life of the party either, but I can hold my own in a group setting.

"What did we order?" King asks.

"Whiskey, neat," I grunt out as the bartender sets three tumblers down.

"Well, here's to putting hair on your chest," King says as he grabs one and raises it high in the air.

"And on your balls," Atom deadpans before throwing his back.

I just sip mine while the two of them gasp as though they've swallowed fire. Fucking amateurs. You never shoot good whiskey. And I never drink less than a decent whiskey when the tab is on the Hounds club card.

"Man, this stuff will kill you." King coughs, and I chuckle.

"Funny. Someone just said the same thing."

"What're we doing tonight?" Atom looks at us as he flags the bartender down once again. "Two beers."

King nods at his new order, and I just shake my head. Fools.

"Same shit, different day," King mutters.

Neither of these boys are officers, but both have been around long enough. I wouldn't be surprised if one day they moved up in the ranks.

Technically, I'm not an officer either. I just have perks that most don't, like a side deal with the president on who will be his next in line. At least, that was the plan when all this started. I signed on for a job with lasting benefits. It got me behind some closed doors quickly, and no one questioned me being there. Law and I haven't spoken on it much since we shook on our deal, but I know he remembers. I also know he's talking to a few other brothers on the topic too. I never asked for it to *only* be me, just wanted a shot. A *healthy* shot for when I make my move. Boss man can talk to anyone he likes. When the time comes for him to step down, he'll get a say. And I know when that happens, it'll be my name that he pitches; then it'll be up to the boys to decide where the chips lie. But like I said, I just wanted an in. If I want the position badly enough when the time comes, I know I'll take it. That's why I have what many don't, including a few Hounds. I've got the drive and the need to put myself before others. To get what I want in the end because I have a plan for shit to work out for everyone involved. A few others have it, like Casper and Bass, but I'm not sure either would ever be up for the challenge when it's presented.

Probably helps that I've sat on this thought for a while now, ever since I took on Ruby. I doubt anyone else is thinking that long term. But that's me, a fucking planner.

"You taking one of these girls or getting a vamp tonight?" King asks Atom.

They know I'm not the type to talk shit like that. I keep things between me and... well, me.

Atom is more reserved than King. He has conquests like any man, but it's King who flaunts it. Not in your face, but he's never one to deny it or say no to a good time. Guy was named King almost the day he came to the club. His actions with the ladies to get almost every vamp in the place on her knees, begging to be the one to take him to bed, were legendary. King of pussy is what he is. And arrogant enough to accept the title with pride.

Kooper

Unlike Atom, who got his name because he's a ticking bomb. He'll put up with a lot of shit and then go nuclear on someone's ass that pushes him too far. Or if he just needs to let off steam. I've been in the ring with him enough times to be grateful that I've never pissed him off and he's on our side.

"Haven't decided. So many pretty things to look at." His eyes roam the place, and I notice when they settle on Ruby. But the guy's smart enough to only look for a few seconds before moving on. Honestly, he was one second shy of getting a fist to the face.

I throw the rest of my drink down my throat to try to cool my fire. I don't get what's going on. Think my protective duty is messing with my brain. I'm seeing Ruby as something more than what she is. And if I see her as anything but annoying, I'm going to be in real trouble.

"I wouldn't say no to Ruby's friend if she gave me the time of day," King says as his eyes flow easily over her. She's joined Abigail and Ruby with the rest of their admirers as they continue to talk in the corner.

"Girl barely speaks. Your ego wouldn't be able to take it," Atom says, but he keeps his eyes on the roommate, assessing her slowly as she smiles and nods but doesn't speak, just as he said.

"I can go for a silent chick. It makes it so much sweeter when I get them screaming my name later." King laughs at his own joke, and I can't help but smirk. He's not wrong.

"You need a loud one. Why not Abigail?" Atom says as he nods at the other girl.

This has me smiling, as I already know the history there. That girl had the biggest crush on King as a kid. They grew up together, him and her and her brother. Then her brother died. Losing him killed any feelings she would have had for King. And King never saw her as anything more than a kid sister. An annoying one, especially since the brothers always teased him about wanting to hook up with her when he first joined the club. It's a sore subject for him.

"That's like telling me to kiss my sister. No fucking thanks." King shakes his head in disgust at whatever image is in there right now.

Atom just shrugs. "She's cute."

"Then you have her. I'm off to get laid." King grabs his beer and heads to the opposite side of the place. He grabs a chick who's in the middle of some girl group and walks out with her, never once saying a thing. The girl doesn't even complain, just grins and waves to her friends as she goes.

Atom and I watch, not surprised, but always impressed at how he does it.

"Guy has a skill," I mutter.

"Amen to that." Atom dips his beer to me, and I clink his glass with mine, even though it's empty.

Laughter pulls my attention, and I see Abigail giggling as the blond dick throws his arm around Ruby like it belongs there and starts leading her, and the entire group, out the back.

"Problem?" Atom was always the smart one.

"Not sure."

I don't know what it is, but I don't like the guys they're with. Call it overprotectiveness or discriminating

Kooper

against outsiders, but something just feels off. This place is swarming with chicks. Hot ones at that. Ruby and her friends fall into that category, sure, but why did they pick the only three girls who were seen with the brothers and yet are alone? No vamps were invited to this, just a group of friends. It's the Flying Monkey. Regulars come in here all the time and don't belong to the club. Not sure if they saw Ruby shake her ass when she did her little part in Troublemaker's dance or not, but I don't know these assholes. But after we just got Troublemaker out of a kidnapping situation, and Ruby's already had an attempt on her life once before, I ain't chancing it again.

"Up for a little exercise?" I stand and toss a few twenties onto the bar. The club might be paying my bill, but I still believe in tipping for the service.

Atom grins, his eyes full of fire like the nuclear bomb he's named after. "Always."

By the time we make it out the back, I see the blond high-fiving his friends as they crawl into an SUV and head out. Atom and I don't give chase. We don't want to spook them. And I've got half a mind to think Ruby will say something if she notices us before they do. They could just be punk kids looking to score, or it could be more. Whatever it is, I'm going to see what they do before I start breaking skulls. 'Cause I'm all civilized and shit.

Not.

Really, I'm just biding my time to see how much they do to warrant a death wish. I can kill a person and not think twice. But if I kill a person and Ruby actually likes them? I'm still debating how I'd feel about that. And if I'm thinking about her feelings, then I'm getting too damn close to my client.

Maybe I should pull back and let Law assign her to someone else. I've done it long enough. If I still want the presidency, I can make my bid for it without him backing me. I've got enough good with the entire club to know I wouldn't be laughed at for wanting the top rocker position.

As we ride just far enough behind other cars for them not to hear the difference in our engines compared to a freaking sedan, I look over at Atom. He's young enough. Got some past issues like the rest of us, but he'd be good on babysitting duty. He was an EOD tech in the Army, so he can be patient and knows how to not buckle under pressure. But he can also go off at a moment's notice and take everyone out within reach. Him being a brother is a no-brainer.

But him being the man to watch over Ruby?

How fucked am I if I say "not over my dead body"?

Pretty fucked.

Pretty fucked indeed.

Chapter 12—Ruby

Lewis is a jerk, but a cute one. Did the typical jock shit back in high school, flirting with everything walking and dating the high school cheerleader type. Doesn't look like much has changed except for his Facebook status of single. Which, to be fair, he was always single. Both he and his girl, Lisa, were never subtle about dating behind the other person's back. It was a big joke, but no one laughed in their faces about it.

Well, I did. But that's me. And since I'm me, I didn't deal with any of Lisa's petty bullshit. Probably helped that I was never interested in Lewis back then. He was like a painting—you looked but never touched. Not for fear of what the curator, aka Lisa, would do, but fear of what you would get on yourself after touching. An STD was a big pass for me.

But that was high school. Years ago. Things change. And with enough drinks in my system, I can agree to be in the car with him and put up with his hand on my thigh as he drives to wherever he said we're going. Some house party or something. I wasn't really listening, but when Abigail said we were going, who was I to turn down a good time?

"Where *are* we going, by the way?" I ask, because while I'm all for living in the moment, shit has gone down with the club lately. I might not know everything, but I'm not about to be a cliché and walk into a problem if I can help it.

Some might think that getting into the car in the first place was a bad idea. But I know these guys from high school.

They all played on the football team. That might intimidate a few peeps, but I'm not exactly the damsel type. These guys know my reputation. They know who my dad is. They would be fools to fuck with me. And if they did, well, I carry a boot knife with me nowadays. A gun might be a safe bet, considering you don't have to be close to aim and shoot. But a knife is easier to hide, and with the ceramic one Fairy gave me, metal detectors don't even buzz when I'm scanned. Might not cause the most damage in comparison, but Fairy gave me some pointers. Of course, with her, that means she did a full report write-up on it and saw it more as a teaching moment. Thankfully, the girl is super smart, but she lacks certain skills. Like realizing I was asking for tips on how to defend myself without alerting my dad.

Not sure which way Dad will go when he finds out about my latest fashion piece. He'll either love it and buy me more in every color or be mad as hell and say I should just call him if there's an issue—or just come home and live in my old room and die of old age because I'll be protected and never let out of my bubble. It could go either way. If I were a betting woman, I'd say he would do a variation of both: be proud and also push for home life.

"Roy's place," Lewis chirps with a squeeze to my thigh and a smirk in the rearview mirror to look at Roy, who's sitting by Natalie with his arm around her back. She looks a little uncomfortable but still smiles. Abigail and another guy, Trevor, got the very back, and from the giggling, I can only guess what they're doing.

"You mean his parents' place." Trevor laughs hard, ignoring the murderous glare from Roy. Guess he isn't so taken with Abigail to not miss a chance to dog on his boy.

Kooper

Lewis howls with laughter, and I instantly remember why I was never interested in him back then. I need a guy with backbone. Or one who doesn't rag on his friends just to be mean.

Sure, the Hounds do it occasionally, but the guy they're ribbing usually laughs too. There's no humor on Roy's face.

"I pay rent," he mutters. "The pool house is all mine. And it's better than that dump you have, Lewis." Roy hits Lewis on the back of the shoulder, and the car swerves.

"Dude, what the fuck?" Lewis looks back and tries to hit Roy.

"Look out," I scream and grab the steering wheel to correct us from going into oncoming traffic.

He pushes my hand back and glares. "Relax, babe. I've got this."

"Really? 'Cause from where I'm sitting, it looks like you were about to cause a wreck to get a hit in. What the fuck is wrong with you?" I'm so mad at myself I could spit. But despite what some say, my dad raised a lady. One who can give you a black eye and steal your car, but not one who spits in public. Unless it's because I ate something gross. I once fell victim to Princess's tactics and took a piece of candy from her after she offered it. Found out after that she'd tried it, spit it out on the ground, and then offered it to me. Seems her dad, Bulldog, taught her not to waste food.

"Man, if you weren't...." He shakes his head as he lets his words just hang in the air between all of us. No one is talking, hardly even breathing.

"Weren't what?" I narrow my eyes at him.

"Lewis," Trevor tries to warn him. From what, I don't know, and I don't let him get away without me throwing a glare at him and his other friend in the back seat.

Abigail is biting her lip, and I see Nat's holding the door handle with white knuckles. She still hasn't forgotten the last car accident she was in.

Seeing her this upset sets me off, and I give all my attention back to Lewis. "No, you can say it. Weren't what, Lewis? Weren't so uptight? Weren't so worried about our lives?"

"Weren't such a bitch." He throws a snarled lip my way, and then his eyes, thankfully, are back on the road.

"Excuse me?" My jaw would be on the floor if I weren't worried about what else is down there. My shoes are sticking enough as it is.

"You've always thought you're too good for us, even back in high school. Just relax for a bit. You don't have to be a bitch all the time. I get that you're a biker bitch and shit because of your dad, but fuck, learn to have some fun. If I'm willing to give you a try, the very least you can do is be grateful for it."

My eyes have got to be out of my head. I look back at my girls and see they're just as shocked as I am. The guys? They're nodding in agreement with the trash coming out of *this* asshole's mouth.

"Grateful?" My breath pushes out of me in disbelief. "You want me to be grateful? For what?"

He looks me over, going from the top of my head to my toes, then back to my tits. "For looking past your issues and offering you some fun."

Kooper

"You need to stop the fucking car. Right now." I'm seething. So much.

"What? I'm not stopping." He looks at me like *I'm* the crazy one.

"Stop the fucking car, Lewis. We're getting out."

"Don't be ridiculous. Roy's place isn't for another fifteen minutes. I'll let you out there."

"No." I take a deep breath to calm my nerves. "You'll let me out here, where I'm still close to fucking civilization and not ten miles out of town."

He shakes his head with a roll of his eyes, and I've had it. I ain't going with this guy any longer than I have to. I unbuckle my seat belt, slide my leg over the console, and try to put my foot on the brake while grabbing the wheel.

"What the fuck!" We swerve, and I hear Nat scream. I'll apologize to her later for this, but after we get out of here.

Lewis tries to push me back, but I elbow him in the nose. He grabs his face as he groans in agony.

Roy yanks my hair, trying to pull me off his friend and push me back into my seat. It works, and he grabs me from behind and holds me back down as Lewis jabs at me with his elbow. Bastard gets lucky and hits me in the eye.

I recoil on instinct. I might know how to throw a punch, but taking an elbow to the eye socket? This shit hurts.

"Goddammit, Ruby. Look what the fuck you made me do," Lewis shouts at me, and it only makes me see red.

Still holding my eye, because I swear it feels like I'm bleeding, I yell, "What *I* did? You're the one who won't stop the fucking car."

"Why the hell—"

"Lewis, man, you hear that?" Trevor says just loud enough to get everyone to stop talking.

Engines. More specifically, the rumble of a motorcycle. More than one.

"Shit." Lewis looks in the rearview mirror, and I look out the back window. I don't know who it is, but I see two, and oh does that make me smile.

"You're fucked now. All of you." I grin as they speed up and flank us on either side. And then my smile is gone. Because now I can see who's gesturing for Lewis to pull over.

Thankfully, Lewis listens. Not sure if it's because the club is here or the murderous look on Kooper's face.

We pull off the road, and the other brother, Atom, parks by Kooper. They get off their bikes and wait. No one from the car moves.

"Get out." Atom says it loud enough that we hear it inside the vehicle, and we all exit. Nat is the first out, then the rest. Even Lewis makes it out before I do. Mostly because I'm already mad, and I know shit's about to go down. While some will go to Lewis, I already know, based on who it is and the fact that since I got out of the damn vehicle, Kooper hasn't taken his eyes off me, that I'm in for a world of hurt.

Before any of us can speak, Kooper growls, "What happened to her eye?"

The boys eye one another. Roy shakes his head, and Trevor says, "Nothing, man."

"Nothing? She got a black eye for nothing?"

"She did it to herself," Lewis states with all the boldness he must have.

Kooper

I still don't speak. Now is not the time for it. One, because I know I'm not the one Kooper wants talking right now. And two, because I have a sense of self-preservation, and I really don't want to alert him that I'm here. I mean, sure, he can see me. But if I'm lucky, he'll only look and not force an interaction between us.

"Say that again?" Kooper takes two steps closer, his hands clenching as if he's holding himself back.

"Ahh...." Lewis glances at his friends, wets his lips, then looks at me as if pleading for me to help.

Yeah, fuck that. And fuck him.

"She grabbed the steering wheel," he finally says. "I was only trying to keep us from hitting anything. She must have gotten hit when I was trying to get us under control."

"That what happened?"

Lewis nods like a bobblehead. "Yeah, man, she went nuts. Total psycho."

"Natalie? Abigail?"

Just their names is enough to get Nat talking. I don't hate her for it at all, because while his story is sort of true, it's also bullshit. And I would say something if Kooper was falling for any of it. But the guy isn't stupid, no matter how much Lewis might think he is.

"He wouldn't let us get out of the car."

That's it. One sentence, and the temperature coming off Kooper, and now Atom as he takes a step closer, rises by twenty degrees.

"You weren't trying to kidnap the president's daughter, were you, Lewis?" I'm not surprised Kooper knows his name. Ten to one he called it in when he first started following us. If I had to guess, half the damn club is headed this way with more information on this guy than even he knows about himself.

But poor little Lewis is dumbstruck. The pained look on his face is almost laughable. And I do in fact giggle, till Kooper's eyes switch to me for half a second, and I clear my throat to cover up my mistake. You know, with finding joy in the fact that the club isn't going to let this dirtbag get away. I mean, there are perks to being the club's first unofficial princess, after all.

"No, no, sir."

Oh, how sweet. Kooper turned Lewis into a boy with manners. I know he didn't have any, despite me busting his nose—which is still bleeding, by the way. No one is even mentioning it, and I'm a bit hurt that I don't get the credit I deserve.

"Good. Now get back in the fucking car and drive away."

"What?" I step forward, my hands flaring out at my sides.

Kooper just turns his head to me and looks on as if his word is gospel or something.

Lewis and his boys look at us and then head for the car. But just as they get in, Lewis looks back and snarls at us all. "Whatever, man. She ain't even worth it."

Slamming the door, he drives off before I think he even had time to put on his seat belt.

I hope he crashes.

"You're just going to let them leave? After he almost poked my eye out? It's bleeding all over the place!" I gesture

Kooper

to the ground, my shirt, and the departing car. It's too dark to see much from where I am, even though both bikes have their headlights on. But I can feel the blood dripping down my face.

"You're not bleeding." Kooper gives me an exaggerated headshake. "You're crying."

His words have my hands balling into fists of their own accord as I stand so still that I could be taken for a statue. "I don't cry," I seethe through my clenched teeth. Not since my mother died. I refuse to. It's a sign of weakness, and that is one thing I never am.

"Fine, you're leaking tears. Better?" *No.* "And what exactly do you want us to do? You wanted out of the car. You're out of the car. End of story." He turns and starts heading to his bike.

"But... but...." I look at the other three, but they just shrug as if unsure what to do or say.

"But what?" He turns back around and comes as close as he can to me. "I told you. The club is done picking up after you. I'm not about to call everyone over just to threaten a guy when you should have known it was a bad idea to get in the car in the first place."

"Seriously? *I'm* to blame?" My neck twitches from the angle I put my head. He's right on top of me but so much taller, using his height to look down on me like some kid.

"If the shoe fits, darling." He speaks so softly, as if giving me a compliment. Asshole.

"Don't 'darling' me. And the damn shoe doesn't fit." *What am I even talking about?* "I was just trying to have some fun. When he started driving crazy the first time, I wanted out. Car accident trauma, remember?" I point to my head, and his eyebrow rises. I take a deep breath and shake my head as I look away from him. "And that wasn't my fault either."

"If I recall from the police report, you ran yourself off the road."

My jaw drops at his words. *How dare he!* "I was trying to run the *other* car off the road. You know, the one with Princess's psycho mom who was trying to kidnap her? I was helping them." I'm yelling, and I don't give a fuck if I wake anyone up as I do it. We're in between town and suburbia. Close enough to get a noise complaint and yet far enough to be mixed into town life.

He takes another step closer and leans down. His boot tops touch mine, his breath fanning my face. "Just like you're helping now, huh? What about the night I got a dislocated shoulder, or when you were giving too much money to your landlord? Were you helping then?"

"I can't believe you actually blame that shit on me," I say with a shake of my head.

"Ain't blaming. Just callin' it for what it is. You don't help problems, you create them. And I'm the one who has to pick up the fucking pieces." He pulls up to his full height, and it makes me want to kick him in the dick.

"Well, who the fuck told you to do that?" I cross my arms more to keep myself from strangling him than out of comfort.

"Your dad."

Chapter 13—Kooper

I watch Ruby deflate at my words. It seems to do a number on me too.

Watching her leave with those kids was one thing. Seeing the car swerve the first time had me calling the club and having them run the license plate to get me the owner's details. The second swerve was all I needed to gun it. Atom was in line with my thoughts, as he didn't hesitate to take flank on the other side of the SUV.

The power of the club had the prick pulling over quickly. I didn't give a fuck about him till I saw her face. Half the time I see her, she seems in one fucked-up position after another. And yet it doesn't deter me from seeing her in a light that I shouldn't.

Our headlights revealed all I needed to see. She was still clothed, nothing missing, but her corset was doing God's work on pushing up her tits, and her eye was already red and swollen. Seeing that had me wanting to take my gun out and shoot the kid on sight. All of them. I didn't care who did it, just wanted them all to pay. But if I did that, Atom would see. And so would Abigail and the roommate.

And Ruby would know.

They all would know.

That somehow, somewhere along the road, I started to have feelings for Ruby. I might not understand them or want them, but I've got them. Reacting the way I wanted would show that. Letting them go was the right move.

I was actually going to let it go, but then that prick had to open his mouth. He had to say that she wasn't worth it. He had to cause a bit of the light to go out in her eyes from the words that she would deny affected her, but I know they did. How could they not? Anytime someone says a person isn't worth it, it hurts. It's a subconscious thing our brains do. We could hate the person talking, but the words? The words fester in the brain and can trick us into believing them.

I'm a bastard. A stone-cold killer. An asshole to anyone and everyone. And I'm a liar. But those are all the things I need to be. And telling her I'm not going after that pissant of a kid is the biggest lie. It would have been the truth till he spoke. Now I'm about to rain a world of hurt down on him. But Ruby doesn't get to know that. She can't.

This will be a solo job. Not even the club will know, but I might get some of my other boys to help. They might not live locally, but they'd be willing to drive or fly out for a little bit of fun.

But that will be later. When he thinks he's safe. When Ruby has him out of her head, and I can do what I need to do to make sure I get my taste of justice.

Right now, I need to back the fuck up. Because while I might say shit to get all this out of her mind in the long run, all it's doing is pulling me in closer.

Her perfume is clogging my senses. Wisps of her hair are floating in the night wind and grazing my cheeks when I bend down. Her breath is giving me life as she pants in my face. Her eyes hold me captive, full of a defiance that I both want to break and define for her.

I'm seconds away from being pulled all the way in and letting myself fall into her space to feel her body pressed against mine as it fights for air through her anger. And so help me, if I touch more than my boot to hers, my control will shatter, and I'll taste the forbidden fruit that is her lips.

Calling out her dad is the breath we both need to take a big fucking step back.

But does that mean I'm done with her? Fuck no.

"Let's go." I turn and head for my bike.

"Go where?" She doesn't move from her spot.

"Call the boys. Get a ride up here to get them home." I nod to Abigail and Natalie as I direct my words at Atom.

"You got it." He's already pulling out his phone and dialing away.

"You can't just tell them what to do." Ruby throws her arms out at her friends as she takes a few steps toward me. Good. She's going in the right direction.

"I can, and I did. Now get on."

She crosses her arms and sticks out her hip. "I ain't going anywhere. Not with you. I'll wait for a ride to go home with Nat."

I lean across my handlebars. "Get the fuck on my bike, Ruby."

I watch her jaw move back and forth as she thinks it over. I don't blink, and I don't hide my anger at all of this. It's not her I'm mad at. Well, it is and it ain't. I'm mad that she was too stupid to see this going anything but sideways when she left the bar. But she's young, and I have to remember that. She might seem older than she is, but she's still very much sheltered in life, and that has to do with both her age and her dad's club shielding her from things.

I'm also plenty mad at the kid still. So, showing all my anger is for her and her actions alone is easy.

With a huff, she gets on the back of my bike. I bite my cheek to keep from grinning. And I'm enough of a prick to gun the engine to force her to wrap her arms around me as we shoot out of there.

It's torture. Pure, blissful torture.

This is what I give myself. This is all I give. I can't take more than this. I can't even *imagine* more than this.

I drive us down the road, then double back down another road and back my bike into a parking spot.

"What're we doing here?"

I don't answer, just get off my bike and walk away. I hear her huff a second before I open the door and the bell overhead jingles.

"Take a seat anywhere, love. Be right with you," one of the waitresses calls out, and I nod at her as I grab a booth toward the back and take a seat so I can see the front. I pull a menu from the holder on the table and glance over it.

"Being an asshole makes you hungry?" Ruby says as she slides onto the seat across from me.

"Being hungry makes me hungry," I reply without looking up.

"What can I get you?"

"I'll take a number five with a Miller," I say to the same waitress who called out when we entered. She's around my age, but the bags under her eyes tell me she's done this job too long.

"And you, hon?"

Kooper

I look at Ruby with a raised eyebrow. She rolls her eyes, shakes her head at me, and then tells the waitress, "Same."

The waitress nods and heads toward the kitchen.

"You even know what the number five is?" I ask.

"Food."

Her response has me huffing out a laugh. When the waitress drops off the beers, I tell her to bring some waters too. Ruby's going to need it, even if she doesn't know it.

We sit in silence during the short wait for our food. I don't mind. Ruby does a great job of looking at everything but me, and I don't hide my looking at her, and everything else. I'm not ogling her, just watching her like I would an asset on a food run.

"Here you go." The waitress sets the plates down, and I smile as I watch Ruby take in what she signed up for.

"Oh dear God, I'm going to die."

I snort. "Not this again."

"How the hell do you expect me to eat all this?"

I shrug. "Didn't tell you to order it."

I've come here a few times. This isn't Ruby's kind of thing. She's never been a wing girl, hates the spicy stuff. She's only eaten it when forced or dared, never on her own. And she just ordered thirty sweet and spicy wings with extra sauce, crisped chips, and a pickle.

I eat while she looks over her food a second before taking a chip and munching on it slowly. I can hear her stomach growling from here, but she's still contemplating if the spice is worth it or not.

When she finally digs in, she's hesitant, then does what she does best: closes her eyes and takes the biggest bite ever. Nothing half-assed about Ruby Hofstadter.

Her groan of pleasure shoots straight to my dick. I didn't expect it and bite my tongue to keep from reacting. Which fucking sucks. Because, like Ruby just realized, the sweet overlays the spice, and it tastes amazing. But it's still spicy enough that with an open wound, it burns badly.

I grab my beer and chug half of it before motioning to the waitress for another. I just need one more now, and then I'll wait till I get back to the clubhouse. I don't need to find a buzz here, not while I'm still driving. But I need something to take the edge off, just a little. And this place doesn't do hard liquor.

"Wow. How have I never known about this place?" Her lips are covered in sauce, like her hands. There's nothing dainty about her eating, and I, unfortunately, find it adorable.

Seriously need my head checked.

"You don't do wings." I say it without thinking.

"How do you know that?"

Dammit. I was hoping she'd let me get away with knowing something about her that I don't even think her dad knows. Or if he does, he doesn't seem to care when he orders a big wing spread for Super Bowl Sunday every year.

I just shrug. I'm not about to answer her.

"Whatever. This place is cute."

She looks around, and I think this is the first time she's actually seeing the place. Before, she was just trying not to see *me*. But now I watch her take it in. It's a small hole-in-the-wall. It popped up five years ago and is conveniently

Kooper

located down the block from my computer area. I try not to come in here a lot; I don't want people to see me as a local and notice when I'm in the area. I prefer when people don't see me. Which is hard enough as it is since I'm a big guy, drive a Harley, and am part of a biker club that's well known around here.

The owners of this place were from up north somewhere. Came down to Kansas to be near their kids when they went to college a few years back and got stuck here making a living instead. Just another family not able to let go of their kids. Reminds me of a few of the brothers back home. Probably why I've got a soft spot for this place. Well, that, and the food's good, plus the price is right. Almost too good to be true, but this is Kansas. Chickens ain't hard to find around here if you know where to look.

"Surprised Dad hasn't put his name up on this place yet."

She isn't wrong. Her dad likes to "welcome" people into the town. Meaning he finds new businesses, introduces himself, and sees how they work. Sees if they're going to be a problem, for the town or the club. And then he likes to take a picture of himself with the owners and put it up somewhere visible. It's his way of showing anyone who comes in that the place is under the club's protection. It might not seem like a lot to some people, but when another club comes in—and not all of them make themselves known to us—they see it, and they know what it means: If they fuck shit up for one of these places, they fuck shit up for themselves.

"He doesn't need to."

Her eyes narrow in confusion, and then they widen as she smiles. "Oh. Well, isn't that interesting?"

"What?"

"Nothing."

"Don't seem like nothing."

"Just noticed that they might not need Daddy's name around here when they've got yours."

"Ain't like that." I shake my head.

"Sure it ain't. Just like the picture back there ain't you."

I turn and see what she's looking at. I should have expected this from her. The only picture of a person on the wall behind me is of some bald, fat guy holding a sign up for winning some damn wing-eating contest.

"Looks just like you."

I turn back to see her smirking. She licks her fingers clean with a glint in her eye before grabbing the neck of her bottle and taking a healthy drink.

I shake my head, and her giggle floats through the air, a sound that has me adjusting in my seat but not biting my tongue. It's a noise I've heard before, so I'm used to it. But this is the first time she's ever done so with just me. Sure, it's because she's laughing *at* me and not with me, but I'll take what I can get. Even then, I know I'm pushing my luck.

We finish up and even box up half a dozen to take back with us. Hers. I ate all of mine. But I've got no problem taking her food for myself. If I'm lucky, she'll forget about it in the morning and I can have a decent lunch tomorrow.

When we head out, she slides easily onto the back of my bike without a fuss. I always knew women were more

Kooper

compliable after they eat. Seen it with Mama Bear a time or two. Figured it was worth a shot. And I'll be damned, it worked.

We ride back to the clubhouse, which is fairly empty. Still pretty early. I expect everyone is still out at the Flying Monkey or back at their own places. Either way, there are only a few brothers around, mostly prospects. A few vamps, too, but one look at Ruby walking through the doors and they make themselves scarce. Seeing them run when she's around always makes me grin to myself.

"Now what?" She flops her fine ass onto the couch as I go to the bar, grabbing her a beer and me a bottle with a glass. I hand her the beer as I put my stuff down and then go to the cabinet under the TV.

"Now"—I grab the controllers and head back to the couch, sitting close but with plenty of space between us—"we play."

The theme song from *Mario Kart* comes on as I pour my first drink.

"Seriously?" She drinks from her beer but doesn't reach for the controllers yet. Which is fine. This isn't her typical gaming experience. She's more computer than console, but she knows how to play. I've seen her do it with the kids.

I grab a controller and fiddle with it before I toss it beside her and pick up my own.

"You can play, or you can watch. Your call."

At the last second before the race starts, she grabs the controller. And the race is on.

"Princess Peach? Seriously? If I'm anything, I'm Mario," she grumbles at the character I locked her into.

"Nah. You don't have a mustache."

"What about you? You got spikes coming out your back? Is this why you have the name Kooper, because you play this old-ass game so much."

I grin as my guy, King Koopa, swerves around her and drops a banana peel that causes her to spin out. "Not spikes, but I am bigger than most guys. And yeah. I made it known from the start that I'm the king around here. No one is going to take me down."

"Big enough to hit, you mean." She tosses a red turtle shell at me and zooms past me to win the game.

She shouts in triumph. "Ha! Princess Peach rules." And then, like the crazy person she is, she sings the damn song that Jack Black made popular a while back. "Peaches, Peaches, Peaches, Peaches, Peaches...." She trails off as the next game starts.

"All right, Peaches," I say after taking a strong sip of my drink. "Let's see what you do when I actually try."

"Ha, you're dead, old man."

If only she really knew how true her words are. Especially if her dad finds out what I'm doing.

Chapter 14—Ruby

Ten months later

Waking up screaming isn't how I like to start the day. It's draining. I'm sure if it was from a scream of passion, I'd think otherwise. But I haven't had that. Screams of passion, yes. Woken up by one? Not so much.

I shuffle out of bed and head to the bathroom across the hall. I still have enough stuff at Dad's place to get ready in the morning. I swear that guy stocks up on my bath supplies once a year just to keep me from complaining that I can't stay over. Well, that, and he bribes me with food any chance he gets. What can I say? I'm a sucker for a good *free* meal. The food on campus is okay, but not something you write home about.

Do people even do that anymore?

My mind wanders as I turn the shower on and get in once it's warm, letting the water wash away the lack of sleep I'm riding high on. Between the late-night gaming last night with Bowser and the nightmare this morning, I can tell it's going to be a long fucking day.

Just like it has been over the past year. I've fallen into a routine. A long, boring routine. It's just the same every day: get up, go to school, study. When I'm not at school, I'm back home watching the club kids along with more studying. I don't know why I thought it would be such a good idea to double the class load to graduate earlier. And then I got the stupid idea to just go straight into my doctorate program without even taking the summer off. Hell, I didn't even celebrate when I graduated from college. Mostly because I thought it was stupid to have a big party for something you were returning to. I promised myself and Dad that when I get my doctorate, that's when we'll celebrate.

He's already making plans. Told me he was even going to take me on a trip. This is his way of telling me that I'm going to take a break after this, but before I start my practice. 'Cause that's the end goal: to have my own place to do what I want to do.

I might not have everything right now, like a building or anything, but this program takes three years. I've got time. And during that time, other than learning the business aspect of what it takes to be a successful physical therapist, I've got a part-time job that's willing to work around my clinical rotations when I start on those next year. I've been there for a month now and already love it. The people are awesome, and I'm learning a lot. It's exactly the type of clinic I want to have when I go solo.

I get that my life is filled with school and my job and babysitting. Some might say, and have said, that it sucks. Do I get lonely at night? Nope. Want to know why? I crash the fuck out. I'm too tired to be missing anything.

I'm keeping my head down. My nose in a book. Even Natalie is doing the same, but she double majored and is taking another full year and a half to finish her bachelor's before moving on. She still hasn't decided, but with an engineering degree and another in English literature, she'll be ready for just about anything. If she ever finishes. I told her to double major in something that had course credits in

Kooper

common, but she wasn't about doubling up. She just wanted options. Her words.

At least the club is still as active as always. Weddings, babies—you name it, we've got it. And it seems we're about to get more old ladies around here. No one is saying it outright, but this new girl, Milly, she's turning heads. Then again, when you take out all but one member of an assassination team by yourself to get you and your kid safe, the brothers are going to talk. And when it's a pretty woman? Yeah, the boys don't shut up much about it. Well, unless Bass is around. It'll be interesting to see how that plays out.

I shut off the water and hear my dad yelling at me from below. I get out of the shower, head to the door, and crack it open.

"Yeah?"

"Leaving in ten. Be ready."

"I'll meet you there." No way am I going to be put together in ten. The water woke me up, but I've still got to put myself together enough to look like something other than a zombie from *Night of the Living Dead*.

"Ten," he calls back, and I shut the door with an eye roll. "Don't roll your eyes," I hear him yell. He might not have seen me, but he knows me well enough.

"I didn't," I say back with a smile. It's all crap. He knows it; I know it. But we still play this game. That's what happens when you raise a strongheaded daughter—you get sass all the livelong day. Lucky him.

I didn't wash my hair, so it doesn't take as long to get ready. More than ten minutes, but less than thirty. I call it a win, even if Dad is grumbling about women taking too damn long as we enter our favorite bakery.

"I told you I would meet you here." The same thing I say every time he mumbles about the exhaustiveness of women or anything about us. And by us women, I mean me. Since Mom died, I'm it for Dad. He can talk to another woman, but he doesn't do more than that. Never even flirts. Vamps know to stay away, not only because he isn't interested, but I might have made a few bold moves when I first started coming along to the clubhouse. I made it very clear I wasn't looking for a new mommy, and any hoochie-coochie who got within spitting distance was getting a knife to the throat. It helped that I punched the bitch I was threatening in front of a lot of them when all she did was say my dad's name. I was only in high school back then, but I still knocked the shit out of her.

And not a single brother punished me for it. That's probably what sealed the deal on the whole thing. If the club ain't willing to step in and correct my actions, that means there's nothing to correct and they stand by it. The Hounds don't force vamps to sleep with members of the club. And since they don't force it, they expect the same courtesy. If a guy ain't interested, move on. If they approach, it's free game. Hell, a vamp can even approach unless they get the shake off. All fair. Even if I'm not a fan of the few who get with vamps when they've got a "townie" on the side. The brothers who like to have a girlfriend but also want someone freaky in bed are not my type. Not sure if I have a true type, but I know what I don't like. And I don't like to share.

Thankfully, none of the brothers who've taken old ladies fall into this category. If they did, I'd cut off more dicks. I like the girls. Everyone who's wrangled a Hound is worth

Kooper

their weight in gold. I can get along with a vamp if forced, but, sorry to say, a girl who spreads her legs for half of the people I see as older stepbrothers isn't someone I want to be friends with and tell my secrets to. Not that I tell anyone my secrets.

They're secret for a reason. If you voice them, that defeats the purpose.

We order the usual, and they're quick to bring out the coffees and pastries: bear claw for Dad and cinnamon roll with cream cheese frosting for me. Oh, and a side of bacon. Because we need protein, and breakfast is the best meal of the day. That, and they add honey and brown sugar to it, so it's just damn amazing. Thankfully, Dad ordered two servings, so we don't have to share. We tried that once with the bacon. Big mistake. It almost split up the family.

Kidding.

Sort of.

Bacon is life in our household, so it's not hard to believe that it could have gone that far.

"What's the plan today?"

I shrug. "Figured I'd stop by the club for a bit and vet the new girl."

Dad just shakes his head. "Not needed. Boys and I already checked her out. She has some mafia ties, but from what we can determine, she's good. Got Bass watching over her."

"That's the point. I need to make sure she's good enough to be old lady material."

"Old lady? To who?"

"Seriously?" The guy looks at me like I'm the one who's lost my mind. But I'm not about to tell him who it is. Let it be a surprise. Even though I think he already knows and just likes playing dumb. "Whatever. If the girl is going to be sticking around, I need to do my part."

"And what part is that?"

"Making sure she can fit in." *Duh.* I do this with every girl who comes in who isn't looking for a quick fuck. They all get vetted by me. Sure, the boys can say they decide on who becomes their old lady or not, but trust me, no one makes it to that stage without getting the green light from me first. If I like them, I do nothing. Let the boys mess it up on their own if they're going to. But if I see them as a problem? I'll make the girl run faster than a gazelle being chased by a lion.

Dad gives me his typical look. The one you see on dads who look at their kids like they just said the moon is made of cheese and one day they're going to eat it.

"Sweetheart, that ain't your part. Your part is to go to school and live a life out of the club."

I snort. "Out of the club? Seriously? I was made from the club. I bleed the club life."

"But you ain't club."

He smiles as he says it. A kind smile. One that reaches his eyes and is paired with a gentle tone. And it makes my blood boil with rage.

I take a bite of my food instead of lashing out and chew it slowly. Even counting to twenty before I give up trying to hold myself back. "You know... you're the president." He looks up from his food but doesn't interrupt as I keep going. "You run the mother chapter. Other chapters turn to you for advice."

He raises one eyebrow, letting me know he's waiting for me to get on with it.

I shrug as I grab my coffee. "Might go over better than you think if you changed a few bylaws." I take a sip and watch his entire body take a deep breath before he pushes back a bit from the table and folds his arms.

"This again?"

"Not really again. You shut me down before you even let me finish last time."

He shakes his head. "You already said your piece a long time before that. I told you then, and I'll tell you now, and again if I need to. Hounds of the Reaper will not let a woman prospect. No change I make will ever let that happen."

"But if you could make the change... would you?"

The silence stretches between us while the rest of the bakery goes about its business. Customers coming in and out, the bell above the door ringing with each passing of the door. Employees cleaning and chatting with everyone, calling out orders to the back when items run out.

But my world starts and ends with this man across from me. I've got a career. A plan in place. But I will always have one dream. A dream that started as a child and never went away.

And with the shake of his head, the dream crumbles.

I hide the hurt his gesture causes. It's soul crushing. He thinks he's doing the right thing. With Mom out of the picture, and the attempts on my life, I'm sure he thinks this is best. But I just feel like a kid told they'll never grow up to be good enough. I don't know why. I can't define it. I just feel it. I won't voice it. I'll eat my emotions, and my breakfast, and just ignore the hole growing inside me that might never be filled. Because that's what this is. His denial for me, his only daughter, to join in is a strike to the heart. A parasite that just eats from the inside out till I wonder if one day I'll have a heart left at all.

"You still having those nightmares?"

His question isn't about finding an easier topic. And I just give him a noncommittal shrug.

"Heard you last night."

"If you heard me, then why ask?" There's a bit of sass in my voice, but if he hears it, he ignores it. He might think it's because he turned down my lifelong dream. But this isn't a subject I want to discuss either.

Ever since the night I was attacked on campus, I've had nightmares. They got worse after Bailey was actually kidnapped and the shit that went down with her and the others who were to be sold into a sex trafficking ring.

They tell me that the person who was behind all of it is dead. That he died in a fire. Bass even told me he saw the police report and everything to confirm that Duke, the Devils Damned VP, is dead and gone. Everything points to my life being able to move on. But I still get the nightmares. Not every night, but enough that Dad and Nat know I have them. It's been a while since the campus incident, and I still can't shake it. It's like a bogeyman takes over my brain twice a week, sometimes more.

At first, I thought it was just the initial trauma. But over time, I've wondered if it has something to do with shows

I watch, games I play. Even the food I eat before bed. Nothing seems to be the key reason for when a dream will come.

The only thing I've figured out is when one *isn't* going to happen. And that's if I see Kooper. Weird, right? Must be because he was there to get me out of that situation. Just my brain recognizing that the threat is gone because Kooper is still around. Or something like that.

I try not to overthink it. But when I go to the club today, besides meeting Milly, I need to get some eyes on Kooper. Just because I have a test tomorrow and need the sleep. No other reason.

"Just want to make sure everything's all right, honey." He reaches out and takes my hand, running his fingers along my knuckles in support.

"You said he was dead. Everyone says that. It's just going to take some time, I guess."

He grips my hand and smiles. "We'll get through it together. No matter how long it takes."

I give him a small smile, but my heart isn't in it. I love how he supports me, but I still feel like I'll never get his full support. Not in everything. Not with what I really want.

"I'm going to sit inside. The dust is killing my eyes today. Let me know when Abigail shows," I say to Natalie as I leave her on the bench at the back of the club. She's soaking in the rays with her eyes shut, but she nods at my words.

I get it. We're inside so much with classes, it seems like a treat to just sit in the sun and bask in its glory. If we were cats, we would be purring right now.

When I get inside, it takes a second for my eyes to adjust to the dimness before I spot a familiar face and make my way over to her table.

"Well, aren't you becoming a regular." I sit in the chair across from Milly as she rolls her eyes.

"Don't get all attached. I'm busting out of here soon."

"That right? You got help, or you need a lookout?" I grin and give her a wink.

"Thanks for the offer, but family's coming in." I raise my eyebrow at her words, and she clarifies. "Don't get your panties in a twist. Your pops was the one who called him, apparently. It's all sanctioned."

"Thank God. I can't deal with any more 'overprotective daddy' moments. Guy's finally been letting the leash out a bit, and I'm not about to get thrown back into the doghouse just when I get some fresh air."

She barely controls her laugh. "That bad?"

You have no idea.

"Ugh, it's the worst. When Mom was around, I had a buffer, you know? Even after cancer took her, he was still reasonable, willing to talk through things. Then things took some turns with the club, got a few enemies, got a bump or two on my head, and bam! Suddenly, I'm five years old and can't cross the street without someone holding my hand."

I rifle through my bag till I find what I need and take my contacts out. Her expression of disgust as I play with my

Kooper

eyeball has me apologizing. "Sorry, but my eyes are killing me. These summer minicourses are great to get in some extra credits, but they force you to take a four-month course in like a week. My eyes are on fire from all the studying I've been doing." The dust outside isn't helping either. When my eyes are already agitated, the dusty air just makes them ten times itchier.

After another rummage in my bag, I pull out my glasses, and she bursts out laughing.

"Yeah, yeah, yeah, laugh it up, Yankee-Doodle. I've worn these maybe three times in my life. I hate them. I look like such a nerd."

"A hot nerd."

I wave her off but smile a bit. "Whatever."

"Ruby?"

We both turn and see Kooper and Domino staring at us as they stand by the pool table, cues in hand.

"Yeah?" I ask, tone laced with annoyance.

"You wear glasses?" Domino asks as Kooper just continues to stare.

I glare at the obvious answer, but the dumbass just keeps looking. "No, I wear stilettos on my head. What the fuck does it look like I'm wearing?"

"Yeah, but... well, I've never seen you with them," he stammers.

"You laugh and I'll bust you *and* your bike up." I turn away from them as I threaten him.

"I wasn't going to laugh. Girl just fucking made all my naughty schoolteacher fantasies come to life." A loud smack has us looking back to see Domino bent over, holding his face. "Not that I was going to do anything about it, man. Jesus Christ," he yells at Kooper, who's already walking away.

"What do you think that was about?" Milly asks.

I shrug. "Koop's in charge of most of my security duty. He probably thought Domino was making a play on the president's daughter. It's a big no-no. I think they've even got it written in the club's charter or something."

She snorts. "Yeah, right."

I roll my eyes. "Dad's strict about that sort of thing."

Before I can say more, Abigail and Nat show. Thank God. Because even though I deny it every time someone hints that Kooper might like me more than the job entails, I know it's false. It has to be.

Over the last year, we've drifted apart. Ever since Bailey's claiming when I got in that car with Lewis, we don't see each other as much. Hence why the nightmares keep coming. He's there, but we talk less. If we talk at all. Mostly just spats here and there. Sort of what it was like before he was given my guard detail.

And maybe that's it. Maybe the job's done. Duke's dead. The threat is gone.

But your dad didn't know about Duke when Kooper started watching you. Why would he stop now?

That one thought is what keeps me up more nights than not.

Chapter 15—Kooper

I watch her from the shadows. Not in a creepy way like a stalker, just because the lights are low and the clubhouse has shadows for many reasons. Usually to hook up with a vamp whenever you want but still be private. I use the shadows as a cover for what I want, though: to watch over *her*. And no one knows. They can't know.

They all get what my job is. They all know I *have* to look out for her. But me watching her like this? When she's safely inside the compound? There isn't a reason for it. None that I'm willing to discuss or even think on, anyway. It's just something I do. And I do it in secret to keep the questions at bay.

After the night I took her for food and we played video games, I knew I'd fucked up. I was treating her as a person and not as an asset to protect. And it was... fun. I can't have fun with an asset. The job requires me to be vigilant. If you start having fun, you forget to look for threats and just live in the moment.

So I've kept my distance. More than ever before. I hardly talk with her. It helps that very little has gone on lately. She's not causing trouble, and trouble isn't looking for her. Means I can define the line between what's right and proper and what I think about at night when I'm alone, watching her on my cameras.

I might seem distant, but I'm closer than I ever was before. This past year has tested my skills. Flexing my abilities to blend in with those around me so no one sees what I'm actually doing. Who I'm actually watching. Listening to. Learning about. It has me invested in new opportunities as well. The boys just think I'm getting better because of the trainings we have with Operation Hell Hound, or OHH. I let them believe my tracking skills and aim have sharpened because I want to be part of the missions that I know I'll never be put on rotation for because of my protection duty over Ruby. They think it's just my desire to be part of the group.

How wrong they are.

When she gets up and walks away with Natalie, leaving Abigail and Milly talking, I follow. To those looking, I'm going for a smoke. I don't smoke for the habit but for the cover. Learned early in life that those who smoke get more breaks. At first, it was just to get a bit of time off the jobs I was on. Bosses never complained when you asked for a smoke break, but they sure as shit had an issue if you took a regular break to check your phone or just sit to get off your feet.

I use smoke breaks still, even within the club. Sometimes it's an excuse to just leave an awkward conversation. Sometimes it's because I need the peace of being alone. But lately? It's to track Ruby without anyone seeing what I'm looking at on my phone.

I don't know when I started acting like this, hiding shit from my brothers. Maybe it's because of *who* it is. Maybe it's because I don't know *what* this is. I have ideas. And if I weren't too busy denying shit to myself, I'd be admitting things. Which I'm not ready to do.

Kooper

I'm looking down at my phone, watching her travel north back to campus. She's got another class to get to this evening. Don't know why she opted for late classes during the summer, but it keeps her out of trouble, and away from boys. Because that's all that is up at the school—boys. Not a single man in sight. And boys get stupid and handsy. I might have stayed away from her these past few months, but that doesn't mean I haven't made it clear to more than one guy that she wasn't interested. She has school to focus on. A career path that's important to her. I'm not about to let some asshole punk kid come in and try to sweet-talk her into losing focus.

Not that Ruby is easily swayed. But some of these guys make a freaking career out of hooking up. They know all the tricks. Ruby isn't fooled easily, but she's still so damn young. She could overlook something if she isn't careful.

And that's where I come in. Really, I'm only doing this to prevent more problems for me. Ruby not dating anyone keeps my job easy. Her dating, hooking up with guys, sleeping somewhere besides her own bed? Yeah, that's a problem.

And not just for the job, but for my own damn sanity as well.

Heading back in after the heat gets to me, I find Bass at the bar with his head hanging low. A beer sits in front of him, but it looks untouched.

"Trouble in paradise?"

He can deny it all he wants, but he has it bad for Milly. The girl is tough, like any of the old ladies. Knows when to protect and when to shoot first. Hounds seem to attract a certain type of woman around here, that's for sure.

"There's a price on Ollie's head," he says without emotion, but the fact that he's closing down his feelings speaks more than he probably wants. Ollie is Milly's. And Milly is Bass's. So that makes Ollie part of the family, and no one comes for our family.

Before I can even think about consoling him, every damn alarm in the place goes off, and a crash from outside tears through the clubhouse.

"Perimeter breach. I repeat, perimeter breach. Multiple assailants. All heavily armed." Flint's voice echoes through the building.

The vamps take off running to the bunk room for safety, screaming like banshees. A few Hounds rush to the place we stash guns. But the rest of us? We just pull out the piece on us and aim it at the door as people come in shooting.

I grab Bass by the collar of his vest and throw him over the bar. He was looking out the back, probably thinking about Milly or some shit, and didn't think to cover his own ass. I hop over, too, and we take cover as bullets and glass rain down on us.

"Shit. Boss is going to be pissed," he says. And he's right. Law doesn't have a ton of rules. But one he does have is to not get blood on the bar. It's a bitch to clean.

"Ask for forgiveness later," I say a second before I stand and start shooting at anything I don't recognize.

Boss can yell his head off later about the amount of blood I spill. But something tells me he'll only be mad if it's mine or another brother's and not the enemy's.

When the last one goes down, silence falls over the place. I look over the dead on the ground. "Call out," I say.

Kooper

"Clear" comes from all around me.

I hop over the bar top as if it's a small fence and move to the guys on the ground. They're all in suits. Looking back over my shoulder, I see Bass doing the same as me, assessing the situation. "These for your girl?" I ask.

He nods. "Think so. Don't know many who wear suits and carry Uzis other than the Russian mafia."

I nod in agreement.

"Sweep inside, groups of two and three. Once clear, head out and bring in our people." I can still hear the war outside, but I don't go running out. We need a secure place to bring in the wounded and protect what's already inside.

The boys fan out. I stick with Bass as he and I head out the back. He's on a mission to get to his woman, and I'm not about to let him go alone. We take a few out as we cross the playground. I see Chains getting dragged inside by General as blood leaks out of one of his legs.

We round the building, and I hear Bass scream at Milly a second before I see her standing in what looks like popping sand as bullets fly around her, catching her a few times. She falls to her knees and then shrieks as she stands and keeps going to a vehicle with a screaming kid being thrown into the back seat. I fire at every one of those assholes, but by the time I get them, the SUV is gone and Milly's in Bass's arms. She looks half dead from what I can see, even as Law comes out and shouts for General to come help.

The plan comes quick from the boss. Our clubhouse is shattered. Our people are down. And a kid is missing. We've got four bikes left that didn't get smashed when the first SUV crashed through the gates. I grab any gear lying around and hop on my bike. Law, Bass, a prospect, and I speed after them. We have a tracker on the vehicle. Flint's telling us where to go, and drones are flying ahead to alert us of ambushes.

We're as prepared as we'll ever be for a rescue mission after being attacked. I don't have time to check my phone like I want. To see if Ruby's safe. I have to trust that she is. She was so far out last time I saw my tracking software, there's no way she was caught up in this.

I have to hope that the pain of what happened is the only pain she'll face. Another thing to keep her up gaming all night to keep the nightmares away. Here's to hoping that knowing her dad's club is no longer untouchable is the only bogeyman to haunt her dreams.

"We've got to tell her." Casper's words have the room going quiet.

I close my eyes and just let it sink in. Everything that's happened in the last few hours. Everything that's happened in the last few weeks, months. Even years. Everything led up to this moment, and yet none of it did.

Law's out. It seems impossible, but it's true. The one pillar the club never thought would fall, has. He's not dead, but that's not the tale we'll spin. And it's all because of her. Ruby.

She has enemies. Duke. The Russians. She's lost so much for this club already, but in order to keep her safe, she's about to lose even more.

Kooper

"I'll tell her." I speak before I realize I've decided. But as I open my eyes and look around at the boys, they all agree. Everyone knows I'm her protector. They don't know all of it, but they know Law has me watching her. They think it's just because of my background with security. They don't know about me getting the club.

But this isn't how I wanted it. And with him in a coma, I doubt Law told anyone of the plan. If I say anything, I'll look like a fucking dick for seeking a position when a body ain't even cold in the ground.

So I keep my mouth shut. General says Law has a chance to pull through. That he could still make it. I've got to hope he does, and then our deal can stick. I'll worry about all the other bullshit between now and then at another time.

Now I've got to lock my shit down. All of us. The small group that knows the truth. We need to walk out of here with sorrow on our faces and hearts and nothing more. No hints of possibilities to change in the future.

And I have to lie and tell a woman that she's all alone in the world now. That she has no one. All because of the club she was born into.

I exit the room and go out to find her. Not a single person follows, knowing this ain't for show. I find her easily. Helping. Fucking Christ, she's always helping this damn club in one way or another. Pushing a vamp off a taken brother, cooking a meal for a sick person, or just watching the kids so couples can have a break. Now she's playing nurse. She might have gone to school for physical therapy, but she's got the basics. Not too hard to put a bandage on something or wipe blood off something else.

The clubhouse is wrecked. Might take a few weeks before we get back up and running. We took a major hit. Casper's already on the horn, calling in other sister chapters for aid. Bulldog said brothers are coming in from all areas to help. No questions asked. No favors requested. Just doing what Hounds do best: standing beside a brother in need.

I get close to her before I speak. Flint must have called in everyone once the place was secure. While I was out trying to rescue someone and instead watched a mentor fall.

"Ruby."

"What?" she barks at me but barely gives me attention. She's stressed. She won't say it, but I see it. This is her entire life—her family. Her salvation. Everything and everyone in here means something to her. Having it destroyed like this is freaking her out, but she's locking it down.

I've been watching her for a while. Did tons of research on her. Even hacked into old computer surveillance from when she would sit with her mom as she went through chemo before she died. She puts on a brave face, but she's hurting. She used to cry when she sat with her mom, but then one day she just stopped and smiled and helped. Since that day, that's been her go-to. Instead of breaking, she fakes it. Instead of crumbling, she stands tall. I don't know if she ever lets it go or not, but when she's around others, she holds her shit together.

"We need to talk."

"A bit busy if you can't tell."

"Won't take long."

Kooper

She pauses and looks back at me, searching my face. I'm not sure what she sees, but something must have shown for her to give me a nod. Turning back, she smiles at the brother she's helping, wrapping the last of the gauze around a knife wound to his forearm and taping it down. "Get over to General in about five minutes. He should have time for you then."

General put the entire clubhouse common room on triage duty. He set up small areas for everything and anything. Milly seems to have taken the worst of it, and he already had an ambulance come and get her after he stabilized her with the aid he could do here. He has a few brothers watching her at the hospital now as she goes through surgery to patch the bullet wounds.

The rest of the boys who got shot were sent to the hospital too. Small lacerations and the like are being treated here by General first and then heading to the hospital. He doesn't want to chance a brother dying from blood loss if it comes to it. He also wants to make sure he can see everyone and get a read on them. If he goes to the hospital, he'll just get one patient and have to trust the others to take care of his men. General might not be into inflicting pain unless it's in the bedroom, as some of us are, but he'll be damned if he allows another doctor to aid his brothers without him first giving them a cursory look.

Standing, Ruby turns and looks at me, waiting for me to speak. But we have too many eyes on us still. I feel it. I know we're being watched. By those who know the truth and those who are still in the dark, like she is.

"Come on."

I walk out the back. A quick glance over my shoulder shows she's following. I walk past the debris that's everywhere. The dead suits have already been removed by brothers. Cops aren't coming, but we don't want the kids to be any more traumatized. The guys we have on the force are doing what they can to help, not put us under red tape. They keep out of our area out of respect for those wounded, leaving us to handle our business. We just need some time to assess before we let unknowns walk in. They have a job to do, and we don't want to cause bad blood. Which is why, when Bulldog spoke to the chief of police earlier, he was able to get a few hours of leeway from them.

I lead her to the rear of the compound, an area Ruby knows well. It was her mom's special place, a small area with twinkle lights around a swinging bench hidden in the forest. It was for Special K to have some peace while she dealt with her cancer, but never too far from her love, from Law.

The brothers have used this spot for a few alone moments too. There's just something special about it that makes the rest of the world sink away, and you can feel as if it's just you and nature, and nothing can hurt you.

And while I want that for her, I know I'm about to ruin the spot for her. A spot she's always felt close to. With the smoke still in the air from what went down and the broken glass from the twinkle lights that must have gotten hit by stray bullets, this place is no longer the heaven I was hoping for.

"So, what's up?" She walks around me and sits on the swing. Surprisingly, it's still intact. She rocks slowly as her toes slide across the ground. "You talk to Dad? My cell service is shitty right now, and I haven't seen him at the clubhouse. I

Kooper

expect he's at the hospital watching over his boys. Figured I'd go there next to give him a break."

I shake my head. "You can't."

She stops swinging and looks up at me as I stand just in front of her. "Can't what? Go to the hospital? I might not be family to everyone here, but I'm pretty sure they allow visitors."

"You can't talk to your dad."

She raises an eyebrow and smirks. "Why?" She thinks I'm messing with her. She expects everything to be fine. If a Hound is hurt, family is notified first. She knows this. But she was never told. No one said anything. Not till now.

"He took a hit. Fell from the second-story landing trying to rescue Milly's kid."

Her face slowly falls. "What are you saying, Koop?"

"Your dad... he's dead."

Chapter 16—Ruby

"Not in the mood for your jokes today." I shake my head as I rise from the swing. Should have known better than to come out here with Kooper. I don't know why I agreed to it. Something on his face, in his eyes, told me he was serious about his request to talk to me. But it was just me needing a bit of normalcy to get me through today.

I was just pulling into my apartment complex with Nat when Flint called me back. I dropped her off and drove back. I even had a few cops chasing after me till I got a hold of Flint and he got word out to call them off me. I would have brought Nat, but she ain't club. And when the club gets attacked, you don't bring in outsiders.

Shit, this has never happened before. I didn't even know it could! After the threat against the club's family with Duke, things were put in place. But that was to protect people outside. Never to protect anyone inside.

I asked about my dad when I got the call, but Flint said he didn't know anything other than that everyone needed to come in. And that spoke more than anything. Unwritten law is that family is notified almost immediately if there's an issue. It's because the club knows how precious life is. And if you've only got a little time left in it, you call in everyone who means a damn to you.

But I never got that call. I was never told anything. Even when I got here, my questions about Dad went unanswered, so I gave up asking and just helped with the chaos. My worries were nothing compared to those who were bleeding and the kids who were screaming.

I did what I always do: I stood up and helped. If Dad wasn't here to show face, then I would do it in his honor.

But this? This is the worst joke a person can play. Not only because the words are awful, but it pulled me away from helping.

"I'm not joking." He blocks my path.

I just shake my head and attempt to walk around him, but he grabs my arm.

"Ruby, he's dead. I saw it myself. He died."

I wrench my arm away and take a few steps before turning back. "How? When?" My arms are waving all over the place as I test his stupid joke. It *has* to be a joke. Anything else will shatter me.

He runs his hands over his head, and dread fills me. I've never seen him look like this before. So unsure, so lost. I start to tremble.

"He was trying to save Ollie. He went up top with the prospect, and Bass and I covered the ground. It was a trap. We would have been dead. Ollie would have died. But your dad…." He takes a minute to smile, but there's no happiness in his face as he does. "He took out the threat and fought hard till he got shot and pushed off the second story. He fell and…." He shakes his head and looks away. There's no reason to say it again. He already said enough.

"Why wasn't I called? Why didn't I know?" My words are nothing more than a whisper on the air.

"We...." He clears his throat, and a bit of emotion seems to crack through his otherwise stoic self. "We thought General could save him. That there was something to do. But then... then we just couldn't believe it. We didn't want to say because we didn't want it to be true. Telling you made it real."

I process his words, and then I glare at him. My jaw tenses. The tears that were starting to fall just sit in my eyes. I refuse to let them drop.

"You didn't want it to be real? You didn't want it to be true? What gives you the right to think you get a say in any of it?"

He steps toward me, and I see anger flash in his eyes to match my own. "I have every right. He was like a father to me."

"He was *my* father!" I yell so loud that birds fly out of the trees.

His anger dies as he looks at the tears on my face. "I know, Peaches. I know." He reaches out to touch my arm, but I don't want softness. I want to hit something, to punch.

This can't be true. It just can't. I can't be alone. I can't be all that's left.

I push him away. Then I do it again, and he takes a step back. "You don't know shit. Where is he?" I start walking back to the compound. "I want to see him."

He's not dead. Just sleeping. Sometimes he sleeps hard. Sure, every time I come in, no matter the time or how softly I shut the door, he hears me. But maybe he just hit his head or something. Or there's a delay, and his guardian angel was on a break but is back now.

Kooper

I don't believe in God. How can I? My mom died when I was young. She told me I should believe. That there were always angels out there to help her, and sometimes she was an angel to others who needed it. She called Mama Bear an angel. I wanted to believe they were real then. To believe that someone was going to help her when the medicine didn't. But they didn't come through. And now?

I'll pray and believe anything if it makes this all a bad dream. The worst dream. A nightmare that I never saw coming.

Dad was invincible. Nothing was going to get him down. He can't be dead. He just can't.

Arms grab me from the back and try to hold me. "No, Ruby. You don't need to see him like this." I struggle in his grasp, but he holds firm, leaning in to speak softly in my ear. "Think of him as you did before all of this. Remember him when he was with you. Don't let your last image of him be of him gone."

A cry of anguish crawls out of my soul as I let my ultimate fear take over. My knees buckle, but strong arms wrap around me and hold me, catching me before I fall. My wails of pain can be heard throughout the state, much less the compound, but no one comes to see. No one comes to figure out what could be my issue. And that makes it so much worse, as they must know. They must all know the truth and that there's nothing they can do for me. Nothing anyone can do.

I wrestle in Kooper's arms, and eventually he releases me. I turn quickly and punch him. Kick him. Smack him in the face. Anything and everything, and he just takes it, making me cry harder as I pound on his chest. My strength drains quickly as my mind explodes with what this means. What it's going to be like for me going forward. Alone. By myself.

I breathe heavily as I let my hands fall to my sides, my head hanging low. A hand pulls my head to his chest, and his fingers scratch at the base of my neck. I feel his lips touch my forehead, and I close my eyes, imagining it's my dad. Something he did so many times that I took it for granted.

"Club's got you, Ruby girl. Club's here for you."

I squeeze my eyes shut tight and let one last tear fall down my cheek before I step away. I look at him. Disheveled from me but still strong and steady as always. A pillar for the club. Someone to hold shit up when everything else falls.

But I can't let him hold me. I've got to learn to hold myself. With Mom and now Dad gone, I need to figure shit out on my own.

I always said I wanted to do it on my own. Never knew this was what they meant when they said to be careful what you wish for.

I turn and start walking back.

"Ruby," he calls out, and I stop. I don't look back, but I stop. "We'll get through this. I promise."

"Okay."

That's all I can say. I don't believe him. That's what Dad would have said. Now look at where he is. Dead. And look at where I am.

Alone. Always alone.

Kooper

The beeping of the machines keeps me grounded in the hospital room as I look out at the storm. We don't get enough rain in Kansas, but it seems to be a constant thing lately. As if the entire state is weeping the loss of one man. That's all we lost in the war the Russians brought to our doorstep, but it was enough.

The door creaking open doesn't disturb me enough to turn and look at whichever nurse has come in for their hourly check. Milly's been under sedation since her last surgery. The internal bleeding did more damage than they wanted. They're hoping to pull her out of it soon, but with the way she moves so much while she's asleep, General's worried she'll pull her stitches. He has his medical team checking on her often, but I stay here when they aren't. I might not have a nursing degree, but I know how to push a call button and assist enough to keep her from bleeding out till someone comes in and takes over.

"Any change?"

I turn at the roughness in Bass's voice. He's staring at his girl as he categorizes every wound he can see. There's so much more that he can't see, but I'm sure he has the full report from General. He's been here a few times. We take turns. But he was called away for Church. Something my dad used to call; now someone else does. Not sure who it is. I'd guess Bulldog, since he's the VP, but who knows for how long. A club can't be without a leader for long. Sooner or later, they're going to have to vote on someone to take Dad's place.

I swallow hard and look back out the window.

"No."

The creak of the door pulls my attention, and I see it's Kooper. We hold each other's stare. I haven't spoken to him since he told me about Dad. We've seen each other, just haven't spoken. When I left him in the clearing, I went back and helped. I did everything asked and not asked. Then, when that was all done, I came here. I go back to the club to rest when Bass comes in. I'm not about to go home. I've got a place at the club. Always did. A room just for me. Dad had it that way. Might seem like torture to go back to the place he ran, but I'd rather be in a bed and a room that has less of me and him than what I have at my childhood home. Where his smell still lingers. Where things he left out in hopes of putting away would still be there. It's what happened when Mom died. I know it'll be the same for him now that he's gone.

I'm strong. Or I like to pretend I am. But I'm not strong enough to go home yet.

Bass sits in the chair beside the bed and pulls Milly's hand to him, kissing her knuckles. "He didn't win, sweetheart. He thinks he has, but he hasn't. I promise you won't wake to having him in your nightmares. I swear it. To both you and Ollie. I'll bring you his damn head to have you rest easy."

Rising, he pushes her hair back and kisses her head before leaning his forehead against hers. I don't know if he whispers something or just soaks in her touch, but he only hovers for a moment before he stands and straightens.

"Look after her for me," he says, and then he's out of the room, leaving me alone with Kooper.

Kooper

I look at him and wait. I know there's more. Bass wouldn't be saying that, leaving like that, if there wasn't.

"We're going after them."

"Who?" He knows I'm asking who's going, not who they're going after.

"Bass, Domino. The prospect who was with us before."

I nod. The prospect will be a brother soon with the way he keeps making waves in the right way. First with going after Ollie to bring him back and now this, it seems.

"And me."

I flex my hands, but he can't see them as I have them folded around me. Seems to be my permanent position of late. Like if I hold myself tight enough, I'll be able to hold myself together. But I can't. Not the way I felt for a split second when I was in his arms. But I hate him. I hate him for telling me my worst fear. I hate him for being the one who was there and didn't call me. I hate that he got to see my dad's last moments.

And I hate that I wake up calling out his name and wanting him there to hold me just for a second longer. To make me feel like I'm truly not alone and that I have the club, and him, behind me.

"When?"

"Tonight. We're on a flight going out in a few hours. Got a few contacts working on getting us somewhere to stay and some intel about Ivan's place. We want to get this done and come back before it's too late."

Too late and miss the funeral.

I've been asked a few times about it, but when someone asks about Dad, I shut down. I try not to, but it just happens. It's like my world closes up shop and all the color is drained from it, and for a moment, I have no idea where I am or who I'm with. Just long enough for them to stop asking me.

I know it'll happen. Casper mentioned that they want to get a few other chapters down here before they do it, to give him the full respect and send-off he deserves. But unless Kooper and his group of men can take out Ivan, the head of the Russian mafia, in a few days or a week tops, I doubt he'll be there.

Which means I'll be doing it alone. Standing alone. At a grave.

The only thing I want is for it to be open casket. But the club refuses. They say he needs to go out with honor. And a busted-up face ain't the respect he deserves.

I don't get it, but I'm not fighting it. Why? To look like a little girl who can't keep her shit together? Half the club already looks at me with pity in their eyes. I heard others say they hate that, but I had never seen it before. Now that I do, I get it. It makes me want to scream at them and then take a bat or a chair, anything I can reach, and just start beating the pity out of their eyes.

Probably not a normal response.

Mama Bear suggested therapy. I think the look I gave her had her running away screaming. She's never mentioned it again. Nor has she approached me alone since. All the old ladies have tried to support me in one way or another, offering food and words. I'm sure I'll appreciate it months, maybe years, from now. But right now, I don't want to think about it. I don't want to be reminded that my world has ended. I want to stare out windows and pretend it's all a bad dream, that Dad's just running late because he doesn't want to drive in the rain.

"Are you going to be okay?"

His words pull a snort, then a smile, then a laugh out of me. More and more laughter, like I'm locked up in the looney bin and was just told that the nurses who give me drugs and tie me down to my bed at night are my friends.

He lets me have the moment. And when it's over, I look back out the window. A fog has set in, preventing me from seeing anything but the rain hitting the glass.

"What do you care?"

I hear his footsteps, and when I turn to look at him standing directly in front of me, I don't flinch. He's close. Like that one time we were arguing over some stupid townie giving me a ride. Our toes touch, but nothing else. It's almost painful how much I resist reaching out.

He must want to hit me. To smack some sense into me or something. No other reason for the vein on his forehead to be ticking. Or his arm muscles to be bulging. I've only seen him like this once before, when a former prospect called me a cunt. Even now I internally flinch at the word. I hate it. It might just be a word, and it's stupid of me, but it holds power over me. It makes me mad on too many levels. I knocked the guy out when he called me that. Kooper was mad till he figured out what happened. Then he got like he is now and knocked the guy out a second time when he woke up and confirmed my story.

Whatever. If he thinks I'll respond better with a bit of slapping around, then I'm all for it. I'm more sick of my mood than he is, and it's only been two days. Two days of nothing but darkness seeping in and showing me how bleak my future is.

"I care, Ruby. We all care."

I look at him. Searching his eyes and seeing he honestly believes it. And it's sweet, I guess, but not what I need right now. I don't want words. I want... I want a hug. But I'll never ask for one. That would make me weak, and I can't deal with that.

Having Kooper see me as weak does things to my stomach. It's as if it would be the worst mistake of my life. He watched me fall apart, but I can rationalize that because I was just told about Dad. Anyone would break down when they're that close to a person. It makes sense. But doing it again? Leaning on him in the process of more falling down and wanting someone to put me back together again?

I don't think I can handle that.

"The job's done. Dad's...." I clear my throat, blink a few times, and shake my head to get rid of the cry that's threatening to come up. "Dad's dead. I'm no longer the club's princess. I'm just a townie now. You don't have to care anymore."

He's quick to reach out and grab the back of my neck, his thumb on my pulse point as he brings me close and leans his head down. My eyes widen at his actions, and I grab his arm with one hand and put the other up to his chest to push him off. But my movements stop at the look of fierceness in his eyes. At the set jawline and his breath fanning my face. His scent, some kind of cologne that I know he likes, clogs my senses and makes things fuzzy.

"You were never just a job. And your dad being dead doesn't kick you out of the club. You will never, ever, be *just* anything. You get me?"

His words are harsh, but the way his eyes look over my face and then land on my lips has me parting them. My tongue flicks out to lick them. A moment hangs between us. I don't know if I sway or if he pulls me closer. But we *get* closer. Barely a hair between us, and yet we remain untouched, just our breaths passing between us, giving life to each other on each exhale and inhale.

A moment that has me wondering where I end and he begins. A moment that's shattered when a nurse comes in.

"Oh, sorry. Just doing a small check. I'll be out in a second."

But a second isn't needed. With one last flick of his eyes to mine, a soft squeeze of my neck, and a caress of his thumb down my pulse point, he's out the door and gone. Never once looking back.

Chapter 17—Kooper

"Anything going on?" Domino asks as he eyes the phone in my hand. We're meant to be radio silent. And we have been.

With the club.

But I'm not talking with the club. I'm checking in with my old team. They're on a job. A boring one based on the comments, but they're doing it. It's easier if they watch her than me trying to keep tabs on her with everything else going on.

"No. Just playing games."

He lets it go. We've been waiting here longer than I think any of us expected to be in Russia. But we want to get it right. And the only way to do that is to wait and not go in guns blazing like we want.

We're here to make sure Milly and Ollie are safe. And to seek club revenge. That's what has Domino, the prospect, Mickey, and me here. Bass and the other mafia guy, Tommy, are here for Milly. I don't really care who's here for what, as long as we have the same end goal.

We're going to destroy the ones who brought pain to our own. Be it the threat of Ollie being taken from Milly or because Law is dead. I'm here to watch the blood drain out of the man who forced my hand in delivering the news to Ruby. Something I should never have had to do.

Kooper

"Sucks that we missed the funeral," Domino says, holding my stare. It's a ploy to keep up the story. Mickey is from a sister club and helps with OHH. We trust him, but he's not part of the mother chapter. And Tommy, well, he's mafia. Not Russian mafia, 'cause I would have shot him on sight if he was, but part of the crime family on the East Coast. His eldest brother is the capo. Oh, and he's Milly's brother. Which sort of makes him family, since Bass wouldn't be out here if Milly wasn't something more than a one-night stand. He all but claimed her with his actions, even if he hasn't brought it to the table to discuss it yet. Kind of hard to discuss much when the table sits without a leader.

"When are you going to vote?" Mickey asks as he watches some soccer game. He calls it football, but he's Irish. And thus has no idea what anything really is.

"After we get back. Club wants us there to vote. But if we take much longer on this, they'll do it without us," I say.

They can wait on a vote. The club, while leaderless, is still running. No one's gunning for the chair right now. Not even me.

I wanted that spot for so long. And now that it's open? Doesn't feel right. Feels like I cheated to get it somehow. I've got time to figure shit out still. Till a vote is called, I don't have to decide on anything just yet. I can still throw my vest in like any of the others when the time comes.

But unlike a vote, a funeral couldn't wait. If we waited, more questions would have been asked. So we did it quick. Quicker than I liked, but I get it. Closed casket, intimate but with a few hundred brothers outside the funeral home in a sign of respect and solidarity. I wanted to be there. For my club. For my brothers.

For her.

My team had eyes on her the whole time. I got pictures. Brothers told me without me asking how she took it. I should have known she'd react like she did. Stood tall. Nodded when expected. Answered questions when asked. But nothing more. She was there, and she showed she could do it. But that didn't mean she had to do it alone. She might have seen the family and friends at her back, all willing to catch her if she needed it, but she refused to fall. Refused to show anything but her strength. Or that's what I'm guessing she told herself. And others might have said the same.

But I saw it for what it was: Her shutting down. Her accepting defeat. Her blocking herself off from the others around her to shelter her own pain and bury it down to not have to live it again. I know she wanted to see her dad. She asked several times for an open casket, but never begged. Still, she was denied. The club wasn't going to make a fool out of her and put a fake in his place just to make her happy. She needs to think he's dead. We need her to think that. Her and the world.

It's the only way to keep her safe. Just because Law is out doesn't mean the threat against her is gone. It never will be. She was part of this world. Still is. A threat is always a possibility. And I will never, ever, let her get hurt because of it.

"Listen up, ladies. We got the intel we needed." Bass comes out the back with Tommy on his heels. They took a call from Tommy's contact earlier, hoping to get some news. Looks like we just got it.

Good thing too. Because I'm ready to go home. Pictures and detailed reports from my team are one thing. But eyes on the target, on *my* target, are even better.

"You're going to need to take it easy."

I grunt at General's words.

"I'm serious. You had a helluva fall. You're lucky you're getting out of here after only two surgeries. A torn shoulder ligament and a pin in the hip to keep the bone fracture from erupting beats a hip and shoulder replacement."

"I get it, Doc. I was there. Remember?" I roll my eyes, but he can't see my face since I turned around to put my vest on. He might think it's to block him out, but really, it's just to hide the pain in my face from showing. I feel like shit. Worse than that. Like roadkill.

We were doing well when we first breached the property. Bass, Domino, and Tommy went one way; Mickey, the prospect, and I went the other. Our job was to destroy everything, while theirs was to find Ivan and end him. I wanted his death to be on my kill count, but Bass got that honor.

Everything was fine. Clearing rooms was simple till they caught on to us and came rushing. We got separated from one another for a moment. I turned a corner, and some mafia asshole shot me in the chest. I fired back because taking a shell, even if wearing Kevlar, is painful. I stepped over him as he fell, but I didn't expect him to still be twitching. I also didn't expect him to pull out a knife and jam it into my hip, then push me over the side of the banister. The weight of him, the fall, and the knife angle did damage. Serious damage. I could barely stand. My right shoulder was dislocated *again*, but this time it felt worse.

I shot the asshole in the head and crawled away. Got my back to a wall, ready to fire at anything and everything. That's where Mickey found me. We both knew enough not to pull out the freaking Rambo knife. It didn't hit an artery, but it wasn't exactly a pocketknife. I felt it in my bones. And for once, I wasn't overexaggerating. Turns out the fall jammed it into my hip and fractured a piece off, which led to me getting a pin as soon as we got back.

Unlike Mickey, who could shake General off, I was in no shape to do the same. His wound was a stable fracture or some shit to the leg. Mine wasn't something General wanted to wait on. He didn't know where the bone chips went, and the Russian doctor we had for a few minutes before we left the country was more attentive to Tommy and him not bleeding out than caring if we all lived or died. We were random bikers. Tommy has a name for himself, even if he was never in Russia. But mafia families like his always get names for themselves.

I prefer how things are done here, though. I like that people know of the Hounds, but not enough to pick me out of a crowd. I like the ability to stay hidden till I do my own reveal.

"You're going to need some physical therapy too."

I turn at his words and pause. *Interesting.*

"Okay."

Kooper

"I'll make a list of a few in town who specialize with this type of wound."

"No need. Already have someone in mind." I start to walk away, grimacing as I go. I take it slow and steady, but I refuse to sit in a damn wheelchair or show anyone that I'm not able to defend myself as needed.

"You going to the club?"

I nod. Sweat is forming on my hairline; I can feel it. General says nothing. I know he sees it, but he also knows I've had enough of all this doctor-patient bullshit. I stayed long enough for him to patch me up, and now I'm out.

"Casper's throwing a party for Walker. Domino told me the story last night about him doing the whole *Walking Dead* zombie thing in Russia. Seems fitting the prospect would move up after that."

And Casper's inauguration, I'm sure. Before I went under the knife, Bulldog asked who my vote for the new president was. I asked who the front-runner was, and when he said it was Casper, I cast my vote for the same. It makes sense right now. And with the amount of pain I was in when I was asked, it didn't seem smart to make a play on the position for myself.

Not just yet. I've still got time. Casper can't hold the position forever. And with him moving up, an officer position is now open. With Law out of commission, I could start the traditional way to the top. Would be more work, but I've never shied away from the hard stuff. I only left the Diplomatic Security Service because of who they wanted me to protect, not because it was hard.

If someone who's an asshole to everyone and his mother is also stealing and raping people, I don't see why I should protect him. It's called karma. You get what you put out in the world. Not that my bosses saw it that way. According to them, I left my post, and the guy got hurt. He's still alive, sort of. On a feeding tube. His delusional wife still pays the bills to keep him alive despite what he did. Love is crazy. Or just blind. Whatever it is, my bosses kicked me out for "failure to perform duties I was hired for." They wanted to throw me in prison to make a point, but unlike Jimmy Travis, Fairy's uncle, there wasn't enough heat on me. It helped that the guy lived through the attack, and I wasn't the one who pulled the trigger. I made sure to cover my bases. It wasn't my fault that some fathers of the people he hurt snuck in when I was on my coffee break. Sure, I rarely drink the stuff, but we were in Italy. It's what you do in that part of the world. At least that's what I told my superiors. They didn't like it. They also didn't like the guy I was protecting. So I got kicked out, lost some of my retirement plans, and found the Hounds. I like to think things worked out for the better for me.

Even with the damn pin in my hip. Fuck. If I have to get hip replacement surgery at my age, I'll be the laughingstock of the brothers. I'm too young for that shit.

When we get to the entrance of the hospital, I'm not surprised to see a car waiting for me. I want my bike, but I know that'll take longer to get. I open the door and, despite my desire to just get in quickly and get the fuck out of here, I take it easy. Even let General help me get into the SUV. I grunt, which he nods to. Our way of saying "thanks" and "you're welcome" without saying it. 'Cause we're men and all.

"You good?" Atom asks as he eases out of the parking lot.

Kooper

"Peachy."

He huffs a laugh, and I look out the window as we drive back home. It's going to suck for a bit, but I'll do what the doc says. I'll get the therapy. Anything it takes to get back to what I was. I don't do well with being down and out. I know Casper, the new boss, will want me to get a full workup from General to get a green light before I can do anything remotely fun. Like go knocking heads in or some shit. Law would have done the same. It's just what a good boss does. And I've got no issues with Casper being the man in charge. I know Law liked him for the job even while I was still biding my time to get my in.

When we pull up to the clubhouse, I see it's busier than ever. Brothers from other chapters are still hanging around, and more protection is on the gates. We're still rebuilding from when they got knocked down by Ivan's men, but we've got things in place now to prevent another attack.

"Party's in the back," Atom says as he slowly gets out. He's not injured as far as I know, so that means he's just keeping pace with me to give me some of my damn dignity back. It's crap but it's appreciated all the same.

I take a breath when I get out of the car and stand tall. Shit hurts, but I'll live. General gave me some meds, and I plan to take them and sleep for a week. After I show face. I need to make sure everyone sees me as the man who's still standing and not lying in a bed somewhere. Well, unless I've got a woman with me, that is.

When I get to the back, I see a sea of faces I know and some I don't. I take it in and give a few chin lifts. I don't see Casper. He must still be inside.

But I do see her.

Ruby's sitting at a table with Milly, Bass, Abigail, and Mickey. She's talking. From the looks of it, even bantering. Small smiles, *forced* smiles, on her lips as she does. Her attire is her usual: tight jeans and a corset top.

"Brooklyn," Chains hollers at Milly. "You got visitors."

I watch, like half the damn place, as the East Coast mafia comes up to join them. Milly seems happy about it. Bass ain't shitting himself, so I guess that's good. But the look Tommy gives Ruby? I don't like it. And when he leans a bit too close, his eyes lingering, I *really* don't like it.

I walk that way and all but turn red when I see him touch her. Just on the back. Just a small amount. But it's not his right to do.

She doesn't see me as she giggles about his manners and runs into me. I could have moved out of the way, but I didn't. Call it what you want. Maybe I wanted her attention on me. Maybe I needed to feel her against me for the brief time I had. All I know is I didn't move, and I let it happen. It hurts a bit. Okay, it hurts a lot. She just ran into my fucked-up shoulder and jammed against my hip that just got a pin in it. Still, the pain is worth it. Even if she's annoyed at me.

"Koop, what do you want?"

I look her over for half a second, then ignore her completely. Or so the others watching would think. But there's no way to ignore or forget a woman like her in your vicinity. Her scent penetrates my brain, and I clench my fists to keep from pulling her close and sinking my nose in her hair. Hair that's down, free of any bindings. I itch to wrap it around my fist and pull her tight to me, just to get a reaction other than snark from her.

Kooper

She's been on my mind a lot. More than usual. Ever since I held her and let her fall apart in my arms, something snapped in me, and I'm almost consumed by the memory. When she fought me, I let her. I was the thing she needed in that moment. A punching bag. Something to let her anger out on.

And I see that right now, she just wants to forget. To pretend for a bit longer that things aren't as bad as I know they are for her. If seeing me causes her strife, then I'll leave. I won't like it, but if that's what she needs, I'll do it.

For now.

I hold my hand out to the man behind her. "Tommy."

He grabs mine in greeting, and I grip his a bit harder.

"'Sup, man."

"How's the neck?" I make a show of looking at his scar as he turns his head to show the bandage on his neck.

"Still hanging. Let me catch up with you later. Got a girl to talk to about a drink." He barely lets me nod before he's ushering Ruby away.

I didn't miss the expression that she was giving me the whole time. Sure, it was a glare, but her eyes were on me and not him.

I take a second to watch them go and then make a beeline for the clubhouse. I stop only once to ask where Casper is, and when I'm told he's in his office, I let myself in despite the door being closed.

"We need to tell her," I bark at Casper. He's sitting with his head in the books, Domino across from him. I sit because I'm in pain, but I won't tell them that.

Casper throws the paperwork down, and I see the tiredness in his eyes. He went from cleanup duty to running the mother chapter overnight. Not an easy task, but one he took on willingly, so my pity for him is nonexistent.

"Tell her what? That we lied to her? That her dad isn't dead, but we need him to look that way? That he's in a coma, and we don't know when he's coming out of it? That we're hiding him from damn near everyone because we can't have our enemies coming after us thinking we're weak, or worse, using his condition to truly end him?"

"If it's the truth," I say with a tight jaw. I want to say so much more, but I keep it together. Barely.

Casper shakes his head. He probably thinks I'm naïve, but I know what I'm doing. He looks at Domino, who just shakes his head. Whatever. They can think what they want about me. I don't like hiding this from her. It doesn't feel right. Never has, even if I agreed to it to begin with.

"The truth? We don't have time to deal with this shit. We've got enemies, and we can't be weak. Telling Ruby is a liability."

"She can keep her mouth shut," I spit back.

"Can she? She's a wild card. Law didn't even know half of the things she was up to. She's unpredictable, unstable. You willing to bet your life on her keeping her trap shut? You willing to bet your brothers' lives? Their wives'? The kids'?"

I cross my arms and look away from them. I can't let them see what I'm feeling. Not sure if I'm able to lock down my emotions right now with all the other pain going on in my system. "Still ain't right."

Kooper

"Maybe so, but unless you want to go against me and take the president's badge, it is what it is. So get on board with it and do it quick. I've got other shit to deal with, and you throwing a hissy fit about having issues with keeping a secret ain't even in the top ten of shitty things I need to deal with today."

I *do* want to challenge him for the badge. I want to do it so I can run this like it should be done. Like telling Ruby the truth. But I'm not strong enough. Not for the club, not for her.

Without saying anything, I leave, slamming the door shut as I go to make one last statement. I'm so close to getting my ass kicked for insubordination right now, but I can't help it. My mind is all over the place. Since Law was shot, I've barely had time to think things through. I went from scrubbing his blood off my hands to feeling Ruby in my arms to rushing off to Russia and getting fucked up. All to come back here and see I lost my possible promotion and watch another mafia prick hang on something I shouldn't want.

I make it to my room, shutting and locking the door behind me. Slowly, I sit on my bed and take the two pills that General said to take with water. I do so with the whiskey on the nightstand. There's water in it, sort of.

I don't bother undressing; it would take too much effort. Instead, I just lean back and close my eyes, willing sleep to come. Once I have the rest, I plan to do some thinking. Planning out what the next steps are and what I need to do.

But all I see when I close my eyes is Ruby.

Chapter 18—Ruby

One minute, I'm sitting down at the table with a burger on my plate next to Abigail, and the next, I see Penny pulling General's niece, Emily, away. I would get up and help, but Emily is a pain in the ass. I know she's young and just in it for the teenage lifestyle of clothes and cute boys, but damn if it ain't annoying. I swear I was never like that. How could I be? When I was a teenager, my mom was going through chemo. Boys and fashion ceased to exist at that moment. Not that I really gave a fuck before that, or after. I dress how I like, and I don't give a shit what others say.

As for boys? I'm still looking for one who turns my head. Not that I'm actually looking. Been busy with school after Mom's death, first trying to catch up on what I missed in high school so I could graduate, then focusing on college. And I did that. The next goal was to get the doctorate. And… well… Dad died.

The drive I had was a part of him. It's kind of hard to find that focus again. It's only been a few weeks, and Abigail says I'm still in shock. Nat says I'll get back to school if it's something I really want. No one is pushing me into one thing or another. I like that, but also hate it. I need a drive, a goal. I feel like I'm in the middle of the sea. On one side is a small island. It can give me cover, but who knows for how long? But just on the other side, and a bit of a swim away, is a boat. It'll take some effort to get to it, and it might not work out in the long run, but it's an option to keep moving. College is the

Kooper

boat, and taking a break is the island. Both give me a rest from what I'm doing now—treading water and barely keeping my head above it.

"Get Billy." Penny's words jar me out of my head.

Who the fuck is Billy?

I know I've been out of it. I put up a front that I think I fool most with. Some see through it; others don't. No one calls me out on it. But even still, we don't have a Billy in the club. I get that we have a few brothers visiting from sister chapters, but not one introduced themselves as Billy. And trust me, I've gotten a ton of introductions over the last few days. Everyone wants to express their condolences, which I appreciate, but I also just want them to fuck off and let me grieve. Or ignore everything. Both work, but I got neither.

Abigail jumps up and starts running to the back of the property. Whatever. Not my problem. Maybe another day I would care, but there's too much going on in my life to think beyond my own issues right now.

The burger is meh at best. Not like how Dad used to cook them. I keep eating, though. I might not know my direction, but one thing I refuse to do is just lie down and not get back up. So I eat. Sleep. Drink water. Do what I need to do to keep my body functioning. It's my heart and head that stopped working. Everything else is fine.

And I can react like everyone else the second we hear a gun go off. Half the tables clear as we duck down. A second passes, and then brothers run for the front as an engine fires up.

"Get inside," someone yells and ushers me and the other women and kids through the back.

I look around and just see scared people, but what can happen to me now? Someone else dies? We all burn and go up like smoke and ash? Honestly, it might make me feel something other than this numbness.

I don't want others to die or to get hurt. But I'm willing to see where things go before I react to anything, sitting my ass down at the bar and reaching around to grab a bottle of beer while I wait.

Minutes go by before Wendi comes in, with a pissed-off Casper behind her and holding a gun to her head. And then I see the same for Abigail. I stand quickly. Not sure what I'm going to do, but seeing one of my best friends like this makes me want to do *something*.

"Don't," I hear the second before I feel a hand wrap around my wrist and pull me back. I didn't even know I took a step in her direction.

I look at the hand, then follow it to an arm and shoulder, then face. Kooper. Haven't seen him for a bit. Someone said he went to lie down or something. Guess this woke him up—whatever this is.

"Sit," Casper barks, and both Abigail and Wendi oblige. "Have Flint lock this place down."

Someone runs off to wherever Flint is. Probably in his little cave of justice with all the computer screens.

"For how long?" a brother, I think it's King, asks.

"Till my bike comes back," Domino grumbles.

My eyes go wide. Domino's bike was stolen? Outside the clubhouse? How the fuck was that pulled off? And why are these two here, sitting at gunpoint? And where's Penny?

Kooper

Kooper lets go of my hand and grabs my beer, taking a swig before giving it back to me. I don't protest. He needs it just as much as I do. Too many questions, not enough answers.

And waiting? Waiting is the worst.

It's been hours of waiting. I switched to water after the second beer. It was going down way too smooth for me to not see it being an issue.

No one has been talking. Not much, anyway. I've moved around the clubhouse's main area a few times. And each time I note that Kooper is close. Not following, but somehow ending up on my side of the room after a while. I refuse to think on it and just roll with it.

When I see Wendi straighten, I look at the door. Seconds tick by before Atom, Penny, and Walker come in. Then Domino runs out, and Penny goes to the bar and starts drinking.

"What'd I miss?"

I've got to hand it to the girl. She's badass. She has to know guns are pointed at her, and she doesn't seem to care. I like that about her. Not that I should. I get that she, her sister Wendi, and Abigail all did something against the club, I just don't know what yet.

The boys start laying into her and Wendi. It seems they're with the Crazy Eights, a group I've heard the brothers mention in passing but nothing more. Somehow it's a group that the brothers get both pissed about and dread.

I'm only half paying attention till I see Wendi is looking at my friend when Casper asks why they pretended to be someone they aren't. Why they hid themselves. What, or who, are they really here for?

"Abigail?" I say her name and watch her flinch.

I didn't think my heart could shatter any more. But hearing it, seeing my best friend betray the club my dad and mom raised me in, is like having it broken all over again. I had no clue I could feel this lost ever again, but here I am as they keep bantering.

They say she was overlooked by the club. That she never betrayed us, just did some intel work, though nothing that had them learning more than they should. That's what "they" say, Penny and Wendi. Who are really Jack and Billy. A cover. Just people pretending to be someone they aren't.

I feel that. It's kind of what I'm doing. I'm Ruby, or at least that's what I answer to. But I don't feel much like myself these days. Just a shell of the person I once was, when I had a family and a home to go to. Now it's just four walls and an empty space.

Even Abigail gets a new name: Rue, a recruit for this C8 group. Whoever the hell they are. They say more are coming too. That this is just the beginning. It feels as if the small world I tried to keep together with tape is tearing away as they speak. Nothing seems right anymore. And as the little salvation I still had falls away, I do the same.

I head for my room. They can deal with this without me. I don't need to be here. More problems are going to come, but they aren't mine. How can they be? I'm not even supposed to be staying at the clubhouse. These rooms are reserved for club members and vamps, not family of dead

Hounds. If they were, Abigail would have had a room. Maybe she wouldn't have gotten to where she is now if we'd let her stay here.

They. If *they* had let her. Nothing about this club is a *we* anymore. I always wanted to be on the inside, but I never was. And now I feel it more than ever before.

"Ruby."

I turn at my name and see Tommy coming down the hall. Forgot that he was held in lockdown, too, till the club figured things out.

"Yeah?"

"Want some company?" He raises an eyebrow and stuffs his hands into his pockets.

He's cute enough. Has the charm and the arrogance that I think I would have gone for if things were different. And maybe after a while, I'll change my mind. But not today.

I shake my head, then turn around and head to my room. I just want to shut things out for a bit. Just a little. I'll pull myself together and go back to pretending enough for others to not notice me tomorrow.

I shut the door and lean my head back against it. Dad would be heartbroken if he were here. He took Abigail in after her brother died. She was like a sister, even though she still stayed away more than not. She said it was too hard to be around us all and not remember him. Maybe we should have tried harder to bring her in. She was like me, an outsider to both the club and the town. Not fitting in. But unlike her, at least I had Dad.

But now, I'm just like her.

Wonder if I'll betray the club too. It's a passing thought. One I know will go nowhere. Because despite losing dad, I still grew up here. I have more good memories here than bad. My friends are here. I might be pushing them away a bit, but they're still here, keeping me grounded in their own way.

A knock at the door makes me sigh. Mafia boy just isn't getting the hint.

"I told you no," I say as I open the door, then stop talking when I see who it is.

"Told who no?" Kooper's eyes narrow. Then his arms cross. "And why?"

I shake my head to dispel the trance I was in for a second from just seeing him here. Last time he was at my door was when he came to my apartment and told me my rent was going down. Since then, he's never actually been on one side of a door and me on the other.

"Nothing."

"Doesn't seem like nothing."

His tone has my teeth clenching. And despite me saying I'm numb, he gets me riled up, and I just start barking back as if nothing's changed between us. "What happens between me and mafia boy ain't your problem."

But things have changed. I just... I just don't understand them. Okay, fine, I do, but I don't want to. It's confusing, and that's one thing I'm not going to focus on. I can't handle confusing after everything else.

He steps into my room, and I back up on autopilot, cursing myself once I realize I let go of the door and it swings shut.

Kooper

Having a man in my room is no big deal. I'm close to the brothers. They stop in all the time to bullshit. But Kooper has never been one of them. And none of them have history with me like he does. No one saw me cry. No one held me. Not one of them was someone I hoped to have close before.

I grew up in the club. Most are family, if not stepbrothers who I've never wanted but learned to deal with. Sure, I had a crush on a few here and there, but nothing came of it, as I knew they were off-limits. My dad would never allow me nor them to do anything.

But... that was when he was alive. With him gone, the rule doesn't seem to apply anymore.

He once told me he didn't want to come into work and hear about me fucking some brother. The thought that I was going to be "office" chatter really bugged him. He didn't want to know about me doing anything with a boy, but definitely not with a brother. Especially since he'd probably seen more than half of them do things with a vamp that no father should ever imagine their little girl doing.

But with him gone, even if the boys talk, he won't hear it.

Not that I plan to go sleeping around with every available brother I see. Though if I did, the brothers I picked wouldn't be dicks enough to talk about it. They respected my father and still do.

Not that I'm thinking about it. And I'm absolutely not thinking about doing anything with Kooper. He was just there when I was vulnerable. He saw me at a weak point, and no pity ever crossed his face. Something I appreciate in him more than any other feature a man can have.

"You and Tommy got something going?"

I glare as I put my hands on my hips. "And if we do? What's it to you?"

"Nothing. Just expected more from you is all."

"What's that supposed to mean?"

"It means your dad would be pissed. He's not even in the ground for a month, and you're looking to replace him."

My jaw goes slack, and I feel it drop. "I am not."

"You sure about that?"

"Look." I move in close and poke him in the chest. "You don't get to tell me what to do. If anyone is trying to replace Dad, it's you. I don't need a daddy. Besides, Tommy is a flirt. That's it. I see his type daily. I'm not going to run after one, especially one who lives so far away. It would be hell on the phone bill from all the phone sex." I smirk as I turn and walk away, only to turn back and drop my smile.

If I thought I'd deterred him, like I would my father, I was mistaken. Because unlike Dad, who hated any talk about sex or kissing or me doing anything with a boy, Kooper just grins.

"If it takes that long on the phone, he ain't doing it right."

My breath stalls in my throat, and I speak before I think better of it.

"How long should it take?"

He takes a step closer to me. "If you have to ask, then you're doing it wrong." He lifts my chin to close my mouth with the underside of his finger. I didn't know it was even down. But as my jaw locks in place, he slowly moves his finger, the one that just touched my skin, to his lips and licks it, then bites the part he licked.

Kooper

I shake my head, trying to... well... shake me out of whatever just happened. I have to have imagined it. That couldn't have happened. Right? I mean, it's almost as if Kooper was coming on to me. Tasting me. Looking at me with want and desire.

But when I look back at him, I don't see any of it but his tilted head.

I must have imagined it.

I'm going crazy. First with Dad dead, and then finding out about Abigail's betraying me and the club, my brain is taking a nosedive into whatever it needs to so I can get through this. I feel hurt all over, and I hug myself tight to try and will myself not to break apart and scatter across the ground.

"What do you want, Koop?"

He moves his head from one side to the other and looks me over. Nothing sexual, just assessing. I hate it because I know he sees more than I want. He doesn't just see me closing myself off like everyone else does. I swear to Christ, he can see my inner child crying and rocking herself in the corner with a stuffie.

"Need some physical therapy. The Russia trip fucked up my hip and shoulder. General wants me to get it worked on so I'm not out of commission. I don't have insurance, thought you'd be willing to help. Could get you the practice you need."

I bite my lip. "Can't the club cover the cost of the PT?"

He shrugs. "Don't know. Figured I'd come to you. If you can't do it, then I can do it on my own. No need to waste club money on me."

I glare. He'd rather hurt himself than take money. Typical biker. "Fine. I'll do it."

He nods and heads out.

I tell myself the glint in his eye was me seeing things. And the flutter in my stomach is just because I'm hungry. Nothing more.

Chapter 19—Kooper

This is a bad idea. It has to be. Anything that makes me second-guess what I'm wearing is probably the worst idea I've ever had. I even freaking googled what to wear. Me. A guy who gives zero fucks about anything. I spent twenty goddamn minutes looking up what's best to wear to physical therapy.

Loose-fitting clothing. No shit.

But still, I dug through my clothes and found some I felt comfortable in. You know, ones that are soft to the touch for anyone to feel. The kind that are tight enough to show my definition without it looking like I'm trying to show off. Some that bring out the color of my eyes.

Yeah, I threw something across the room at that last thought. I would puke if I could at how stupid I'm acting, but I haven't eaten this morning. I read somewhere that PT can lead to expressing yourself in other ways. Last thing I want is to fart when Ruby has my legs spread and her face close.

And yeah, I looked up what some of the moves are going to be. This will be a testament in strength, I know. I also hope that it helps expel whatever it is I'm feeling toward her. If I get her close for a bit, have that feeling, then I can just get it over with and go back to wanting her out of my way.

Again, I know how stupid that sounds. I'm not fooling anyone, not even myself anymore. I want her.

I want Ruby.

Still can't have her, though. And that's what I need to focus on to get over this so I can move on and live life beyond all this bull.

I drive to her work. She prefers to do this where someone can step in if she messes things up. Though I doubt she's the type to. If I spent twenty minutes looking up how to dress, I know she spent hours researching how to do the moves properly. That's just the way she is. She never does anything half-assed.

I wish I had my bike, but I read that some people are sore after these sessions. I don't need to cause further issues by straddling a bike after I was just stretched wide.

"Can I help you?" a young kid asks as I walk in.

There doesn't seem to be anyone else here. Not sure if that means this place sucks or that it's just a time that no one wants to come. 8:00 a.m. is a bit rich for my blood, too, but it was all Ruby gave me. She called yesterday, told me the address and the time of the appointment, and then hung up. Never took any of my calls when I tried to get a different time.

She thinks it's an issue for me. That I would be the type to sleep in because of a long night of drinking or something. What she doesn't know is that I had to switch shifts at the gate for this, and *that* was the headache. Nothing more, nothing less.

"I got him, Alister." Ruby comes out from the back hall, and I just stare. I've never seen her in professional attire before. Her pink scrubs are tight in so many places and loose in others.

"Right-o, boss lady." Alister smiles at her and nods me in her direction. "Just follow her, and she'll get you all fixed up."

I nod once and move to where Ruby's standing. When I get close, she turns and walks down the hallway. I keep a close distance. You know, in case I get lost in this one-hallway place.

"Boss lady?" I ask.

She turns, seeing my smirk, and rolls her eyes. "You tell one Gen Z to stop playing on their phone and actually do work they were hired for, and they get all fussy about it." She opens the door marked five and allows me to enter first before she follows and shuts it. "Unfortunately for him, I don't let a few eye rolls and small jabs at my age deter me. After he saw I wasn't having it and the others were asking me to deal with him, he just started calling me that. Has a nice ring to it, don't you think?"

I chuckle. She almost sounds like herself. Except her eyes didn't light up as they would have if she were her true normal self.

"I had General send me your notes on what happened." She holds up a hand before I even open my mouth. "No, he didn't tell me anything more than what the injuries are, where they're located, and how he treated them so I can do my job. The guy's not one to blab secrets, unlike others. Take a seat."

"Still mad about Abigail?" I slowly sit on the treatment table and ignore the way the plastic creaks and starts sticking to my legs almost immediately.

"Still mad? It happened a week ago. Actually, it's been longer than that. Months or who knows. We just found out. How can you be over it already?"

I shrug. "I'm not."

She purses her lips and folds her arms, pushing her boobs together. In the tight scrubs, there's major pulling on the fabric to keep them confined.

"If you don't get to be over it, then neither do I. Plus, I get to be pissed off more. Lie back."

"How so?" I ease myself down and let my feet dangle over the side.

"Scoot up more so your head's at the top and your legs are mostly flat on the table." I do as she says and adjust when she moves me a bit. "And I can be mad because she *was* my best friend. We practically grew up together. She could have told me. She could have told me there were issues with her landlord or the town, or whatever Jack said she was having issues with. I would have helped. But no. She went it alone, and then she just rolled over to this C8 group without a second thought for me or anyone. It's utter bullshit."

I grunt as she starts moving my leg.

"Oh, sorry. Try to relax. I'm going to move you around to work on some areas to see how tight you are. Then we'll do some moves so I can fully stretch you out. We'll finish with me showing you a few moves to do at home. Next time you come back, you can show me what you did. The moves are to be done slowly and consistently. You should get more flexibility each time you do. So while today might suck, and, well, tomorrow and a few days from now, by next week, you'll be able to do things you can't do today."

Kooper

I nod but don't speak. I can't. Not when she's this close, her scent in the air and her heat hitting my body. Then she does the unimaginable. She drapes herself across me and starts stretching both my shoulder and then—fucking hell—my hip. I bite my cheek. I claw my nails against my palms. I pinch my toes together. Anything I can do to cause pain to myself.

Sure, she's doing that too. But with her doing it, it hurts so good. I get the whole pain-pleasure aspect on a whole other level.

And holy shit, she just instructed me as to what she's doing next. I need to run out of here. To make up an excuse that I have to go. But my brain freezes on any ideas other than "ahhh" when she lifts my leg, puts it over her shoulder, and leans down to me. Her fingers interlock around my upper thigh, and she holds the position.

With. Her. Hand. Touching. My. Dick.

If it were a guy, or hell, anyone but her, this would be no issue. I could overlook it as a gentle graze. A subtle shift and I could move it enough that she wouldn't feel it.

Till it starts to grow.

I want to die, but I also want to watch how she reacts. I look at the ceiling, seeing a poster of a damn possum hanging upside down. It's ridiculous but better than the overused cat hanging from the tree branch.

I take a chance and look at her. Her head is bowed down, looking away from me as she holds her position. I will myself to remain flaccid, but it's not happening.

So, I do what I always do: say *fuck it* in my mind and go at this head-on.

I stare her down and wait for the moment that she either feels more of me or notices the tent growing in my shorts. I don't have to wait long. And her response? Not something I would have expected.

Her head turns, and she looks at my cock, not moving other than a small gasp leaving her lips. Just watching and watching. The more she looks, the harder I get. And when she licks her lips, fuck, I feel myself leak a bit.

But then she snaps out of it and jumps back, no longer touching me as her eyes bounce around the room till they land back on me. She seems flustered. Either this has never happened to her at work, or….

She clears her throat. "I'll, uh, get you some pamphlets." She all but runs out of the room.

Sitting up, I wait. And wait some more. Just when I'm about to go find her, the door opens and Alister from the front walks in.

"Here you go. Take these home and do the stretches every other night if you can. We'll have you back at the end of the week." He slips me an appointment card and then walks out, leaving the door open.

I grab my shit and follow him.

I look around, but Ruby is nowhere to be seen. I get to my truck and pull up my app. She's still in the building. Well, her phone is. Either she left it, or she got scared and wasn't going back in there. Not till I left.

No idea why, but that makes me smile as I start the engine and head home. After all, I've got some stretches to practice. And some Google searches to run on how to prevent what just happened. Because while I don't give a shit about getting a boner, I'd rather not have one if it lets me see Ruby longer.

It's gotten easier over the past few weeks. Still get a boner, but I've willed it down to a solid chub most of the time. It helps when I close my eyes and just picture Law dying. It's morbid and fucked up and just what I need.

We don't talk about that first session. I don't bring it up, and neither does Ruby. But she does blush. Not that I call her out on it, but I do smile. And she glares when she sees my smile. It's there, but it's unspoken.

My hip and shoulder are doing better. I've never believed in all this doctor mumbo jumbo before. Not that I was against modern medicine, but I never saw stretching to be anything more than what you do to limber up for a run. Like a marathon run. Not that I ever did one. Hence the no-stretching thing.

But I guess I'm a walking billboard advocating it now. Well, I'm not saying shit, but the brothers know I come here. I can't hide it. And they know who's working on me. They think it's just my way of keeping an eye on her.

And it is. And it ain't, all at once.

Duke is still out there. That's the intel C8 gave us. He might be hunkered down with his club, the Devils Damned, but he's still out there. He could have friends willing to make enemies with the Hounds. Half the reason we said Law was dead and hid it from her that actually he's in a coma is because we know enemies like to prey on the weak. If it got out that he's just sleeping till who the fuck knows when, more attempts would be made on his life, and hers.

By lying to her, we're keeping her safe. And with me doing weekly check-ins, as far as the club knows, I'm watching the shadows. Looking for anyone who thinks it's a good idea to finish what Duke started a while back. Every brother with a family is doing the same. Even though, for all Ruby knows, she has no family, the club still considers her one of our own.

After the shit that went down with Abigail, we realized we'd fucked up. We let someone get close, but not close enough to protect. We don't want Ruby to fall into the same things Abigail did. We know she'd never turn on us, never betray the club in that way; there's too much club blood in her to even try. But her being outcast by townies and us? Yeah, we aren't going to let that happen.

I'm not going to let it happen.

"How's that new stretch I showed you last week working out for you?" she asks as she does the basic movements for my arm before moving to my hip. We do it this way each time. I might not need the extra stretch in my shoulder, but with the dislocation a while back and then the torn ligament, I'm not against making sure it's all in working order. We all know shit ain't going to get easier for me. I need to be in top shape at all times with how the club works.

"It's fine."

She has me doing the fucking butterfly. Something I hate saying, but I've gotten used to doing. It sucks, but every day I get my legs lower. She focuses on my hip, but last week she started adding in other stretches to work the entire lower region. I want to start lifting again, and she's willing to help

Kooper

me get back into it. It's been weeks, almost the entire time Casper and Billy were in Michigan for a job, that I've kept my workouts to just a few small reps. I feel as if I've lost some muscle mass already, and it's only been a little while. I don't like it and want to get back to it.

General still bitches that it's too soon, whereas Ruby knows she can't control me but just make suggestions. Hers is that I go slow and do more stretches in other areas since it's been a while. I hate to break it to her that even if it was a year, and I was stuck in bed, I'd never go easy in my life. I wouldn't do the stretches either, but I know she monitors my progress and can tell when I don't do them, and she gives me hell.

Did that the first week. She said to either do the homework or stop wasting her time and find someone else to work on my hip. Not sure if that's a tactic they teach at her school or not, but I'm all for that type of bedside manner. Tell it to me straight. Do it or don't. But if the results are either staying with her or not? We all know what I'm choosing.

"Show me." I sit cross-legged and grab my toes as I push my elbows down on my knees. Slow. She likes it when I go slow.

We moved off the table a week back and do most of the shit on the floor now. She prefers it if I do most of the stretching on my own, and she only guides me here and there. Less touching for her, I think. But I still get a chub just being close to her. Smelling her. Seeing her.

She leans forward and pushes down a bit. We hold the position, and I do what I always do when she does this. When she gets close, she just focuses on the stretch, while I look at her. I memorize everything about her in those moments. I can do it a hundred times a day. I file the memory away for when I'm not here and I want to be.

She's gotten braver lately, holding my stare for a few seconds at the end each time. Till she looks away and we switch to another move.

Twenty more minutes on the floor, and now we're up. She wants to do a balance test with me today, so I stand on a rubber bubble with one foot bent, and her hands rest on my hips from behind. I look back to see her kneeling down to check my hips, and I tighten up. Having her below me while I'm standing is one thing I can't ever get over.

I close my eyes and will my dick to deflate. But it doesn't, and I lose my balance.

"Whoa, I got you." She grabs my hips as she stands quickly.

She's shorter than me, coming up just over my shoulder.

"You good?" she asks.

I look back and down at her and nod. Just once. Her eyes aren't on mine, though, but on my lips.

I don't look away as she watches me. I just bask in this. In this weak spot for her, because I know she likes to pretend I don't have any influence on her. Maybe I didn't when I started the job. Maybe not even after her dad died. But recently? After she can tell I'm turned the fuck on with her hands on me two to three times a week? She can't deny how I feel. She can chalk it up to just a momentary thing. To me being a horndog or whatever. But it's not true. If another woman touched me like she does, I wouldn't be so hard all the time. I wouldn't be seeking relief after each session in the shower like I do now.

I especially wouldn't be mad the second she turns and starts to walk away.

"Right, I think—"

I don't let her finish. I grab her arm, spin her around, and use my other hand to palm the back of her head and pull her lips to mine.

I hold her tight to me as she struggles for a second. Her mouth opens in protest, and my tongue slips in. I grab her around the waist with my other arm and pull her flush against me. Her arms are between us, and she uses them to push me back, but I just pull her closer. Her fingers turn into claws to dig into my chest.

But then her fight dies. Her claws flatten, and the pads of her fingers press into me. Her mouth responds. Her tongue, tentative at first, glides against my own. The hand on her neck starts to massage the base of her hairline while I rub my other thumb over the small bit of skin that was revealed at her waist when I pulled her into my arms.

She fits perfectly. I knew she would. And her taste? Fucking unimaginable. Like forbidden fruit and sweetness. Peaches and cream.

And when she moans? If she didn't feel my dick against her before, she sure as hell does now. No way to hide what that noise from her does to me.

Knock knock.

"Boss lady, your next appointment is here."

She pulls away, panting. I let her go because I know now isn't the time to force this.

I had a taste. A sample.

But so did she.

I hold her stare as she looks at me with wide eyes as if she's never seen me before. Maybe she hasn't. Not like this. Not with desire and want clear in my gaze.

She licks her lips, and her eyes dip to my cock. Seeing it still straining to get to her, she snaps them back up to mine.

"Um, keep up the stretches." She grips the handle of the door behind her and pulls it open, then practically runs out.

I smile as she goes. She might not know it, but Ruby just made the biggest mistake of her life.

Not running from me. Oh no. I knew she'd do that.

But she didn't tell me to stop.

And I don't plan to.

Chapter 20—Ruby

"It's just a normal day. Completely normal."

But it's not. How can it be? I still feel Kooper against my lips. The ghost of his hands is still imprinted on me. Everything about this morning is on repeat in my head.

And I hate it. Hate it all.

How dare he kiss me! How dare I let him? And no, I didn't moan. I didn't respond. I just... I just...

Fuck. I bang my head against the steering wheel.

I *did* kiss him. I responded.

And fucking hell, I enjoyed it.

But I shouldn't. I can't. Not just because of Dad, but because of everything else. He's club. I don't mess with club. Sure, Dad's dead, but I should honor his wishes. Right?

"Ugh." Stupid Kooper. Had to go and make things complicated.

Him getting a boner when I worked on his hip? Shocking. Totally unexpected. That first day, I ran out like I've never seen a dick before. A freaking schoolgirl action. But the more I thought on it, the more it made sense. The guy's a biker. A freaking Hound. They have vamps at their place all the time. He's probably still either suffering from morning wood or just used to getting hard when a woman gets close to his dick. Just a physical response, not the want or desire.

No way he wanted me. No way did he see me as anything but a female who was so close to his dick that he'd get a hand job from her.

Or that's what I thought.

But that was before he kissed me. Before he made little sparks flash behind my eyes and my always-active brain stop thinking. It took a second, maybe more than that, but then it all clicked. I stopped fighting and started feeling. And fuck if I didn't feel everything.

He made me wet. And not just with his mouth. Him being pressed against me like that? His hands holding me possessively? It's how every girl dreams of being kissed.

I did.

Just never thought it would be with him.

Which is why I came to the club after my appointments. I should be home studying. Got a test in two days. But I'm here. I need to clear the air. Need him to explain it to me, that he was just horny, and he'd do it with anyone. That I'm not special. That he didn't think and just reacted. Anything that I can actually handle. Because if Kooper likes me? Wants me?

I just don't know. But I don't think I can handle it. Hell, it's been five hours since then, and I've done nothing but think of him. I can't have that. I have to focus on school. To make Mom and Dad proud as they watch over me.

I might not know what direction my life is going, but I know I want to finish school. It's paid for, after all. Part of Dad's will. Domino has it. I told him not to tell me all of it, just what I needed to know right now, which is that the house is paid for and so is school. Once I'm done with that, I can figure everything else out. One step at a time. Or in my case, one deep breath at a time, and minimize the issues.

Like Kooper kissing me.

It can't happen again.

With new resolve, I get out of the car and head inside the club. I don't see my girls here, but that doesn't stop me from making myself known. The boys have kept to themselves these past few weeks. I get it. I'm a reminder of the man who used to lead them. I don't begrudge them for keeping me at arm's length.

Well, everyone but Kooper. There was nothing arm's length about this morning.

I clear my throat, push the thoughts away, and smile wide. "Hey, losers, what'd I miss?"

I don't miss the boys looking at everyone but me. Except for Kooper. He has eyes on me, but I refuse to be held captive by him. At least not till I get him alone to talk.

"Don't."

My head turns at Bulldog's voice. He isn't looking at me, but at Casper.

It's Kooper who looks between the two and asks, "What? Don't what?" But then he looks at me again and shakes his head. There's a plea in his voice as he looks down at the table he's sitting at. "No. Don't do this. Casper... shit, man, don't."

"Don't what?" I ask, clueless, but not one to be left out. If it was secret club stuff, it would be done in Church. With it out in the open like this, that means it's fair game to ask.

"Don't tell me what to do, Koop," Casper grits out. "I'm in charge of this club."

"Come on, man," Kooper begs as his eyes shift to me and then back to the new president. He almost seems desperate to keep whatever the hell it is from my ears. "You're hung up on your old lady walking out. This has nothing to do with her."

"Whoa, big man got hitched? So soon? Who's the lucky bitch?" I grin as I pull out the seat between them and sit. I even make myself comfortable by grabbing the whiskey and taking a deep pull. I need a hard burn after this morning. Being close to Kooper is doing weird things to my libido.

"No one," Casper barks before taking the bottle away. "I ain't chained up. Not now, not going to be."

"Well, with that attitude, you won't. Might try loosening up a bit. Maybe you should call that vet girly, the badass one, and see if she's still interested."

"Billy's dead to me." He seems lost in his head, and his words are a complete lie based on the heartbreak written clearly on his face.

And instead of giving him the easy way out, I push. It's what I'm good at.

"Why? Y'all seemed good together. Even when I saw she pulled that gun on you. Pretty hot."

"She left."

"Oh, was it something you said?" I lean back in the chair, kicking my feet up on the table, undeterred by Casper's foul mood. I'm used to bikers being grumpy. It's when they're sweet and kissing me that I get flustered and can't think straight. "You guys sure know how to fuck up a good thing."

"It was what she did."

"Can't be that bad."

"She lied," Casper spits out.

"So?" The guy's stupid to think a lie would be enough to keep me away from someone I love. Which is clearly how he feels about Billy.

"So?" he scoffs. "Lying isn't a deal-breaker for you?"

I think about it for a second. I've never had anyone lie to me. Well, Abigail did, but I'm not in love with her. She's a friend. And it hurts. Maybe I'll get over it, maybe I won't. But if I really loved someone? Like how Mom and Dad loved? I heard them fight a few times. They weren't the perfect couple, but they were a real one. Things were said often, actions done. No one ever cheated, which I think would be the deal-breaker for them. But lying? I think they would have worked through it. And I hope to be as good as them one day.

"If it was to help in a roundabout way, nah."

He tilts his head at me and just stares.

"Don't, man." Kooper's jaw is so tight, his mouth hardly moves when he makes his demand.

"Jesus, what has you in such a panty-twisting mood, Koop? Just relax for a fucking sec. Hell, go get your dick sucked if you think it'll help." I give him a side-eye.

He's acting weird. I don't want anyone to know what happened this morning. Because it won't be happening again. And if he keeps acting like this, the brothers are bound to ask him what's going on. Them knowing is the last thing I want.

"Your dad's alive."

Those words. Words I never thought would be said. Words I never gave myself hope to think.

They sink in, and I blink. Once, twice. My feet drop, and I lean close, eyeing everything and everyone. No one is laughing. Everyone is looking at me. No one even seems to be breathing.

"Wh-what?"

"He's at St. James Hospital. In a coma." Casper says it like that explains everything.

"What? Why?"

I look at someone I consider my friend and new president of the club, then at Kooper. He doesn't look at me, like a coward. They're all cowards. My hands ball into fists under the table as I look at everyone. They're people I've called family. Friends. Hell, some even helped raise me. But how can family do this to me?

As if reading my thoughts, Bulldog speaks. "Club thought it best to keep it under wraps."

"With him dead, the threat goes with it," Domino offers.

"Without him, the club—" Kooper takes a second to look at me with a nod to include me without saying it. "—everything and everyone would be fine. The threats already high on him would be limited, or even gone."

"Once it was gone, we were going to tell you. After some time," Casper says.

"We don't even know when he'll wake up. We're keeping it quiet for his protection," Chains says as he puts a hand on my shoulder. He probably meant it to be in support, but it just feels like a brick hitting me.

Kooper

Like everything they just said. A ton of bricks hitting me over and over. Each time I think it can't get worse, it does.

"Ruby." Kooper nudges my knee with his hand, and the feel of him on my skin has me swatting it away and then pushing Chains away as well.

"Get your hands off me." I can't be here. I can't. This isn't a safe haven for me. It's a torture chamber. Every time I'm here, something bad happens. I have to get out of here.

I turn and head for the door. No one stops me, but I feel their eyes on me till I hear Kooper speak up.

"We don't even know if he'll wake up," he says.

The plea in his voice. The desperation. I hear it. Not sure if it's because of what happened this morning between us or because of what all this means for the club. But I don't care. He doesn't get to make me see it from his point of view. I can never forgive him, or any of them, for this.

I guess I'm a liar. A foolish girl who said a lie wouldn't change anything if it really mattered. A big fucking liar. Because this changes *everything*.

"Yeah, but there's a chance, right?" I look back, catching Kooper's eye first, then Chains' and Casper's. "Right?"

They all nod.

Swallowing hard, I walk out. But not before giving them my parting words that I hope they take for the truth they are, 'cause I'm not coming back. "So, why the fuck should I waste my time with you all when I can be with him?"

I get to the hospital on autopilot. Once I'm inside, I realize I won't have to play games trying to figure out what name they stashed my dad under. Because General is here, waiting for me. The club probably called him. I should be grateful, but I don't care.

"Where is he?"

"Ruby, sweetie, you have to listen."

"Where. Is. He!" I yell in his face, and everyone on the floor turns to look at me.

To his credit, General doesn't even flinch. I'm sure he's heard worse.

"This way." He turns on his heel, and I follow.

We take turns, go up some stairs and down others. I'm not even paying attention. How can I? Twenty minutes ago, I was trying to live a life without Dad, and now I've found out he's alive. In a coma, but alive.

General finally stops at a closed door, opens it, and then steps aside. I take a second, but then I walk through. First thing I notice is Mad Max. He's here. Which means this is real. It's all real. Dad's really here, and he's alive.

Mad Max was his personal enforcer. A man who did everything for my dad. Who saw him as the reason to get up in the morning, before he met his Fairy. And he's here. Watching a man who's lying in a bed with tubes coming out of his mouth and arms.

Dad seems so fragile. A man who was always larger than life is just a shell of what he was. But the beeping? That beautiful noise? Some might find it annoying, but I find it holy.

Kooper

I bring my hand to my mouth, but I refuse to break. He might not know I'm here, but he can hear me. I have to believe he hears me. So while I hold in my sobs of relief and grief, I move to his bedside.

Mad Max rises but says nothing. The silent watchdog as always. He doesn't even try to apologize like General did. He just moves aside, and I grab my dad's hand, tracing the veins along the top of his hand as I let the tears fall.

"Hi, Daddy. I'm here. Your little girl is here. And I'm not going anywhere." I lean forward and kiss his forehead, then sit on the bed.

I stay there for hours, just watching him breathe through his tubes. I take in everything. And when my stomach protests and my eyelids begin to droop, I rise and look at Mad Max. He never left.

"You can have tonight, but starting tomorrow, you're out of this room. Only family is allowed in here, and I'm the only one he has. You and the others can go. We don't need you anymore. We don't want you. So get lost and stay there."

I turn to leave, reaching the door before he speaks. "You can be mad. It's your right. You can disagree with what happened, but it happened. The Hounds won't be leaving. We'll give you space, but we ain't leaving." He pauses long enough that I look over my shoulder and see him watching Dad. "And he is family. Just like you."

He turns back to me and holds my stare under his heavy demeanor. The guy has always been scary, but I've never felt his full intensity before. It sends a shiver down my spine.

I don't answer, just turn and walk out, taking my time and memorizing the way out so I can come back in the morning. I find my car and get in, driving home in silence.

And all but ignoring the sound of a motorcycle following me all the way.

Chapter 21—Kooper

Four months later

I pour the milk over my second bowl of Cocoa Puffs and let it sit for a second. I like the crunch of the cereal, but I also like the chocolate-tasting milk. Call it a kid food or whatever, but I like it, and I'll stab anyone who says shit to me about it.

Especially this morning.

I got in about two hours ago. Had an hour of rest before my phone went off, alerting me that she was heading to class. Been up ever since.

"You look like shit," Casper says as he slides into the seat at the bar next to me. It's early. Well, early for most brothers. Just after seven in the morning.

"Surprised you got yourself an old lady with the way you say sweet nothings so early in the day," I grumble before putting another spoonful of goodness in my mouth.

"She likes me for what I don't say."

I grunt at his words. I don't have a response for him, and I'm not sure if he wants me to say anything anyway. Brothers can be weird about talking about their old ladies. Either they can take the trash talk as long as someone doesn't cross the line, or they can't. Any of it. It's all or nothing for them, and any sign of disrespect is met with a fist to the face. And despite how eloquently Casper said it, I look and *feel* like shit. No way do I need him to add to it this morning.

Plus, anything this early can be taken the wrong way. Some say it's worse in the evening, but nah. Drinks flow in the evening—people are looking for a good time then. In the morning? No one wants to deal with shit. "You hear about Domino?" Casper asks.

I nod and swallow what's in my mouth. "Jumper filled me in."

If Domino can't find his girl in the next twenty-four hours, Jumper and I are headed up north to Michigan to help look. A few of the other brothers from OHH will join us. We don't react without thought, and Domino said he wanted more details before we all just start burning down buildings in the search for her.

We know how fast someone can get transported out of state, or out of the country, once they go missing. We just shut down several sex trafficking transports abroad thanks to the work with OHH.

Sending Domino up north was just to close out the chapter there. To get all the bad seeds who infected the Hounds of the Reaper MC out for good. Learning we had some of our own involved in that shit put a foul taste in my mouth. In all our mouths.

I voted on just demolishing everyone in that club on sight. Especially with Domino being the one who went up there. The guy's crazy awesome with his explosions. But Casper had other thoughts. He didn't see the need to destroy everything and everyone unless there was proof.

It's bullshit. But it's political bullshit. I get it. Well, now I do. I've had time to think it over when I was first told about Domino heading up north a few months back. Despite what so many think, running the mother chapter, or any chapter of a biker club, isn't about just doing what you want. Sure, we've got a fair share of that, but the rest is just like it is everywhere else—political.

If Casper sanctions wiping out an entire chapter, others might pull away or just go silent on us. Or try to take us out. We all have a creed, but pushing the Hound laws only goes so far. By doing an investigation on the club, and disbanding it if that's what's needed, it's a move that the other chapters can get behind. But it has Casper pushing more and more for a national presidency and chapter.

The mother chapter has a good head on most things, but this Michigan shit, with the former VP selling people for sex trafficking? It showed us we need more vigilance. More eyes on a wider scale to make sure all Hounds are represented in a way the mother chapter and most of the others agree to.

"Think it's going to be an issue?"

My spoon is halfway to my mouth before I stop it and turn my head to look at Casper. He's not looking at the bar top like a coward, but at me.

"You asking about Domino getting an old lady or something else?" My voice is just barely hiding a bit of an edge to it.

Guy's ballsy, as he doesn't blink when he speaks again. "Something else."

I shake my head and put the spoonful in my mouth. "I ought to bust you just for asking," I mumble around my food.

Ain't a secret, no matter that I don't talk about it. It's my business, so I don't see how it's anyone else's. But apparently everyone else thinks differently.

Once Ruby found out about Law, you could say that our little weekly ritual of playing doctor and patient ended. Abruptly.

No more stretches, no more physical therapy. No more accidental touches. And no more kissing.

Hell, she hardly looks at me these days. And when she does, she looks away so quickly that I almost miss the color of her eyes. Lucky for me, I already know what they are, and my memory is the best. I can get any details I want from my memory bank. Like the way she looked after I kissed her soft lips. Or how she tasted like peaches and cream. Or the small, soft groan that left her lips when I had her in my arms.

That one gets played on a loop in my head every night. I would say I can't help it, but it's a lie. I know it, and I do it. I'm a grown-ass man. I can do whatever I want in my head. Fuck anyone else.

Despite the loss of what we had, or at least could have, I refuse to go to another physical therapist. General bitches about it all the time. Whatever. That's his issue. I still do the stretches she taught me and the other things I found online. I'm not letting my past injuries keep me down. They won't affect how I do my Hound job.

Or how I keep protecting Ruby.

Duke is still out there. No idea if he's hunting her or not, but if I were him, I'd still have unfinished business with the Hounds. And I won't let Ruby be that for him.

I tried talking to her about it. Once.

Kooper

I cornered her after she came out of her father's room. She'd just finished her shift. She learned quickly that despite what she wanted, Mad Max wasn't going to let her dad sit without a brother. If he isn't there, he has another brother on the door. Most of the brothers, out of respect for Ruby, sit outside the room. Mad Max doesn't give a fuck what she wants. He has his own personal issues for being there, and he isn't about to let her change his mind. He was the boss's personal security. He wasn't there to take the bullet for Law like he had planned to all his life. So he sits by his side and waits. If Law never wakes up, I've got a feeling that Mad Max will sit there till one or both take their last breath.

Once she learned the brothers were taking watch over her dad, she kept her mouth shut like we asked, never once telling anyone that her dad is actually alive. I checked several times. She doesn't talk to anyone, not even the old ladies. Everyone's at arm's length and then some. I know they all try, but she doesn't respond.

Except when she said who she doesn't want on the door. Told everyone she'd stop throwing a fit every time she sees a brother at the hospital as long as I'm never there.

The boys think it's because it was me who told her he died. That she's taking the bulk of her anger at the club out on me. But I know it's more. It's because of what I started. What we shared just hours before she found out the truth.

But, just like eating a kid cereal and not giving a rat's ass what people say, I did the same to Ruby. I had Atom take a walk when it was his turn one day, and when she came out of the room, I was there.

She took one look at me and started heading for the exit. Fast. I grabbed her arm and pulled her into an empty room before she could do anything. I knew Atom was only waiting long enough for me to get Ruby, and then he was on guard duty for our former president.

"Get your hands off me." She wiggled out of my grasp, and I let her go. The room was empty—I checked before I planned this out—and she walked to the farthest spot away from me. There were no windows in this room, just fluorescent lighting.

"We need to talk." I crossed my arms and planted myself in front of the door. I wouldn't put it past her to run at me to get out of this room.

"Like hell we do. You lied to me. You all lied to me. You can go walk off a fucking bridge and drown for all I care."

I shook my head at her, and she snorted. Nothing sexy about it, but I'd rather get a response than nothing at all. "No, we didn't. He did die. Twice. Once on the floor of the warehouse, then coded on the operating table."

She didn't like that. I knew she read the charts. She'd demanded that General give her everything. She's smart enough to read it all and understand it, while most of that shit is mumbo jumbo to me. "That's bullshit. You know it's bullshit."

It might have been bullshit wording, but it was the truth. And I needed her to see it from our standpoint. To understand that what we said wasn't a lie. A fabricated truth? Yeah. But we never lied to her.

I never lied. Not directly. Everything I've ever said to her has been the truth. She might not see it that way, but I do.

Kooper

I remember her anger dying out at my words. Her arms coming up in a cross over her body to hold herself. Something I wished I'd done for her. Even if she fought me, I could have held her till the fight went out of her or till she felt like things weren't falling apart. Or just accepting my embrace, or me.

But none of that happened. I just stood and watched her from a distance. I could see her. Shattered. Hurting. Bleeding out. And yet I did nothing, unsure of what would be the right move. Tell her more? Tell her how I feel? Have her lash out at me and dispute my feelings or just crush them because she's hurting? I can see her doing either. Or nothing.

She hasn't said anything about the kiss. The one that kept me up for hours. Still does. Maybe it meant nothing to her.

"I know you're hurting. We all do. We did what we did to keep you safe. We're still doing that. Once your dad wakes, he'll tell you the same thing. This was all for your protection. And maybe then you can see it from our side, and things will go back to the way they were."

She slowly raised her face, her eyes menacing as she looked at me. If she were a witch, I'd have been smitten on the spot. "What if I don't want it to go back? What if I want a change?"

I shrugged and let my hands fall. "That's your choice. I'll support whatever it is you want." And if she so happened to want things to change between us and not just get back to babysitting duty, I'd be okay with that too. Way okay with it.

She snorted a laugh that didn't sound as amusing as it was haunting. "Oh, I just bet."

My head went back as if I'd been hit in slow motion as I looked at the ceiling briefly. I got it. She didn't want *that* kind of change either. I stuck my hands in my pockets and waited for her to say more. I knew she wasn't done when her hands fell to her sides and she took a step in my direction.

"Look, *when* my dad wakes up, the only thing I want from you or the club is to pay the damn hospital bill and then get the fuck out of our lives. You've done enough. First Mom, and now Dad. I'm sick and tired of the club taking everything from me and getting nothing in return. Maybe Abigail was right to reach out to a more accepting group. At least with them, you know going in it's all smoke screens and daggers. They don't pretend to like you and treat you differently just to get a cheap thrill."

She was centimeters away from me, her face tilted up to look at me while mine was tipped down.

"It was never a cheap thrill." My voice was soft but held weight.

Her eyes flared for only a second.

"I don't care. Don't want to hear it. Won't happen again, so why the fuck bring it up? Never happened in my mind, so keep it that way with yours."

We were so close. A hairsbreadth apart. She swayed toward me and then back. I held as still as I could and tried not to fall for the magnetic pull of her lips on mine. I wanted to crash down on them so badly that I felt physical pain. But I didn't. And after a few blinks, she realized it too.

"Now get the fuck out of my way. I've got class."

She pushed past me, and I watched her go, not giving a fuck if a brother saw me looking at her. Atom might have

Kooper

heard what was said, maybe guessed on the context. But he knew shit about what was really going on.

How could he when I don't know what the fuck is happening either? Over the last few months, I've kept out of her way. Mostly. I watch her. When I'm not physically there, I have cameras. Systems tracking. And when the Hounds pull me for club work, I've got people willing to come in and take over for me.

Once Jumper and I get the green light, I've got a team ready on standby. The brothers don't know about it. It's not that I don't trust them—they can keep their mouths shut if they try—I just don't want to involve anyone just yet. Having my team step in is easy work compared to telling the Hounds that I'm interested in Law's daughter.

Might be more expensive and a fuck ton of logistics to get people in place when I need them, but that seems like a piece of cake compared to bringing in family.

This is messy. All of it. I get that. And I've gone to great pains to keep it away from everyone. Not that I'm ashamed of what I feel or for how I feel, but because of who I feel it for. She doesn't need this shit. *My* shit. Till I know what she wants, without the anger and grief and pain, I'll hold back.

But the second I see her shift an inch in my direction, the kid gloves are off and I'm all in. I'm just waiting for that moment. No matter how long it takes.

Everyone thinks a sniper is the most long-gamed person on the battlefield. And sure, they wait and are patient most of the time. But a Diplomatic Security Service member? Our long game comes in the form of thinking ten steps ahead. Of having contingencies for contingencies. We have an endgame—keep the assignment alive. No matter how long or how difficult it is. We look and plan for every possibility. Ones we like and ones we don't.

And we never stop. Not till the assignment is dead or a new one takes over. Law gave me one assignment. No one has taken me off it. And while my job is to keep Ruby alive, I also plan to be by her side while I do it.

"If you want me off the roster sheet, say it. Don't pussyfoot your way around it," I say to Casper but don't look at him. My jaw is tight from him thinking I'm not ready. I'm more than ready. Bass even cleared me of all physical shit two months ago. Sure, I take it easy, and General bitches that I need more help, but I'm cleared to do jobs.

Unless the president says otherwise.

I look at him out of the corner of my eye and watch him weigh his words before he speaks. "Flint has a call with Domino in an hour. You'll know then if you're going." He pats me on the back and leaves. Taking my appetite with him.

I pull out my phone and check the feeds. Ruby's in class right now. She hates this teacher, but she goes, determined to get her doctorate and making plans to take care of her dad when he wakes up.

Just like *I'm* making plans for when he wakes up. But not for him.

For her.

Chapter 22—Ruby

A few weeks later

"Ms. Hofstadter, do you think the rules don't apply to you?"

I glare at my bag and keep searching through it to find my phone. I thought I silenced it. But of course it goes off in the one classroom where the professor is a dick. Most would just give a student a minute to silence it or some shit, but the second it went off, I got singled out. Of course, it's obviously mine. I'm sitting alone in the back. Everyone else sits close. But I refuse to look at the guy if I can help it. He's an egotistical jerk. Got tenure last year, so he thinks he can do whatever the fuck he wants—like talk down to his students when he's not even ten years our senior.

He knows his stuff, I'll give him that, but he's only book smart. He couldn't hack it in the real world. And didn't, obviously. No other reason for why he's teaching us how to be a successful business owner and not running one himself.

Guess the old saying is true: Those who can't do, teach.

The guy's also been a major prick since the moment he saw me. Could be my hair, or my clothes. I get looks for those. But I think it's the fact that I haven't taken off Dad's old leather jacket much. I do when it's hot, but the classrooms are always freezing, so I wear it. Almost religiously. And there's no hiding the Hounds of the Reaper

MC logo on it. There's no president rocker, or any rocker, to be fair. Casper had it changed so I could be allowed to wear it and not disrespect the club in some way. Well, when I was still on speaking terms with them.

You know, before they confessed that it was all a lie and my dad's not dead. He's just in a coma, and no one knows when he'll wake up, if ever. I try not to be morbid about it. I have a dad. Sure, it's a one-sided conversation every time I see him, but I like to think that if he *could* talk, he'd just listen to my rants and raves like usual and then add a little input here and there. He always was the best listener.

Even more so now.

"We're all waiting, Ms. Hofstadter."

I bite my tongue and silence the call at the same time, looking up with a plastic smile. He nods once, like he won or some shit, and goes back to his lecture.

I look at the screen and see the call was from the hospital. My heart stops. Nothing good can come from that. But before I can panic and dial the number, I get a text.

He's awake.

I read it. Again and again. It's not sinking in. And then it does. I gather my stuff, not caring how much noise I'm making or that I'm disturbing class. I have to leave, and I have to do it now.

"Ms. Hofstadter, please sit down. Class isn't over."

I put my backpack on my shoulders and look at the text once more to make sure I'm not imagining it. But it's there. Clear as day. And from Mad Max. He wouldn't fuck around with something like this.

"Ms. Hofstadter."

Kooper

I look at the professor, who's red in the face. No clue if he yelled my name or just said it a ton before I looked up at him.

"My dad's awake," I say without thinking.

"Your what?" He looks confused, but that's his problem.

I rush from the room, hearing murmurs from my classmates, but who cares what they say or think. My dad's awake, and I'm finally going to tell him something I've held back each time I've talked to him since learning about his coma.

That I love him. And if he pulls this shit again, I'm going to kill him.

Getting to the hospital is easy. It's all autopilot now. I know when to speed and when to slow down. I don't even flinch at the number of bikes I see when I pull up. They're closer, so it makes sense that they got here first. I might not like it, but until I can get Dad to see it my way, I have to live with it.

But not much longer. Soon the club will be out of our lives. I refuse to let this happen again. And I'll do what Mom should have done so long ago: I'll demand that he lose the club or lose me. It won't be easy, but I need him to do it. To keep him alive. Because life without him is unbearable.

When I enter the building, Hounds are everywhere. But they all give me space. Well, everyone but Kooper. He walks right up to me.

"They just took him back. General wanted to run some tests real quick."

I nod but keep walking. The entrance isn't his room. I need to be in his room.

I practically sprint back there, Kooper hot on my heels. Neither of us says anything, and when we get back to the room Dad has called his own for more than half a year, a nurse is there changing the bedding.

She gives me a kind smile as she continues. I've seen her a few times but never spoken to her. She knows who I am well enough to know I don't like idle chitchat. Something a few of her colleagues don't get.

"He should be back soon," she says to me as she leaves.

I look at the empty room and see Kooper is still here with me. Mad Max must be with Dad or something. I start to pace, bringing my thumb up to my mouth and nibbling on it. Since the call, everything has been a blur. And now that I'm here, it's all just hitting me.

Dad's awake. Dad's going to live.

I won't be alone anymore.

"Shit," I mumble to myself, but Kooper hears it. He's been watching me not so subtly this whole time.

"What?"

I shake my head.

"What, Ruby?" He takes a step, just one, toward me.

I bite my lip and stop pacing to look at him. "I told them. I didn't mean to, but I told them."

He looks confused, and when I don't say more, he shakes his head as if he doesn't understand. How can he? I'm so lost in my head with everything going on, I'm speaking in half-truths. "Told who what?"

"My class. I said my dad was awake. But I wasn't meant to, was I?" I turn and start pacing again, running my hands through my hair and pulling at it. "Shit, what if I fucked it up? What if I caused him harm now that he's awake?"

"It's okay. I'll take care of it."

I hear his words but don't stop to look at him as a thousand and one thoughts go through my head. "How? How are you going to take care of it?"

"Don't worry about that."

This time I do look at him and see him shrugging with a soft smile on his face. As if he really thinks he can just take care of something like this for me. He's either a magician or a psycho killer.

"Sure, I'll not worry about you killing twenty-five people."

His deep chuckle has me stopping my pacing completely to look at him in wonder. It's been so long since I've heard a man laugh. Something deep and throaty. Something that sends goose bumps down my arms.

"While I'm flattered that you think I can kill that many for you, I was thinking about just talking to them first and doing some background checks, seeing if any of them are a threat or not. Then, and only then, I'll take out those who are. Might be a handful, tops." He winks at me as he puts his hands in his pockets.

I huff out a laugh. He's completely right. I'm being an idiot.

"No, you aren't." He takes a step closer, and I realize I was talking out loud. "You have a lot going on. This, this is huge. It's okay that you spoke up. You should be able to talk about this stuff. The club will deal with anything that isn't right. We got you. We got you and your dad."

I nod and let him pull me into his arms. He feels so warm as he wraps them around me, and I do the same, tentatively at best. I close my eyes and breathe in his scent—leather, just like Dad. He's tall like Dad and has muscles like him too. But unlike Dad, he has an underlying scent. I can't describe it, but it's different. It's not bad, though. Makes me want to nestle my nose into the crook of his neck and lick him. And other things.

My eyes spring open, and I push him away and step back all in one movement.

"Fuck, what am I doing? Why do I always go to you? What kind of sick game are you playing?"

"No game, Ruby." He's locked down his emotions, and I hate it. I can't do that, and I want to. I can get there, but I don't do instant shutdown well, like him.

I shake myself out of whatever that was and cross my arms to keep from reaching out to him.

"Whatever, I can't deal with this right now. Dad's awake. I need to find out what condition he's in and then talk to General about his PT plan. He won't be down for long, and I want to make sure he gets the best from me so I can help. We both know he'll start running before he even attempts to go easy."

Kooper

I'm saved from having to say anything else to Kooper as Dad is wheeled back in by General and a nurse. Mad Max, Casper, Bulldog, and Chains are right behind him.

I twist my hands together as I wait for them to put Dad back into the bed, then wait some more for General to give his doctor speech.

"Well, everything looks good. No major swelling or anything. I still want to monitor you for another week here, but unless your PT doc has any more issues—" He nods to me with a warm smile, one I return and then step up a bit when I see Dad looking at me. "—you should be able to do your physical therapy at home."

"The club will make sure everything is set up for you," Casper says, and Dad nods.

I take that as my cue and sit on his bed, grabbing his hand. "I've missed you so much. You can't ever do that again to me. I swear I almost died right alongside you."

Dad's eyes flicker to my hand holding his and then to me. His head tilts a bit, and his smile is hesitant, but there.

"Sorry."

"It's okay." I shake my head. Now isn't the time to berate him for being a hero to a little kid. He did good. Any of the brothers could be here right now. It just happens to be my dad, and I'm taking it harder than the others. "We can talk about it later. All that matters is you're awake, and I'm going to make sure you're up and running in no time."

"No." He pulls his hand out of my grasp. "I meant, sorry, but do I know you?"

The room quiets. The brothers were murmuring to one another but have stopped. There's a buzzing noise, but I'm not sure if it's from a machine or just in my own head.

"Who are you?"

"Funny, Daddy." I huff out a laugh.

He doesn't. He shakes his head and looks at the others around us. "Ain't laughing. Are we together or something?"

My head tilts down at the implication of his words. "Seriously?" I look at him and then General, catching Kooper's eye for a second before looking back at Dad. "I'm Ruby, Dad. Your daughter. You and Mom had me like a million years ago."

"Who?"

I blink back the sudden emotions clogging my throat and threatening to spill out of my eyes. "Your wife—Katrina."

He shakes his head as if he's as clueless as the rest of us feel right now.

I feel myself panicking, and I look at General. He seems lost, and then he steps into doctor mode. Someone pulls me off the bed, and I go to the window, half listening to General ask Dad a few things.

If it were anyone else, I'd think they were joking. But Dad would know never to pull a stunt like that. Especially after all that's happened.

"Ruby?"

I look up and see everyone staring at me. Did he ask me a question, or did he just say my name a few times?

I shake my head to show I don't know what's going on. "What?"

Kooper

"Want to take a walk with me?" General asks. Not one of the brothers, but a doctor. And as I look at everyone in the room, nothing on their faces says it's a good thing to take a walk. But as I look at Dad, I see something else too.

Zero recognition. I'm just a stranger to him.

Tears prick my eyes, and I nod at General while not looking away from Dad.

It takes him coming toward me and ushering me out the door for me to move.

"What's going on?" My voice is small. I hold myself together, but just barely.

Dad's door opens, and out comes Kooper. He shuts the door and leans against it. He might act like he's on sentinel duty, but it doesn't matter why he's here. He seems to always be here every time I'm about to fall. Only once did I let him catch me. I refuse to do so now, even if I'm trembling to keep from running into his arms.

"I'll run some more tests, but my initial diagnosis is dissociative amnesia," General says.

"What's that?"

"It's when someone forgets personal information, memories, sometimes entire people."

"Even Mom? He loved her. Said she was the love of his life."

"We know a lot about the brain, but we will never understand it all. No one knows why some get forgotten and others don't. He had a lot of blood loss, and there was some brain injury. The stress of his death, the two times he coded, could have been traumatic enough to add more stress on the brain and cause more issues."

"But why me? Why Mom? Why not you? The club? You're the ones who did this to him! I was the only one who cared. Who loved him like... like Mom." My voice cracks on a sob, and I close my mouth tight to swallow it.

General just shakes his head. "I don't know, kid. I don't. We can try a few things, see if that triggers it."

I brush the stupid tears that breach my eyelids off my face. I didn't allow them to fall. There are just too many to keep them from overflowing. "How long?"

"For what?" General moves his head to look me in the eye. I keep looking away from him, not liking what he's saying. "Till he gets it back?"

I nod and wipe more tears.

He's silent. So silent that I have to look up and keep eye contact with him before he continues. "Sometimes days. Sometimes longer."

"Is it permanent?"

"In rare cases."

At least he's telling me the truth. I close my eyes and let it sink in. All of it. Everything for the past few months. His death. His "rebirth." And now this. Awake but doesn't know me.

Jesus, how much more can I take?

I turn and walk away.

"Where're you going?" General calls out.

"I have class," I mumble. Then I stop and stare back at General before my eyes flick to Kooper. "If he starts to remember me, call me. I'll be back later."

Kooper

Both of them nod, and I head back to the parking lot. I ignore every person who tries to talk to me, asking about dad, seeing if he's okay. I walk around them all and get into my car. I hear the rumble of a motorcycle close by but don't pay it any mind as I drive away.

It's been pure hell these last months. If I thought losing my dad and best friend was bad, I was wrong. Seeing him awake gave me so much hope, but then having him forget me? Forget Mom? Forget everything but the damn club?

I can't function.

So when I get home, not to class, I don't berate myself as I head upstairs and into my house, not paying enough attention to know if I shut and locked doors behind me, or even if Nat's here.

I just fall onto my bed, close my eyes, and pray that I wake up from this nightmare.

Chapter 23—Kooper

Amnesia? Fuck. That's the last thing anyone ever thought. Death would have been kinder to her than this. I saw it the moment she shattered. The moment her bubble popped and pain ate at her heart.

I follow her home. I can't trust my equipment. I need to see with my own eyes that she makes it back okay.

And when I see her leave almost every door open as she goes into her place, I know I need to do more. Not just to keep her safe, but to let her know she isn't alone. I lock her car and shut the door, then go upstairs and do the same with her apartment.

I make a note that her place is empty and get to her room. I don't know if she hears me or not. I see her shaking, trembling, and then I hear it. Her cries. The pain of losing her dad all over again.

I shut her bedroom door, kick off my shoes, hang up my vest on the back of her desk chair, and curl myself around her.

She doesn't even flinch as I hold her. And that scares me. She's so lost in her grief that she's left herself unprotected. But that's what I'm here for—to protect her when she can't protect herself.

"Shh, Peaches, shh."

My words have her crying more, and then she turns and buries herself in my chest. I try not to find joy in this. Try

Kooper

not to see it as anything but her seeking out human touch in her time of need.

But I fail. Because while I try to be a good guy, I'm not. I'm a selfish prick. And having Ruby in my arms brings a soft sigh from my lips.

I hold her for hours, well into the night. She falls asleep at some point. I should wake her, knowing she'll want to check back in on her dad, but I don't. She hasn't slept well in months, just short naps and less than five hours a night. She's running on fumes, if that. She needs time to rest. To fully rest.

I have no idea what the weeks ahead hold for her, but I know she'll need her strength, both mentally and physically. Her class load is lighter this semester, as she wanted to get more time with her dad at the hospital. But now that he's back, I've got a sick feeling in the pit of my stomach that she's going to push herself harder. If she can't put all her energy into helping her dad, she'll do it in whatever is next on her list. And that's school.

The girl goes hard when she needs to focus on something. But she also crashes harder. I've known her to take a weekend off here and there, to veg in front of her gaming system for hours on end and then rest longer than usual. But this? Cuddling up to me? Sleeping on my chest and allowing me to be in her space?

This isn't like her. And that's what worries me.

I didn't think anything could break her, and I've seen her go through a lot. She cracked but never broke. I wonder if this has finally tipped her over.

And if it has, I'm still not sure if I should be thankful for it or not. This closeness? Her allowing this? It could change the second she wakes up. I've been mentally preparing for the sparring. For her to push me away.

Something I don't want her to do but know will be the right move. And for her? I'd do anything. Even if it kills me.

I slowly move my head and tilt it down to look at her. I learned quickly since being here that she frowns when I move too much, as if I've disturbed her slumber in some way. And her frowning is something I don't like causing. Not anymore. I used to find joy in bringing it to her face. But like everything else, that's changed.

Her face is inches from mine as it rests on my shoulder, her hand on my chest and one of her legs bent over mine. I have my arm wrapped around her. It's completely numb from the position, but a lost limb is a small price to pay.

I move my free hand and brush the small hairs off her face. I'm gentle. Soft. Barely touching her. But I can't let go. Now that I've touched her, it seems impossible to stop. I lower my hand and tentatively touch the tips of her braids, playing with the ends after the bindings. It's coarser at the tips, but I like the feeling of it stabbing my hand softly.

"Any news on my dad?"

I don't jump or stop what I'm doing. I don't even look at her. Her breathing changed the second I pushed her hair off her face. I should have known she would wake soon after. I was just hoping I had more time. Still, it doesn't deter me in the slightest.

"General texted a while back. They have him resting."

Kooper

"Any memory change?" The small bit of hope that I'm sure she's trying hard to hide from me snuck through in those three words. Enough that I stop touching her hair and look her in the eyes when I shake my head.

She breaks first and looks away. But she doesn't move. Not off me, anyway. Just her hand, and she plays with the fabric of my gray T-shirt. I swallow and will my body not to react. Not to think what it would feel like if my shirt was gone and her hand was on my bare chest.

Her stomach grumbling has me reacting more than anything.

"You need food."

"I need a lot of things," she mumbles, but doesn't move off me.

I slowly move my arm, the one she slept on, and let my hand glide over her locks. I don't run my hands through it like I want. She's not ready for this. But a soft glide she allows.

When her stomach breaks the silence again, I smile. "Got any preferences?"

"Wings." It's instant, and my hand stills for a second. She tilts her head up and looks me in the eye, challenging me and yet daring me to call her out on it. But I don't.

"I might know a place."

A small smirk hits her lips for a second. "Of course you do." It's gone in the next breath, just like her, rolling off me and the bed. "Going to change." She pulls some clothes from her drawers and keeps her back to me. "Check on Dad, will you?"

I nod, not that she can see. I roll off opposite her and grab my stuff as I head for the door. "Take your time."

"Always do," she mutters just before I close the door, and I breathe a sigh of relief. That one quip lets me know that while Ruby is broken, she's not lost. Not completely.

I dial up General, but he doesn't answer. Could be a million and one reasons why. That it's close to the middle of the night and he's sleeping is logical. But most likely, he's in the middle of some doctor thing and can't take the call.

I text Mad Max next. Law might be awake, but till he's able to handle shit on his own, Mad Max will be there to protect him.

Anything new?

No.

I know he won't elaborate. He's a man of few words. However, when he has something to say, he does. That's why I don't push it. His answer is all I need to know. There's nothing Ruby or I can do tonight to help if we go back there.

I put on my vest and finish lacing up my boots when she comes into the living room. Her usual getup is gone. No corset, nothing tight. Just baggy joggers and an oversized shirt that's so faded I can't tell what the name going down the side of it is.

"Ready?"

She nods, and I head for the door, but it opens before we get there. Natalie comes in with a pile of books in her arms.

She sets them on the counter with a huff of annoyance or maybe just exhaustion from carrying so much up two flights of stairs before she even notices us.

"Oh, hey. Sorry, didn't know you'd still be up. I hope I didn't wake you."

Kooper

When Ruby doesn't say anything back, I look at her and see she's not really here. She's moving, but that's about it.

"We were headed to get food. Want any?" I offer. Not that I want her to come. I'm not sure if having me for company is what Ruby wants, and she's too stuck in her own head to tell me right now. But I'm saved from having to make small talk with the roommate as she shakes her head.

"No, but thanks. I'm just going to crash. Been up for what feels like days trying to get this research paper written. Next time, though."

I give her a chin lift and open the door. Ruby walks out it without a look or a word to Natalie. She notices, based on the frown on her face, and I just shake my head.

"Bad day is all. Nothing against you."

I know she and Ruby are close, but not close enough that she knows what's going on. They used to be closer, and I know they're busy, but I can tell there's a strain in their relationship that wasn't there at the beginning. Not sure if it's because Ruby's holding back from telling an outsider club stuff or if she's making sure Natalie doesn't turn into another Abigail issue and cause problems.

Ruby might not like the club right now, but she seems to never lose her loyalty to it.

"Okay. Drive safe." Her voice is small, like her smile.

I give her another chin lift and leave, shutting the door softly on the way.

When I get to the bottom of the stairs, I make sure not to trip over my feet when I see Ruby. She isn't in her car like I expected but on the back of my bike. Waiting. For me.

Again, I just chalk it up to me knowing where we're going, and she's still too out of it to be driving. This is not her claiming me. This is not her saying that she wants to be on the back of my bike forevermore.

This is just a ride. One of convenience. That's it.

And I keep telling myself that when I get on and start her up. Even before I back out of the parking spot, her arms are around me and her head's pressed to my back. I should make her use a helmet, but I can't find it in me to tell her to move. It feels too good.

Instead, I do something I rarely do: I drive the speed limit the entire way, even slowing down at yellow lights and not racing through them like usual.

When we arrive at the all-night diner on the opposite side of town from her place, she doesn't bat an eye. It might not look like more than a run-down place with a handful of people and cheap plastic on the furniture, but it's open.

She slides into the booth, knowing to take the one opposite the one with the clear line of sight. The waiter is quick to come over, asking us what we want.

I expected her to say something about needing more than the five seconds it took to get in here, but all she does is look at me.

"He's ordering for both of us."

My eyes widen a fraction at her words before I turn to the server and order. Her trusting me with making this decision? Just another thing I've wanted to do for months, maybe even years, yet never expected. Now I don't hesitate to do it, and I cherish it as I do.

Kooper

Ruby isn't ready for everything I have planned. She might never be. But these small things? Letting me hold her? Having me drive? Knowing I'll get something that not only she wants but needs? Well, shit, it brings a warm fuzzy feeling to my chest.

I like providing for her. Watching over her. Taking care of her. Anticipating her wants, her needs.

It's empowering. I've never felt this way about a woman before. Never cared enough to learn about them like this. Even when the job was to watch and protect a female client in danger, it never went this deep. It was always just a job.

But now it's more.

When the waiter puts down our food, she sneers at her plate.

"I wanted wings."

"These are boneless."

"But I wanted wings."

"Trust me. This is what you want."

She's upset with the world still. And since I'm the only one near, she's lashing out at me like a child. Something I don't put up with. Usually. But instead of barking back, giving her the fight she somehow created in her mind that she needs right now, I shut it down and just tell her to eat.

I pick up a boneless wing with a fork and bite into it. She glares at me and then at her food before finally picking up her fork and using it to push things around her plate.

I swallow and take a sip of water. "It's the sauce you like. This one is even sweeter. And you don't like wings, not the bone-in ones, because it gets your hands messy. And while you can sit there all you like and say you don't mind getting your hands dirty, the truth is, you don't like it when it gets under your nails and you have to wait till you get home to scrub them completely."

Her eyebrows go up and then narrow as my words sink in. She knows I'm right, but she won't say it, and I'm okay with that. I don't need her to say it. Just need her to eat. She used a lot of energy today, and she needs to replenish at least some of it.

She pops a wing into her mouth and mumbles a "Whatever" around chewing it. I cover my mouth with my napkin to hide my smirk as I wipe my mouth clean.

Just like the last time we ate together, the conversation is nonexistent. Doesn't bother me. Some can't handle that, but I know that's what she needs right now. To just sit and eat, knowing that nothing can touch her with me here and she can think in her own head without me asking or judging.

When the check comes, I pay it quickly, and we go back to her place. I follow her up the stairs and don't even hide that I'm staying. Nat's door is shut as we pass it, and I head to the bathroom while Ruby goes to her room.

Once I'm done, I check the house to make sure it's secure, set my alarms on my phone for issues, and go to her room. Where the door was left cracked open.

I take off my vest and rehang it on her chair, then my shirt. I put my wallet and phone on her desk, along with my keys. Sitting on her bed, I unlace my boots. From the angle, it strains my hips a bit, and I hear a crack but ignore it. Nothing I haven't heard before. Just like the one I heard in my shoulder when I took off my shirt.

Kooper

"You need physical therapy."

I look back at her and see she's on her side, under the covers, looking at me.

I shake my head. "Fuck off." There's no heat to it at all as I stand and turn toward the bed to raise the covers.

She scoots back a bit. "Seriously. It could be getting worse."

I settle into her bed and lie on my side, looking at her. I don't reach for her; I'm already pushing my luck with being here. "What can I say? My doc dropped me as a client." I smile at her, knowing she can still see me with the illumination from the twinkle stars she has set on a timer. They should go off soon.

She looks at me. I see her eyes roam my face, and then she turns over and faces the other way. I close my eyes and let myself get comfortable. I hear the click of the stars turning off from the timer.

"I could help."

My eyes spring open at her words. It could have been a trick. Something my mind played on me in a cruel joke. I could have misheard or misunderstood.

But as her breathing evens out and she falls into slumber land, all I can do is wish. And hope.

And dream.

Chapter 24—Ruby

When I wake up, I expect him to be there. I know I didn't imagine him staying the night. I didn't lose my memory with everything going on and forget all that happened. I remember—everything. The feel of him holding me. The silent freedom of not having to decide and just being able to focus on what I wanted. Okay, not what I wanted, but what I needed.

Skipping class to have a meltdown wasn't the wisest. I know I can get notes from my classmates, but I hate asking anyone for anything.

Which is probably why I let Kooper stay last night. He didn't ask, just did. No permission was requested. He also didn't take anything. Nothing was done for his benefit that I saw. It was all for me.

I know it's because of what happened with Dad. He pities me. That's it. That's all there is to it. Yet when he held me and then made sure I ate and finally slept beside me but never touched me? There was nothing about pity in his arms or his actions.

I shake my head out. I need coffee. Any type of caffeine, really. I'll even settle for chocolate. Not that that's settling, but it would be nice.

I get up and head to the kitchen. Finding a skillet on the stove isn't unusual. But seeing the lid on it? Well, I

Kooper

honestly thought we didn't have tops to these things. I lift it and see an omelet. A perfect omelet.

"Nat," I call out. I look back and call her name again as I put the cover back on the skillet and then go to her room.

I knock on the door, and it pushes open to reveal an empty room. Taking a quick look in our bathroom, I see it's open. I spin, though I have no idea why, since it's not like she's hiding; our place is too small for that without it being obvious where she was.

Nat is nowhere to be found. I'm alone.

And there's food. Perfect and waiting.

Screw it.

I pull a plate out of the cabinet and slide the omelet onto it. I open the fridge, grab the ketchup, and then stop. Right in front on the top row is an iced coffee. And from the label on it, it's my exact order.

Either I've got a stalker, or I've started to sleepwalk and get things together before waking. Not one to ignore gifts, I pick it up hesitantly. Not sure why. It's just an iced coffee. Nothing scary or hidden about that.

I bring the coffee, ketchup, and omelet to the table and pull my laptop out of my bag. As it powers up, I squeeze out a nice layer of ketchup goodness onto my eggs. I take my first bite and open my emails, only stopping at the second bite when I see two messages, both from my professors. One from the class I missed completely and the other from the one I walked out of.

The first just has the notes from the class with a note saying they hope I'm feeling better. Odd, but I guess it makes sense to think I was out sick. Especially since I make a point to never miss a class, even showing up ten minutes early every day and sitting in the first row. I guess being that kind of student has its perks.

But the second email? Surprising. The guy made it clear from day one that he wasn't going to go easy on anyone or help. Either do the assignments or get out—his exact words. So, seeing an email from him, with his personal notes of the lecture I walked out of, is beyond anything. There's no note included, just the attachment.

"Must be my lucky day." And after the last year of having more bad luck than good, I think I'm entitled to this. I'm also completely fine with not overthinking how all this happened and just accepting it.

Tomorrow. Tomorrow I'll worry about things and what they mean. But today? I'm just going to eat food, drink caffeine, and review what I missed. Today is a nonthinking day. Just one. Tomorrow I can feel the world falling apart.

But today is for me. Only me.

Two weeks. I've had to deal with this for two weeks. And I'm done. I'm completely done. Done with the bullshit. Done with the waiting. Done with the unknown. Just all of it.

At least when Dad was in a coma, there was hope. And while everyone keeps telling me there's *still* hope, I call BS on it.

Kitten lost her memory when she fell down a cliff and into the club, almost literally. Got the coffee mug and the markings to prove it. She also got herself an old man from it.

Kooper

But there was a difference with her and her memory. Sure, it was everything for her and not selective like Dad's, but she *wanted* to get her memory back.

Nothing that Dad is doing shows he wants that. Especially when I walk in on him flirting with a fucking nurse. Again.

It makes me sick. Visibly sick and angry. It's always the same nurse. The one I used to think understood the silent cues. But she seems to have ignored all my glares up to this point.

And after finding out I got a fucking C on my latest paper today, I'm no longer in the mood to be nice. General told me to just let things play out. To come as much as I wanted. Share memories, bring pictures. Do what I want, just don't push it. Too much could do more harm than good.

It's her giggle that sets me off. Before I fully walk through the door, I hear it. And the sneer on my face doesn't hide any of my feelings.

"Pretty sure you're not being paid to drool over the patients," I say by way of greeting. I drop my bag at the door and cross my arms.

Dad looks at me from his spot on the bed, frowning, while the nurse gives me a wide-eyed innocent look as she stands beside him at the machines.

"I... I wasn't drooling."

"Don't lie, honey. Men of the club don't like it, and it won't get you special dicking for the effort."

"Ruby!" Dad berates me, but it's not like it used to be. His bark to me is what he uses on strangers. On prospects of the club. On anyone but me.

I glare harder but don't apologize.

"You did your job, now get. I'll make sure General knows just how much *special* treatment you're giving to your patients. Pretty sure he'll side with me and see that you're just a waste of the hospital's time and money."

"Girl, you better get your mouth right," Dad seethes, and the nurse shrinks in on herself. He isn't looking at me, though, but at *her*.

"Why? Six months ago, you wouldn't have even looked at this... this... hussy. You wouldn't have seen her at all. But now? You forget me. Fine. Whatever. I have no dad. I'll live. But Mom? You forget her? The woman you joined the club for? The one you put up with all the bullshit for, everything her uncle threw at you to get you to sway off her. You didn't even see her in that time. You spent one weekend together. *One.* And that was it for you. You never looked at another woman. Ever. Not when you were apart. Not when you got the presidency and every damn bimbo in the state threw themselves at you, naked even. Not even when she said to get laid because she was as big as a house because she was pregnant with me."

I'm screaming and watching him finally, *finally* look at me. He's glaring, but at least he's listening.

At some point, Atom came into the room, probably to see what all the noise was about. He was on guard duty when I came in. I'm guessing Mad Max had something else to do. Good for him for having a life outside of here. Something I can't seem to do yet. But I'm getting close. So close.

"And when she got sick?" I swallow the emotion in my voice, but the tears don't listen to my silent plea to stay put and start leaking down my face. "When she lost her hair and went through chemo? When she died? Not once. Not once did you see another woman." I sniff and use the back of my hand to wipe my nose. Super classy, but I don't care.

"You used to say that you had already found the perfect woman. That she was the love of your life and there was no one who could compare, so there's no use looking. That the memories you shared are enough to keep you warm at night."

He looks away, breaking eye contact. Breaking me.

"Guess that was all a lie. A little amnesia and it's all gone. Or maybe it's not amnesia. Maybe you're just hard up. Need to get your dick wet, Dad? Is that it? Well, have at it." I gesture to the nurse, who has tears in her eyes, but she's still here. When any normal person would go screaming for the door, she stayed. And I hate her. "You won't even have to pay her like the others do."

"Ruby." Atom's harsh tone makes me flinch more than any look Dad could give me right now. Because he knows. He knows I'm not like this. That I don't lash out at strangers unless they deserve it.

Well, from my point of view, she does. This and a keyed car. Maybe even a black eye.

"Fuck this." I grab my bag off the ground. "If you don't want to remember, that's your issue. I'm done trying to keep a memory of someone who doesn't even want to try. He's all yours." I nod at the nurse. "I'm done with him."

Walking out of the room doesn't hurt. It's the fact that only Atom called me back. Not Dad. Not a single word from him.

I'm not paying attention, which seems more normal for me than not lately. I used to be so good at knowing everything that was going on in my surroundings. But now I just don't seem to care. Which my subconscious yells at me all the time for. I need to be smart. I really do. But it's hard to care with everything going on.

A hand stops me, and I pull away before I see who it is. At least I still care enough to react once touched. Too bad I don't follow it up with a punch.

Abigail.

Of course. If this day could get any worse, I'm sure God will find a way to do it. Starting with her being at the hospital.

"What?"

She flinches back at my hard tone but doesn't seem deterred enough to leave me the fuck alone.

"I called out to you a few times."

"Ever think that I just don't want to talk to you?" Not that I heard her, but she doesn't need to know that. If I did, I'm sure she would have met the same result.

"You look like you've been crying." She ignores my brush-off, and I just roll my eyes.

"Captain Obvious, you aren't." I turn to walk away, pushing my bag higher on my shoulder as I go. "Tell the Crazy Eights to get their money back. You're not worth the price." I smirk. Twice now I've made references to women not being worth the money. Wonder if I can make it three for three before the day's over.

"How's your dad?"

I stop.

Kooper

Turn.

And take two steps back toward her. Close enough to be in her face.

"What the fuck are you talking about?"

Six months ago, she would have flinched and backed away. Would have backpedaled so fast and apologized in seconds. Even before I questioned her. But now? She stands tall. She doesn't back down. She even maintains eye contact.

"Your dad. Is he doing better?"

"He's dead," I spit out. To which she tilts her head, keeping her expression neutral.

"Okay. And the John Doe?"

Fuck. She knows. I don't know how, but she does. The club, Casper, Kooper—they all made it clear that this was still to be kept quiet. Or is that no longer a thing now that he doesn't remember me? Maybe I'm the only one who's still in the dark.

It's not like I've talked to anyone. Not even Kooper. Since the night he stayed over, it's been radio silence. Not that I'm looking at my phone or checking it every time I get out of the shower to see if I missed a call or a text.

I don't reach out to him because I don't need to. I don't need him. He did what I needed that night. He held me and let me fall apart. Just like he did when he told me Dad was dead.

Whatever. I'm dealing with my feelings and thoughts about him lying to me. Things are murky at best. One moment, I'm all against him saying it was a lie, and the next, I see it as a truth that Dad *did* die, and he just left out the part that he was brought back to the land of the living but in a coma after that. Which is still a lie. A lie of omission.

Or is it?

See? I'm all confused. And it's all because of Dad. And Abigail. Seriously, if I can just have one issue at a time to think through, I could figure everything out. I wouldn't react so rashly and lash out.

Okay, maybe I would. But we'll never know. Just like we'll never know what life would be like if you didn't eat the ice cream out of the pint container it came in. Maybe the world would survive if you put it in a bowl. Maybe not. Best not to chance it and change things up or think differently.

"Who?" I don't need to elaborate, and her answer is the only thing that has her facial expression changing. From neutral to caring. Something that used to happen when she talked about me. I saw it from a distance. But now it's for someone else.

"Billy."

I should have known. Her boss is also the new president's old lady. The boys might say they keep shit away from the women, but I've seen more than one brother break that rule when it comes to keeping their old ladies in the know. Usually it's just for a safety thing. Telling them to keep them safe.

But now? This? How the fuck is Billy even a part of this? Or Abigail? Or any of the Crazy Eights, for that matter.

I turn and walk away, making it to my car without anyone else approaching me. I take a moment and then pick up my phone and dial one number. When Nat answers, I put it on speaker and peel out of the parking lot.

Kooper

"Get dressed. We're going out."

"Where're we going?" I can hear her already wrestling through her clothes to find something. And that makes me smile. That was the exact answer I needed from her. No questions, just acceptance.

"Anywhere that I can get plastered and make bad decisions."

If the world is going to throw me a bad day, I better make the most of it. And if I'm lucky, I'll get drunk enough to forget it all.

Chapter 25—Kooper

I was already planning on heading up north even before Natalie called. I knew after Atom texted that I needed to be there. I stayed away too long. Left her alone with her thoughts too much.

She's a strong woman. Nothing Ruby does is because someone tells her to do it. She can be a *willing* person or as stubborn as a mule. But she's never a pushover. Her thoughts are her own, and she says and does what she wants. Pushing her into something is the easiest way to see her walk away and never look back.

That's why I kept myself away. She had a lot going on, and she needed to focus on other things. I know she was thinking about me. I zoomed in enough times on my surveillance cameras to see her start a text with a message to me and then close it out without sending it at least half a dozen times. Something I've been doing, too, but double the amount.

Okay, fine. Triple.

I might not have reached out, but that didn't mean I wasn't watching. I think I've watched her more in the last two weeks than I did that first year I was on her detail. Things have changed. Even if I wanted to go back, I can't. Something has turned the tide, and there's no stopping what's coming.

I track her location and am happy to see that it doesn't change as I make the long-ass drive up. Nat gave me the address, said they were at some house party. That things were getting out of control, and she was worried.

That she called was what had me running to my bike. I just got out of Church. Issues are going on with the Devils Damned. Their president wants a sit-down, something I don't like. And I wasn't the only one. But with the shit that happened between Psy and Casper's old lady, it's murky waters. Church was put on hold when a vote couldn't settle things after three attempts. Stalemate each time. Club has a rule: When it's something this big, the majority needs to be on board.

We rescheduled Church for another day, and as soon as I collected my phone on the way out, since they ain't allowed in Church, it rang. The name had me speeding past everyone. No one protested. A few asked if they were needed, and I shook my head.

Nat's voice was panicked, but nothing too frightening. I got the details: Ruby went looking for a good time and found trouble. Same MO as usual.

After hanging up with Nat, I checked my apps, then called my contact. He has eyes on her. So far, she's fine. A few college boys are talking to her, but nothing more. Not that he can see much more from the scope he has on her from across the street.

My guys don't engage. They survey. I might not have been the one close to Ruby these past weeks, but that doesn't mean I didn't have a team on her at all times to keep her safe. Despite what she might think, there's still a target on her back. Might always be there.

I park behind Ruby's car and head inside the only house on the block with people spilling out of it. The sign above the door lets me know it's a damn fraternity. I was never in one, just knew pricks who were. I don't know everyone, but if I haven't met a single decent guy who was in a frat, what does that say about them?

The place is packed, but not enough that I miss Ruby. Especially since she's on a table dancing with two other girls I don't know. I look to the side and see Nat, biting her lip and looking worried as she stands close enough to catch our girl if she falls.

She's in her typical armor: corset, tight pants, thigh-high boots with fucking tall heels. You'd think she'd break her neck in them, but apparently they've been her staple since high school.

Her moves are coordinated. No teeters. No falls. And when one girl stumbles, my girl just shakes her off and keeps going. Those fucking Misfits must still be teaching her dance moves. No way she learned to bend over and snap up with her ass in the air from TV. Not that I'm complaining about the view. But I'm not the only one who notices. Or admires. I sneer at everyone, enough that a few back away from me, but it doesn't deter them all.

She twirls, puts her hands up, and shakes her hips. Her eyes are half closed, and then her head rolls and she sees me. A grin, a sultry devilish one, touches her lips before she overdramatizes her movements.

I get closer, standing by Nat with my arms crossed. Ruby looks down at me but keeps dancing.

"Kooper, thank God. I've never seen her like this. She's danced before and we've partied before, but she's like a whole other person right now."

Kooper

"She been drinking?" I glance at Nat out of the corner of my eye and see her nod.

"Yeah, a bit. But no more than usual."

I hold out my hand and wait. Ruby doesn't take it at first, but I raise my eyebrow in challenge, and she takes the bait, grabbing my hand and then putting her foot down on a chair that must have been used to get them up there. It's dainty as fuck how she takes two large yet graceful steps down and doesn't once stumble. As soon as both feet are on the ground, she's in my space.

"Koop. What are you doing here?" She's all smiles and breathless words. Something that has my dick taking notice.

"My job," I grind out and clench my hand that isn't holding hers. Because she hasn't let it go, and I refuse to be the first to do so.

"Your job?" Her eyebrows rise. Then her head shakes. "Didn't you hear? I no longer have a dad. So that means"—she lets go of my hand and wraps her arms around my neck—"there's no reason for you to watch over me." She moves in close to my ear, her breath tickling my skin. "Unless you like to watch."

She pulls back and flicks her tongue over my nose before detangling herself from around me and sauntering away, hips shaking and every damn eye in the place on her ass.

I follow her and feel Nat hot on my heels. By the time I'm next to Ruby again, she has a cup in her hand. I take it from her, sloshing a bit over the side.

"Hey," she cries in protest before she grabs it back. "That's mine."

"We need to leave." Another growl. One that should have her quaking in her boots. But she just smiles around the rim of her drink as she sips on it.

"After this one."

Never say I was never one to compromise. I grab the cup out of her hand one last time, chug it, and then crush it with my hand before throwing it on the ground.

"There—it's done." I grab her upper arm, and for a second, she sways into me. "Let's go."

She pouts. Literally pouts. One fucking big-ass lip pout. Something that shouldn't be cute and a fucking turn-on but is. And as I move through the people to the door, I slide my other hand over my dick and push it down. Now isn't the time.

"You're no fun."

"You're having enough fun for the both of us," I mutter a second before I'm greeted with a wall. Not just any wall. A frat wall of drunken college kids who think they know best.

"Hey, man, what's the rush? Why not stay a bit longer?"

"Yay to staying," Ruby chimes in, and I roll my eyes.

The prick who's the ballsiest of them all for even saying anything to me lights up at her voice. "See? Stay. And if you've got somewhere to go, at least let her have some fun."

Another guy smirks a second before he speaks. "Yeah, we'll make sure she gets home. Won't we, boys?"

Kooper

Some think that if you go to college, you become smart. Or that only smart kids go to college. For a few, that might be true. For others, it's their daddies' money that got them into college. Not a single brain cell was used. Just like now.

Because if they had even half a thought between the five of them, they would see me as more than just some guy dragging a girl out of this place. They'd see my vest. My attire. They would understand that my entire vibe right now is not to be fucked with.

But they're idiots. The whole lot.

And when they look at one another and grin some more, I've had enough.

I turn back and hand Ruby to Natalie. "Don't let her go."

I wait till she nods, and then I turn back and let my fists do the talking.

The first one goes down easily; he wasn't paying attention. The second throws a right hook, which I block and counter with my own. I swing low and punch the third with a jab to the stomach, and as he bends over in pain, I grab his head and ram it into my knee as I pull up. His head bounces off me, and then he falls back.

That leaves two: the one who spoke the last time and some other asshole who's too stupid to run when he's in a losing match. They look at each other and then put their fists up like good little boys who learned how to box from their fathers.

The music is still going, but we have a wide area to work with, as everyone backed up. And not a single person is coming to these two dipsticks' aid.

I see the moment the talker makes his move. He holds his breath and punches out. I block and then see a fist coming at me from the other side. I block again, but it leaves me open, and I take a jab to the ribs. I grunt and see the talker smile wide as if he just won.

Celebrating too early. Big mistake. I'm just getting warmed up.

I stop messing with the no-name and uppercut him, sending him flying through the air and landing on a few girls, who scream. Then I turn, all my anger focused on the last man standing.

He backs up a step and then lunges. I grab his fist, and he stops. But I don't. I use it to hit him in the face. Once. Twice. Then I spin him till his back is to me and kick him in the spine. He stumbles into the crowd, which parts like the Red Sea, and smacks into a wooden wall before falling backward.

Everyone here has held their breath as I breathe and look around, waiting for the next attack. I eye a few, who just shake their heads. Seems there are some with brains after all.

I go back to Nat and see her eyes wide with fear, but she doesn't back down, just blinks it away and hands me Ruby. Who stumbles more than I've ever seen in my life. I bend down and throw her over my shoulder before turning and heading for the door, which is now standing wide the fuck open without a single person in my way.

Kooper

"That looked like fun. I want to do that. Put me down so I can do that," Ruby says as she pushes off my back to look around.

I just keep walking, and Nat meets my stride as we get outside and make our way to the car.

"Think we could charge money for that? I bet we'd make more than they do each night. Ha! I'm three for three. Hashtag winning."

I look at Natalie over Ruby's rump, and she shrugs. She's just as clueless about Ruby's rambling as I am.

"Ooh, you know what we should do? We should get tacos. No, wings! I love wings."

I grin at her drunken words as I lower her beside the passenger door of her car.

"You good to drive?"

At Nat's nod, I reach into Ruby's front pocket and pull out her key fob.

The outline was clear to see when she was dancing, and since Ruby isn't a girl who brings a purse to a party, I don't even hesitate to get them.

But maybe I should have. Or at least thought this through. Because while Nat was on the other side of the car, and the music from the house party was loud enough to cover most of what someone said to another person when close, I did not miss Ruby's moan. Or the soft rotation of her hips as she tried to get my fingers to move to areas that, if sober, she'd never let me touch.

I toss Nat the keys after unlocking the door, then pull Ruby to me so I can get her door open. She comes willingly, pressing her entire body to me and even rubbing against me.

I should get fucking sainthood after this shit.

Getting Ruby into the car is easy, if not a bit rough. To keep things the way they should be, I might have pushed her in. And while she tried to fumble herself into a sitting position, I put her seat belt on and shut the door. If she touched me one more time, I don't know what I would do. She's definitely on something. I need to prepare for what the night will bring.

I tap the hood of her car and head to my bike behind them. Nat sticks her head out the window when I mount up.

"Head home. I'll follow you."

She nods and drives off.

I take a second to check my phone.

Nice hostage rescue.

Dick. Of course he was watching. And not helping. Not that I needed him to.

Shut it down.

His response is a meme of the Grinch smiling with plotting fingers in front of him. I don't care what he does, just want this place to learn a lesson. One being that you don't do this shit to anyone. Two, you don't fuck with a Hound. And three, that Ruby is off-limits.

My guy might not be a Hound, but that's just because he likes to travel too much. I told him to become a nomad, but even then he'd have to prospect in one spot for a year. He isn't the type that can stay still for a month, let alone twelve.

The drive to Ruby's isn't long, thank fuck. I must be tired, because my vision blurs a bit. I have to adjust more times than not and almost wreck at the last turn.

Kooper

I pull up just in time to see Nat trying to get Ruby to stand long enough for her to close the passenger door.

I park my bike and walk, stumbling a bit, over to them.

"You get the doors. I'll get her," I tell Nat, who nods.

Once again, I bend down and put Ruby on my shoulder. I need her secure so I can use the banister on the stairs to help guide me. I must have gotten a taste of what she had in that last drink.

Shit.

"Did you know your ass is really nice? I bet I could bounce a quarter off it. Hey, Nat, do you have any quarters?"

"Shhh. And no, all out. Sorry, hon." At least Nat's smiling at Ruby's antics and not berating her as she opens the door and lets us pass through.

I march down the small hallway and drop Ruby onto the bed hard enough that she bounces and giggles with glee. And I fucking stumble into the damn wall.

"Are you all right?" Nat asks.

I shake my head, then hold it to stop it from spinning. "You guys take anything tonight?"

Maybe she and Ruby wanted to have their own party. It happens. No judgment here. Just need to know what it is so I can plan for how to get it out of our systems.

Nat shakes her head, unfortunately. "No."

"How may drinks did you have?"

"I had three. And I don't know about Ruby. I went to the bathroom at one point, and when I came back, I saw her drinking with those guys you, uh... you punched out. They tried to get me a drink, too, but I wasn't feeling it, so I called you."

Awesome. So they gave her something, and I took it too. Could be a whole lot of somethings. Only cure for most of it is time and flushing out the system.

"Get her to bed. I'll get some water."

I leave them to it as I lock down the place. I refuse to sway even a bit. Even if the floor slopes at some points tonight like it never did before. I grab a bottle of water, chug it all, then grab three more before I head back to her room.

"All I could get off her was her boots. She's too wiggly."

I nod at Nat. "Go get some sleep. I'll watch over her."

"Okay. Night, Ruby. Night, Kooper." She turns and starts down the hall but stops when I call out to her.

"You did good in reaching out. Shit could have gotten worse if you hadn't."

She licks her lips and seems to gather some courage before she speaks. "I know she's had a hard time with her dad being gone. I just want her to be safe. Losing family is never easy." She goes into her room, shutting her door before I can question anything.

Her words feel odd to my ears. The background on her says she's an orphan. But what she just said makes me think she had family. At least once.

"It's so hot. Why is it so hot?"

All thoughts of Nat die as Ruby's struggles pull me back to her. I close the door and then look at her. She's writhing on her bed and clawing at her corset. Soon it's off, leaving only pasties to cover her nipples. The next second, she kicks her pants off, and the smallest bikini briefs ever made lie against her pale skin.

God—if there is a God—give me strength.

Chapter 26—Ruby

Why is it so hot? I feel like I'm burning up. Taking off my clothes helps, but it's not enough.

"Turn the fan on. Jesus, it's like a sauna in here."

Kooper turns and starts the fan, then comes over and puts two bottles of water on the nightstand and opens the third.

"Here. You need to drink. You took something, and we need to flush it out of your system."

I sit up and take the bottle, guzzling to quench my parched throat. A bit spills out of my mouth. It feels good against my skin, and I groan at the coolness.

I move to pour the rest of it on me, and my eyes snap to Kooper when he grabs my hand in mid-tilt. He shakes his head.

"Drink."

Unlike before, he doesn't let go of the bottle. He brings it to my lips, tilting it up as I swallow it down. We don't break eye contact, and I don't tell him to stop. When it's empty, he pulls it away and then uses the pad of his thumb to brush away the few drops that were on the rim of the bottle and trickled down my chin.

He moves his thumb to my mouth. It's wet, and he runs it across my lower lip as if making sure every drop is used on me.

Kooper

With my eyes on his, I open my mouth a bit and bend forward, sucking his thumb. His breath hitches, and a deep rumble comes out of him. It makes me wet.

"Lie down." He slides his thumb out and looks down at me as he takes a step back. God only knows what he sees. He says I'm on something. Maybe I am. I've never felt like this. Like I could fly. Things are hot, but colorful. Like rays of sunshine bursting with each blink. And when I touch things? The sheets? The water? Him?

It sends sensations through my body. Things that set me on fire in other ways. I thought being drugged meant things were blurry and I would forget what was going on. But this? It's as if each sense is heightened to the ultimate. And all in good ways. Nothing feels rough against my skin or too bright to see. It's as if my own perfect bubble has been placed around me, and everything is just wonderful. Sensational. Arousing.

"You need sleep. I don't know what they gave you, but sleep and water will help get most of it out."

"Those dicks," I mutter as I scoot to the top of my bed and push my covers down enough to put my legs under them.

"Yeah." He turns and starts putting his stuff on my desk.

I like that he does that. It means he's staying. Good. I could use a cuddle right now. I know last time we didn't, except for when I was crying. And maybe he only cuddles when someone is having a meltdown. But coming off a drug is kind of like a breaking point, right?

He gets into bed, and I roll into him and then frown.

"You have clothes on."

"Yes."

"But it's hot." This makes no sense.

"You're on drugs. It's messing with your system."

I think on his words and then tilt my head. "Didn't you drink my drink?" He nods, and I sit up on my heels. "You could be drugged too." I smile.

"Doubtful." He closes his eyes and puts an arm above his head as if he's going to fall asleep.

I keep watching him, and then I see it—sweat trickling down his forehead. I reach out and catch it with my finger, and his eyes open, watching as I lick it off my skin.

"You're hot."

"Thanks," he grunts.

Rolling my eyes, I snort. "We're grown adults. We can sleep next to each other in our underwear and have nothing happen. Seriously. The only reason you're still dressed is you're scared I'll jump you. Or..." I lean down close to his face and smile wide. "You don't trust yourself. Hmmm, is that it, Koop?" I run my nose along his jaw and feel it clench. "You think that once you have me so close, you'd snap and have your way with me?"

"Right." He's out of bed and taking off his clothes in the next second. If he's trying to prove something, I have no idea what it is. I lost all focus the second his shirt came off and then his pants. His tight black boxer briefs leave nothing to the imagination, and I swallow unconsciously at the sight.

"Scoot over and behave." He pushes me back, and I roll a bit as he turns off the table lamp and gets under the covers. "Now, go to sleep."

I should. I really should. But I've never been one who does things she should. Where's the fun in that?

I slide my body over him and grin as his eyes snap open.

"What are you doing? You said we could be adults about this."

"Sure, we *could*. But why should we?" I lean down and snuggle against him. "Damn, you feel good." I run my hands all over his body. It's like little zings hitting me every place I touch. I can't get enough of how awesome it feels.

"You're high," he grits out through clenched teeth.

I shake my head. "No, I'm not." He glares, and I just smile. One that's evil and wicked. "I'm low." I move myself on top of him and then lower on his frame, sliding my pussy along his cock, moaning at the feel of it.

"Shit."

We both say it at the same time. I can't stop rubbing against him. It feels too good. His hands bunch in the sheet between us, and then he pulls it down. It was a thin sheet, but it managed to hide his ridges. Now my lower lips wrap around his cock as I slide on it in my panties.

"Fuck, fuck, fuck," he chants as he grabs my hips and tilts his head back, closing his eyes. He doesn't move me. Not in encouragement or to push off. I know it's coming. His rejection. But not yet. Not just yet.

"Don't. Please don't stop. I need more," I plead before he can say anything. I keep moving, rubbing on him faster and harder. It pulls groans from him and pants from me. His nails dig deep into my hips, and I find my release.

But it's not enough.

"More. I need more."

His eyes open, and I move slowly. He's still hard, and I'm wet. But the ache, it's still there.

"Please, Koop. Please make it go away."

He squeezes his eyes tight and shakes his head as if at war with himself.

"Please. I'll be good. Just one more and I'll stop."

He looks at me again, a set determination on his face. "Just one."

Then he pulls me up to him. I open my mouth in protest till he sits me on his face and begins to lick me through my drenched panties. My hands fall behind me, resting on his abs that flex as I grind my core over him.

I'm close, but it's not enough.

I change positions, then pull off the pasties covering most of my boobs and grab my nipples, twisting them and rocking. His eyes flare at the sight. I grab his hand, bringing his fingers to my lips and sucking on them before moving them slowly down my body till they touch me where I want.

The ferociousness in his gaze makes this ten times hotter. And forbidden. So forbidden that I shudder in ecstasy from the very thought.

But still, it's not enough.

I push his hand off, grabbing the iron bedframe for leverage as I stand tall above Kooper. His face is wet from both of us. My panties are almost pushed to the side. He licked me through them so well that they're molded to my lips, my clit outlined as if it were braille. I bite my lip as I pull one side of them and then the other down my hips, shimmying till they fall onto his face. I lift one leg, then the other, to step out of them.

What I don't expect is for him to squeeze them tight against his face and inhale, shuddering on the exhale as if he just came. I look at his boxers and see a bit of a wet spot, but I don't know if that's from me or him.

I look back at him, and our gazes collide. He tosses the panties aside and pulls me down. I land hard on his face, but if I hurt him, he doesn't say it. Doesn't even grunt from the weight of me sitting on him. He just devours.

Everything.

I scream and don't care if anyone can hear. In fact, I want them to. I want them to know what's going on. That a god is eating me out. Because heaven can only be like this.

His mouth covers me completely, and his tongue works magic over me.

"I'm so close." I grab my breasts and massage them as I close my eyes and ride his face. His hands grab my hips and cant me so I go faster to his wicked tongue as it flicks against my clit.

"Yes, right there. Yes. Yes. Yessss." I wither against him, and still, he doesn't stop. Not yet. Just closes his eyes as if he's having his favorite dessert.

He hums and moves me off his face. My juices flow down his chin and then his chest as he puts me back into my first position, sitting on his stomach, just above his massive cock.

"Peaches and cream. Just like your mouth, but sweeter." He licks his lips and chin as he savors the taste of me.

The sight has me saying one word. "More."

He shakes his head. "No, honey, we can't."

But I'm not having it. I move lower, below his dick, and rub my hand over it, pulling a hiss from his lips.

"Fuck, your hand feels good."

"It could feel better." I get to the top of his boxers and grab the waistband, pulling it down, stretching it below his third leg. And that's no exaggeration. The thing is massive, and it makes me even wetter, if that's possible.

"Shit, you're fucked up." He shakes his head against the pillow below him, but his hands don't stop me. "But so am I." He rubs his hands up and down my arms as I gently glide mine down his cock once more before I move up on my knees.

I grab his cock and rub the head of it against my clit, moaning and groaning at the feel of him against me.

"Shit," he grits out as I keep doing it over and over. I hold it up against my pussy and rub myself along him with no barrier between us. It feels so good.

"Please, just give me a little more. Just a little."

He pants as he watches me, and I bite my lip, looking at him with hope in my eyes, begging with everything I have but not saying the words.

"Okay," he huffs out as if it's the hardest thing he's ever done. "Just a little."

I dip his dick inside me. Just the tip. It's a stretch, and I grimace, but it feels good. Too good.

"How's that, Peaches? That good for you? Shit, we need to stop." He's panting and gripping my hips so hard I'll have bruises in the morning.

Kooper

"Just a little more. It feels so good. God, you're so big. How do you even fit?" The tip is pushing me to my limits, and it's barely in. The burn is like what I feel when I've been out in the sun too long. It tingles, and I should step away. Go inside or at least put more sunscreen on. But just like when I'm getting burned, I stay.

I push forward.

Or in this case, down.

"Ahhh!" I scream as I seal his cock all the way inside me. He's so big. And with me on top, I swear a part of him is touching the back of my throat as I bounce on him.

"Shit. Fuck, what did you do? Goddammit. You're tight, Peaches. Fucking tight." He's protesting with his mouth, but his hands are still on me, moving me back and forth, just like when I was riding his cloth-covered dick the first time.

Having him inside me is what dreams are made of, even if I've never dreamed this. It's better than sex, because this isn't just sex. It can't be. The colors are too bright. The feel of his hands on me is sparking into my soul so much that it's almost a problem.

And still...

"More," I moan.

He pinches my clit between two knuckles, and I come hard. I fall forward and take his mouth in a full-on kiss. Something we haven't done since all this started. Something that should have happened at the start, but it seems to be our ending.

Or maybe just the midpoint. Because while I saw heaven in his arms, Kooper is still rock-hard and pushing into me over and over.

We roll, and he grabs my head, holding it in the perfect position as he takes what he wants and finds his release, shaking and shivering on bated breath but never once stopping our kiss.

His body stills over mine, but we don't separate. We stay locked in each other's arms and continue kissing. Doing what we should have *only* done from the start, though we seem to be making up for it now.

And when he grows hard again inside me?

I lock my ankles behind his back, and we ride the wave of pleasure together till the heat dies down and we fall asleep in each other's arms, never once detaching.

Chapter 27—Kooper

I must be dreaming. That's the only reason I wake in the middle of the night and smell peaches and cream and feel a warm body wrapped around mine. One that's soft and naked. That fits perfectly in my arms as she lies on me. Whose soft snores bring a smile to my lips.

And because of who I think it is in my arms, I refuse to open my eyes and wake from this slumber land.

The world isn't the same anymore. I woke up the morning before thinking one way. Having a plan and a focus. And now this. The plan? Out the window. Completely fucked. There's no way I'm going back to what it was before.

In my dream, I had a taste. More than a taste—I ate the whole damn peach and rolled in the juices. I took everything I wanted and let her take as well. She flourished without me lifting a hand. It was amazing to see. And imagining what it could be like if I had directed, if I had taken control? It could only have been better.

If that's even possible.

The dream—fuck, okay, the reality of it was more than I could have thought. She surpassed everything I thought. Every wish. Every hope. Her tight pussy clamped around me as if it was begging me to never let it go. Just the thought has me getting hard against her leg that's thrown over my hip.

Not sure if it's me or she just starts having the same thought. But slowly at first, she rocks her sweet cunt along my leg. She gets bolder as she goes, rougher, chasing the friction to get herself off.

With my eyes still closed, I shift her till she's lying away from me. She whimpers in protest till I lift her leg and slide right in. It's like coming home with how wet and welcoming it is.

I'm half asleep, and so is she. Our movements are slow, but there's no less spark than before. My hand is on her hip, rocking her back and forth till her hand reaches back and grabs my ass for leverage as she takes over. I lower my hand, using only touch to dictate where to go, and explore her thighs till I move higher and find her apex.

I slide two fingers into the top of her slit. I can feel my dick touch my fingertips as she glides back and forth. I press down hard and let her motion shift my hand up and down on her clit.

She moans and arches her head back. I wrestle with her hair, moving it with my chin and nose till I find a patch of her skin and bite hard before sucking.

Her breath hitches, and then she stills before giving a short burst as if she's having a seizure as she comes on my dick, squeezing my cum from me with each pulse.

I let go of her neck, licking and then kissing it before settling. I don't move any other part of myself. My hand is still squeezed between her pussy lips, and my dick is still inside her, just like it was the last time we fell asleep.

I never thought I was one to enjoy having my dick inside a woman all night. Usually I'm the first one in the

Kooper

bathroom, removing the condom and washing off any remnants of the night before as quickly as possible.

But with Peaches? Not only did we not use protection, but the idea of wiping any part of her essence away brings me to anger. I should be worried about the no-condom thing. I should. But I know we're both clean. I got tested a while back and haven't been with another since. And I've made sure that Ruby hasn't been with anyone in months. I haven't let a guy come around in over a year. The one tonight? He got too close. If my guy wasn't there to teach them a lesson, I would have left earlier and dealt with it.

But I have a team that handles that shit. They're happy to do so. Which means I can be here. In this dream of perfection. With Ruby keeping my dick warm all night long.

I stretch and feel things pop, but nothing hurts. Just the typical aging sounds I've gotten used to over the years. As I roll, I grin when my face lands against a pillow and the peaches and cream scent fills my brain. Memories of the entire night replay on fast-forward in my mind.

But why have a memory when I can have the real thing?

I reach out across the sheet and feel only coldness. I stretch to the far edges of the bed and find nothing.

I sit up so fast that I have to grab my head as it splits open. The damn drugs that started all this are still messing with me. I could blame our being horny on whatever it was. I did feel out of it more than usual, as if just a breath on my neck had my dick standing erect. If neither of us had anything in our system, I honestly don't know if we would have taken it that far. Hell, if I just hadn't downed her drink, I could have resisted. Or at least appeased her just enough to get her to sleep.

But both of us? Fuck, everything about last night was memorable. I might hate how it happened, and that I was fucking drugged, but I like that I remember everything. Every sight. Every touch. Every taste.

And the way she kept asking for more. I don't think I ever heard her say my name as she came, but that just gives me something to look forward to for next time.

I grab my phone off the desk and check her location. She's still in the apartment. Good. All I need to do is relax for ten seconds, let this migraine pass, drink a gallon of water, and then we can get back to where we started.

She's probably in the bathroom cleaning up. I've never slept with my dick buried in someone most of the night. And I liked it a hell of a lot more than I thought I would when I heard one of the brothers talk about it. Just sounded unsanitary. Now I get it. My dick was nice and warm, like being hugged in a special room all for him.

I probably need a shower before we start round two. Or is it round five? When do rounds start? After an orgasm or after you've slept for a bit? Something to debate with Ruby when I find her.

I scoot to the end of the bed and put my feet on the ground. Just that much movement hurts my head. How the fuck could I *fuck* all night and not feel like this, but now I do? Is the world trying to punish me for what happened?

Kooper

Sure, this wasn't how I wanted it to go, but do I regret it? Fuck no. I wanted it. Have for a while. Now that I've had it? Well, at least I know that all the bullshit it'll cause will be worth it. But I already knew she was. I didn't go into this blind. I waited. Plotted. Prepped. Made sure that if I was going to risk everything for a girl, she'd be worth it.

Because that's how Ruby is, all or nothing. Either you're in it for the win or not. Don't expect a fling with her. She's not the type. And I wouldn't disrespect her like that. Also, I don't want to.

Ruby's mine. She just needs to figure that out. Hopefully, when I find her, she'll already have that thought, and I won't have to fuck it into her. Although that could be fun.

I grin as I look down at my feet, and something catches my eye: my dick. Not because I've never seen it before, but there's something on it.

"What the fuck?" I wipe off the dark stain and bring it closer to my eyes to see. Blood.

Was Ruby a—

I don't finish the thought before I'm standing, swaying but determined. I can't find my briefs, but I locate my jeans. I pull them on, not even bothering to button them as I storm out of her room and to the bathroom.

Which is open. And empty.

I go to her living room and look through it to the kitchen.

Also empty.

I walk over and open Nat's door. She's still asleep in her bed and is alone.

High-stepping it back to the bedroom, I grab my phone and check again. But there's no change. She's here. Or at least her phone is.

I dial her number and hear the buzzing. I look around and find it on the floor.

Fucking awesome.

I pull up the security feeds outside her place and see she left over an hour ago. A fucking hour!

I grab my shirt and my keys. I have no clue where she went, but I'm not about to just sit on my ass and wait. I just found what perfection, what home, could feel like. What if she gets hit by a car? Or someone snatched her? What if Duke is out there somewhere? My boys aren't watching her because they know I took her last night. But I fucking lost her this morning.

I still at the sound of my phone chirping. Opening it once more, I see that she's outside. I'm so lost on everything that I can't seem to get my shit together when it comes to her.

Hearing the door open and shut has me forcing myself to breathe. To take a second and not go out screaming. Or grab her, throw her over the couch, smack her ass, and then fuck it. I'm both raging and horny as fuck. The drug is still in my system. And what we did, what I saw on my dick... it's making me more possessive than I thought I could be. I need answers. And I'm not going to get them standing here, looking at four walls.

I walk into the kitchen and lean against the breakfast nook, watching her cute ass as she's bent over to look in the fridge, pulling out a Gatorade from the back. A purple one. Her favorite. She hides them from herself to keep more on hand and uses them as a treat when she pushes herself running.

She uncaps it and chugs half of it before turning and letting the door close, her eyes locking on me. Lowering the drink, she wipes the back of her hand over her mouth, taking the sweat with her. She should be gross looking. She went running. Long and hard from the looks of her hair, as half of it's sticking up, the rest plastered to her skin, molded there by the sweat.

Despite what most might think, Ruby's never the type to run in skimpy outfits. She's more covered now than I've seen her at the clubhouse. Biker shorts that are closer to her knees than her crotch. Her sleeveless shirt covers her entire mid-frame. The only skin you see is her arms and below her knees. She's almost a nun compared to her usual attire.

And it's hot as fuck. She's panting and sweaty. I can smell her, and it ain't cute, but her clothes? While the shirt was once loose at the start, it's clinging to her now. Her biker shorts, which she uses to cut down the chafing on her legs, have created an amazing outline of her pussy.

I should demand that she shower right now. But why? I just want to fuck her standing. But I can't. Not till I get answers.

I cross my arms and stare, hoping if I do nothing, I might make it out of this unscathed. I'm a heartbeat away from saying "fuck it" and taking her here and now. Especially as I see her eyes taking in my shirtless chest and the fact that my jeans are still unfastened.

I watch her swallow and wonder what it would feel like to have her try to swallow down my cock.

I cough and adjust. I need to focus. My moment has her eyes snapping back to mine.

"You forgot your phone," I growl.

She shrugs. "Oops." She brings the bottle back to her lips and walks past me.

But I stop her before she can make it farther than a few steps, grabbing her arm and spinning her a bit.

"There's still a threat out there. You need to be safe."

She rolls her eyes and pulls away as she heads to the couch and sinks into the cushions. "What threat? I'm no longer part of the club, remember? I'm sure Atom told you. Dad's dead." She looks me in the eye with a furious expression. "He's gone, and I'm out."

I know what she said yesterday. Atom told me everything. Even if he hadn't, I had Flint show me the surveillance tapes. We put the cameras up the second Law went into a coma. We might have had a guy on the door or in the room the entire time, but we still wanted more eyes on everything. We had to watch the hospital staff too. Anyone can be bought for the right price or with the right threat.

Despite what she says, I know she doesn't mean it. She can't. Her dad is her whole life. Him being gone was more painful than she'll ever say. Then having him back? It was like a breath of life back to her. I know this hurts. Having anyone forget you, but especially family, has to be hard.

Ruby's stubborn, though. She told him off. Said he was dead to her. And she'll stick to it for a while. But not forever. At least I hope not. She might not know it, but her dad has a bigger impact on her happiness than she says. She wants his approval. I know that. Everyone can see that she does. She probably wishes she'd been born a boy. Things would be different if she were.

I, for one, am grateful as fuck she wasn't. Instead of gaining a brother, I gain my forever kind of girl.

Eventually.

"You don't mean that."

"It's the truth. Right?" She tilts her head, and a glint takes over her eye. Not a nice one. "That's what you said. That's what the club said. Dad's dead." The look on her face lets me know she's going somewhere with this—I just don't know where yet.

I nod, even if it wasn't a question.

"Funny. Seems that Abigail and the Crazy Eights think something different."

Shit. I run my hand over my head. "Look, Ruby, you don't...."

"Don't what? Don't know what's going on? Well, of course not. I'm kept out of the fucking loop every way this goes. But hey, now that we've slept together, maybe I can get some perks. That's how it works, right? Sleep with a club brother and gain some knowledge? Well, go on. Tell me something I don't know."

I just look at her. I can understand her anger. It's normal. What I can't do? I can't show her that what happened last night had an effect on me. Not till I know she felt something more than a dick inside her. What happened for me last night was life-altering. But for her? With the way she's acting, it's as if I'm just a notch on the bedpost. And for someone who used to live that life, I can't say I'm happy about being on the other side of it for once.

"What? Nothing to share?" She huffs and turns away with a shake of her head. "Well, now that the ban of 'no fucking the president's daughter' has been lifted, maybe I'll find someone who has more to say, or is at least willing to fool around a bit for the right incentive."

I'm on her before she can say another thing. My hands cage her in on the couch as I put one on each side of her head and lean down.

Fear coats her eyes for a second before she blinks and an easy smile lifts her lips.

"Oh, so you *do* have something to say after all?"

"Don't." That's all I'm going to say. Just one word. And it's enough for her to drop her smile and glare. But I match it with my own.

She can be pissed. She can be petty and a bitch and get wild and crazy. Whatever the fuck she wants. But she will *not* go find another brother, or anyone, for that reason.

"Um...." A cough has me turning to see Natalie holding my phone out. "It kept ringing."

As if on cue, it does it again. I look back at Ruby once more before pushing away and grabbing the phone to answer.

"Yeah?" I don't check who it is, but I've got a feeling.

Casper's voice comes in loud and clear. "Church. Now. Bring Ruby."

Chapter 28—Ruby

"Get dressed," he barks at me.

I just raise an eyebrow. "Get bent."

Oh, he doesn't like that. His whole body seems to inflate from the deep breath to... I don't know. Calm down? He doesn't seem calm. Not one little bit. Kind of like me.

Feeling like shit after a night out only means one thing: running till you throw up to teach yourself a lesson. At least, that was the plan. I rolled out of bed this morning, ignoring everything around me, including what was sticky on my legs. Gross, I know, but I just needed out. So I grabbed my running stuff and left. I should have brought music or something, but I was in such a rush to escape before anyone told me I couldn't that I didn't think.

I left Kooper naked in my bed and went running, pushing myself hard so I wouldn't think so damn much. I didn't want to do anything but focus on breathing. But my head hurt the entire time. So much that I was begging to throw up, but I didn't. There was nothing in my stomach to do so.

So I pushed on, forgetting anything and everything. If I had timed myself, I might have gotten a new personal record out of it. But I left my watch at home in my rush.

When I got back, I was left staring at a glaring Kooper standing in my kitchen, with his shirt off and his jeans on but the top button unfastened.

A yummy sight for sure.

And then everything came rushing back. What happened last night. What happened at the hospital. My anger at everything I was hoping to avoid for as long as I could just surfaced unbidden. And no one else was around to let it out on, so he got it. And took it. And still I wanted to drag him close and climb him like a pole.

But I can't do that. So I glare and tell him to fuck off. Something he doesn't do. Typical.

"Casper called Church."

"So?" How does that have anything to do with me? It never has before. One night of dicking—no matter how fantastic and amazing it was—doesn't mean I'm riding on the back of his bike everywhere he goes. The guy's whacked in the head if he thinks that.

"He wants you there too."

This has my jaw dropping. Literally. "I'm not some damn dog who gets called into the house like a good little boy. Tell Casper to fuck off. I'm not part of the club, and he can't tell me shit."

"You're either coming on your own, or I'm dragging you there. Figure it out while I shower." He goes into my room and comes out a second later before heading into the bathroom. "And if you think for one goddamn second about running, I'll chase you down and strap you to my damn bike."

He slams the door to the bathroom, and I glare as I see Natalie jump. She's still here. Listening and watching all

Kooper

this bullshit and not saying anything. She looks at me, and I sigh. I'm over all this drama, and it's not even eight in the morning.

"I think we need coffee," she says before going into the kitchen and starting a pot.

Some days I don't trust her. Things she does or says make me question her. Especially with everything that went down with Abigail and then the club lying about Dad. It's easier to question things now. To question people. Things I might have only thought odd before are now suspicious.

Like when she sees a random person and just goes off on them, telling them to back up when I never even saw them get close to her. It's like a switch that flips in her brain. It seems random at best when it happens. And then she disappears for a few days. Not completely gone, just avoiding me and locking her door and shit.

But when she comes over and hands me a cup of coffee fixed how I like, I can't help but be grateful that she's in my life right now. I might not know her, not everything. But when I need her? She seems always to be there, even if I do keep her at arm's length and don't tell her a lot. Similar to what she does with me.

It's probably why I decide now is the time to share. Because after everything that went down this morning, Nat was content to just sit on the couch and drink coffee in silence with me.

"I think I raped Koop."

The amount of coffee that spews over our table is hilarious. Disgusting and not something I want to clean, but funny all the same.

"I'm sorry, what?" She shakes her head as she sets down her mug and wipes off the liquid she spat out on herself.

"He said to stop, but I stuck it in any way."

Last night, I was cognitive. I was horny like I've never been horny before in my life, but I was able to make up my own mind. I could have opened the nightstand drawer and pulled out my nighttime toy. I could have used my own hand. Or hell, gone into the shower and used the detachable spray. It's always hit all the right spots before.

But I didn't.

Instead, I begged. Something I never thought I would do in my life. I begged and pleaded. And when that didn't get me an immediate answer, I pounced. I took matters into my own hands and made sure he couldn't refuse.

That's probably why he was so mad at me this morning. I got him drugged. I know he was as messed up as I was. Maybe it was a different reaction for him, though. Maybe he wasn't all there like I was, and I took advantage. I forced him to do something he hated, and when I woke up, the spell was broken.

But then why did he wake you in the middle of night to do it again? Why did he call you Peaches if he was forced? Why did he grab your hips and keep you there as he pounded into you?

My brain is telling me it was a mistake. My heart? Well, that bitch is saying something else. Something I'm not ready for. Especially not after I just cut myself off from my dad and the club.

Kooper

That was the plan last night, anyway. Leaving the hospital, calling Nat, and going out was meant to be my big "welcome to reality" party. A party where I said goodbye to club life and hello to townie life. Sure, I got drugged on my first big adventure, but that's just how life goes. Just when you think it can't get worse, it does.

But it didn't. Kooper showed. He stayed. He's here.

I shake my head at my heart's speech. Some people say it's your conscience that talks to you. I say it's your heart. She and my brain are usually on the same page, so I rarely have these internal arguments. But that seems to be something of the past. No more peaceful moments with everything in sync. Now it's all out of balance and shit.

"I doubt he saw it like that."

I shrug. "Guys are weird. If they get raped, I bet they tell themselves they wanted to do it anyway or something."

Nat shakes her head. "Trust me, girl. Kooper wasn't raped by you or anyone last night. He has, what, a hundred-plus pounds on you? You really think you could have overpowered him and forced him to do something?"

I bite my lip, and my shrug is smaller as I sink lower into the couch. "We were drugged."

"Again, have you seen that man? Goliath doesn't even begin to describe him. He had your drink. Which was already like a third gone from what you drank of it. Who knows what was in it? Even then, I highly doubt that there was enough in there to affect you and him the same. It doesn't make sense in a scientific way at all. The math doesn't add up. Trust me, if the guy wanted to stop it, he could have."

I let her words sink in and really listen to them. It quiets parts of my brain I didn't know were screaming at me till then.

"So...." I look at her as she picks up her drink, taking smaller sips than before, I note. "You and Kooper really had sex?"

On any other day, I would have pointed out the obviousness of her question. Like the fact that I just admitted it. Or that I'm sure she heard it, and that's what had her sleeping in past her 7:00 a.m. ritual wake-up time.

But all I do is nod. And when the shower cuts off, I look at the bathroom door. I feel something on the horizon. Something big is coming, and I don't know how I feel about it. Either with the club, or with Kooper, or both.

And I don't know if I like it or hate it.

"Want to go for a drive?"

"You want me to go to the club?" Her eyes bug out.

I get it. I haven't invited her there in months. Not with how things have been going. But I need a friend, and I'm not sure how many I have at the club anymore. I pushed a lot of people away. I don't plan on building bridges today either, which means I'm about to burn a few more. And I think I might need some help in the getaway process when I do.

The bathroom door opens and Kooper walks out, pulling on the same shirt from yesterday. I would offer him one of the club's tees I've stolen over the years. I make sure to get the extra large; they make comfy sleep shirts and loungewear, as they're soft as hell, and when they're that big, shorts aren't needed. It hangs so low I can walk bare underneath if I want and none would be the wiser. But I don't

Kooper

because I don't live alone, and going without underwear feels weird.

"Leaving in ten."

I stand, putting my empty coffee mug in the sink and my empty Gatorade bottle in the trash. "Nat's coming."

His back is to me as he bends over his phone. I see him tense before he looks at me over his shoulder, then at Nat. She's biting her lip and holding her coffee as if she were about to sip it. Not sure if he sees the mess on the coffee table or not. He could have heard us, but I don't think so. Kooper snoops to keep me safe, not to just be nosy. Or I hope not.

"Ten." That's all he says as he walks to my room.

Nat looks at me and nods. "Right. I'll go get changed. You take a shower, and I'll...." She looks at the coffee table and her nose wrinkles. "I'll clean this. Think he'd be willing to stop on the way for breakfast?"

"He better. I'm close to dying if I don't get a breakfast taco soon. With more bacon on it than what comes out of a pig."

"Yuck. You're gross." She laughs at the thought but goes to get changed.

I head to my room, glancing at Kooper as he sits on my unmade bed and laces up his boots. An unmade bed with my panties hanging off one side and my pasties next to it. I look back at him and see he's watching me take it all in.

I should make a joke about it. Something like how I expect him to clean up after or at least make the bed when he sleeps in it. But a single eyebrow raise lets me know he's not in the mood for any smart comments right now.

So I turn and open my drawers, pulling out my normal clothes. Kooper might be bringing me in, but it's on my terms. And in my way. No one will know anything is different. No one will see a girl who's done with everything. Or someone confused about what last night meant.

No one will see the coward I've become as I tuck tail and go into the bathroom to shut everyone and everything out. They'll see what they always see. What I make sure they see.

A woman who knows what she wants. Who takes no crap from anyone. Who's untouchable. Who doesn't cry. Who can stand on her own feet without a man, father or other, holding her hand.

That's what they'll see. I just have to hold that image for a little while. Just long enough to make them believe.

Just long enough for Kooper to not see under the mask. Seeing that while I was broken last night, he made me whole after. That being his, even with the drugs, having him call me something other than Ruby, was what I needed. What I'll dream about later in the night when I sleep alone.

That my desire to be more than what I am now is just that. And I won't look for it to be a reality. Even if it felt like that all night. Like I could be someone new. Someone strong and willing to break away from what I forced myself to be once I learned Dad wasn't going to let me in the club. When Mom left me and Dad had to raise someone who wasn't a boy, and he had to be soft when he wasn't the soft type.

He could be caring and sweet, but he was never Mom. We both knew that. His love was more than tough love, but it wasn't sweet like a mother's. We made it work.

Kooper

Till we didn't. He doesn't love me anymore. He doesn't *know* me. How can you love someone you don't know?

They say he could regain his memory. And maybe one day he will. But till then, I don't think I'm strong enough to love him for both of us. I'm not even strong enough to love myself right now.

Loving for two seems impossible.

As I wash away my fears, hopes of what I thought the future would be so many months ago, I feel small stings of pain from the soap on my skin. Parts of me where Kooper's nail went a bit too deep. Where his teeth left a bit too much bite.

The pain recedes, and with it comes a thought. I don't know if it's from my head or my heart, but it's there. That the pain is the past leaving. And the bruises? The scabs? They're the start of something new.

Something new with *someone* new.

Not new in my life, but new in my mind. New in my heart. Or maybe he was always there in some way before. I just didn't know it till now. I never unlocked that type of pain before. Maybe I couldn't. Perhaps releasing Dad and my past is what I need to move forward.

Or maybe I'm still so fucked up on drugs that I don't know anything anymore.

"Two minutes, Ruby." A bang on the door has me shutting off the water.

If it were Dad, I'd take my time. But it's not. It's *him*. Kooper. A man who shouldn't be in my house, or in my bed. One who shouldn't even be on my mind. And one who especially shouldn't be leaving himself behind in small parts after coming inside me last night.

The thought of being pregnant is a passing scare. One I don't think about more than a second. The mark on my underarm from my birth control reassures me enough not to worry about it. I got it a while back, and the doctors said it would make my life simpler. At the time, I was thinking about being regular, but I guess this is what they had more in mind. No fuss, no baby mess.

'Cause being pregnant right now will just fuck things up. Even more than they already are. And that's already too much as it is.

Chapter 29—Kooper

I leave Natalie and Ruby in the clubhouse common room, munching on breakfast tacos we stopped and got when we were closer to the club. I wasn't about to waste time waiting in a line close to a college town on a Saturday. College kids might sleep in, but as soon as Saturday happens, I swear half of them are out looking for greasy food in the wee morning hours.

I'm the last to arrive in Church before the door closes. No one even bats an eye that I brought in food. What can I say? I'm hungry.

I sit by General, wanting to talk to him after this is done. Makes it easier if the guy's close enough for me to get his attention without alerting everyone else.

Casper hits the gavel on the table, silencing everyone.

"Billy spoke to the Crazy Eights last night."

Some mumbles go around, but I keep my thoughts to myself. I'm pissed. I voted against letting C8 know about Law as a sign of good faith. Even if I already think Casper spilled the beans to his girl before he brought it to the table. Casper's play on it was that it made sense if we wanted more eyes on Law, as well as to strengthen the new bond between our two groups. It's still rocky, like the mountains between us.

We've had OHH run a few missions with them. All have been successful. So I guess they've got that going for them.

My issue is that it's only been a few months. We're still in the freaking honeymoon stage with them. They don't need to know everything just because they give us intel on the Devils Damned and Duke when we ask about them.

Sure, it could be seen as one-sided. And it is. But fuck, we're the Hounds. They put plants in our home and expected us to roll with it. And we did, for the most part. But that doesn't mean we can't still hold shit back in my opinion. And some brothers too.

But it still got the majority vote to tell them. And from the way Ruby spoke this morning, I guess it's all over their news bulletin already.

Really, all I see is another thing the club did that fucked Ruby over. We should have told her first, let her know we were going to say something. If anyone had a right to know, it was her. Especially with the way we held her to a gag order on all of this. Forced to deal with all this on her own and not talk to anyone. Well, anyone but us. We wanted her to come to us. *I* did.

But she didn't. If her dad was still in a coma, I suspect we'd still not be talking.

And despite the pain of his waking and forgetting her, I'd still do it all over again to get what we had last night. One perfect night, drugs and all. Because they led to it. And I can't be mad when I got what I wanted in the end because of them.

Which reminds me, I need to check in with my guy and find out what went down after we left the house party. I

Kooper

make a mental note to do it after this, since I had to drop my phone at the entrance before I entered Church.

"Psy is adamant about talking with the club. C8 confirms it ain't a trap, just talking. Seems a person went missing, and they're looking for some details."

"Interesting twist of events," Gator snarls. "They think to look within first?"

For a while, we thought the Devils Damned as a whole were part of the people trafficking. Men, women, kids. If it was for sale, they were part of it. Or so we thought. But it was just one man. One man tied to them—Duke, their VP.

We found out a few weeks before Ruby learned about her dad that Duke's still alive. Alive and in Devils Damned custody. And staying that way under rules set by C8, who declared him to be untouchable. Someone who fucked with more than one Hound's old lady, and we're just supposed to sit on our asses and do nothing.

Not a single brother was okay with it. We all hated it. We almost said "fuck you" to the entire C8 group over that one point. But they swore he would never be an issue again. That the Devils Damned had him contained.

Perhaps containment was the issue. Now he might be poaching from within his own walls to fill supply orders for the right price. Who the fuck knows? But I don't want to do shit to help them in any way. They don't deserve it.

"Show me Duke's head, and then we can talk. Till then, I'm out," I mutter, loud enough for everyone to hear and to take a moment to think on.

A few brothers nod in agreement while others look at Casper. He's the president and has the ultimate say. His loyalty is to the club. But his old lady is part of C8. She moved out of an operative role and into a consulting one, a link between the two groups. They say they can be neutral enough to make things work for both, but can they? So far, nothing has been called to question their loyalty. This will be the first real test.

"Boss." Chains pulls Casper's gaze. He might no longer be an officer, but Chains' voice is always one the club respects. "Might want to draw a line on how involved we are with your girl's group. They're good with the OHH shit, but this? This is personal. Having them side with someone we always saw as an enemy might put a strain on things within the club. You might want to consider keeping the pillow talk to a minimum till we figure this shit out."

The boys adjust at the table and look away. Calling a brother's relationship into question is always… challenging? That doesn't seem right. More like insulting.

"Chains… brother," Casper growls and then takes a deep breath. "Glad to have you at the table. I appreciate your thoughts and want to keep hearing them. But if you bring up me and my old lady's relationship again, I swear to every Hound here, I'll beat you with this gavel and then go fuck her after without an ounce of shame."

They level a stare at each other for more than a beat before Chains nods. "Fair."

And just like that, the tension is gone and we're moving on.

We're guys. We move on quickly. Half the reason we don't let chicks in the club is because we all know they can hold a grudge longer than it takes a star to die out. That, and fucking a member of the club would just complicate things.

Kooper

That's what vamps are for—to fuck and toss out. If a woman was in the club, you'd have to see them all the time. See them getting with someone else, or just have to remember what life was like buried in their cunt while trying not to be biased if dishing out punishment. It complicates things.

That's why women's roles are reserved to vamps or old ladies. Anything else just isn't needed.

That's why what Ruby is makes things complicated on so many levels. She's neither of those things, but she's more than a civilian. She's part club but not *in* the club. What I did should have *me* taking the gavel to the face from every brother here. Most, if not all, see Ruby as their sister in some way. If they were ever attracted to her, they got over it quickly with Law's decree.

I was the one who fucked shit up. I saw her as annoying at first, not someone I could end up admiring. She was a pain in the ass to me and not someone I wanted to get to know. But slowly, over time, things changed. My allegiance changed. I was no longer protecting her because it was my job; I was protecting her because she became more than a job.

She became what I wanted to come home to. What I needed to feel at peace with. Acceptance in. Before, I didn't give two shits about anything and anyone. Having the respect of my brothers was enough. Till one day it wasn't. I needed more. And that came with the need for Ruby to see me as something other than her shadow. As more than just a club brother following her father's rules. To see that I was my own man. One who she could come to if she needed help. Someone besides her father. Someone to lean on. To trust.

I've broken her more times than fixed her. But with each break, I'm building her stronger. Making her see beyond her bubble that was popped. That she's more than just a president's daughter. More than just someone attached to the club. That she can be anything.

And I'll be right beside her the whole way, pushing her to what she wants. Even dragging her if I think she needs it.

"Maybe—" King coughs a bit, as if he's surprised more than the rest of us that he spoke up. He usually keeps quiet, listening and assessing. He speaks when he needs to, but he's never the idea man. More the kind to follow up on if things could work with the details he's provided for manpower on missions. "Maybe we pass on the meeting and tell C8 to take it on. If they want to be buddies with them, that's their thing. They said we were partners. That they wouldn't go with our enemy, and we wouldn't go against theirs. So let them have the ball. See what they do with it. You got your girl. We got our liaison person telling us details. Think she'd lie if C8 decided to switch sides?"

Casper waits a beat, then shakes his head. I would have to agree on that. Billy might be manipulative, but her love for Casper is stronger than I think C8 expected. If they'd lasted undercover another month, I truly think Billy would have flipped sides and turned on C8 just to be with him. She might not have said it, but I think her allegiance has already shifted.

"Let them fuss it out. If we're really needed, then they *both* come to us. Together. None of this one-on-one, 'he said, she said' bullshit."

Kooper

"When did you grow a brain?" Bass smirks, and King takes it well with a shake of his head as the others chuckle at his expense.

"About the time we all learned you were more than just a mouth," he shoots back, gaining even more laughs as Bass's smile drops.

"Settle." Casper bangs the gavel twice before we do. "King's got a point. Who knew?" Another round of smirks, even Bass as he quietly gets over his little tiff. "I'll talk to Billy and let her know the club's ruling. We'll wait till they get back to us on it. Meeting adjourned." He smacks the gavel hard. "Kooper, stick around. Someone bring in Ruby."

Most of the boys head out, but Atom sticks around, as well as Bulldog and Flint. Before General gets up, I tag him on the leg, and he leans in.

"Need a tox screen," I say.

His eyes get wide, but he keeps his voice low, like mine. "Issues?"

I shake my head. "Solo thing. I'll get with you after this."

"How long was it in your system?"

"Last night. Felt like shit again this morning. Still do a bit. Might not be a ton, but I'm hoping you can at least get me an idea of what it is."

He nods. "You know where to find me." He slaps my back and exits just as Ruby walks through the door.

"You rang, Your Majesty?" The girl even bows a bit, her hands rolling at her sides. Like a freaking court jester being summoned before a king.

"Save the sass and have a seat," he barks at her. He doesn't even stand, just folds his arms and leans back in his chair.

Ruby raises an eyebrow. I doubt she expected Casper to ever speak so harshly to her. But things are changing. The sooner she gets that, the better for me.

"Last time I checked, I already had a daddy. And you weren't looking for a sub."

Casper's hands come to the table, and he stands slowly. "Let's get a few things straight, little girl. You have a dad, not a daddy. A daddy is someone who cares, guides, and even adjusts behavior. Your dad raised you till you could take care of yourself. A daddy sees that, despite your age, you still need a firm hand to guide you into decisions that others would leave you on your own to make. They mold you into the best of what you can become and tan your ass if need be, if not other things. They create a safe, trusting place for someone to grow beyond what they thought without fear of failure or disappointing someone. Unless it goes against a rule, a rule that's put in place to keep you safe. *You* don't have a daddy. You might need one, but you don't. And I am not the caregiving type. I have my own demands and needs, and not one of them can you even attempt to satisfy like my girl does. Now sit the fuck down and shut your mouth if you know what's good for you."

It's either the sass from Ruby getting to him or the fact that his relationship got called into play twice within the hour that sets off Casper. He ain't wrong, though. On any count.

With a huff and a puff, she sits. At the opposite end of the table. The door ain't closed, so this isn't an official meeting. If it were, she wouldn't be here. We don't let women in Church—well, not usually. Fairy was invited in once because of her entanglement. And the Crazy Eights meet with Casper and the boys in here, but that's just because it's the biggest room and has wheelchair access for Charles, their leader.

"Want to tell me what happened yesterday?" Casper's still standing as he asks. Bulldog, Flint, and I are still in our seats, and Atom is holding up a wall close to the back by Ruby.

She shakes her head, glancing at me and then at the table. For a second, my heart stops beating, and I hold my breath. I look at the boys, then the boss. No one is looking at me, just at her.

They can't know. They can't possibly be asking about what went down between us. I've made sure that nothing we did was caught on camera. I'm the only one with cameras in her place, and they're only at the front door and by her sliding back door to the tiny balcony. If cameras saw me, all they would have seen is me coming and leaving. Nothing else. And me sleeping on the couch ain't a hard concept to understand. I've got no doubt that no one in their right mind would think I was in her bed, letting her fuck me all night long before I took over and did the same to her.

"Why not just check the feeds? I know you have cameras at the hospital."

I try to let the air out softly and not all in a rush so no one knows how long I've held my breath. A dead giveaway.

This is just about her dad. Not me.

Jesus, man. Get out of your own fucking head. No one cares if you fuck Ruby. They only care if you fuck her over. And they care far more about Law's recovery than anything else.

Which is how it should be. A brother's care over another. But when it comes to Ruby, putting anyone, even her dad, before her doesn't sit well with me.

"We saw the feed," Casper replies, acknowledging that they were eavesdropping. That this is what they wanted to talk to her about. "We still want to know what your thinking is. Why you thought it was okay to talk to him like that."

"Talk to *him* like that? My own dad? You're really going to stand there and tell me how to talk to him?"

"Yes."

"You're unbelievable," she mutters under her breath.

"What did you say?" Casper quirks an eyebrow, and maybe on a submissive it might work. But Ruby ain't a submissive. On a good day, she's a brat. But that's about it.

"You heard me. You ain't deaf, none of you are, but you might be going mental. The lot of you. You really think you can stand there and tell me what I can or can't do with my own dad when you keep lying to me? Keeping things from me?"

Casper huffs. "What did we hide this time?" He seems annoyed, like he's talking to a child.

"Oh, I don't know. What about telling me to keep all this to myself when you blab to your woman and her group, huh? So you can do what the fuck you want, but me telling my old man off, who doesn't even remember me at all, is a bad thing? Fucking one-sided assholes."

"They're talking?" Bulldog growls and turns his gaze to Casper, who looks equally pissed.

"Abigail sure had no problem blabbing it all over the hospital. Or should we be calling her Rue now?" Ruby looks away with disgust, and the boys look at Casper.

"The club voted." That's all he says, but there's grit in his voice.

"Kind of shitty that you didn't take the gag order off Ruby first, though," Flint says.

Whether Ruby wants to acknowledge it or not, she has allies here. And I don't think Casper expected any of this to go the way it's going.

But there's a reason why Casper is the president. He knows when to take a step back and say when he's wrong. Or at least attempt an apology.

"You're right. It should have gone differently, but it didn't. The club fucked up. Again, where you're concerned. I get it. And you can be mad at us."

She scoffs. "I am, dumbass."

"But..." He looks at her with an intensity to keep her from interrupting again. "Don't let your anger at me, at us"—he gestures to those around the table—"affect how you treat your father. You're going to regret it. He's your dad. He might not remember who you are now, but he will. Just give it time."

Ruby shakes her head. "I've given this club plenty of time. Him too. What else do you expect from me?"

"To keep trying," Atom says, pulling her gaze.

"Trying? He forgot me. He forgot Mom. All he cares about is some ditzy nurse. If he came to the clubhouse right now, I swear he'd hook up with the first vamp he saw."

"You don't know that," Flint says with a shake of his head.

She looks at the others at the table. Everyone but me. "And you don't know it either."

When no one answers to deny her, she stands and exits in a flourish. And I don't even hide that I watch her go.

Chapter 30—Ruby

Oh my God, this place is nuts. *Looney Tunes* in the crazy house. They honestly think they can pull me in here and tell me what I can and can't do? How to act and talk to my dad? When they've done nothing but pull bullshit over bullshit on me?

"Let's go, Nat. We're leaving." I say the words loud enough so that by the time I get to the table where I left her, she'll have gathered her things and will be ready to go.

But I don't get that far across the clubhouse before someone grabs my arm.

"What the—" I yank, but there's no give, and I turn to see Kooper holding me tight. "Let go, asshole," I say between clenched teeth. He's the last person I want to see or talk to right now.

Instead of answering, he just pulls me back. He's stronger than me, and the fight I give isn't enough to do more than just piss him off.

"Let go. Get your hands off me."

Unless the entire place has lost its hearing, not a single brother is willing to step in and stop me from being manhandled.

And I'm just about done with all this bullshit.

So I swing. I give Kooper a good left hook to the face, and it has his head turning. But his grip doesn't falter. It only gets tighter till he uses the force to swing me over his shoulder. I'm screaming and hitting him, and not a single goddamn person hears me. Or cares.

"I hate you. I hate you all," I shout as I'm carried past everyone and into the hallway that leads to a few of the rooms. We pass mine, and I already know where we're going before we get there.

As soon as my feet are on the ground, I push him away, but really it's me who bounces back in my stumble. I pretend as if I meant to step back, that walking away from the door, my escape, was what I wanted.

I watch him lock the door and then turn to look at me. There's anger in his eyes, but also desire. And I hate that I feel it too. I should be pissed the fuck off, not turned on. I can't help but look at the bed and then scream in my head before looking back. His damn smirk has me clenching my fists tight.

"Wipe that shit off your face before I show you why my right hook is better than my left."

"You need to calm down."

"And you need to go fuck yourself."

He tilts his head and looks at me. I don't like it. He always sees more than I want. More than I usually know what *I* want till he tells me later.

"Is that it?"

"Is what what? Skip the code talk and speak English for once," I huff as I run my fingers through my hair and push it off my face.

"You need me to fuck you again to get you to calm down?"

Kooper

A laugh literally bursts from my mouth. "Ah, no. That is not it at all."

"I think it is." He steps off the wall and moves closer, like a predator hunting his prey.

I put up one hand and shake my head.

"No, seriously. I don't want that." How can he think I want that right now? I'm pissed off. His *buddies* just tried to tell me what to do with my dad. My dad! They know nothing. They can do whatever the hell they want in the club, but they can't overstep into my life. Only Dad could do that when he was president, and he isn't anymore. I'm no one. No longer part of this group. So they can all get fucked.

"You don't?"

He's so close now that I have to put both hands up. But he just runs into them and keeps walking. I counter till I hit the wall next to his bathroom. He leans in and runs his nose along my neck. I arch only because I don't want him to touch me. That's it. It's not to give him better access. Especially not when he flicks his tongue out and runs it along my skin. And that moan? That wasn't a moan. It was a war cry. A cry of anguish and disgust. Not of want or need.

"I think you lie, Peaches."

"I'm not Peaches."

He grabs my hips and pulls them flush to his. "You're right. You're not just *any* Peaches. You're *my* Peaches."

His lips cover mine before I can protest further, invading my mouth with his tongue and plundering it like it's a damn castle. Destroying my resolve as he continues his onslaught. I'm like a damn maiden, helpless to resist as he grabs my hands and holds them against his chest, pressing his weight down on me, preventing me from leaving. Preventing me from moving. To do anything but accept this... this... punishment from him.

And it *is* a punishment. Something I don't want. Something that's meant to correct my behavior in some way. To force me to do what he, what the club, wants. How dare he use his lips against me. His perfect soft lips that I remember sucking on my clit for what felt like hours as I came on him last night.

I shake my head and tear my mouth from his. Enough to breathe but barely enough to think, as his lips just move to my neck.

"I'm mad at you." I'm telling him but reminding myself as well. "You and your brothers can't tell me what to do." *Damn, he's really good with his mouth.*

"You're right."

I pull back, as does he. I know I am, but never in a million years would I have thought Kooper would ever agree with me. Especially about his club brothers being wrong.

"They can't tell you what to do." I'm confused by his words till I see his lips curl up in a cruel smile that's almost charming. Devilish is more like it. "But I can."

"You're being delusional. Yeah, you stuck your dick in me, but that means nothing." I lock down my reactions. Turn cold to him. I've learned how to wear this mask, how to pull this sheep's clothing on when I need to. To let my frosty bitch side out when things hit too close to home and I don't want others to know.

The last time I used it was back in high school when someone referred to my mom dying. Back then, I was told the same as today: "Keep your head down." "Keep trying." "Don't make waves." Back then, it was to reserve my energy for Mom. To save myself from getting locked up for giving someone a massive beatdown so I could be there for her. To make it easier for her, not having to worry about me.

Now it's to save Dad. To keep my shit together so he can recover with ease. To have him focus on his healing and shit.

It's always about someone else. "Ruby, do this for so-and-so." "Ruby, act this way so the club looks this way." Ruby. Ruby! *Ruby!*

I bang my head against the wall. Then do it a few more times. I'm surprised he lets me. But I don't look at him. I keep my eyes closed as I try to either beat sense into myself or just whack myself hard enough to get out of this pity party.

Finally, I open my eyes. I see his ceiling, and then I roll my head down to meet his eyes. There's no pity in them. No fear or horror. No anger or frustration. Just him looking at me. It's a neutral face, but I swear he understands me. Understands me on so many levels that I should be hiding from it.

"It means nothing," I say again. I don't know why, but I do.

His response? A blink. Then he lets go of my hands that are still on his chest, moving his own down till he gets to my jeans and unsnaps the buttons. His movements aren't rough, but there's nothing suave or romantic about the way he jerks my pants open and slides his palm flat against my stomach, down beneath my panties. How he parts my nether lips, grazes my clit with his nail, and slides two fingers into my sopping wet pussy.

The second he touches my clit, I'm shivering. Him going straight inside without a buildup has me shaking. I move my hands to grab each bicep to hold myself up. I'm going to fall. There's no other way to describe it. My legs have turned weak. I'm wobbling on them, and he's only stuck his fingers in. No movement, just holding them there.

He steps closer, pushing his thighs tight to mine to keep my legs straight. His other hand grabs my hip, and the indents from last night are like a finger groove for him to find. I should wince when he touches my bruises, but I just groan at the feel of his hands on me again. But it's involuntary, and I close my mouth as soon as I hear it.

But not before he does too.

I glare at him as he starts pumping his thick fingers inside me, sending shivers racing up and down my spine. I shake my head over and over again. "It means nothing." It's a chant. A plea from me to my own ears. For it to be true. That I don't care. That Kooper is just a random guy, and none of this means more than it should. It can't. No matter how much I wished for something like this in my deepest, darkest thoughts. No matter how much I begged for this kind of attention from someone. It was never Kooper in my mind when I did. It was never him.

Just a dark shadow. A random person who was meant to put me on a pedestal and never let me fall. Someone who could make me feel as if I was enough while putting me first in everything.

But it can't be Kooper. He has the club. I'll never be more than the club. Ever.

"Tell yourself." He leans closer, his breath brushing my ear. He nibbles it just a bit, making me arch into his fingers, which seem to go faster. "Tell yourself anything you need to hear. But it's all a lie. Everything you say is a lie. Because you're mine, Peaches. Completely mine."

I shake my head just a little. I can't do more than that. I'm so close to coming, it's ridiculous. I'm both sore and craving the burn he's bringing me with each movement. And when his fingers flutter inside me and somehow change positions to hit a secret spot I had no idea I had, I whimper.

"You are. The sooner you get it, the sooner we can move past this."

"When?"

"When what?" I feel his smile against my neck a second before he kisses me. "When did you become mine?"

I nod and grip his arms tighter as I try to climb away from his fingers and yet sink down on them faster. So close. So goddamn close.

He growls in my ear. A whispered growl that makes me even wetter. The nibbles, licks, and kisses aid in his assault on my body.

"Maybe it was the first time your dad gave me you to protect. Or when I fucked up your landlord for fucking you over. Or when you were grinding this hot little pussy on me while claiming to fix my hip. That kiss we had? That was the start of it. But I claimed you the second I stuck my dick in this tight little pussy and it bled all over my cock. The moment you gave yourself to me, just me, and no other. You're fucking mine now, Peaches. You had your chance to be with another, and you chose me. And I'm choosing you right back."

He does a twisting motion, and I'm coming. My mouth opens to let out a scream, and he covers it with his own, taking my breath, pants, whimpers, and release all in one passionate kiss that leaves me seeing spots as he takes too much oxygen from me.

When his mouth releases mine, I embarrassingly give chase to his lips for another kiss. One he doesn't deny me. It's slower, like how his fingers glide in and out of me. Petting me like a good little kitten for not biting.

Which makes me frown. I ain't no damn animal. And I don't need a pet. No matter how good it feels.

I must be hormonal as shit, because I'm back to being pissed. The orgasm seemed to only give me a small, very short reprieve. Maybe I really do need a good dicking to get in a better mood.

"Fight me all you want, Peaches. But I was your first, and I'm going to be your last," he murmurs as he pulls away.

"Not happening. For one, I've got plans that don't involve you in the future. And two, you weren't my first. Ever heard of a period?"

He pulls his hand out of my pants, looks at it, then shows me. "Well, look at that. Clean fingers." He then sucks them fully into his mouth, and my hoo-ha flutters a bit at the sight. "Tastes like peaches and cream. Just like last night. Not a hint of copper."

Fuck, I'm turned on again. So much that you'd think he'd been teasing me for an hour and I didn't just come on his fingers.

"You really need to get over yourself." I wanted it to be haughty, but it just comes out breathless, because, well, I am. I swallow hard, my mouth dry from watching him lick his fingers clean. "Learn some biology too. I thought my period was over. You must have just gotten a little on yourself when you stuck your dick so far up."

He grins, laughing at me. "Did you just try to school me in biology and compliment my dick size all in one go?"

Probably. I can't think right now. I'm just trying to get out of here without jumping him a second time. Nat says I didn't rape him. And his actions right now show he's a willing partner. But if he doesn't back up in the next five seconds, I'm liable to just force myself on him again.

"It wasn't a compliment," I grit out, but it's a contradiction. I want to deny it. To deny how he was. But I felt it. Might not have gotten up close and personal, but I swear a part of me got tattooed by his cock last night.

Chapter 31—Kooper

She's scared. I never thought I'd see her scared, but she is. She fears this. Her and me. And what that means for her.

But she doesn't have to be scared. I've got her, and I'm not letting go. But I see she isn't ready for that. Not yet. But soon.

The way she chased after my lips told me we're closer than I thought when we left her place this morning. I figured she'd put up a wall. And she did. But I broke it down quickly.

She's trying to build another. To tell me a lie. But I know what I saw. I know I was her first. No man has ever gotten inside her before. And no other man ever will.

Do I wish I'd known it was her first time? No, this was better. Her wanting me and pushing past the fear and the pain to keep going all night? That's the memory of her first time. Not the fumbled fingers in a dark room with someone unsure of themselves.

It was my first time too. The first time I let a girl on top. Let someone else take the lead and be in charge. We shared more than just a bed last night. We shared our firsts. But she's freaking out too much, what with me knowing she was a virgin and probably the fact that I just fingered her in the club, to really appreciate that. So I keep it to myself.

She's still mad. I get it. The boys bombarded her. I'm pissed off for her. But I'm smart enough not to go out there half-cocked without cooling down first. Leaving like that can be reckless. She could do something rash, like drive away and not stop till she's in Canada. Nothing against the North Country, just not really in the mood to go someplace cold.

So I need her here, calmed down enough to at least have the sense to stay close to home.

I thought I broke her spirit for a moment. But the fire in her eyes tells me she's still turned on, and that makes her mad. She needs to get even. To somehow get on better ground. To think she's on top of the world for a bit.

And God as my witness, I'm willing to make the ultimate sacrifice.

"Maybe you need to see it to really understand the size we're talking about."

I step back, undo my belt buckle, and pop open my jeans. Her eyes follow my movements as I drag my zipper down. My dick is already fat, hard, and ready to be inside her.

"Or are you too scared?" Her eyes snap up to me, and I shrug as they narrow. "Virgins are always scared of a dick." My smile turns wicked. "But you aren't a virgin, right? Nothing you haven't seen before, right? So why don't you prove it? Prove you know what you're doing."

"You just want to get off."

"Seems fair. Consider it a reciprocal exchange. You got what you wanted. Now it's my turn."

She stares at my barely contained dick. Even jumps a bit when I move it. She's completely full of shit. She has no clue what to do. Any vamp would be pulling on my chain without me even suggesting it. Hell, wouldn't have to be a vamp. I don't have a big enough ego to think I'm irresistible to women, but the vest is like a damn chick magnet.

Not even Ruby's immune. I've seen her over the years. I know she looks. Especially when it's a brother who comes in from a sister chapter. She looks all right, but she never touches. The vest might attract her, but she has enough willpower to say no to a brother.

Till me.

Not sure if she was always planning on saving herself or if it just happened. I, probably like everyone else, expected her to have experience. Not vamp level, but more than a blushing bride. I was mistaken.

A bit of hate trickles inside me for thinking that about her. No shame if a woman fucks a man, but I never imagined she'd been untouched. I assumed so much about her, just like what others do all the time.

Was our kiss her first too? When I ate her out, was that another one? What about when I took her for wings and paid? Has she even gone on a date before?

I've watched her. For years. It started as protection and morphed into something else. Something more. At first, I figured she was just sneaking out and getting her time with others when I thought she was in class or with a group of friends. Then, when I started watching closer, I assumed her focus was just on school. Then her dad. But what if it wasn't? What if all the expectations, all the rumors about her and the clothes she wears, are just an act? One to fit the mold people assume so they don't look closer?

Could I be so lucky?

Kooper

Could I be blessed enough to have all her firsts and seconds, and a hundred other firsts? What was it in my past life that gave me this... this... gift? One I should cherish.

But I won't. Not because I'm a jackass, but because she won't want the fuss. She doesn't flaunt things. She doesn't goad people. She tells it like it is and hints at what things are that aren't. All her quips about sex and giving head and dating were all just for show. Something she put on to fit into a group that lives half its life with sex on display.

She grew up in the club. Saw more of it than most people do in their entire lifetimes, and she isn't even a quarter of her way through life yet. She did what she had to do. Either to blend or survive, I don't know.

But she doesn't need to pretend anymore. Not because I popped her cherry, but because I won't let her just exist anymore. We all saw her. We *dealt* with her. But just like Abigail, we kept her at arm's length. She got close to us because of time and space, not because we let her in. Not really. Not like how some of the old ladies are.

And that stops now.

The very thought makes me smirk. She sees it and must think I'm challenging her still. Calling her bluff. I'm about to step back and just say fuck the blue balls, but she surprises me.

She sinks to her knees, pulling my pants down as she goes.

Finding the flap on my briefs, she guides her skilled fingers in and pulls me out. Her hand runs up and down my length, and her thumb traces around the ridge at the top before moving over my slit.

"Try not to come too fast," she says a second before she takes me all the way into her mouth and chokes, coughing and gagging but not releasing me.

I lock my knees to keep myself standing. Her kisses are amazing. Having sex with her is phenomenal. But her mouth? I've never had anything better in my life.

If she's done this before, I don't care. If she hasn't, I also don't give a flying rat's ass. Skill or no, having her gag on my dick has me counting in Spanish, backward, to keep from blowing my load.

Her warning might have been another bullshit move or the warning it was meant to be. I can't tell right now. I can't tell anything. All I know is I don't want her to stop. I *can't* have her stop. I might die if she does.

I grab her head and hold tight, not directing her, but just needing something to make sure I'm in the present and didn't die and go to heaven.

I'm so fucking close that I start chanting her name. The name of my old lady.

"Jesus, Peaches. Your mouth... fuck. So good, Peaches. Don't stop. Never stop. Oh, Peaches."

But then she does.

She pulls off my cock, rolls away, and is by my door a second later.

"What the hell?" My dick is still out of my pants, and I shimmy to turn. I'm confused, turned on, and starting to get mad. Really mad.

"What? You got what you wanted. I sucked your cock."

Kooper

I grind my teeth together. Never in my life have I been denied before. And from the smirk on her face, she knows that.

"What? Used to getting everything you want? Welcome to my world, asshole. Taught to me by this club." She gestures to the walls surrounding us. "You get half-truths. And just when you think you're about to find peace, someone comes along and takes it away, leaving you standing there with your pants down and fucked over but with zero satisfaction."

She unlocks the door and opens it a second before she's out of the room. I'm tucking myself back into my damn pants with the door still open as I chase after her.

"Ruby," I bellow down the hall.

She turns to glare at me for a second before she rounds the corner. I quicken my pace, knowing she ain't stopping for me anytime soon.

"Nat, we're going. For real this time." She gets to her friend and picks up her bag.

"Where're you going?" I ask. Half the damn club is here, and not a single person seems to be doing anything but looking at us.

"To see Dad. Like a good little cunt." She flinches at the word she hates more than she hates asparagus. And she really doesn't like that stuff.

"Your dad?" Nat questions.

"Oh, right," she huffs and looks around. Seeing Casper, she holds his gaze while she talks to her roommate. "You don't know. Well, it's not a secret anymore." Casper shakes his head, which she ignores as she turns back to look at Nat. "Dad's alive. Just got out of a coma. It was all a cover-up concocted by this place." Another hand movement to show which place, and with whom the blame sits. All of us. "He's out of it now. Everything is fine, except he doesn't remember me or Mom and wants to get his dick wet. So I've got to go play nice with him and his new side dish to make sure the club's *beloved* brother doesn't get worse or something. 'Cause we wouldn't want him to suffer. Who gives a fuck about anyone else as long as he's alive and kicking."

"Ruby," Casper barks. His face is as red as a beet.

She turns and has her mouth open to snap back, but Billy draws her attention as she walks into the clubhouse with Jack in tow. I shake my head, anticipating the shitstorm we're about to have as the tide shifts and Ruby's anger moves to a new target.

"Woo, did it just get chilly in here, or is it me?" Jack half jokes as she looks around and sees everyone not talking, with Casper and Ruby standing on either side of the room and me halfway between.

"I think it might be me," Billy says, as she doesn't miss the glare Ruby isn't hiding that well each time she looks at her. "Something on your mind, Ruby?" Girl definitely has balls, thick as steel. Not only for having to deal with Casper and his dominant ass, but to call out Ruby right away and not wait for some of the tension to die down.

"A lot, actually. But since I'm not fucking the president, I have to keep my mouth shut. Unlike you," Ruby sneers.

Billy looks at Casper, and it seems Ruby isn't the only one mad at her. Casper's glare doesn't dissipate as he

Kooper

catches his old lady's eye, and I see Billy's shoulders drop as if realizing it.

"Law, right? Rue say something?" No one nods, but the unspoken is enough to say it all. She takes a step in Ruby's direction. "Look, I'm sorry—"

"Save it. Tell your sad story to someone who gives a damn. And that ain't me."

"Hey," Jack barks and steps in front of her sister as if she needs to protect her. When we all know that no one will lay a hand on an old lady. Even Ruby. She might want to hit Billy, or all of us, but she won't. "Billy only told me and Rue to have us keep an eye out. Not only on your dad, but on you too. You've got people after you who you need to watch out for. We made the call. Not the Crazy Eights. They would have told us to forget the protection and care about ourselves. We have our own threats to worry about. Bigger than some girl's daddy who doesn't love her anymore. So get off your fucking high horse and look around. This place, all these people? They did it to protect you. To care for you. You think they do that easily? Fuck no. You think they care about me? About Rue? Hell, Billy would be out on her ass if she wasn't with Casper. No one in this place cares if we live or die, but they do you. So stop throwing your pity party and do the right thing."

"Right thing?" Ruby's head twitches as she looks around at us—at all of us—nodding as she goes.

Jack, a bit harsh in her words, said what's been said behind closed doors. What's been whispered about. Not by me, but by others. And those who don't meet Ruby's eye as she looks around are the ones who agree. And Ruby sees that. She sees everything.

"Right. Got it. Let's go, Nat." She starts to walk away. "Give my room to someone who matters. Give it to Jack for all the fucks I give. I won't be back," she tosses over her shoulder as she reaches the door.

"Ruby," I call out to her as she pushes the door open and Nat goes through first.

She looks at me, and I see the sadness in her eyes. "What? No Peaches?" She shakes her head as if she's disappointed in me. "How quickly the tides turn. Find someone else to fuck, Koop, because it ain't me. Not anymore."

With those parting words, she walks out, and the door swings closed.

I stare at the door, hoping for her to come back through it as I feel every eye in this place turn on me.

"You fucked Ruby?" I hear the anger in Bass's voice as I look at him, then see half the damn brothers rise, one after another. Their anger is clear in their unison against me.

I don't deny it. And they don't need me to say it.

And when the first fist comes at me from the VP, I welcome it.

Chapter 32—Ruby

"Are you okay?" Nat's hesitation is clear. Well, that, and it took her five minutes to say anything after we both got into the car and drove away from a place I once called my home. Not anymore.

I shake my head. "Not even close."

"Yeah. Didn't think so." I see her look out the window from the corner of my eye. But she must have decided the silent game is no longer needed, as she turned back to ask, "Is your dad really alive?"

"Yup." I pop the *P* more out of the anger still coursing through my veins than to emphasize the point.

"And did you really just... break up with Kooper?"

"Yup," I say with a tired sigh. But is it really a breakup if we were never actually together? Sure, we've been together for years, but not *together* together till last night. A long night, but it was only one night. We shared a kiss before that. Some meals too.

Wait. Were Kooper and I dating? Thinking back on it, every time we were together, it was more than just a check-in. Check-ins don't take people out for dinner and pay. Check-ins don't play video games with them on a Saturday night while their boys are out partying.

Fuck. I think we were dating. I was just too stupid to notice.

"Damn."

"That about sums it up," I mutter.

I can't believe I didn't see it before. Next thing I know, I'll find out my favorite gamer is him. Wouldn't that be funny?

Fuck. The name is Bowser. It is him.

I'm such an idiot.

I shake my head at myself and everything else. I was so wrapped up in expecting people to tell me the truth that I overlooked the lies. "I'm over the secrecy. All the lies. The half-truths. I can't take it anymore. So if you've got something to say, now is the time to say it."

I glance at her and hold her eyes for longer than I should while driving before I look back at the road. But I don't miss her shaking her head out of the corner of my eye.

"Good."

The rest of the drive is quiet as we head to the hospital. I don't know why I came. Maybe because I really am a glutton for punishment. I know Dad hasn't gotten his memory back yet. I would have been called, despite everything going on.

But I still want to see him. I might not talk to him, but I will see him. I just haven't decided what I want to do yet.

Nat follows me into the hospital and down all the corridors that lead to my dad's room. King's sitting outside, so Mad Max must be in there. He gives me a chin lift but says nothing. Either someone texted him about what went down, or he just remembers my original decree. I don't want to talk to any of them. Now more than ever.

Kooper

As I get close to the door, the handle moves, and out walks the nurse. *The* nurse. One look at her has me spinning on my heels.

"I'm not trying to replace your mom," she calls out, obviously not caring if she causes a scene or even loses her job over this with all the rules about decorum and other professional bullshit they always seem to have in workplaces.

She's bold. Bold enough to get me to turn back and put my hands on my hips before I reply. "How can you? He doesn't even recall who she is. If there is no Mom, there is no me."

She opens her mouth to protest, I'm sure. To give me some sad little speech about how my dad needs me and he'll remember. How everything will be okay. But it's all a lie. Complete and utter shit.

I take three steps and get right in her face, jabbing my finger at the door that's just to our left. "And there sure ain't any him. Not in there. No Dad. Only Law. Because if that was the man I knew, my dad, he would never, ever, look at another woman." I look her over like the trash she is. Or what I want her to be. Her makeup isn't harsh like the vamps. She's not slutting it up or even attempting to make this about her. But I can't look past my own anger to see her as anything but not being my mom. "He loved Mom so much that even in death, she was his whole world. You aren't her. And him?" I point to his room. "He isn't him either. He died, just like I did."

The door opens on my last words, and I see Mad Max on the other side. Not only him, but my dad, who's sitting up in bed and staring at me. He heard me. I'm sure the whole damn place heard me. Because when I talk lately, everyone else shuts up and listens. Swell time for that to start. Why couldn't it have been sooner? When I gave a damn. Or had the strength to, anyhow. Now, all I want to do is go home, crawl under the covers, and never come out. Ever.

"Let's go, Nat. This is another place I no longer need to be."

I decide on the way out that I need to get Nat a gift. At the very least, I'll spring for her favorite pizza. With all the shit going on today, she keeps going, standing beside me the whole way. She doesn't say a lot, but I don't need words. I just need someone to be with me and walk when I say walk. Might seem like I'm in need of a control thing, and maybe I am. Everything else is spiraling; I have to know that I can get something my way. No matter how childish and barbaric it sounds that bossing around my roommate makes me feel as if I have some control in life.

As we pass through the glass doors, I see Atom walking up.

"Surprised you're not Koop."

The guy really doesn't know when to stop coming after me. I can't tell if I like that or not. Okay, fine, I do. But right now, I'm happy it isn't him I have to deal with. Instead, I get to deal with a biker who knows I slept with someone in the club. Not my finest moment, telling everyone. But again, I'm over the secrets.

"He's getting his ass kicked for touching Law's kid."

"What?" I look at Natalie as if she'd have some clue on how that makes sense, but her mouth is hanging open just as much as mine is. "We're adults. We can do whatever the fuck we want. It's not like he did anything when I was underage or some shit."

Kooper

He crosses his arms in indifference. "Doesn't matter. He knows he can't touch you."

"Seriously? Dad has no clue who I am. The rule is null and void."

"He might not, but we do. He went against Law. He went against us all. You really think we think so little of you that we wouldn't care if some guy touched you? You don't think we wouldn't have vetted him? Like we did with every other guy who's come close to you? But he was in the club. *Pretending* to be your protection, when in fact he was just playing daddy to a girl who didn't know better. Sick fuck will get everything he deserves. He manipulated you."

"He was protecting me. And he didn't make me do anything. No one can."

"Says the woman who's here at the hospital when she said she was done." He raises an eyebrow to prove a point. The only point I see him proving is that he's an ass.

"Hey, Natalie." He tosses her a chin lift, and the surprised look on her face is almost comical. Not sure if it's because of what he just said to me, calling me out on doing everything I denied earlier, or that he remembered her name. I know they've met before, but I don't think they've said more than a handful of words to each other.

Hearing about Kooper is not helping me figure anything out. I'm confused about my feelings. Do I like him? Have we been dating? Was I manipulated?

Is Kooper my daddy?

Okay, that last thought can get fucked. I'm not some submissive type. I don't need a man like that. Having him take care of me in his way... was... nice, somewhat. But that

347

doesn't make him my daddy. I'm not about to be sucking on a bottle or wearing diapers.

Get a fucking clue, woman.

My brain is screaming at me from one side and yelling at me from another. I squeeze the bridge between my nose to quell the headache. I've read enough and seen enough to know there's more than one type of "daddy" out there, but now is not the time to focus on that.

Especially with Abigail, aka Rue, bouncing up with a smile on her face.

"What's up, peeps?"

"Get fucked."

I turn at King's tone behind me and sigh as he joins our little group outside the hospital. Thankfully, it's just him and not Mad Max or that fucking nurse.

"Already did that. You said never again unless I was willing to vamp it up, and that's one thing I won't do."

Okay, what? My head turns so fast to Abigail that I feel it kink a bit. Her smugness reminds me of my own, but somehow I've lost mine over the last few days. Maybe she and I are more alike than I want to admit. And despite me hating everything Jack said, maybe she was right. Maybe I do need to get over a few things.

"Look out!" Nat shouts, then shoves us all apart.

I look at her and then feel things fly by my face. Someone pushes me down to the ground as I look the other way and see a white van with the bay doors open and guns firing. I can't even scream, the air knocked out of me from the impact.

Kooper

"Stay down," Atom orders, and I do, rolling onto my stomach and moving behind one of the large square cement planters that line the hospital entrance.

I look over and see Nat hunkered down two planters over, covering her head with her arms as she takes the bulk of the shots.

Atom fires and starts running to her only to get hit. He moves as if his shoulders are dancing back and forth before he collapses to the ground. Nat screams as she stares at him, and I lose my hearing as a loud ringing takes over.

I look the other way and see both Abigail and King firing back. They seem to be shouting, but I don't know what they're saying.

I need to help. I need to do something. Something other than just watching this happen.

Looking back at Nat, I decide I have to save her. She isn't part of this. She's just here because of me. Like everyone else.

But a moment later, I see her getting grabbed. I shout, but then I feel arms on me as someone comes up from behind. I elbow them, and they loosen their grip. I wiggle out of their grasp till I get pulled back and backhanded across the face with enough force to push my head to the side. I watch helplessly as Abigail stands, shoots, and then falls.

Not like Atom, though, who's bleeding out. Or maybe he's dead already. There's so much blood under him as he lies on the concrete.

Why isn't there anyone helping us? Why hasn't someone come out of the hospital?

Where are the Harley engines that come to the rescue? Where is everyone?

Abigail crawls for cover, dragging herself along the concrete.

King is still shooting, and when Nat and I get pulled into the van, I see him make a break for Atom and pull him inside the hospital.

Once I'm inside the van, it's like a vacuum. But instead of removing the noise, it all comes back. I hear everything. The screams. The shouts. The shooting.

And Abigail.

Pleading. Begging for King to come back. To help her.

But she can't see what I can.

She doesn't know what I know.

That he's club.

And club looks after club. Period.

So while she might cry out for help, he's just looking out the side of the door, watching and waiting. Not to help but to get the license plate. Something to help him find out who did this to his brother.

Not for me. Not for Abigail or Nat. But for Atom. For the Hound who's bleeding out.

Because he's club.

And I'm not. I'm just a girl. Not good enough for the club. Not good enough for my dad.

Not good enough for anything.

Chapter 33—Kooper

I know the second she's taken. Not only because my phone is chirping like a damn alarm, but because the siren goes off in the clubhouse the second shit goes down.

Mad Max called it in, said shots were fired at the hospital. No one thinks twice about hopping onto their bikes and going.

But I already know we're too late. Too much time has gone by. If things were okay, my team would have told me. Them not calling is all the information I need. Still, I'm not prepared to see it.

The Crazy Eights are on the scene too. I see them, Jack and Billy, run down one hallway, while I go another. Word is that Law is fine. No one came that way, but Mad Max still has shit locked down. A few brothers head to his room anyway. The blood trail I'm following is from another brother. Atom. He got hit multiple times from what I heard over comms.

I'm stopped by a wall of vests, but my eyes go to King. He sees me coming and moves in front to get to me quicker.

"Five, maybe six people came out of a van. No plates. It was white with a blue racing stripe. Nothing on the outside to distinguish it. Went south at the entrance. Told Flint what I could."

I nod. I get it. Even with the call, the van was gone before Flint could track it. The satellites weren't in the positions we needed.

"Casper." I look over at the prez, who's talking to General. He holds up a finger, and I wait.

"Atom took three shots through and through. The fourth is dug in deep. Going in now. Should be out soon," General tells Casper.

A day without losing a brother is always a good day.

But losing Ruby? My Peaches? Fuck it all to hell.

The boys are still riled from earlier. They got their punches in. Not all, but a few. I let Bulldog, Chains, and even Bass have a hit. When a line formed, I punched back. I'm not about to get a beatdown over falling for some girl. I can understand the first few hits. I get it. She's family. And despite everything, they think I fucked her over. Actually, I don't know what they think. They just got mad at her leaving, and, instead of taking it out on themselves, I was the easy target.

A willing one, because the woman was right. I should have just claimed her, then and there. Should have done anything, even groveled, to keep her there. But I didn't. Not sure if it's because I still don't think I deserve her after all the shit that went down. After I wanted to use her to get the presidency.

I saw her as a thing to use. To dispose of after I got what I wanted. But somehow along the way, I fell in love with her. Not the sweet kind that gives flowers and recites poetry. The hard kind. The gritty kind. The kind people burn bridges for and end up locked behind bars. The obsessive kind.

Kooper

I was shook when she left. When she called out what we did and threw it away so quickly. In one breath, she acknowledged what we had and tossed it aside. In that moment of weakness was when my brothers attacked. Just three times. Enough for me to get my head on straight and tell them to fuck off. But enough for the damage to be done already.

She's gone.

"Casper," I say again, and he looks at me. He knows what I want. He got the same debrief from King like I did just seconds before.

"Yeah, I'll ask Billy, see what C8 can do."

I nod because I appreciate it. It means the club will owe the Crazy Eights again. That they'll have something over on us like before. When all this started and old ladies became part of the damn club and not just a fable a vamp dreamed about when she was in a brother's arms for a minute.

"Like fuck you'll ask us."

We all turn at Jack's words as she storms down the hall. Billy's close by her, but not with as much pep. Tears are leaking down her face, and I know they ain't for our own.

"You had one job. One goddamn job." Jack gets close to Casper and pushes him.

One push, and that's all it takes for another brother, Walker, to get in front of her and push her back. For the brothers to realize that we're no longer friends. No one touches, let alone pushes, a president.

Walker holds her back, but I see the struggle as she keeps trying to get out of his hold.

"You won't get shit from us. None of you. You can suck a dick for all we care."

"Settle the fuck down," Casper booms, then looks at his woman. "Krista?" His voice is softer as he uses her real name, something I know isn't used often between them unless it's just them. Or in sweet moments behind the bar or in a dark corner when they think it's the two of them against the world. But the stricken look on her face has him coming over to her and cradling her in his arms as he tries to get an idea of what's going on.

"She's dead. Rue's dead."

Shit. This complicates things. Of course, the Crazy Eights will be out for blood. They lost one of their own. But maybe we can pool our resources. Use that hatred to find my girl.

"We said we would work with you. We said we would do shit your way. You were told that the only thing we wanted was the same protection for our people as you gave the others," Jack snaps.

"We did." Casper looks confused, and Jack turns to King, whose face is stoic as he looks on.

"Did you? 'Cause the security feed I saw showed you leaving her there to bleed out while you helped your friend. Even after they left, you stayed away."

She pushes Walker's arms off her and takes a few steps away, then comes back. Walker holds his hands out wide to block her from coming close to any other brother, but that doesn't keep her from pointing her finger right at King as she speaks.

"Her death is on you. Hers and your kid's."

Kooper

We all turn to King. He looks stricken as his eyes go wide.

"That's right. She was pregnant. Your kid, King. *Yours*. No one else's. And you left him to die. Just like her. The Crazy Eights are done with the Hounds of the Reaper. You need to find someone? Find them your fucking selves."

She turns and walks away, muttering and cursing as she goes. Billy turns her head into her man, away from the rest of us, and cries. We can't hear it, but we see the shakes.

I look at King and feel sadness. Dread. The guy had no clue. None of us knew they had hooked up. Was it before she told us who she was or after?

Does it matter?

King looks at us. None of us have judgment in our eyes. How can we? This shit is serious.

"I didn't know," he says with a shake of his head. "I... I didn't know." He turns and walks a bit, shaking his head. Then he slams a fist into the wall, smashing through the plaster. It comes out bloody, but he doesn't even stop for aid, just pushes off a nurse who comes to help and walks out. Walker and a few of the other brothers follow.

No one left behind. No matter how fucked up that is to say or think right now, it's the truth. Hounds don't do shit alone.

"Casper." This time when I say his name, I give him the time he needs to pull away from his woman and look at me. I don't know what this will mean for them. And honestly, at this second, I don't care. I need my girl. I need to have her in my arms. Till I do, not much else matters. "I need a few brothers to come check on my team."

I'm asking for help. I'm letting him know that I have others. Others I trust beyond the Hounds to help. Does that make me an outsider? Someone not fit for the club because of who I ask for help and who I don't?

I see the anger flare in his eyes before he nods. But that look lets me know the conversation isn't done. That there will be a shit ton more to talk about when we all get the chance to catch a fucking breath.

"Bass, Gator, Jumper, go with him. Report back once it's done."

I nod and head out, not questioning who he chose. I get it. Gator's good with tech. Bass knows his weapons. And Jumper is crazy enough to survive anything thrown his way. He jumps off buildings for fun. Going to look at the damage to my team and what I might have caused this club is a walk in the park compared to what he's used to.

Finding my team is easy. I track them just like I do with Peaches. But unlike Peaches, whose phone was tossed before she even got into the van, they just left my guys' phones next to their bodies.

"Jesus," Jumper says as he takes in the scene.

My team had the trackers too. They followed her from the club to the hospital. They must have expected her to be there for a while, like she usually is. That explains why they're both on the roof across the street.

Doesn't explain the other body, though. But if you take in every part of the scene—the carnage, the empty shell

Kooper

casings—you get the picture. Someone was up here to take out Ruby. Or to just be the eye in the sky. They weren't expecting my guys to show. To deem that the same building had the best vantage point to see who was coming and going from the hospital.

I check one of my guys, then the next. My brothers stand around and assess while I confirm what's obvious. My team is dead.

"This the whole team?" Bass asks.

I shake my head. "Two more. One got called away to do another gig, and the other had the day off. Fuck."

I stand and kick at the gravel on the roof. This wasn't how it was supposed to go down. My team was good. We survived worse than this in the Middle East.

"They trained?" Gator questions with an eyebrow raise, and it pricks at my anger.

"Watch your mouth, boy."

He holds up his hands in surrender. "No mouth, just questions. If they were just some flyby boys, this can be tossed aside as a sloppy mess. If they were trained, then we have to assume that there was more than one guy up here to get the drop on your team. And if that's the case, we might need to think on whether they knew about them before they came up here."

"What are you saying?" Jumper asks as he kneels beside the guy I don't know. One who must have been with the team that nabbed Ruby.

"This was planned. They've been watching her. And they're good. So good that you and your team didn't notice. They saw her leave, saw an opportunity, and took it."

I nod but then shake my head. "These guys trained with me. No way they got taken out by a rookie."

"Exactly. This was planned and well organized. King picked a fucking great time to screw us all over," Bass mutters as he steps over a body and goes to look at something across the way.

Having the Crazy Eights would have helped us. They have resources. They can get into places—*have* gotten into places—without others noticing. They play at being weak, exploiting a person's desire to look away from the uncomfortable, like someone with a disability or smelling of garbage. They hide that way. They do it well too. We never saw it coming when they pulled that shit on us. And from the OHH debriefing forms I've looked into, they still make it work.

"There a reason why you picked them?" Bass stands tall and nods to the bodies on the ground. "Why you asked for their help and not ours?"

The club. The brotherhood.

"You know why." I hold his stare, which isn't easy to do. Hounds have an ability to make anyone uncomfortable just by looking at them. Even another Hound.

"You ever think that was your sign? That if you had to hide it from us, you shouldn't be messing around in it?"

Bass, like everyone else, has a right to what he feels. Hell, I know he was close to my girl. He's always seen her as a baby sister and ragged on her enough that it was a mutual thing for her. He has a right to have thoughts, feelings, and whatnot. But he doesn't get a say in how I feel. In *what* I feel.

"You might think you know what happened, but you don't," I say with a shake of my head. "It was never meant to

Kooper

be like this. What I feel for her...." I hang my head as I put my hands on my hips and look at the bodies. "It didn't start out that way. She was a job. Just a job. They were called in when I wanted a night off. I still did the job, just outsourced when I got tired, or bored. But then...."

"Things changed." This from Gator, and I see that he's starting to get it. He's newer to the club. Prospected a few years back. Not as much history as some brothers have with Ruby, but still close. They all got close to her. She was around. She was nice. She fit in with the old ladies. Still does.

I nod. "Yeah. Things changed." I look back at Bass. "I needed them to protect her when the club couldn't. Or wouldn't."

Bass looks away first, then turns back and nods. He understands now.

"What now?" This from Jumper.

I don't answer, because I don't know. Hunt, obviously. But where? Which direction? We're blind.

"We call our friends." Bass pulls my attention, along with Gator's and Jumper's. "We pool our resources. We do what we have to do. Ruby's family. She might not like us right now, but she is."

The boys nod and pull out their phones to make calls. Bass pats me on the back as he walks by.

"Don't worry, brother. We'll get your old lady back. Kicking and screaming if we have to."

While I appreciate his call that I'm still his brother, I doubt his words. Getting Peaches back won't be easy. And there's no doubt that she's doing a fair amount of kicking and screaming. The girl doesn't like to be pinned down. From my experience, she's the one who does the holding down.

And I'm the only one who gets to enjoy that. I promised myself I would be her first and last. And I don't break promises.

I break necks.

Chapter 34—Ruby

Have you ever been hungry? Like you could throw up from craving food so much? That type of hunger when you question if you can feel full from eating your fingernail?

I've never gone without before. I've been hungry, sure. Skipped meals here and there because I was busy and wanted to push through. But I always knew at the end I could eat. That there would be something to fill my stomach.

Now I don't know when it will come.

Once we were in the van, I fought. I fought long and hard and got beaten down easily. Everything hurt—my face, my stomach, my legs. I was kicked and punched so much that I feared I would die in that van. But I didn't know then that I would soon wish it were true.

Someone was mad. And they took that out on me. But I never saw a face. Never heard a word. They wore ski masks and spoke so quietly that I never got anything more than a word here and there. And when I did think I heard something, it was in Spanish. Something I never learned. I chose French in high school because I liked to talk about pastries and say I was speaking in French when I ordered them.

I don't know how long we were in the van. Seemed like days. Natalie and I were both stuck with something at one point, and I only remember flashes of what happened between then and now. I think we were put on some kind of cargo plane. I remember looking out a window at some point and seeing trees from high up like we were flying. But the rest of it was just being carried from one place to another. And not in friendly arms. Arms that had hands with roaming fingers that dug deep, and when I pushed them off, their owner's deep laugh rolled through me before I was tossed onto the ground. I banged my head more times than I can count. I don't even know if I *can* count anymore or if it's just brain damage.

Because if there is damage, that would explain what I'm seeing. Or what I'm not. Just gray. Everything is gray. The walls. The floor. Even my skin looks gray.

Nat doesn't look any better than me. She got hit a few times, based on the swelling on her face, but I didn't see when it happened. They threw us both in here, wherever here is.

I hurt still, but it seems that time has been a friend to me, as some of the swelling has gone down enough that I can open both eyes. After we got here, the beating I had in the van seemed liked child's play compared to what I was put through. And for no other reason than they could.

"You okay, Nat?" It's a stupid thing to say, but I need something stupid. Something to ground me. Anything to keep me focused on this and not the pain in my stomach.

"No," she croaks out, then licks her lips only to wince at the crack in them. "You?"

"Same girl. Same." I place my head against the wall and pull my knees up to rest my arms on. There isn't an ounce of hospitality in here. Not even a piss bucket. Not that I have to go. You need food and water for that. I've had none since the breakfast tacos.

Kooper

Just the thought brings a rumble from my stomach. I ignore it. Or try to.

"It goes away." I turn to Nat and give her a questioning look. "The hunger. Eventually, it goes away."

"How would—" I don't finish my sentence as a flap at the bottom of the door opens, and a tray is pushed through. Two bowls of soup and what looks like bread sit on it. The smell coming off it is better than the smell in here, but not by much.

I look at Nat, who looks at me. We wait, and then I move to the door. I look it over and reach out tentatively to touch the flap. My hand shakes as the fear that it'll be snatched up the second I get too close to it rises. We didn't hear any footsteps leaving. But we didn't hear them come either.

I push on the wood, and it doesn't budge. I try to use the tips of my fingers to pry it up, but there's no give. They locked it somehow. I look at the food, and my stomach gurgles once more.

"Hungry?" I ask Nat and give her half a smile.

She shakes her head, fear clear on her face. She must be thinking what I am—that it's poison. Something to take us out. I'm tempted. More tempted than anything in my life. More than when Dad told me girls couldn't ride motorcycles, and then he left the keys to his bike just sitting on the table. I would have taken it out that night if Mom hadn't come in and noticed. But Mom isn't here to tell me it's a bad idea. She's dead. Like Dad. Like I will be, too, if I don't eat.

"Fuck it," I say and grab the bread. Slowly, I bring it to my mouth.

"Don't eat it."

I look at Nat, but her eyes are as wide as mine.

That voice.

It wasn't hers.

"Who's that? Who's there?" I stand and walk to the wall. The one Nat was leaning on, opposite the one I was at. There's a grate there, above my head.

"Don't eat it."

"Eat what?"

"The bread. They lace it with something. One minute you're awake, the next you're not. It knocks you out."

"For how long?"

"Don't know. Seems like a second, but then you wake up and feel cold, as if the sun went down."

There aren't any windows, but there's a light. Nothing bright to push the gray away, but enough to see what's in front of you. But I get what she's saying. I feel hot in here. Sweat trickles down my spine. Not blazing, but not comfortable. If it feels like this in what I can only assume is the daytime, then nights would feel considerably cooler. It's not much, but at least it's a way to track time in the outside world.

Nat's still sitting, watching me as I stand beside her. I look at the vent, then back at her. I press my finger to my lips to keep her quiet, then gesture for her to come closer. She scoots quietly over, and I point to myself and then to the ceiling. She nods in understanding as she stands and braces her legs before cupping her hands together over her knee.

I grab her shoulders, put one foot in her grasp, and bounce. One, two, and on three, I rise and Nat pushes me

Kooper

high. I bring my other foot to her shoulder and stand on them as I reach for the vent. I can see through it, as it's mostly just a hole between the two rooms covered by a small grate like you find at the bottom of a shower drain.

The room is similar in every way to ours. Nothing on the floor. No window to look out of. Everything's the same, but there's only one girl in this one, not two.

She's walking in a circle. Barefoot, like us. They took my boots and boot knife the second they got us into the van. Well, after the first beating.

She's wrapped in leather pants that are fitted to her legs and a tank top that's tight and low. She looks like a vamp. Bet she even paid for her chest. The long black hair against her pale skin probably looks sexy as hell if she curls the ends and has the right amount of eyeliner to go with it.

But that's not what's happening. Her hair looks limp. Dirt covers a lot of her. And her mascara—well, if she had any makeup, it's gone by now.

She looks just as scared as we do, but strong enough to speak up, and she's not leaning against the wall and wallowing in pity like me. I don't begrudge myself for doing it. I'm strong; I know I am. But I was taken. Saw people I know get shot and probably killed. I was beaten. Drugged. Flown somewhere, and that can't be good. Hunger was the easiest thing to hyperfocus on, and now I have another.

Like what got her grabbed. Was this all random or selective?

"Hi."

She stops at my voice and looks at her grate, seeing my face. She backs up a step to get more of a view.

"Hi." Her smile is brief and tentative. Like mine.

"Do you know where we are?"

She shakes her head.

I lick my lips as I try to think beyond my panic. "How long have you been here?"

She shakes her head. "I don't know. What day is it?"

"I don't know. It was the twenty-fifth when we, um… when we were taken."

"Okay, I guess a few weeks, then. It was Valentine's Day when I woke to… well, this."

I look down at Nat. Not because I'm worried she can't hold me, but because I want to make sure she heard. The look on her face as she stares at me lets me know she did. And that she fears for us too.

I swallow and look back at the other woman. I don't want to crush her hope, but she needs to know. "It's April."

"What?"

"April 25. Before… before all this."

She walks a step back till she hits the wall and sinks to the floor. "Two months? I've been here that long?"

The strength she once had evaporates before my eyes.

"What's your name?" I ask.

Tears escape her eyes as she looks at me and doesn't even bother to wipe them away.

"Ava." She sniffs. "What's yours."

"Peaches," Nat says loud enough to carry through the vent. I look at her in confusion.

Kooper

"What?" Ava asks as if she didn't hear.

Nat's eyes narrow, and she nods at me as if to say, *"Continue with the lie."* Something in her gaze has me complying. "Peaches." I look back at Ava. "Call me Peaches. And my friend, um, I mean, her name is... Daisy."

No idea why I'm giving out a *Mario Kart* name for Nat, but she doesn't protest. Ava either doesn't see through it or just doesn't care for the mind games when she's dealing with the ultimate mindfuck of finding out how long she's been here.

Which gives me zero hope. Especially since I have no one looking. I just walked out on everyone that I ever cared about. If Dad was still... Dad, I would have an army looking for me. I would have zero doubts.

But the way I left? The things I said? To Dad? To the club? To Kooper?

That last one has me slouching, deflated, and Nat lowers me.

We've said enough to our new roommate. She doesn't seem like she's up for a little girl talk. I'm not either.

I sink to the ground and sit by Nat, our shoulders touching. I speak softly. Not only because I don't want Ava to hear, but I've run out of energy after thinking of what all I've thrown away.

"Why the lie?"

I feel her shrug, moving my shoulder as she does it, but I keep looking ahead at the blank wall in front of me.

"We don't know her. It could be a trap."

"You really think they would do that?"

Another shrug. "I don't know anything. All I know is that we're here, and we need to survive. Sometimes, most times, that comes at a price."

I turn to her, face scrunched in confusion at her words. She rolls her head on the brick wall behind her to turn my way.

"They took us. They could have killed us, but they didn't. They want us alive. Not sure for how long or why. We need to survive till we do. We need to know what they want."

"How are we going to find that out?"

She lets out a breath and looks forward again, closing her eyes as if she's about to sleep. "They always tell you. It's no fun for them if we don't know what to fear. And if their words don't do it, they'll pit our relationships against us. Both new and old. Making us fear for the other."

"How do you know all this?"

She shrugs but says nothing more.

"What about the soup?" she calls out to Ava.

There's a pause before she answers. "Not drugged, but it tastes like piss."

Nat opens her eyes and looks at me, then moves to the tray, pulling it closer to us. There's no spoon. Guess we're meant to use the bread to scoop it up. Instead, Nat leans down and smells it, then tilts to the side and gags a bit.

"Told ya," Ava says as she hears Nat. "But it's kept me alive all this time."

The hollowness in her voice brings a pit to my stomach. Will I be like that? Will I still be here in two months? Will Ava? Will Nat?

Kooper

"Right," Nat says as she squares her shoulders and pinches her nose. Then she leans close and sips at the soup. She keeps gagging but doesn't let any of it come up. I guess forcing it down once is enough for her, as she leaves the rest for me and sits back on the wall.

"Your turn," she says, and it brings a surprised smirk to my lips. One that has her lips twitching in return. Who knew we could find humor in this?

"It wasn't a lie." Her voice is soft again. Quiet, but not out of fear of Ava hearing. Just softly as if she's afraid to tell the truth.

I just stare at her, and she takes a second before she looks at me. "You really are Peaches. *His* Peaches."

I blink back the wave of emotion that her words bring. I lean over and rest my head on her legs as she runs her hands through my hair.

And then I let the tears fall. Not sobs. Just tears. Tears that I'm lost. That I'm forgotten.

But also tears that she's right, and I never got to tell Kooper that I claimed him, too, just as much as he claimed me.

Chapter 35—Kooper

Two weeks. It's been over two weeks. Sixteen days, thirteen hours, and ten minutes of pure hell, to be exact.

I've lost her. Every single favor the club has, personal or not, has been called in. Operation Hell Hound has been put on hold, as we're using all resources to track down Ruby. Mad Max has called in his father-in-law, the ex-CIA operative, but even *he* can't seem to find anything out. We even contacted the mafia for help.

Nothing.

What's worse is that her dad still has no clue who she is. Maybe that's a good thing. It spares him this feeling of helplessness. Something I've never had before. The guys with old ladies keep telling me they know what I'm dealing with. That I just need to have faith.

Funny, I'm pretty sure we all said the same thing to Ruby about her dad's memory coming back the day she went missing.

But with each hour, each day that passes without a single speck of hope, the fear builds. That my once perfectly imperfect Peaches is lost. And I'm going to be lost without her. Forever.

"Kooper," Mad Max calls from across the yard. He's standing with his girl, and they make no move to come to me.

I mosey over to them after I toss my cigarette. Been smoking a bit more lately. I see Mama Bear's worry each time

Kooper

she catches me lighting one, but she knows to keep her trap closed. Smoking brings me out of the clubhouse. And usually if I'm out, then I'm driving around looking for my girl. Taking these few moments, as unhealthy as they are for me, is at least giving me some time to stop running around and finding nothing at each end of the trail.

"Yeah?"

"Think you can give Fairy a lift to the bakery? She put in an order for some fresh shit and needs to pick it up. I've got to head to the hospital."

We've all been taking turns watching over Atom. He's recovering, but slowly. The guy got lucky. One bullet can kill you, but sometimes four just leave scars.

Law's out of the hospital now. He's been at his place and the club a few times. With everything going on, it's hard to welcome him back in when he doesn't have a connection like the rest of us. Like he should. He stays away more to ease the guilt on our faces than his.

As for the brothers, none are taking things for granted. Protection duty is on all of them till this is sorted. Hell, Mad Max was like this with his old lady even before this shit. Always wanting her covered when he wasn't there, even if she can handle herself like a pro with her throwing knives—something I've seen her carry more and more lately. I'm not sure if that's at her request or his, but it's something I wish I had Ruby learn how to use. Anything, really, that could have been used as a weapon to help her.

"Sure." I catch the keys he tosses me to one of the club trucks we keep around for shit that needs moving.

He grabs his woman and, in no hurry, seals his lips to hers. She hops into his arms easily as he lifts her under her thighs. She's tiny compared to him, and this isn't something new. I look away while they groan and moan into each other.

Another time, my dick would have taken notice. What can I say? If something sounds like porn, my body reacts. Even if I ain't interested in the parties involved. But without Peaches, nothing is fulfilling. I can't even seem to get hard enough to jack off.

Guess I finally understand how Law felt. Well, when he remembered Special K. He always said he never needed another woman once she died. That he had enough memories to satisfy him. Though maybe it wasn't the spank bank keeping him out of the dating life but the fact that without her here, he just didn't have a desire to get hard. She took a part of him—the part that can make life—away when she went.

Like Ruby has.

"Be safe," Mad Max says as he sets her down, and her head twitches to mold to the hand he places on her cheek.

"We're in the truck, and it has the best features for a collision, should one occur, with multiple airbags and a steel frame to keep from tipping. It also has protective glass to prevent bullets or other things from getting at me through the window."

"I know." He doesn't laugh at her. None of us do. It's just Fairy being Fairy. Saying the facts and not giving in to the emotion behind things.

He nods at me and then walks back into the clubhouse.

Kooper

I head toward the trucks, using the fob to start it up before we get close to verify which one it is. I don't mind doing side shit like this. It keeps me busy. The first five days, I was riding everywhere. Didn't sleep. Hardly ate. It was Mama Bear who sat me down and said that if I was going to kill myself, I should just let the brothers do it already so they could plan the funeral and get back to work. She was pissed. At me. At the club. Everyone. Ruby called Mama Bear her sister once. Special K was a savior to Mama Bear before she became part of the club and even before Mama Bear knew anything about this place. But they had a connection. One Ruby used and embraced like a true sister. And that sister was mad.

And she let me have it. Mostly calling me stupid if she thought her sister, my woman, was going to be okay with coming home and seeing me as just half a man. Someone lost in the hunt and barely recognizable.

So I ate. I slept. I spoke to my brothers. I did things asked of me. But I still hunted. I still thought about her. I did everything for her. I called the school and put a hold on her shit. Got her and Nat's apartment sorted. Had the guys take out her trash and clean out her fridge. I buried my friends and brought in my others. They're with us, but not in the club. I keep looking at data, at all the feeds, over and over. I have Flint send me everything he goes through each day, and I go over it again.

No one asks me to stop. They know I won't listen. I barely listened to Mama Bear, but she got through to me when the others didn't. Not because she begged me to stop. Not because she told me to. It was because she said I was doing it for my old lady, and *she'd* be the one who would be pissed at me.

That's why I keep going. For Peaches. She might never come home. I might never find her. But it's that "might" that keeps me going. That keeps me strong. And it's also that "might" that I fear. Because a pissed-off Ruby is as terrifying as it is a turn-on.

"Hey, Fairy, Kooper." I open the truck door and look back to see Kitten running after us. "Wait up." She hops into the truck a second later. "I forgot to add a hot chocolate to the order."

The girl has a sweet tooth issue for sure. But what do I care? If driving Miss Daisy around is what's needed today, then that's what I'll do. After, I can go back to looking for my girl.

The drive takes no time. We don't have a ton of variety in our town. A few things here and there, enough to not be upset that we live out here. Couple of places to eat, a few chain restaurants, but only one bakery on this side of town. And the only decent one in a fifty-mile radius.

A spot is open in the front, and I pull into it. The girls give me the decency of staying in the truck while I check things out before I walk over and let them both out. They know the drill—quick and to the point. We enter the bakery with no fuss. This place knows the club, and we know it. Enough to know that we feel good here. I've also got a ten-to-one bet that Flint has already hacked their surveillance and is watching everything. Like Mad Max, he worries about his old lady and keeps a close eye on his Kitten when he can.

The owner, Dom, tells us to wait as he goes into the back for our order, and Kitten orders a very large hot chocolate at the register. When we get our shit, I walk to the door first. I don't hold anything, keeping my hands free in case I need to pull the weapon that I've kept strapped to me for days.

"It's you."

Kitten's words have me turning to see her staring at some Asian businesswoman drinking a coffee and reading a book.

"I'm sorry, do we know each other?" She gives a pleasant smile but doesn't seem to really dive into whatever Kitten is going on about.

"It's you. You're the one she yelled at."

I get closer to Kitten and put my hand on her shoulder. I don't want to be here any longer. I want to be back at the clubhouse or on the road looking for my girl, not dealing with whatever the hell this is.

She shrugs me off instead and takes a seat at the woman's table. To her credit, the woman doesn't demand that we leave, but she scoots back a bit as if she's afraid Kitten will spill her drink on her white blouse.

"You're the one Natalie argued with. The one she told to tell someone to mind their own business. To stop looking for her."

Now I'm looking at the other woman with both intrigue and suspicion. Is she another C8 operative?

Jack wasn't lying when she said her group was done with us. They packed up and left without a second thought. Not even a Dear John letter. Just ghosted us in the night. If it weren't for Billy still with Casper, you'd think it was all a dream. But Billy stayed. I think that means she chose him over her group. No one talks about it. Not really a conversation to bring up over a beer. Maybe a few, but I haven't been interested. Some might get drunk in a moment like this. I just get a clear head and keep it that way.

"I'm sorry, I think you have me confused with someone else." The woman closes her book and grabs her purse while standing. She's about to leave, but Kitten doesn't let her. She grasps the woman's hand so tight, I almost fear she might get sued for physical abuse.

"Please. Natalie is missing. She was taken. Along with his woman, her roommate."

They both look at me, and I just stare, not agreeing or disagreeing. I would never deny Ruby being mine, but I don't know this woman. Maybe she's in on it. Maybe everyone is. Till I clear a person, everyone is under suspicion. Ruby was here one minute, gone the next. That takes planning. Skills. And people working with them to make it happen so that the Hounds can't find them. I'm not about to say shit to people I don't know because of that.

"No one knows where she and Ruby are. If you can find them, if you know anything about where they are, please tell us. We just want them back. We just want them home."

The woman stares at Kitten for a couple of seconds before pulling her hand back and walking quickly away. Probably out of fear of us manhandling her some more.

"What was that about?" Fairy asks. She's carrying like six muffin boxes that come close to covering her entire face. We—well, Kitten—offered to help, but she insisted on doing it herself. Something about a mathematical geometry shape and the load of each box that distributed things for easier accessibility.

Kooper

"I thought she could help." Kitten's still staring out the window, as if she expects the woman to come back at any moment.

"Come on. Let's get going. Maybe your old man found something," I say to cheer her up. To cheer me up. I doubt it, but it's all I've got right now.

As we all pile back into the truck, I don't miss that four cars down is the Asian woman. Her car is still parked, but it's clear she's looking right at us. And she's on the phone. Could be calling the police. Could be calling someone else. All I know is that I still don't know shit, and staying outside a bakery is doing nothing to help.

"She's here." Kitten comes running down the hall, yelling it over and over till she finds me just as I come out of my room. I had just gotten out of the shower and heard her yelling. Never got ready so fast in my life.

"Who?" My heart stops for a second, thinking it's my girl, but Kitten must know my thoughts because she shakes her head.

"No, not Ruby. That girl we saw at the bakery yesterday. She's here. The Asian businesswoman."

"Okay...." I'm not really sure what she's going on about, but this doesn't concern me at all. I need to get back out there and find Ruby.

"Come on." For a small little thing, she has some muscle on her and pulls me along. All the way through the clubhouse and to the gate, where the other woman is waiting.

We're on lockdown for the families. No one goes out without a brother, and no one comes in who we don't know. No one.

"Hey!" She waves and smiles like we're long-lost friends. "I brought those clothes you wanted to try on." She holds up a brown sack filled with clothes.

"Ah." Kitten looks at me but moves closer to the gate. I walk with her, as I'm not about to have something happen to an old lady. No doubt Flint's watching the cameras, and with Walker on the gate, we should be good, but you never know.

The woman is smiling wide and tilts her head down as if she wants to have a private conversation. Kitten falls for it and leans in, as if they're conspiring over clothes.

"Get me inside." She says it between her teeth, her smile never faltering. Her lips never move so no one can see what she said, only hear it if they're close. And I'm close.

I look her over skeptically. She's small, but we've been fooled before by size and other things around here.

She sees my look and doesn't bat an eye at it. "I promise you, sweetie. I have exactly what you're looking for." Her words are for Kitten, but her eyes never leave mine.

A spark of hope flourishes inside me. It might be the biggest mistake I've ever made with the club, but I make the call.

"Open it up, Walker."

He doesn't hesitate, and in walks the woman, giving Kitten an enthusiastic hug. To Kitten's credit, she plays along,

Kooper

going so far as to gush over the clothes that could be in the bag and being so grateful she brought them. That she has nothing to wear or some shit.

I don't know what they say, as I'm only half listening. If the woman doesn't want to talk outside, then she must know we're being watched or something. I look at the cameras that I know Flint is using to watch us walk inside, then move my finger to my nose and rub it in a circular motion. A yellow light flickers on the camera, and I know he understood my cue to scan the surrounding area.

I hear the drones take off a second later and hope they can catch whoever's watching.

When we get inside, the woman keeps walking toward the back like she knows where she's going, which pulls a ton of attention. "All right, sweetie, I'm going to get set up in the back. I think your man is just going to love the lingerie sets we picked out for you. And don't worry, I brought some for your girls too. Why don't you go get your man, and you can try it on for him. Oh, and bring that boss man you've got around here. I heard he's got an eye for this stuff."

Kitten stills and looks at me, and I nod. Then she races down to her man's place, and I follow this woman, whoever she is, as she makes her way into our Church room. Bass and Jumper come too.

She just smiles at everyone as she dumps her bag open on the table and starts sorting things out as if she really is showing clothes. We wait a minute, maybe two, before Flint, Kitten, and Casper join us, shutting the door behind them.

"Boss man?" The woman smiles at Casper, and his eyes narrow.

I step in front of him. If she's looking to take out one of our own, she's mistaken. We'd all take a bullet for the president. Even Kitten. And when she tries to step in front of Casper, too, Flint pulls her back enough to take the head position.

"Cute. But also revealing." The woman pulls something out of her pocket and puts it on the table. It lights up from red to green.

"What's that?" Jumper asks.

"A jammer," Flint says.

"Smart man. And yes, it is. But it can also do this." She pushes another button, and a 3D blueprint of a building pops up above the table. It looks like something Tony Stark has. "We think they're being held here." She points to a room. "It's underground, but it makes the most sense. Our intel hasn't seen any women in the top facility since we started looking."

"Who the fuck are you?" Casper growls.

"Name's Gina. As far as you and I are concerned, we're friends." She tilts her head as if debating. "Well, more or less. We're not in your area to take over or make a connection. I was here only to keep an eye on one person. Nothing more."

"Natalie," Kitten says in a rushed whisper as she takes a seat.

Gina nods solemnly. "I only do eyes-on every few weeks. I've got other jobs that take me out of the area.

Kooper

Haven't seen her in a bit at the college, so I figured I'd make a play here and see if something turned up."

"How did you find her?" I ask. Her being Ruby, but she thinks it's Natalie and speaks hesitantly.

She releases an audible breath. "Without answering more questions than not, let's just say we have a way to track Natalie." When no one says anything, she shrugs and adds more. "We turned it on and got a hit on her location. Here." She gestures to the screen. "Colombia."

I fall into the nearest seat.

Colombia? South America?

Shit. No wonder we couldn't find her. She's in a different fucking country.

I look to my left and see the same disbelief on my brothers' faces. We assumed she'd be here. In America. We've got friends all over the world, but we didn't expect this.

I look back to the one person who seems to know more than we do. The one who might have an idea about how to get Natalie and Ruby out. If she's there. There's a chance they aren't together, but it's one I'm willing to take.

"What's the plan?"

Gina grins. It's borderline crazy, and I kind of like it. And her next words bring a matching one out of me.

"I've got a plane. Leaves in two hours."

Chapter 36—Ruby

This place? Not my favorite. As Kitten would say, zero stars, would not recommend.

Kitten. Jesus, I miss her. And Mama Bear, Izzy, Fairy—hell, just everyone. We've been here for… shit, I don't know how long. It seems like forever one moment and like no time has passed the next. I can't even count the length of a day by our meals, as they seem to come at different times. Sometimes it feels like we get another a minute after they take the first. Other times, it's as if I haven't eaten for days.

Same thing with the bathroom breaks. Ava said we get them, so Nat and I were never forced to just do the deed out in the open. Someone comes, grabs one of us, and takes us to a bathroom. A place with no doors or windows. Not even a sink or toilet paper. We've got a toilet that I swear has never been cleaned, but at least it flushes. And the people who take us? They watch. I gave up yelling at them to look away. It did nothing but get me a fat lip and a black eye each time.

The people are covered from head to toe. No skin is shown, so I can't tell anything about them. They dress in military getup and ski masks, like the ones the guys who nabbed us wore. Not sure if they're the same people or different ones. No way to tell. We can see their eyes, but knowing one is blue or green doesn't tell me shit when they seem to vary in height. Just when I think it's someone I know

Kooper

from before, the eye color is different. I try to figure out how many are here to find some way to differentiate one from another. Who is quicker to slap me and who just stays silent as I rant.

It might seem stupid to waste my time on this, but it's all I've got. There's nothing else to do. No big escape plan to come up with. The room is locked all the time. They slide the food tray through the door when they give us something. When they want the tray back, they open it and wait thirty seconds. If nothing's there, then they come and take it. But they leave us in bruises.

I ache. Some days are better than others. So far, all they seem to do to Nat and me is hit us. Beat on us. They don't say anything when they do it. Even after. But we get the message. We learned quickly to be compliant. Maybe that seems like giving up to some people, but I can't take it. There, I said it. I can't take this much abuse. I hate crying, and I cry a lot here. Mostly silent, dry tears, as we rarely get enough food or even water to stay hydrated.

And I know this makes me weak. It makes me the worst of the worst. But I will gladly take this over anything that Ava has going on.

We talk. She's become a friend of survival. We share stories to keep us from going crazy. She doesn't have parents, only a brother. One she was close to. But, like us, she doesn't know if he'll come for her. She says he has friends, but she doesn't know, like us, if he'd be able to find her. She was living in El Paso before this, which is far enough away from Kansas that I'm thinking we aren't close to either of our homes.

I should probably do something to help her. To call out when she needs it. But I don't. I stay in the cocoon that I put myself in, covering my head and holding my knees to my face when it begins for her.

When her door opens and someone comes in, we don't look, Nat and I, but we hear. We hear what they do to her. Her screams. Her pleas to stop. Whoever does it laughs. Laughs as he... they—who knows how many—use her.

The sounds. I can't block them out no matter how much I try. They seem to echo. The plea in her voice. The slapping of skin on skin. The gagging....

She says it only happened after we got here. That she never had to do it before. That she was like us, just held and pushed around. Somehow, we caused this for her.

I'm scared. I never thought I would be in my life, but I am. And I fucking pray they never tire of her. That she keeps their attention forever. Because when they're done with her, I know they'll come for us next.

They haven't separated Nat and me. I'm not sure why, but I don't even think it out loud to whatever spirits of the world are listening. It's a blessing. I know it is. But if they move on from Ava, I wonder if they would separate us then or make us... perform together. Either on each other or with someone else while the other watches.

The mind is a terrible, scary thing to have. Just when you think you've imagined the worst thing possible, a new thought comes up. And you know you aren't sick enough to think you're the only one in existence to have that thought. To come up with the concept solo. Which means if you thought it, that at least one of the other people in this place thought it too. And I don't think a single one has enough of a conscience to be put off by the idea.

"Peaches?" Ava hasn't said much since the guy left this last time. But she calls out to us when she's ready. And despite us being horrible for not wanting it to end for her, we let her know we're here for her.

"I'm here. We're here." I never know what to say to her after she's... raped. I need to name it. Say it in my head. It's the truth. And no matter how many times I hear it, I still fear it. I don't think there's anything wrong with fearing things.

Before, I did. Before all this, I thought I was untouchable. I knew things happened. Heard about. Had people tell me. What happened to Troublemaker and Mama Bear was harsh. But that was all I thought. I was still too far removed. Too many degrees of separation. And I still am, if I'm honest.

I only hear what's going on. I don't see it. I know I couldn't handle that. All that shit about me being tough, it's out the window. I just want my dad. My mom. Anyone to come and put me back in the box I once was in. This is torment. When I sleep—which is never a good sleep or long enough—I wake to her screams. Some of them real, but most of them phantom. Memories and fears plague me all the time.

When the time comes—and I'm not a fool to think it won't—I know I'm not going to go quietly. I'll kick and scream like Ava. I'll plead and beg. But I'll still get used. Every place they can abuse, I know they will. Just like they do with her. But unlike her, I don't know if I'll be strong enough after. To keep eating the slop they give us. To keep doing what they want to avoid the beatings. I think a part of me hopes I'll fight harder. I'll refuse the food. I'll force their hand. I might even try the bread. Because if there's no one coming, then I have to find my own escape.

And if that's with death?

I don't know. I keep telling myself I'm not ready for that. That I can survive this. That so many have survived this before me. That it would be a selfish, coward's way out.

But then I hear her screams and pleas again, and I don't know. I just don't know if I could take it. And if I do, I don't know how long I'll last.

"Do you think you can get a message to my brother? If I don't make it, can you tell him?"

"Don't talk like that," Nat tells her as she stands by the wall and looks up at the grate. "We can make it. We can. I know it seems bleak right now, but we have to keep trying."

I can hear Ava's sad laughter through the wall. "Bleak, huh? What are you, a poet?"

"Give me a lift," Nat says to me, and I nod before I scoot into position.

We take turns looking over at her. We might be losing weight from the lack of food, and it might seem easier to lift each other than it did the first day, but we're losing muscle too. The motivation to do anything physical like a push-up or something is too tiring to think about. I don't know how prisoners do it.

They get three meals a day regulated by the state. My mind reminds me that an inmate and I are not alike. I'm a prisoner. A plaything for whoever is on the other side of the

Kooper

walls. I did nothing to deserve to be here. Other than giving up on my family because I was mad that they lied.

I'd forgive them if they were here. I'd forgive everyone. Even Dad. Though thoughts of him hurt too much. He probably doesn't even know I'm gone. Or if he does, he doesn't care. Not like the rest. Not like Kooper.

I dream and wish for him more than anything. He was a nuisance at the beginning, but then he became the person I relied on. The one I looked for over Dad. The one I wanted to see over anyone else. He was there when I needed him more times than not. He accepted me for me, never asking me to be more and giving me everything I wanted before I knew I wanted it. He knew me better than I knew myself.

And I told him to fuck off. Made it clear I was done with him. I was hurt, obviously, but I should have seen that he was never against me. Not like I thought everyone else was. He was there, standing guard, caring, guiding, doing everything for me, and I took it for granted.

"Hey." Nat's voice is soft as she holds on to the grate and talks to Ava.

She's been the strongest out of all of us. Telling us to keep going. Making sure we eat the pig piss they give us. Reminding us that one meal at a time is what we need to do to get through this. I should question this. Should be worried that she seems almost at home in this place. Like nothing fazes her when she was such a shy, jumpy type at home. But I don't. And you want to know why? 'Cause I don't care. I don't care if she had issues before like this or is just a better person than me. I don't care what she had in her past to give her the strength now. I'm just grateful for it.

If I were taken without Nat, things would be different. And I don't know if I would be here, wherever here is, or for how long I've been here if it weren't for her.

"Hey." Ava's voice is weak. Weaker than usual. I hear her sniff, and then she's crying. "He called me Duch... Duchess." She stumbles over her words as she cries harder. I can only imagine what Nat is seeing. I've looked over before and seen her cry. She gets to the corner where we can see her more times than not. It's her way of making sure she's always in view when we look over.

She'll be clutching her knees, crying into them as she holds herself as close together as possible. They took her clothes a while ago. She doesn't have any to cover herself with. Once in a while, they come in and pour water on her. Freezing water, from the sound of it. But I guess they'd rather keep her clean that way than provide her with a stitch of clothing.

Easier to fuck her if nothing's in the way.

I swallow the vomit that rises at the thought. Not that I have much in my stomach to come up. It's been a few days since we last ate, I think.

I hear the door open on the other side of the wall and freeze, holding Nat so she doesn't move an inch to draw their eye.

I scream with Nat at the sound of a shot and wobble, forcing her to tumble down. She falls hard, and I look at her, but she's shaking her head.

"They killed her. They shot her."

Oh my God.

Kooper

I start to hyperventilate. They just killed Ava. For nothing. Nothing!

When our door starts to open, I panic. I shift back to the far corner of the room, just like Nat. Two guys come in, one moving toward each of us.

I scream. I kick. I hit. I cry. I do everything. My fingers try to grip the concrete as I'm dragged from the room. I feel my skin tear at the nail as I go, but the pain is nothing compared to what I think will happen to me.

Nat is screaming too. Fighting. I see her kick the other guy in the head so hard he stumbles. She stands and runs for the door. I don't give a fuck that she's leaving me. I just want her out. I want someone to get out. To get help. To get freedom. Anything but this.

I see more than hear when she gets punched in the face with a gun and falls back into the room as a third person steps in.

I still.

No one has brought a gun close to us before. Was he the one who shot Ava? Will he shoot us next?

He looks around, and I'm so transfixed on his gun that I'm compliant enough for the guy who was dragging me to grab my hands behind my back and lift me till I'm standing.

Gun guy looks at Nat on the ground, me, then his other man, who's moaning and groaning and holding his head. He shakes his own before he shoots him in the forehead. I squeak at the brutality of it, and fear racks my core.

He just shot his own man. His own man! We're nothing to them, and he shot his own guy.

I want to go home. I want this all to be a dream. I don't want to be brave anymore. I want to be free. I want Kooper.

I'm shaking from crying, but I keep my mouth closed to keep the sobs out of the predators' ears and hopefully draw less attention.

I'm broken. They broke me. They didn't even have to do anything, and I'm broken.

God, I'm so pathetic. All this talk about me being tough. About being able to be good enough like a man to take on the club, and I crumble at this. Being kidnapped. Taken hostage. Treated worse than any animal and forced to listen to someone I've come to know as a friend get raped repeatedly. To hear and watch people die.

If a man can handle this and not be affected, then he can have it. He can keep his boy clubs and exclusive shit. I'm done with wanting to be in the *in crowd*. I just want to be out of here.

The guy with the gun backs up and out the doorway. Another appears, and any hope that we might be dealing with just a few assholes is very slim from the number of people who seem to be down here.

The new guy picks up Nat, who still hasn't moved since she got hit in the face with the gun and fell back on her head, hitting it hard enough that it bounced. I hope she's alive, but if she isn't, maybe she got lucky.

Because as they take us down the hall, her one way, me another, I know that whatever luck I had has run its course. It's just me now. On my own.

Kooper

I swallow my fear. I have to. I have no one left. And I'm not going to meet my mom with tears in my eyes. If I go out, I'm going out like the warrior woman she taught me to be.

I steel my nerves and remember what Nat said about surviving and needing to just get through one meal at a time. One deed at a time. If I die, I die or... well. But I'll do it without letting these bastards see me cry. They've seen it enough already. The only tears I'll cry from now on are tears of joy. Of finding peace. Of coming home.

Be it in life or death.

Chapter 37—Kooper

Every rescue gets the best of the Hounds. When Operation Hell Hound gets a job, we take it like it's one of our own behind the line who needs to get out if it's a rescue mission. Sometimes it's not. Sometimes it's something else. But it's a job. Each one is vetted to the extreme to see if we agree with what the plan is.

And recently, C8 was with us in that plan. But not this one. Not today. Never more, in fact.

That's fine. The club still has friends. Who the fuck ever thought we would work with the mafia or... well, we don't know who Gina works for, but she has connections. The boys and I are suspicious, but we all agreed: Till we get eyes on Ruby, we're playing nice.

After that? Honestly, all I care about is Ruby. So does the club. If others get tagged in this mission and taken out, it's not something I'm going to lose sleep over. OHH was called after Gina gave us details. They were ready before the plane landed in Kansas. They've actually been on ready alert for weeks now, just needed a direction.

Like me.

They went ahead and are scouting the area, feeding Flint, Gator, and every other person we've got working on this intel. We have half the damn club in the cargo plane. Gina has a few guys, but our seven to her four has the odds in our favor.

Kooper

We've all kept our distance. We're sharing space, but I've got a feeling we both have our own agendas. Their allegiance is to Natalie, or whoever was tracking her. Makes me wonder if she was the target and Ruby was just a decoy to throw suspicion.

It's a question for another time.

A red light starts blinking a second before a buzzing alarm starts. Then the damn rear ramp starts to lower.

"What the fuck?" Bulldog snarls, but Jumper grins and hops up.

"Sit down, pretty boy. This one ain't for you," Gina says with a smile and a wink at my brother, who only pouts. "We're just doing a drop-off." She goes and stands by the ramp as it lowers.

My boys and I look at one another, and more than one pulls a gun. I do the same. We aren't about to be the ones who drop off. Jumper might get a thrill out of this kind of shit, but the rest of us don't jump out of planes for fun. Or ever. I know how. It was part of the things we did with OHH a few months back. Training, just in case. But I never expected to actually need it.

The team of four we met on the plane make their way to the back. Without ceremony, three jump. The fourth just watches, and when he sees them clear, he pushes the button to close the ramp.

"They know something we don't?" Bass asks no one in particular.

Casper looks at King, and that has him going to the cockpit. We need to know what the hell is going on. So far, they've run this shit, but they've also told us what's going on. We didn't trust them, but we didn't expect this either.

"Don't worry, boys," Gina says. "We're still on target to hit our flight time."

"What was that?" Casper asks as he nods to the back of the plane, which is now closed.

"That?" She gestures behind her like she's confused. "That was a drop-off. The boys had another plane to catch." Her smile is Cheshire-like at best.

"We going to see them later?" Bulldog asks.

"What for? You already got me and Big Mike." She points to the other guy, who just crosses his arms over his chest. "What else do you need?"

"You said this place was a fortress. Heavily armed and dangerous," Bass says, tilting his head.

"Yeah." She nods, waiting for the question.

"So why only bring two people to get your girl out?" Casper asks what we're all thinking after King returns with a nod. All's good up front.

"Job's to get you in. I'm not being paid to get her out."

Okay, what the actual fuck is going on with Natalie? My brothers and I glance at one another to see if anyone understands what's going on.

I don't know what the rest of them are thinking, but my goal is to find Ruby, then get her and my brothers out safely. If we find Natalie in the process, then I'll call it a double win. Again, we don't know if Ruby is still with her. This might just be a rescue mission for Natalie. But I hope we're wrong and they're both in this place.

Kooper

Our team did the surveillance, though we only got a bit before we went radio silent due to passing over the border, and we want to keep off as many channels as possible. Not that we didn't bribe everyone possible to look the other way, but still, we're keeping off the frequencies. When we land, we'll get more details.

OHH will set up and do a perimeter sweep. Orders are for them to hold and only to breach before we get there if something goes down. I really don't care if they wait on us. I just want Ruby in the arms of someone I trust, be it mine or a brother's. Just so long as she's safe.

But from the sound of it, unless something went extremely right, the other team would only be wheels down about thirty minutes before us. They might have left earlier, but they're flying from North Dakota, while we came in from Kansas.

"All right, boys, time to go," Gina says, and we all stand, going to the Hummers in the bay.

The plane isn't going to do a full stop for us to get off. We have less than a minute to drive the three vehicles off this thing. I'm hoping the pilot is as good as Gina thinks to be able to do a stop-and-go long enough for us to get our wheels on solid ground and not just fall out of the damn plane.

The only warm and fuzzy I get is that her man, Mike, takes the first Hummer, and she gets into the last one.

I take the wheel of the second one, and Bass and Jumper get in with me. Casper is in the back with Gina and Walker. Bulldog and King are in the front with Mike.

The ramp starts to lower, and I turn on the vehicle. I glance at Jumper, who's riding shotgun, bouncing on his seat like a fucking crazy kid as the night sky is revealed. It's so dark, I've got no clue if we're close to the ground or not.

The Hummer in front of me floors it, and I follow right on his ass. I glance in the rearview mirror to make sure the boss is also with us and see headlights.

The second we're off the ramp, I feel weightless while still strapped to my seat. The wheels have zero traction, and we're flying through the air till we take a hard hit and bounce. Every one of us. I hit my fucking head on the roof, but other than cursing at it, I keep my foot on the gas pedal and swerve to correct and keep us from tipping over while following the other car.

"Shit, now we're having fun." Jumper's giddy with excitement.

I look at him and then at Bass in the back seat. He's shaking his head.

"Fucking adrenaline junkie," he mumbles, but it doesn't faze Jumper in the slightest.

"Hell yeah. Think we can try it backward?" Out of the corner of my eye, I see him look at me. I just give him a small shake of my head.

The radio sparks to life, and Jumper grabs it before anyone else does. "Can we go again?"

"We're having General give you a psych eval after this," Bulldog mutters over the comms.

"Oh, you boys are fun. We might have to do this again," Gina laughs.

Casper must have been holding the button to talk, but Gina spoke before he could. I know Walker's driving, and she's in the back.

Kooper

"Shut it, all of you. Flint's got eyes in the sky. We're clear the whole way through. Going to pull off about six klicks before the turnoff and meet up with our team. Follow the map just sent over."

Each Hummer is not only equipped with radios between cars but also GPS synced to a satellite, courtesy of Fairy's uncle, Jimmy Travis. He got us the eyes in the sky while the mafia, thanks to Brooklyn's family running the entire East Coast and looking to merge with the West Coast, got us the names and numbers of the people to bribe.

Billy wanted to help, but C8 cut ties with her once she chose sides. We don't fault her for it. King is the one who seems to be doubling down on this job to make up for what happened. Not that it was his fault. People die. He made a call. He sent out the medical team to get to her as soon as the threat was gone. He did what he could without injuring anyone else. He had no idea how bad she was till Jack told us. If Abigail had been open about being pregnant, maybe things would have gone differently. But they didn't. C8 can't blame him for not knowing and choosing his brother over a lay. Because as shitty as it sounds, that's what she was at the time. He only realized too late that it was more.

Listening to the others talk keeps me just focused enough to not break protocol and just ram into the building myself. This Hummer is equipped with a shit ton of things, thanks not only to Bass, our weapons specialist, but me and my team. My guys wanted to come. They wanted to get some blood on their hands for what was done to their fallen brethren. But I said it was my call, my job, and thus my blood to spill. They backed down, not liking it but getting it all at once.

Casper wants a meetup with them after this. He wants to know everything. And I told him I'll tell him everything. After. After we get Peaches. Alive or dead, she's coming home, to me.

"Next left," Bass says from the back seat.

I can see it just as well as he can on the screen, but I don't point that out. I'm not in a talking mood.

We drive for about ten more minutes before we pull up to what looks like an abandoned house. The front wall is down, though the others are standing, but nothing shows life. Other than the two other Hummers parked out front.

We get out slowly. Just because we're expected doesn't mean we aren't compromised. Things are going too well for me to think shit is fine and dandy. Especially after that little drop-off stunt Gina pulled earlier. It would have been fine if she had told us before, but there was no warning. When we left the compound and followed her, she introduced them as her team and said they were coming with. That was it, and we didn't ask for signed affidavits on the matter.

Don't get me wrong, Flint scanned them all with facial recognition. Unfortunately for us, there wasn't a single thing on them. As if they're ghosts, all of them. They're either criminals or worked with them. But what choice do we have? They have more intel than we do. Not only do they have a tracker on Natalie, or so they claim, but they also have video footage. They found the girls on some surveillance from CCTV at an airport once they landed. Both of them appeared to be unconscious as they were taken from a plane to a car. We followed the car to the place Gina had shown us, but we had no other footage. They could have taken Ruby out someplace along the road and we missed it, or they could have taken her through a tunnel. Apparently, under the building they're occupying is a series of tunnels the cartel used before it was shut down by a military raid.

Or so they say. For all we know, they could still be operational. Casper told me about the tunnels he had to deal with when he went after Billy. That's why we have so many brothers with us. If we each have to take a tunnel, then we will. No one is coming home unless it's with Ruby.

Sometimes it takes a second, but we always find everyone—covert ops at its finest. Even from those we consider friends.

A flash of light has Bulldog signaling back before two people come out of the dark, holding guns pointed straight at us.

"Casper?" one says. I can't make out anything about them, as we shut the vehicles off and were driving without headlights to keep us off anyone's radar. Apparently, the road we used isn't often traveled, and the less light the better.

"Hoss?" Casper calls out, and the two figures lower their weapons.

I wasn't worried. Okay, fine, I had my gun out and a knife at the ready, but we planned to meet here. This group of OHH operatives specializes in the seek-and-find type of job. They were pulled from another mission they were planning in Asia to do this one. We have plenty of Hounds from the other sister chapters champing at the bit to get involved with OHH. We pulled in the best for this and started training up the second best for the other mission.

Just because my world stopped rotating the second Peaches was taken doesn't mean everyone else's did too.

"This way."

We follow Hoss, the other guy he appeared with staying put before bringing up the rear once we all fall into line. The place looks wrecked except for the staircase leading down. We take it and turn a few times before we come to an open area. Looks more like a bomb shelter than anything else. No windows, cots on one side, a radio mount at the back, and a huge table with maps already on display. Oh, and a wall of weapons.

Either the boys have been busy since they landed, or this was set up by someone else. Maybe we've got more friends worldwide than I thought.

Now that I can see, even if it's a dim light, I take in our team. No need to think too hard on how Hoss got his name. He's a big-ass dude who might even put Mad Max to shame.

I look around as Hoss motions to the others who are already in the room.

"That there is Switch. He's our tech guy and can hack into anything like turning on a light switch."

"Already got a line in," Switch says. "So far, there's nothing to pinpoint where they are. Got a call in to Flint, and we're going to use some other tech to see if we can get a body count from some infrared."

Casper nods, and I just take it all in. My prez is leading the mission. He's in charge. But he knows I got one thought and one thought only. Ruby. Till then, I'm keeping my mouth shut most of the time.

Kooper

"The guy behind you"—Hoss points to the guy who followed us in here—"is Havoc—demolition expert. And these idiots," he continues, tossing his head behind him to twins sitting on a bed, shining up their guns with a rag, "are Viper and Venom. Where one goes, the other follows."

They give me a chin lift, and I give them the courtesy of one back. I might not know this team, but I've heard of them. Flint even gave us a small history lesson on each member so we know how to play to everyone's strengths. Just like I'm sure they got one for each of us.

"Right. This is Bulldog, Walker, Jumper, Bass, King, and Kooper. It's his girl we're going in to find. And this is Gina and Mike." Casper points to each of us and then flings his other hand to the other two.

"Big Mike," Gina interrupts with a smile that wouldn't be deemed nice but also not cruel. Like one gives a hostess who pronounces the party name wrong when their table is available.

"Right, Big Mike." Casper lifts his eyebrow at her and then looks back at Hoss. "They're the ones who provided us with this information."

"No need to thank us just yet. We're still not able to confirm if your girl is in there, only ours," Gina says.

I don't know if she means it, but there's a hint of glee in her voice. Something that makes my blood run cold. And the others sense it, too, as we all stop moving, the air seeming to suspend in time above us.

Big Mike stands at her back, arms crossed. Like a warrior waiting to attack.

Too bad for him, I'm about a minute out from breaking everything, including him and her, to get my girl. Nothing will stop me.

Nothing.

Chapter 38—Kooper

"What's that?" Havoc asks as he comes closer, as do Viper and Venom.

Bulldog speaks for the group. "They've got a tracker on the roommate, Natalie. They know she's there, and we've got nothing else to go on till then to assume Ruby isn't."

"Might be a good idea to start tracking the whole damn lot," a voice says from the left, and we all turn to see three others emerge out of what I thought was a bunk area.

"Mickey? What the fuck are you doing here?" Bass grabs him hard and gives him a hug. They got close when we were in Russia for his woman. Now he's in Michigan, taking on an officer's position, last I heard from Domino.

"Domino sends his regrets and says me, Lucky, and Rooster"—he points to himself and the other two—"were the best he could do to replace him."

"Glad to have you," Casper says with a nod. They've worked together before, when he was getting his woman too. The guy gets around, it seems.

Damn, just how many times is the cavalry going in to help get a brother's woman? Maybe Mickey's right. Maybe the whole lot needs embedded trackers. Would save us time and solve a few issues before they become them.

"Okay, now that the bromance is done, let's get to it. Our intel says they have a shift change coming in." Gina moves to the table and looks over the maps, pulling up a building schematic.

"Shift change?" This from Walker.

"Yeah. Every few weeks, another group comes in."

"Comes in from where? What's the details on this place? Who are we raiding?" Viper—or is it Venom—speaks up. They need their vests back on and not the Kevlar. Hard as hell to tell who's who.

"These men are locals for hire. They go where the money is. Some days they're freedom fighters. The next, drug lord cartel men. If the money's good enough, they do what's needed. But they all have a common problem."

"Let me guess—death to Americans," Bulldog grumbles.

"Actually, they've just got a thing against borders. They see one, they want to knock it down. They're as free as gypsies in their mind and hate to be confined."

"They would suck at prison," Havoc comments, earning a few grunts in agreement.

"Where do you think most of them came from?" Gina asks as if she's genuinely curious before she explains more. "They either snuck out or were let out by the government. Who knows? But they don't like people getting in their way."

"Good thing Hoss is good at being a wall, aren't you, big fella?" One of the twins slaps him on the back.

"Fuck off, Viper." He pushes him back, and the guy falls to the floor. At least I know which one is which now. That, and Viper has a deep red strip down the side of his Kevlar.

"And if they don't like it, that's why we've got Havoc. He's really good at taking them down." The other twin, Venom, grins at Havoc as if nothing just happened to his brother. Guess this shit happens often.

"Damn, Domino is going to be pissed he missed this," Mickey says with a wide grin and a shake of his head.

Casper puts both hands on the table and looks everything over before pulling out an aerial view of the place where Nat's being held.

"I want four teams. Three snipers with spotters up at the tree line. Here, here, and here." He points to three spots that have the best vantage points. "King is with me. Bulldog on the second, and if you're willing to part with one of yours, Mickey, he can be Bulldog's spotter."

"Take Lucky. He's pretty good on a gun if you want to switch."

Bulldog nods, and the two eye each other in understanding.

"You want the third?" Casper looks at Gina, who nods. "We don't start shooting till the welcome team gets there."

"Welcome team?" This from Lucky.

"Yeah—nothing says 'welcome to the party' like explosives."

"Ah, the nice way to let yourself in." Viper grins.

"Exactly. Get set up and then double back." Casper looks like Havoc, Viper, and Venom as he speaks. Our group already discussed on the plane that we were going to let the professionals handle this part. While we all know how to throw a grenade, those with OHH train on stealth. Getting in and out. By having them set the charges, we have a better shot of sticking to a timetable.

"When we blow it, I want you to double back and help the ground team. If we plan this right, we can get them all looking left while..."

"While I go right," I say. Finally, we're getting to the part that I want. The part that gets me in and looking for my girl.

Casper nods. "I want a four-man team to go through these tunnels. We don't know if they're blocked or not, but it's a start. We suspect two people are in there. We get in and get them out. Kooper and Walker already volunteered for this. Any others?"

Rooster looks at Hoss. "Might be easier to break down the walls with you on the inside."

Hoss, who seems to be a man of few words, similar to Mad Max, nods. "Even better if I had some cover."

Rooster knocks his knuckles against Hoss's and grins. "Deal."

"What if we find more?" King asks. He's been quiet. He wants to be here, but he's still fucked up about what happened with him and Abigail. And their kid. We all told him to hang back, to deal with his own shit. His response was "They're dead. Shit's dealt with."

If I were one to suggest therapy, it would be to him. But I'm not, and I've got my own issues to work through, so I kept my yap shut and didn't blink when he got on his bike and drove beside me to the airfield.

Kooper

"Do what you have to. But the priority, gentlemen—" Casper looks at everyone, landing on me last. "—is Ruby. The rest is bonus. That clear?"

Nods all around.

"What about the roommate?" Walker asks, looking at the two who aren't part of our group.

We all do. But Gina keeps her face clear, no emotion at all, and just blinks. No response. And after we wait half a minute for them to demand we get Natalie out or something, Casper continues.

"Do what you can, but you know what I want."

The boys nod again.

"Hoss?" Casper turns it back over to the big guy. Pun intended.

"Right." He takes a step forward and points to a few spots on the map that are circled in red. "We've got vehicles stashed here and here. Find one and get on it. Wheels are up at 0400. If you aren't back at the rendezvous, find another way home. You need a lift, darling?" He looks across the table at Gina as he says the last bit. Maybe he likes her. Maybe he's just trying to be a nice guy. Or maybe he's trying to figure out just what the fuck is going on with her and her friend, Big Mike.

"Thanks, sugar, but I'm all set." She winks at him, and then she and Big Mike walk away from our group. Far enough that we can talk without them hearing. Just like I'm sure they're doing.

"We good with them?" Mickey asks, voice low.

Casper looks around, and Jumper shrugs, feeling what we all are. Casper is the one to speak. "Not sure. Best to keep an eye out. That's why I want a spotter. Not only to help with targets, but to watch our backs."

"Got it. Let's get busy," Hoss says.

"Seriously? 'Let's get busy'? What kind of morale boost is that?" Viper quips as he and his brother move away.

"What would you prefer he say? 'Let's get howling'?" Venom asks.

"Oh, I like that. What about 'let's get barking'?"

"Doesn't work. We're Hounds, not dogs. And specific to the Reaper," Walker says as he goes to the wall of weapons and looks them over.

Viper glances at Venom and shrugs. "Maybe we should say 'let's get to killing'?"

"Too morbid," Venom comments offhandedly.

"Says the guy strapping three grenades to his belt."

"Better than the rope. Seriously, what're you going to need the rope for?"

"Don't know. But if I don't have it and we need it, won't you feel like a fool?"

"Already do when I see your ugly ass every day."

"Oh, Mom is so going to hear about this."

"They always like this?" I ask no one in particular, as most of us are just watching the antics play out as they suit up.

"Worse," Switch says before turning back to his computer.

Kooper

"Think they can pull it off?" Rooster asks as we make our way through debris to get into position. We have the farthest to go. Comms are on, but we're keeping the talking to a minimum between the teams.

Mostly to keep Gina and Big Mike out of our heads. So far, they're playing ball. But who knows if they'll be switch hitters when things start happening.

"The twins might be annoying, but they get shit right," Hoss grumbles, then pauses. I do, too, watching him take a second to think before he continues to walk. "Well, when it comes to this. They suck at pulling a chick."

Rooster chuckles, and I grunt. "Reminds me of Lucky," he says.

"Figured with the name, he got laid all the time," Walker says.

"It's become more of a staple that he won't. He gets punched more times than not, and by women lately. He only got the name because his dad was named Lucky. Guy grew up being Lucky Jr. till his pops died, and then the Jr. died too."

The chatter between us slows as we head into the tunnels as planned. We've got a rough idea of when shit is going to start popping off, but we don't know how long it'll take to find them. And our "get out of Colombia" card is already stamped. Our timetable is limited.

We keep to a tight formation as we go in, noting any issues with infrared to make sure we don't trip on anything. Switch has already hacked their system and found zero feeds of the tunnels. Either the reception sucks down here, they don't know about the tunnels, or they're blocked off and not a threat to them. Which is a problem for us.

"Hold position," Switch says through the comms. "I see lights coming in from the courtyard."

We hold. The courtyard is at the back of the facility, where we plan to enter.

After a few moments, I signal for us to continue. It's dark as hell, but I see the light Switch mentioned. Which means we're about to get to the courtyard and not continue to go underground. I guess "tunnel" doesn't mean the same thing here as it does back home.

Rooster attaches a mirror to the end of his AR-15, then slowly puts it on the ground and moves it around the corner for him to see.

"Two smoking out back. About fifteen feet to the left," he whispers.

Walker holsters his gun and unsheathes his knife. Hoss moves his shoulder holster so his gun is now on his back as he puts his fingers in brass knuckles.

Rooster pulls back from the opening as they take point.

I check my watch, hold my hand up to show five, and then count down. With one left, I signal for them to go. A second later, explosions start going off.

I pop out just in time to see Walker come up behind one of them who's looking at the house. He slides his knife across the man's jugular while holding his mouth to muffle his scream. Hoss crouches a bit, and as soon as the other guy turns back to his friend, he hits him. Hard.

I don't question if the guy is alive or not. You don't get that kind of head turn if you're alive. One-punch kill? Guy really is a hoss.

Kooper

We go in a two-by-two formation and enter the building. As soon as we see stairs heading down, we take them.

Switch had already scanned the entire building, at least what he could see. There isn't any indication of anyone aboveground who seems to be of the hostage nature. Sure, he only had heat signatures, but his system is damn good. He and Flint worked together enough that we got to see full-body imagery, and there was no one in any position other than walking freely around in groups of three or four.

If they had Ruby up here, she wouldn't be calm. She would be a terror. I know my girl. She might freak for a second, get in her head, but if she saw freedom, she'd fight for it.

We can hear our boys fighting off any who run out to see what the issue is, falling like ants in the trap we set. But the lower we go, the less noise we hear.

We hit the bottom of the stairs and scan the hallway. Footsteps have us doubling back to get cover as four men run by, their walkie-talkies screaming in Spanish.

I look at Walker, who knows the language better than me.

"Calling for help."

I nod, and we keep going.

They're going to need help. Lots of it. Because the second I find my Peaches, I'm burning this place to the ground.

Chapter 39—Ruby

Something's happening.

I don't know what, but I can feel it.

I can't see anything. They put a blindfold on me, then tied me up and hung me from the ceiling like an animal. My toes just barely touch the ground. I'm still clothed, but for how long, I don't know.

I don't know if this is how it starts. If Ava got this instead of bathroom breaks.

But I've been here for a while. Long enough for some parts to go numb. But not my mind. Something changed in me. I'm not sure if it's because of what happened to Ava or because now I don't have Nat's strength to lean on. But there's a resolve in me. A steady beat telling me that I will survive. That I *can* survive. One breath at a time. Even when they beat me, I'm still taking a breath.

I've been hit more times than I can count since they took Nat from me. Each time I screamed, I took a hit. I must be getting used to the pain they put me through since I got here, because I had enough balls to fight back. Not a lot, since my hands were tied, and I was being held. But when I spat, I made sure it was in the direction I thought someone was. I hope they got blood all over their shoes or wherever offended them the most. It's not much, but it's what I have. And I must have hit the mark, because the next hit I got was in the stomach so hard that I think it broke a rib. It at least cracked one, based on the pain.

But I'm alone now. Or I think I am. I can hear still. I heard people running. People speaking in frantic tones. Still no clue what's being said, but something must be happening.

I can only hope.

But I'm not sure if that's too much to do. Too much to wish for right now.

I hear the door open, and this time, I don't speak. I learned my lesson the last time, unfortunately. Especially since I took the last smack across the face after they hung me up, and I dislocated my shoulder. I hurt. A lot. But I refuse to cry. I promised myself I won't. Not yet.

So I wait in silence.

"Pinche puta," I hear before I get slapped again. A cry escapes my lips at the sudden attack, and he pulls another from me when he hits me in the stomach. I can't move with it from how I'm hanging, and it hurts even more than before.

I pant for breath, feeling lightheaded and dreading passing out. That's one thing I fight for. One thing I refuse to do. Who knows what the fuck will happen when I can't protect myself. Not that I can right now, but I'd rather be awake and remember than have to wonder about the horrors that are inflicted on me.

I hold my breath, waiting for the next hit. But it doesn't come. Instead, I hear fists, but nothing touches me.

God, I wish I could see.

I focus on my hearing and not the pain or the blood rushing to fill my ears. I can only guess at what's happening.

Gunshots. I hear a lot of gunshots. More fists on flesh. Some screams.

Then I don't have to guess. My blindfold is lifted, and my eyes gloss over with tears. Fresh ones. Ones I willingly let fall.

"Koop," I sob as he grabs my face and kisses me. It hurts because of the split lip—and because everything fucking hurts—but I welcome the pain. I welcome everything, because I feel him. He's not made up. He's not a dream that'll fade away when I open my eyes. He's here. He came.

For me.

"Oh, baby, what did they do to you? Oh, my sweet Peaches, I've got you. Help me get her down."

Another guy comes into view, one I don't know, but together they slowly lower me to the floor.

I grunt in agony, and Kooper sees. He sees everything. Always.

"Don't untie her hands yet, Rooster."

The guy, Rooster, nods and moves back to the door, leaning out and then shooting a second later before leaning out again. No shots this time. Either he got the guy he was aiming for, or they ran off.

"Okay, baby girl, I'm going to put your hands over my head and hold you. Try to stay as tight to me as you can."

I nod but still cry out a bit when my arms shift to fit over his head. The tingles of numbness feel like spider bites and nails being embedded into my skin again and again.

"I know, Peaches. I know." He kisses my forehead, and I swear everything is fine. The pain, the anguish, all of it. I have him. I'm in his arms. It's all fine.

Kooper

I hold tight as Rooster takes the lead. At first, I keep my eyes shut, but I need to look. I need to see what's going on. To see that we're actually leaving.

"Nat? Did you find Nat?" The thought is a whisper on my lips. I'm scared we'll get caught. That we won't make it if I bring too much attention to us.

"Walker and Hoss already got her out."

They could have left. They could have taken her and gone. But they kept looking for me.

He must see the expression on my face because he holds me tighter. "I'm never leaving you behind, Peaches. You're mine. Always have been. Always will be." His words are rushed, and I feel them on my skin, even if he's focused on looking around to keep us from being ambushed.

I nod, and I'm sure he can feel it. Just as I can feel my tears slide down my neck.

Bodies. I see so many. We get to the stairs and go up quickly. I would joke about him obviously not skipping leg day from the ease with which he carries me up them, taking two at a time, but as we round the top, Kooper's ducking low, almost dropping me as we take fire. I hunker down closer to his chest and hold on tight. If this is where we die, I want it to be in his arms. I'm not letting him go, just like I know he won't let me go.

"Go out the front. The back's compromised," Rooster yells. "Switch, we're coming out the front," he says, but I've got no clue who he's talking to. I see the earpiece in Kooper's ear, but I thought Flint would be here.

"You better get your ass out, too, Rooster, or Domino's going to skin me alive," Kooper says a second before he shifts me. He's only using one hand to hold me, like he did when we were leaving the hospital after the shooting on campus. That was so long ago. But even then, I knew I was safe. That with Kooper, I'm always safe.

He pulls a gun from his belt and holds it out as he jogs us to the exit. So many people are there, but they don't see us. They're shooting at whoever's in front of us. I can only hope it's the Hounds. Family that's come to get me out.

As Kooper runs, I'm jostled, but I hang on tight and keep my pain inside.

Bodies seem to drop around us as he runs for the tree line. A second later, he swings around and shoots as he runs backward, and I hold tight as both his hands seem to be firing now. No idea when he pulled the other gun, but I refuse to be the reason we slow down. I wrap my legs around him like a damn spider monkey, clinging for dear life.

"Attagirl," he says, bringing a huff to my lips. The stupid guy is taking the time to praise me while he's the one shooting and running backward. Always making sure I feel my worth, no matter the cause.

Everything. Everything he does is for me. To make me feel special in some way. To let me know how much he cares. How he's always cared. I could never have imagined I'd find someone like Mom had. And I didn't find him. He found me.

Or more to the point, he was forced to protect me. And he stayed. Long after the job was done, he stayed.

He turns back, and I can now see the whole house. The place I was held hostage in for who knows how long. It's half on fire, just like my world felt a few minutes before. And through that fire, I see someone running toward us. Someone I don't know.

I open my mouth to scream, but a hole appears in his forehead a second before he drops, and in his place is Rooster running straight at us.

Thank fuck he's on our side.

We keep running for who knows how long. Eventually, the gunfire coming our way dies out. No one seems to be chasing us anymore, but we keep going. Till we don't. Kooper stops, and I turn my head to see we're in a small clearing.

"Put your feet down, Peaches."

I do as he says, and he gently leans down and pulls his head out from between my arms.

"Here." Another guy steps forward and hands him a knife. A very large knife like you'd see in an alligator hunter movie. Kooper uses it to easily cut the rope keeping my hands together.

"The others?" Kooper asks.

"Out. Venom and I wanted to stay for some fun."

"I have to say, though, I'd have more fun at home than this," another guy—who must be Venom, as he looks identical to this one—says as he comes out from behind a tree.

"What's left?" Rooster asks.

"Bikes. Got three. One of us is riding bitch." Venom grins and winks at me.

"She's with me," Kooper says. "Rooster will take lead. You two follow up."

"Damn, how did I become the bitch in this?" the other twin, not Venom, complains.

"You're lucky, I guess." Venom smirks as he turns to get the bike.

Kooper unstraps his Kevlar and puts it on me. I don't protest, not when he palms my cheek and kisses me before turning at the sound of a bike being rolled over to us. His kisses are over too quickly. But now isn't the time to demand his lips on me. Later. When we're safe. Then I'll demand. I'll make all sorts of demands then. One being me sitting on his face again. That particular memory got in my head a lot here. Something to keep me going, to focus on. Mostly just the feeling of rightness with him. And feeling safe in his arms. I want to see if it's as good as what I remember. If I'm lucky, it'll be even better.

Kooper lifts me easily and puts me on a bike, then gets on it himself. "Can you hold on?"

I try, but it hurts. He sees the look on my face without me even voicing my protest. I'll hold him even if it hurts. I will survive this.

He just turns to the twin who isn't Venom. "Let me get that rope."

"See? Told you." He sticks his tongue out at his brother and flutters it a second before he unfastens a piece of rope.

"What do you mean, you told me? I was the one who told you to grab the rope, Viper," Venom says as he drops the kickstand to hold up the last bike he rolls out. Rooster is already on his.

Kooper

"No, you didn't," Viper snaps, but his fingers belie the anger in his voice. They're soft and gentle as he ties the rope around me and Kooper at our stomachs, securing us together. If we fall, we're screwed, but I'd rather that than bouncing off the bike. I lean in close once Viper's done and grab what I can of the back of Kooper's shirt.

"You good, doll?" Viper asks with a small look of concern.

I give him a thumbs-up, and he grins. "Classic 80s move there. Love it."

He hops onto the back of his brother's bike, and then we take off.

The road is bumpy, and I hold on for all the life I have. Which is a lot considering the shame I felt back in that place when I almost wanted to give up. Something I'll deal with later when I can care about more than hanging on.

We're on dirt bikes, and while great for off-roading, they're not meant as two-seaters. My ass is basically off the damn back but for a fraction of cheek. Everything hurts, but pain means life. Pain means something to live for.

I hear gunfire, but we never see anyone. Not that the boys aren't looking. Rooster has one hand on a gun, the other on his throttle. Only Kooper and the twin driving, Venom, have both hands on their handlebars. Viper is looking around, tracking everything to see if it's moving or not.

I don't know where we're headed. I can't see, but they seem to know where we're going. I close my eyes briefly and just sink into the ride. I've been riding behind a man all my life. Even with Kooper. But never like this. Never because he came for me and I was his. I try to find some joy in this, thinking that I need to find more joy in the small moments. You don't know when they'll be your last.

In what feels like a mix between hours and minutes, the grass gives way to a clearing, and I see a cargo plane sitting with the bay door open at the back. The boys don't even stop, just drive up the ramp.

Shots ring out, and they seem to be getting closer. I duck as I look back to the clearing we just left. A Hummer is coming our way, but it doesn't look like it's alone.

I turn back around in time to see Bulldog come rushing toward us. "It's Casper," he shouts, then goes out halfway and starts firing. The others get off their bikes and start shooting while Kooper cuts the rope and then pulls me off the bike, dragging me behind a crate.

"Stay here, Peaches."

I grab his shirt, scared that once he leaves, I won't see him again.

He puts his hand on mine and pulls it away slowly, looking me in the eye as he does. "I'm coming back, Peaches. I'm coming back. You're my old lady now, and I'm not about to let you get away from me again."

I nod, and then he's gone.

I can't see what's happening, and I'm too afraid to look out. A few others run by, but they're too fast for me to see who they are. I hear the guns, the shouts. Something pings against the plane, and I cover myself. To get hit by a stray bullet and bleed out when I'm so close to freedom would be the crown on a horribly bad day if there ever was one.

Kooper

But then the shooting stops. The yelling dies down. And I'm picked up and pulled into arms I know. Smelling a scent I adore and feeling warmth for the first time in what seems like forever.

"She good?" someone asks, and I hear the plane's engines purring to life, then a noise that sounds like something closing.

We're going. We're finally going.

"Give me a second," Kooper says to whoever asked. I don't look, my face buried in his neck as I hold on tight and give thanks to whoever is listening that I'm out. That I have him. That I'm not alone.

I hold on tight as he moves and sinks into a seat. My legs are straddling his, and I couldn't give two shits who sees.

I need this moment. I need to feel him as the plane rushes down the runway and takes off. I need to find my peace as I break down.

And I do. I cry so hard, and for who knows how long. He lets me. And I let myself. I told myself I would. I saved it for this moment. I gave myself a reprieve when I saw him, letting those tears fall for joy. And these fall for everything else that happened.

Later, they can check me. Look me over and see what hurts. See what they can do to fix me. But for now? Now I get to be in my old man's arms and just feel him hold me. Openly in front of his brothers. In front of family.

And know that everything is finally going to be all right.

Chapter 40—Kooper

I love my club. I love everything about it. I fuck up sometimes, and when I do, I know my club will deal with it. I'm not going to fuck it up so much that I get kicked out. But not talking about my feelings for Ruby? Hell, *having* feelings for Ruby at all? Using my own team because I hid shit from them that I knew they wouldn't like?

Not only do they get it, but they get over it. Sort of. The free shots to the face probably helped too.

But for all the love I have, if Casper doesn't fucking hurry the fuck up and end this meeting, I'm going to lose my shit.

At least he was willing to move it to the hospital. I haven't left it. If Ruby's here, then so am I. I lost her for seventeen days. Never again.

"Any word on Gina or Big Mike?" he asks.

Bulldog shakes his head. "Saw them leave before us. They took off to the west." Opposite where we took off. They probably planned it that way.

"You see them?" Casper asks Walker.

He nods. "Got eyes on them for a second. They saw we had the roommate, and that was it. No looking back, not even to see if she was alive as I fireman-carried her out."

"Probably able to check vitals on that tracking system they have on her," Flint adds.

"We know what that's about?" I ask. I want my girl to have answers when she wakes up, not more questions. And I know she'll be asking. Ruby isn't the type to sit in the dark and be happy about it. And I've got no issues with sharing with her. I trust her. I know she'll keep her shit together if needed.

"None. Still got jack shit back on facial recognition. Want me to put the feed out to our friends?" Flint asks the boss.

We didn't tell the other groups who we were working with. Especially since we don't know either. Not that they asked. They answered when we called, and that was all we wanted.

Casper shakes his head. "No, not yet. They didn't ask for a favor, just gave us intel. My guess is that the favor was in getting Natalie out for them. We did that. As far as I'm concerned, we're square."

"How's she doing?" I ask.

General answers. "Still running scans. She got it worse than Ruby; that much is clear. Initial report shows a fractured fibula and three broken ribs. Fractured jaw as well. We've set the leg and have a call out to a plastic surgeon to come in to help us after we reset her jaw. I'm hoping to keep her here for a few weeks just to be on the safe side."

"And Ruby?" Casper asks. Everyone looks at me when he says it. I feel the eyes as I stare at my hands.

I know some of it. We agreed she'd find out most of it when she wakes up. After we got back, we came straight here. General put her under to give her body time to sleep a bit and give me time to talk. Also, so he could run some tests without freaking her out.

"Broken ribs. Broken nose. Torn rotator cuff. She got off easy in comparison."

"Nothing easy about it," Walker says, and I look at him, giving him a nod in appreciation. He gets it. Just because you don't wear that many war wounds doesn't mean you didn't feel all of it.

"And the rest?" Bass asks.

They all want to know something. Even I do. We found a third woman, naked and cold on the floor. That could have been Peaches. Maybe it was. Either way, she's mine. No matter what happened there, she's mine, and I'll hold her through whatever the answer is.

"Still waiting on results. But...." I look up at General when he pauses and see his eyes on me, waiting for me to look at him when he speaks. "No initial findings."

I hear the collective sigh, and I just nod.

"We done?" I look at Casper, ever the respectful bastard that I am.

"Go see your girl. I'll let Law know she's back."

He should be here. Law should be by her side through this, but he's not. Still no memory. But that's fine. I'm here for her. I'll be all she needs till he remembers. Even then, I'll still stand by her side.

"I'll be in later to check on her," General says, and I pause at the way he stands. Something's off. Something he isn't saying. Something he wants her to know before the rest of the brothers. Before me.

I nod, and then I'm out, heading down the hall and giving King a chin lift as a greeting before I walk into her room.

Kooper

Her open eyes greet me, and it's like the sun is finally shining after years of rain.

I go to her and kiss her forehead. She's multicolored but still the most beautiful thing I've ever seen.

"Hey, Peaches."

"Hey." Her voice is soft and rough. I grab the water on the table beside her and hold the straw for her while she takes a sip.

When she's finished, I set it down and look her over once more before I speak. "How're you feeling?"

She closes her eyes and breathes. I watch her chest rise and fall and look at the monitor. Steady breath. Thank fuck. Hearing her breathe is like damn birds singing and angels spouting poetry. It's the best damn thing I've heard in my life.

"Like shit." That pulls a chuckle from me, and she cracks an eye open. "And I know I look it, so don't try to say anything nice."

I hold my hands up in surrender. "Not my style."

She smiles, knowing it's bull. I'll tell her anything she wants to hear, lies or truth, just as long as I get to talk to her.

I sit on the side of the bed and grab her hand, running my fingers over her skin gently.

"Is my dad here?" She's looking at my hand, not my face. But I know she can see me when I shake my head, and I watch as a bit of hope dies in her eyes.

"That's okay. I... I guess it's better that he doesn't see me like this. I wouldn't want this to be the reason he gets his memory back. He might think you did it." She huffs out a sad, pitiful laugh as she looks up at me.

Her dad would for sure beat my ass if he remembered her and knew about us. No doubt about it.

"Then we could match." I give her a wink and a small smile. One I only give to her. I doubt she knows that. Not yet. But she will. She'll know everything about me. I already know everything about her. It'll take time, but I know that one day she'll get it. She'll understand that all I see is her. That all I *want* is her. And if I have to take a beating to get her dad to remember her, I will.

"Nat okay?"

"Yeah. General says she'll need some surgeries but will live."

She nods. "She was tough. She kept me sane in there. Kept me from losing my mind. I…. Things got dark. I had thoughts. She made sure I didn't act on them."

"No shame in that, Peaches. Shit *was* dark. Every man here, brother or not, will never begrudge you of what you thought. You didn't know we were coming. You had no idea what was going on. Braver men than you or I take that step. The one you didn't. So hold your head high, baby girl. You survived. Doesn't matter how, just that you did."

I brush away the tear she lets slip down her face away.

"Still, I need to thank her. Maybe you can get me over there later to see her?"

I run my hand through my short hair and take a beat. "Honestly, Peaches, I'm not sure if that's such a good idea. You can thank her and all, but wait till we know more."

"More what?"

Kooper

I shake my head. "I don't know. More about her? Know what's true or not."

She tilts her head at my words. "What's true?"

"How well do you know her?"

"We've lived together for six years." She says it as if that explains everything, and I give her an eyebrow lift. She shakes her head. "Not well. We both kept things to ourselves, and I... I didn't push. I wanted to just be me with her and not have to deal with... well, everything else. I kept my distance, and she did the same."

"She has a tracker on her. I don't know where or why, but Kitten found a woman who knew her. Or yelled at her or something. Not really sure about the connection. All I know is that she said they turned the tracker on, and that's how we found you." I take a breath, steeling myself to tell her the truth. She deserves it. "We were looking for Natalie. But we were hoping for you."

Her hand tightens on mine. "It's okay. I don't care who you went there for, as long as I got out."

I lean in close and press my lips to hers. Softly, like she deserves, before pulling back just a little. "You. It's always you I'm looking for."

She smiles as I lean away and sit back a bit. "She must have someone watching her. You think she's in trouble?"

"No, they didn't seem to care if she lived or died. Or so they said, but they waited to get eyes on her before leaving."

"Probably family."

I nod in agreement. "Probably."

She licks her lips. I already know she's going to ask me something, so I bring her hand to my lips and kiss her knuckles. "The answer is yes. Just ask."

She smiles. "Can you keep looking? She always said she was an orphan. But if she has family, I don't want her to be alone. Like... like I was." She corrects herself before I can do more than part my lips. "Like I *thought* I was. I know I wasn't. I never was. Not with you in my life."

I rub her hand again, keeping it warm between mine as she closes her eyes to rest. But I can't wait. I know I should, but I can't. "Peaches...."

"Yeah?" She keeps her eyes closed as she speaks.

"There was a woman." Her eyes flutter open. "She didn't make it."

A soft smile touches her lips as she nods. "Her name was Ava."

"When did she die? She...." I look for a polite way to say this.

"Wasn't decomposing?" Ruby supplies.

I shake my head.

"It was right before they moved us. I'm not sure how long ago it was, but I think it was the same day, or the day before. Time was different down there. I don't know. But I wasn't moved long before you found me. And she was—" She swallows her emotions. "She was shot before that."

Something to tell Casper. It might be a coincidence, or they got wind that we were coming and were taking out liabilities. But if that was the case, why not kill Ruby or Natalie? Why just this other person? We didn't have time to do more than see that she didn't have a pulse before we moved on. Maybe if we had, we could have gotten prints to find out who she was. Tell whoever was looking for her that she was found. That she had some peace finally.

"They…." Again, she takes a second to control her emotions, even closing her eyes, removing the tears that had appeared a second before. "They raped her. Not sure how many, but we heard. We heard it all. They killed her and then separated us. I think… I think we were next. If you hadn't shown up when you did, I don't—"

"Shhh." I shift closer to her. "You never have to think about the what-ifs. I did show. And I always will."

"Oh good, you're both here," General says, interrupting our closeness.

I glare, and he only smiles.

"Did I come at a bad time?"

"Yes."

"No," Peaches says at the same time and swats at me. I move down a bit so she can see him a bit more but still hold my glare.

General's smile widens. "Ah, patient wins."

"What's the verdict, General. Am I going to live?" Her joke makes my heart stutter a bit at the thought. Something I won't get over soon, I'm sure.

"Wouldn't be here if you weren't. I still want to keep you for a few days to get your fluids back up and make sure you put on a few more pounds before I let you go."

"Trust me, I am willing and ready to eat. Just not Jell-O. You bring it and I'm chucking it at your head. You get me?"

He grins, as do I. "Noted."

"There something else?" He wouldn't be here just to say that. I know him. Not as well as my girl, but enough to know when he's stalling.

"Yeah." He looks at his clipboard and then back at us, resolve showing on his face as if he battled with a decision and just now made the call. "We did a full scan when you were out. We wanted to make sure there wasn't anything in your system that we didn't know about that could be harmful to you. We took some blood."

"Okay." She doesn't seem worried but still looks at me for guidance. Something I find pride in.

"What'd you find, Doc?" No need to pussyfoot around this. I hold her hand tighter. Whatever it is, we can do this together.

"We found a higher-than-average level of hCG, or human chorionic gonadotropin."

"English, Doc," I grumble. Stupid doctors are always saying shit that no one understands.

"You're pregnant."

Chapter 41—Ruby

"Run it again," I blurt, so quick that I feel as if I'm out a breath. Or maybe that's just because my heart stopped pumping, and the oxygen isn't circulating.

I can't be pregnant. I just can't. I had sex… what? Once?

Technically, it was like nine times.

Shut up, brain. It was once. One night. Sure, we went at it all night, but that still counts as once. Right?

"I ran it three times to be sure." General looks at me with kind eyes. Something I'm sure he does with all his patients who receive news like this.

Like… shit. Is this good news or bad? I don't know.

"But I'm on birth control. I have the implant." I move my arm a bit to show him the small lift in my skin.

"Funny thing about implants is they only work a few years before they expire."

"Expire?" My eyes are as wide as saucers. I had no idea they expired. Did I? I don't know.

"From what we can figure out, it would have expired right around the time your dad—I mean Law, ah…."

When Dad died, but didn't die. I was too lost in my grief to do much then. If my doctor had called to set up a replacement, I would have missed it. Shit.

I look at Kooper, who's still staring at General. Maybe he didn't hear him. Maybe he's doing the math, like I am, and trying to figure this out.

What math, girl? You've been with one *guy.*

"Wait." Dread trickles into my mind. "Could it be...?" I close my eyes and shake out the shudder. I feel Kooper squeeze my hand, but I can't look at him when I say this. I just can't. "Do you know how long? Like, when it happened. I didn't sleep much, but... but... something could have happened. Something when I didn't think it did."

God, to be pregnant by one of them, one of my captors. Just the thought has me hyperventilating.

"Breathe, Ruby. I need you to breathe," General says.

I blink and, I swear, he's by my side in a second, holding my shoulder and trying to calm me down. It's not working.

"I'm going to be sick," I say a second before I lean over and throw up the water I drank earlier. Thank God General is quick, because I would have hit his shoes if he hadn't grabbed a kidney-shaped bowl for me to upchuck into.

I keep gagging, but there isn't anything in my stomach. Eventually, I roll back over onto my back, exhausted from that small effort. A cool cloth touches my forehead and cheeks before Kooper wipes my mouth and then tosses it away.

"We did an initial check when you were out. There were no signs of rape. However, we can still do a paternity test, though we won't be able to do so for a few more weeks. You're still in the early stages of the first trimester. We'll keep

Kooper

you on fluids and get you some actual food. I'll have one of our OB/GYN doctors come by, and you can go over things with them. They can give you a better idea of what to expect now that you're... well, expecting."

General smiles, but I don't.

Finding out I'm pregnant wasn't the plan.

But they ran blood work on me. Checked and double-checked. They're sure, they say.

And when General found out, he told me first. Well, me and Kooper.

Kooper. A minute ago, things were different. It was just him and me. Starting something. The possibilities were different. They were endless. Now? Shit, it looks like we started something weeks ago, and now we have to pay for it. Literally. Babies are expensive.

Oh God, what about school? Where am I going to live? I have no home. Dad doesn't know me. I've got nothing. I'm not going to raise this kid in the clubhouse, and Nat's and my place is too small. If we're even still going to be living together. If I trust her enough to be around my kid.

Double shit.

"Right, well, I'm going to get a nurse in here to start you on some prenatal vitamins and set up a menu for lunch to start getting you where you need to be for that healthy little one inside." General turns to leave with a pep in his step that I don't seem to have in my heart.

"General." He turns, and I watch his smile fade as he takes in my expression. Which I'm sure is full of panic. I glance at Kooper, who's watching me but saying nothing. Just listening.

I look back at General. "Is it too late? Too late to... you know?" I tilt my head back and forth and gesture to my stomach.

He doesn't frown. He doesn't get angry. He just looks on with respect. "No, sweetie. It's not too late to terminate if that's what you want. If you're thinking that because you don't know whose it is, I suggest you wait till we get a paternity test done first. We can get that done and then make that call. But the decision is yours. And I, and the club, will stand by your choice."

Tears fall down my cheeks as I nod. My voice is gone, floating away in fear of everything.

His smile is sad, but his eyes are those of someone who cares about my well-being and not the world's opinion on what I should do.

Then he leaves. And the quietness in the room is deafening.

"We'll get through this, Peaches."

Kooper's words draw my eye. I didn't want to look at him when I asked. I didn't want to see what would be on his face. But I should have known that he would have held his feelings, his thoughts to himself. It's what he does. He keeps a part of himself hidden from me, but only so I can shine a little bit more.

He'll let me decide. I know he will. Any choice I make, I know not a single Hound will think less of me. They'll support me through it all.

But what will I feel?

Kooper

"Was I raped?" I ask him. General already said it doesn't look like it, but I need to hear it from him. I need to know his thoughts.

He shakes his head.

"So... so it's yours?" I'm not sure why I'm questioning it. It's obvious when you do the math. Which is as simple as one plus one. But in this case, one woman plus one man makes three.

A small smile lifts his lips. "Unless you really weren't a virgin."

Even in this, after everything, he can pull a reaction from me without me thinking. I roll my eyes and push his chest. It's weak, but the impact is there.

"You know I was." No use in denying it now.

Before I can pull my hand back, he holds it close to his chest. Right over his heart.

"You want this?"

I don't know if he's asking about him or the kid.

I bite my lip and regret it. It's only been a day at the most since I was saved. My lip still hasn't healed enough for me to do anything but pout.

"Do you?" It's a total cop-out to answer his question with one of my own. But I need to know what he's thinking. He buries parts of himself for me, and while I appreciate being put first, in this I want to be second.

"I'll take you however I can get you."

My jaw drops at his open declaration. I know he said things when he got me out of there, but that was different. That was in the moment. In a battle when we didn't know if

435

we'd live or die. After not seeing each other for so long, it was a heat-of-the-moment thing. Or so I thought.

Even if my heart knew it was more. Hoped and begged for it to be more.

"You're it for me, Peaches. I don't want anyone else. I want you. And I'll take you however you want me to. I'll be your protector, your bodyguard. Your King Koopa to my Princess Peach. Your friend. Your teammate. I'll be your old man and the father of your kids. Hell, I'll even be the stay-at-home kind so you can go off and live your dream or whatever the hell you want."

A surprised laugh pulls from my lips at his words, and his grin widens. "You are *not* a stay-at-home kind of guy."

His smile drops as he brings my fingertips to his lips and kisses each pad before looking at me with such intensity that it feels as if I'm about to be set on fire. "For you I would."

"I don't know what I want," I whisper. It's the truth.

What felt like five seconds ago, I thought I did. But now? There's a kid inside me. A *kid*.

How can this be happening? I'm not ready to be a mom. I'm not ready for this. I'm a kid myself. Just ask my dad.

Dad.

He won't know. He might never know he's a grandpa. I could tell him, but would it be the same? Would he even care?

And does Kooper even want this? This is sudden. We had sex once. *Once.*

I guess they were speaking the truth when they said it only takes one time in Sex-Ed class. Of course it would be me who's the statistic in all of this.

Kooper

Kooper, for all his faults, is honorable. Loyal. He would stick by me. By the kid. I have zero thoughts that he would abandon him or her if we don't last. And who knows if we will.

We fucked once.

Jesus, I'm not going to be able to get over that part.

He'll tire of me. He's used to experience. To a fast-paced life. Saying you'll stay home is one thing compared to the reality of actually doing it.

Tell him he has to watch the kid and not go to the club because I'm in class or at my job? That's laughable. Something that would never happen.

And me staying home? I know people do it. Mom did. But that's not me. I've worked hard for what I have. Real hard. I didn't know what I wanted before all this, but being locked up for days gave me time to think about everything. To really see what matters most. And my own practice? Yeah, I want that.

I want the long hours. The grueling schedule. The complaining about paperwork and wondering if we'll make rent.

Okay, not the last part, but I want all the rest. I want a boring job to do in the day.

And at night... I want Kooper.

I've wanted him for a while. He became my world, even before it turned to shit with Dad and everything else.

But I don't know if I can give him what he wants.

"What if the kid isn't yours?"

I'm 98 percent sure it is, but there's still the unknown. Till I get the test results, it'll always be a what-if.

Even after, I've got no misconceptions that I won't wake screaming to nightmares that could be memories or just my mind playing tricks on me, giving me details of what could have happened or did when I thought I was protected. When I thought I was safe in that cell and things were happening next door to Ava. I'm naïve in a few things, but not enough to fully believe I came out of that place untouched. Mentally or physically.

"It would be yours. If you choose to have it, it would be your kid, Peaches. I can't think of a better thing to watch over than something that belongs to you."

"Do you… do you want it?" Another whisper. This time because the emotions are holding my voice hostage and not allowing me to speak louder without releasing a sob.

"Whatever you want."

"No." I shake my head and close my eyes before looking back at him. "No. You can't do that. You can't be the one putting me first in this. I need to know what you think. What you want." His head tilts as he stares at me. "Please," I beg.

"I do."

I let out a breath at his words.

"Like I said, I'll take you any way I can get you. If you don't want a kid right now, I get that. Shit happened to you. Bringing in a life after that is not easy. But I'm not going anywhere. So if you choose not to have this one, I'll still be here for the next one."

He palms my face and rubs his fingers over my cheek. "And the next. And the next."

"Jesus, how many are you expecting?"

"Kids are going to need friends."

I shake my head, but it's with a smile. He leans in and presses a kiss to my forehead and then a peck on my lips.

"I feel different now. I don't feel like me, like Ruby," I confess to him as we're inches apart. A secret for his ears alone.

"Then don't be. Be Peaches. Be *my* Peaches."

"What... what are you saying?"

"I think you know."

"Say it." I glare at him, but he just leans back and shakes his head.

"No."

"Why? Scared?" Calling him that puts my fear at bay a bit. I'd rather us both be scared than just me.

He shakes his head again. "Never. I can say it, scream it, tattoo it. It won't change anything. All that matters is if *you* say it. If *you* feel it."

I swallow, even if it's hard to do. I don't know why calling him something other than Kooper scares me more than thinking about having a kid, but it does. Maybe because I know this is it. Once it's said out loud, once *I* say it, there's no going back. It'll be him and me forever. If I call him my old man, and he calls me his old lady.

Even if he tried to end it, I have too much of my mom and dad in me to let it go peacefully. I'd kill the bastard before I let him get away from me. *If* I'm willing to call it for what it is right now.

"Say it."

"I... I—"

A nurse comes in at that moment, and Kooper backs up enough to give her room to check me over. She stays for a minute and then says she'll be back in a second with the menu.

As soon as she leaves, I speak before Kooper can sit down and get close. When he's close, I can't think straight. And I need to. We both do.

"I need time to think. About this. About us. And you do too."

"I just told you what I want."

"But I want you to be sure. To know what it means. We *both* need to be sure that if we do this, that... that we *do* this. I don't know what that will look like in a year or, hell, a month. There could still be issues, complications with the... with the baby." Saying it doesn't make it any easier. It's weird, all weird. "Please, Koop. Please."

He looks me in the eye, seeing more than I know before he nods.

And then he walks away.

Was that my answer?

Chapter 42—Kooper

She thinks I don't want this. Us.

That I'll pick someone or something over her.

She's wrong.

But I'll give her time.

She wants that.

So I'll give it to her.

When she told me to think about it, I knew I didn't need to. I've already thought about it. For months, maybe even years if I do the math between when my feelings changed for her. But she needs space. Without saying it, that's what she needs.

She wants to think without me standing over her shoulder, assessing every move, every thought she might have.

She doesn't think she can be herself. And maybe she can't. People change. Some over time. Some in an instant.

Every day, I come to visit her. Every day, I check that she's okay. I don't bring up the things left unsaid between us. And she doesn't either.

We keep our distance. Sort of. I cave more than I should with a touch here, a handhold there. I'm distant only because she wants me to be. She needs that wall right now. She needs to rebuild herself and find a way to stand on her own feet.

In her mind, at least.

General had her discharged as soon as he was happy with the weight gain. Natalie had some complications during her surgery and is still there. In another few days, she'll be released.

Ruby hasn't gone to see her. Not yet anyway. We found her family and got a call out to them. We're waiting for their response before we talk to her. Might seem shady, but Ruby has a right to call the plays here. Well, that, and General keeps saying that visitors could upset Natalie's progress. That her nightmares have become night terrors, and they have to medicate her a bit more to keep her calm enough to heal.

I guess other shit went down with her that not even Ruby knows about. Could have been during their hostage moment or something else. My gut feeling is it's a combination of both.

But I keep it to myself.

I park my truck and head up to her apartment. She's taken some time off school, mostly because she missed the start of the summer semester. But she's also playing catch-up with what she missed. Her professors were cool about her extending her spring semester into a summer session. Even the dickhead who usually gave her a hard time about shit. Of course, a few choice words from me and the boys helped a bit. Well, that, and a generous donation to the school, which made sure they were also on board with the decision. All she had left was a paper to write and a final for each of her three classes. Today, she submitted her last paper, so she's officially done.

Just in time for us to drive to the hospital and do the paternity test. General says he can get us the results quickly,

Kooper

which is what we want. I don't care what it says; I already know what I want. But if it eases her mind, I'm all for it.

"Coming," she calls out when I knock on her door.

She opens it and gives me a smile that lights up the darkest corners of my soul. "Hey," she says on a breath.

And I can't help it. I just can't. I lean in, grab her face with both hands, and pull her lips tight to mine.

Her squeak of surprise is enough to give me room to sweep my tongue inside her mouth to taste her. Her moan as she wraps her hands around me has me pushing her against the wall and moving my hands down to her ass to lift her legs around me.

I'm so hard that I'm surprised I'm not already inside her at this point.

She's fully recovered. Well, enough that she's only doing some physical therapy stretches for her shoulder. The rest of her is back together enough that I know I can do this without causing too much damage. Her bruises are gone, and her ribs, though still healing, are good enough to have some of my weight on them.

She pulls her mouth away and catches her breath as I move my lips down her neck and throat, nibbling at her skin as I go.

"Fuck, that feels good. Shit. Right there. No, stop. We have to go. Oh God, don't stop." She pushes me away and then pulls me back as she debates what she wants. I'm not letting my lips rest for one second. Now that I have them on her, it feels impossible to stop.

Till she pushes me hard enough to peel me off her. I'm still holding her up, but now her arms are fully extended and she's looking at me. I feel wild, like an animal, and the desire swirling in her eyes matches what I feel inside. Especially in my dick.

I grind against her and watch her eyes roll back on a groan and smile. I love that I pull that out of her.

"We're going to be late," she grits out between her teeth as she rotates her hips to get my cock in the spot she wants.

She's right, so I let her feet drop and kiss her nose before turning for the door. It closed when we came in, so I open it and turn back to her.

She's still standing by the wall, holding on for support as her breathing returns to normal. Then her eyes meet mine, and I see the fire in them as she glares, making my dick jump in intrigue.

"You'll pay for that."

"Looking forward to it, Peaches."

She shakes her head, but I don't miss the smile on her lips as she crosses over the threshold and heads to my truck. We spoke about it a long time ago. No bike on the highways. Not when a car can fuck shit up for the both of us, and the kid, if it hits us when we take my bike.

If she keeps it.

The drive is quiet, rock music playing in the background as we pass mile after mile of cows and cornfields till we get to the hospital.

Once we're inside, the test is quick. We could have done it at the hospital by the school, but we both wanted General to do it. He's still the only one who knows. No need to talk about it till she makes her choice.

Kooper

When we get back into the car, I drive home.

Not to the clubhouse, but to home.

"What's this?" she asks as I pull up the drive and park.

I look at her and then just get out of the truck.

Like usual, she doesn't wait for me to get to the door before she's hopping out. I've got half a mind to get the truck lifted so she'll have to stay in there till I get her down. But I know, pregnant or not, she'd still hop down on her own.

She doesn't need a man. But if I'm lucky, she'll want one.

I grab her hand and don't say anything as I move to the walkway that leads to the front door instead of the garage that we parked by.

It's a single-story farmhouse design with a black roof and clean white lines. The entire thing is a mirror of itself if you cut it down the middle. I pull her along as we walk the path to the front door. I take a second to key in the door code, then open it and step back, letting her go in first.

She gives me half a smirk and an eyebrow raise but steps in. The main area has an open floor plan, and she can see the royal blue bottom kitchen cabinets on the left and the large sectional leather sofa on the right.

"You trying to compete with Bass and his place?"

I shrug. Of course she's been to his house. She was usually the one stocking the fridge when he was getting back into town after being on a mission before he and Brooklyn got together.

"This is a few hundred square feet bigger. Behind the kitchen are three extra rooms and the attachment to the garage."

"And over here?" She shimmies her delectable ass to the right, pointing past the brick fireplace to the hallway behind.

"Why don't you go and see?"

With the squeal of a small child, she takes off at a jog and runs down the hall. As if I'd change my mind and demand she stay put.

I follow easily. Nothing much back here, just the laundry room and an extra bathroom. Oh, and the massive primary bedroom.

I find her there, jaw wide open, as she takes in the sitting area, the platform up to the bed, and then the bath. At least the closet doors are closed, or I'm sure she might have an aneurysm with the size of it. If I know one thing about my girl, she's a sucker for a good-size closet.

"What size bed is that?"

"It's a Wyoming king." I move up behind her and wrap my arms around her as I place my chin on her shoulder.

"It's bigger than a California."

"Still smaller than an Alaskan."

She turns in my arms. "They have bigger?"

I chuckle as I brush a piece of hair behind her ear. "Yup. But I think those sizes are usually reserved for those who share."

"Oh." Her hands come up to my chest and fiddle with the buttons there. "And do you share?"

Kooper

"Yup."

"You do?" Her eyes go wide, and then she rolls them and shakes her head as if she just got it. "I mean other than with you and the brothers."

I shake my head. "I only share with you." That gets a smile out of her. "And I don't have brothers."

"You've got the club."

"Do I?"

I raise an eyebrow at her, and she smiles, but then looks down, then back up, and her eyes are wide.

"What happened? Where's your vest?" She pushes out of my arms and paces. "Did Casper kick you out? Because of me? Because of us?" She points at herself, then me. "Oh, he better not. Get your keys, King Koopa. We're about to whip some ass." She starts marching for the door, and I can't help but feel happiness burst from the inside out.

"Hold up. No need to go all Donkey Kong on someone who had nothing to do with it."

"What? Casper wasn't the one? Does he know? Because only the president can kick you out. God, was it my father?" The blood drains from her face, and I pull her in for a quick hug and a kiss before she passes out.

"No, Peaches, nothing like that."

"Then what was it?"

"I'm out."

She's it for me. And she needs to feel like someone put her first. Her and our kid. I don't care what the damn blood test says. I know what I know. That's my kid inside her. It might not share my DNA, but it will be mine.

"What did you do?" She takes a step back, horror on her face.

"I chose." I say it simply, because it is.

"You chose? You chose what?"

"You." I nod and gesture to her.

"Me."

"You."

"What about the club?"

"What about it?" I say with a shrug.

She shakes her head and paces again. "You can't do that. I don't want you to. We need to call Casper, tell him this was all a mistake. He can overlook this. You can still be part of the club."

I walk to her and put my hands on her shoulders, stopping her in her tracks. "I can, and I did. I choose you. I will always choose you. I love you."

She blinks. Several times. I know how much she hates crying, though it seems to happen a lot more now. She blames it on the pregnancy. I don't care what the reason is, but I don't bring it up. She likes to pretend she doesn't have feelings. That she's as tough as nails and more. And she is.

"I love you too."

Four small words that shatter me completely.

"Damn right you do. Now give me those lips."

I pull her close and resolve then and there to never let go.

Ever.

Chapter 43—Ruby

I know we've done this before. Hell, I play it on repeat every night and sometimes during the day. Or twice a day depending on what's going on.

I've talked to people. Something Troublemaker and Mama Bear convinced me to do. And it's helped. I don't think I'm "healed" or whatever you call it after therapy, but I feel… okay with what happened. With it all. My therapist still thinks I'm holding on to some guilt and anger at myself for how non-badass I was, but hey, that's why she gets paid the big bucks. To sort out my head for me so I don't have to. And if she wants to keep the money coming in, she needs to figure out real quick that being okay with something is sometimes the best I can do in the moment.

But what can I say? Not everyone is Kooper. My man. The one who knows me. Who gets me. Who sees me and my self-esteem issues. The one who noticed I always felt like I was playing second fiddle to something I could never be part of. I'm still not sure if I'm okay with him leaving the club, but this? Him doing it and not seeming to give a fuck that I'm not okay with it?

God, I love this man.

He pulls me flush to him, and I go with ease, like a rag doll moving as he directs.

He lifts my feet off the floor, and for a second, I'm just hanging in his arms with mine around his shoulders, and we kiss as if there's nothing else to do. Because there isn't. It's just him and me. And the peanut.

But even that nut can't distract me from the feel of Kooper holding me in his arms so tight, like I'm precious. No, not like that. Like I'm *his*. Because I am.

He bends, and only then do I realize we moved. I thought it was just the way he kissed that had me thinking the earth was spinning. He sets me down gently, pushing me back as he scoots us both up the bed.

I hear his shoes hit the floor as he kicks them off, and I do the same. The weather is hot outside, but it's nothing compared to what it feels like in here. I always thought it was a joke when I saw in movies or read in books that they ripped each other's clothes off. But I get it now. I want to feel him, all of him. And I can't do that with all this damn fabric on him.

The second his shirt is off, I'm biting his chest, kissing his abs. Anything I can get my hand and mouth on, I'm doing it. He does the same, and it's a fight over who can kiss where. And honestly, I don't know who's going to win, but I'm all too happy to play the game.

The rest of our clothes go just as quickly, and then I'm straddling him as I kiss him with everything I have. He holds me close, his hands on my back and then moving to my ass to give it a tight squeeze. I lift, and that's the opening he needs to move his lips off mine to my nipples, kissing, sucking, and then squeezing them as his hands continue to roam.

I'm not going to last long if he keeps this up.

Fuck it.

Kooper

I don't have to play fair. I don't have to play by his rules. Never did before. Not really.

I wiggle my hand between us and stroke his hard cock. He groans around my breast in his mouth a second before I sink down on him. He pops off my tit with a moan as I arch my back in pleasure.

"So good. God, you feel so good."

"It's this slick pussy. You got it all wet for me. Next time I'll be the one to get it wet."

"Promises," I murmur as I move on him, rocking back and forth like I remember. Moving to what feels good.

"Always, Peaches. I'm always going to want to eat out that sweet peach between your legs." He grabs my ass and helps move me.

We rock together as our lips crash against each other like waves on the shore. I chase my release, and I feel him do the same as his movements get frantic. We can do slow and easy next time. Or even the time after that.

All I want now is to explode in his arms.

I cry out his name as I come, and he matches my release with his own.

I lock my lips onto his and kiss him slowly. This is not the end. This is just the beginning.

For tonight and every night after.

"Tell them to fuck off," Kooper grumbles from behind me, but at least he releases me from his hold enough for me to reach over the edge of the bed and pull my phone out of my discarded shorts.

I read the name on the caller ID and look at Kooper as I answer. "Yes, General?"

Kooper sits up and pulls me slowly to him. I allow it, but my mind is on the call. I touch his chest to hold him at bay as I listen to what General's saying.

"Okay, thanks. Yeah, talk soon."

I hang up and look at my phone as if I can see the call, replaying it back like a damn TikTok video in my head.

"What did he say?" Kooper runs his hands up and down my thighs as I sit cross-legged in front of him.

"It's yours." I finally look up at him as I repeat myself. "You're going to be a dad."

"And you a mom."

I huff out a breath as it hits me. Just like that. A mom.

As soon as General said it was Kooper's, I knew I could never get rid of it. Hell, I knew I wasn't going to do that at the hospital when I asked, but I wanted to give myself an out. Just in case. But we knew. We all knew it was never really someone else's. It was Kooper. Always Kooper.

I lean up and get onto my knees, shuffling the few inches separating us and wrapping my hands around him. I play with his hair as he pulls me even closer to kiss my chest, right where my heart is, before pulling back and looking at me.

"We really doing this?" I ask, more in awe than anything else.

"Yeah, Peaches, we really are."

Kooper

"And this house?"

"It's yours."

I smile. "Ours."

He shrugs. "I'm happy to share it with you. But it's your birth date on the lock. Your name on the deed. I just bought it for you."

I run my fingers through his hair and hold him still, looking deep into his eyes to see his soul. "You know I don't need all this, right? The big house? The grand gesture? I just need you."

"Lucky for you, you don't have to choose. You get both. All and more."

My smile perks up. "Oh, there's more?"

He smirks. "Maybe you should check out the rest of the house."

The way his eyes sparkle has mine going wide. With a squeal, I grab the sheet out from under him, wrapping it around me as I laugh at him falling off the bed before running to the other side of the house.

The first room just has a bed. The second? A crib. Nothing else, but it's enough to get my heart beating. But the third? The third room leaves me speechless.

I feel arms wrap around me from behind as I take it all in.

"Like it?"

I just nod. How could I not? It's every gamer's dream console, all done up in flashing lights around a sign with my username in bold red highlights. Hell, it even has one of those super-awesome comfy chairs. And right next to it is one for him with his username: Bowser.

I *knew* it was him.

"Good. Because the warranty went out on it last month, and I can't take it back."

He chuckles as he kisses my cheek before releasing me to fiddle with a few keys to power up one of the systems.

"Warranty? How long have you had this?"

"I got it for you last year. Thought it could be a Christmas gift."

"What?" I whisper.

"Huh?" He looks back at me and blinks. "You okay?"

Okay? This guy bought me my dream gift when I was mad at him. When I wasn't even talking to him. He spent way more than a few grand, and he didn't even know if we would be together.

I turn on my heel and head for the bedroom.

"Peaches?" he calls after me, but I don't stop. I keep marching till I get to my room. I mean ours.

I grab my panties and bra, pulling them and my shorts on. But when I pick up my shirt, it's ripped. Like seriously ripped. I guess we really were in the moment.

"Peaches?" he repeats as he comes into the room. His jeans are on, not buttoned, and he looks yummy as hell. Still, I glare.

"What now?"

I don't say anything as I head to what I can only assume is the closet through the massive bedroom. And I was right. And like everything else, it's huge and perfect and just about everything I could ever dream of.

Kooper

I curse as I stomp over to a set of drawers and start opening them till I find one filled with his shirts. I grab the top one and put it on.

"You going to tell me what has you in a tizzy?"

"Not in a tizzy. Just pissed. Now get your shit. We're going."

"And where is it we're headed?"

"The clubhouse."

"You going to tell me why?"

"Nope. Now hurry the fuck up. I don't got all day."

And like the fucker he is, he does as I say without so much as a hitch. Fucking bastard.

The drive is quick because the town is small, and despite what he said, we're close to the clubhouse in case he ever wants to go say hi.

As soon as we park, I'm out and walking through the door. Kooper yells at me the whole way to stop, but I don't.

I'm a girl on a mission, and I'm not about to stop till I get what I want.

As soon as I see who I'm looking for, I walk right up to him and glare. "Give my old man his vest back. We both know this club needs him more than he needs you."

I don't give a fuck that I broke up poker night with the boys. I need Casper to give Kooper his shit so we can get going. I want food. Wings, preferably.

He gives me a side-eye, then tilts his head to the side. "Lose something, Dixon?"

I stomp my foot. "His name is Kooper, not Dixon. He's a brother, and he deserves the respect of the name given to him."

"That right?" Casper gives me a look of childish disbelief. "And who might you be?"

"Peaches," Kooper says before I do. He comes up to me and pulls me back to him.

"You sure about this? I've got no problem living as Dixon for you," he says into my ear before I turn in his arms.

"I want you to be happy."

"I'm happy with you."

Fucking asshole keeps saying sweet things, and I'm going to cry. Which I really hate doing, no matter how many times the baby forces me to.

"You can have both. All of it, whatever you want. But we both know I'm going to piss you off. You're going to need to vent to someone. So join your little club. Talk your little talk. And come home to me each night."

The boys around us chuckle, and I get close, blocking them out as I hold my hand to the side of his face. "I don't need a knight to fight my dragons. I just need you. If that means I get a Hound in leather with chrome for a steed, I'll take it."

"Deal," he growls a second before he kisses me soundly as the entire place erupts with cheers.

"About damn time. Bulldog, go get Kooper's vest off my desk. And get the one that says 'Peaches' with it."

I break my kiss and turn to Casper, who grins. "Welcome to the family."

Kooper

Family. I had one growing up. Thought I lost it. But then I found it again. With Kooper.

Because I became his.

As if reading my mind, he pulls me close and sings in my ear, pulling a giggle from my lips and joy from my heart.

"Peaches, Peaches, Peaches, Peaches, Peaches, Peaches, Peaches, Peaches, Peaches, Peaches, I love you."

Chapter 44—Natalie

The beeping of the hospital machines brings me out of my sleep. Every time I fall asleep with it, I swear I won't get more than an hour. But the sun is shining through the blinds, and I know I must have slept for a solid eight hours, if not more.

The doctors keep giving me things to help me sleep. They say I have night terrors and wake up and start moving. But that's the issue. I can't move. I've got a broken leg, so I keep causing more damage to myself.

I feel like I've been in here for years, but I'm told it's been closer to a month. I just hope I get out soon.

"Hey, Nat."

I look left and feel my face light up. Ruby. She hasn't come to see me at all, but I didn't blame her for it. Shit went down for us. I don't want her to see me and think ill will. Being kidnapped is no joke. Everyone processes it differently.

Still, I wouldn't have minded if she'd showed a little earlier. I can only take so much daytime television. At least there was a nice volunteer nurse who came in a while back and showed me how to crochet. I suck at it, but it keeps my mind focused on something other than living in that damn cell.

And even though I have a hospital bed to sleep in and fresh food every day, I still feel like I'm in that that room.

"Hi! How are you?"

Kooper

She moves closer to my bed but doesn't meet my hand when I reach out for her.

My gut sinks at her reaction to me. Something is off, and I just feel the need to cry.

"Wh-what's wrong?" I stumble over my lips as I lick them to keep the dryness at bay.

"You have a visitor."

I tilt my head in confusion. Maybe she's more messed up than me, because as far as I'm concerned, *she's* my visitor.

"Your sister."

My concerned expression drops, along with my voice. "I don't have a sister."

"Oh, don't say that."

The voice. The voice I refuse to think is real speaks as she enters my room. My hands are in fists, ready to attack if she gets too close. But she knows me well enough and doesn't get closer than just behind Ruby, keeping her between us.

"I know you never liked me since my mom married your dad, but I'm still family. I care about you. We all do. We've missed you since you ran away." Her sugary-sweet voice is lost on me, as are her fake-ass tears.

"What are you running from?" Ruby's face contorts as if she's been betrayed. As if I were the one who did that.

I just shake my head. "I wasn't running."

"It's okay, Barbra. You don't have to be embarrassed. These things happen all the time to people."

"Your name isn't Natalie?" Ruby's expression changes quickly to one of rage, and again I shake my head.

"It is. Barbra is the name *she* gave me. How did you find her?"

"We found you, actually. They put out enough information on the web for us to realize it was you and not some random person. We contacted them. And Barb, seriously, we've been over this. Mom and Dad changed your name legally. You are Barbra."

"They had no right."

The face she puts on for Ruby is comical. Acting like I'm a silly child throwing a fit. They decided to change my name when I was nine. Nine! Why? Because they felt like it. Because my bitch of a stepmom didn't want to be reminded that my dad was with someone before her. That *she* was second in his life. So they picked a name she wanted. And it was a name that made her smile a cruel smile. I don't think she even liked the name, but she liked it better than me being named after my mom, Natala.

"Are you ever going to stop punishing us? Me?" She sniffs, and Ruby looks back, fucking falling for this bullshit. "We tried not to. We really did. But we fell in love, Barb. Real love. I told him we shouldn't. I knew he was promised to you, but he chose to leave his family's job to be with me. He sacrificed everything for love. I know you wanted to marry him, get the cushy lifestyle and all that he brought with it, but he chose to be poor for me. Can't you just be happy for us? I'm sorry that he was your fiancé. We should have—I know we should have told you we were together when Mom and Dad announced your engagement. We had no idea Dad would force you into marrying him. I thought I was doing you

Kooper

a favor when we spoke up. We thought you'd be happy. We had no idea you would be so upset. If it were just money that you wanted, you could have asked for it. You didn't need to steal it from us. From Mom and Dad. They would have understood."

I just can't stop shaking my head. What complete and utter crap.

And from the look Ruby just gave her, I know she doesn't believe it. Not all of it. She's known me for over six years. Money has never been a thing I'm after. Ever.

And my evil stepsister must realize she pushed the wrong con, as her eyes shift to Ruby and see she isn't buying it.

"But don't you worry. Everything will be fine now. I'm here. I'll take you back."

"To what? To watch you and him be together? Why would she be down for that?" Ruby asks with a skeptical look on her face. One I want to cheer at but don't because I'm still so mad at all of this.

Why is she even here? I made sure that no one knew where I was. Or so I thought. Sure, I saw a few people who might be part of the family, but I scared them off.

Fucking hell, I was kidnapped for like three weeks. There was no way anyone was looking for me. How did Ruby find her?

"No. I wanted my sister, not him. I decided to turn down love and pushed him away. But she had already run before I could tell her." She sniffs again and touches her eyes like she's trying to hold her tears in. "I want to get her home. She needs to rest. Regroup. So do I. It's been a long road getting her back. I can see why she likes it here. It's… peaceful. I guess that's why she stayed. It's just what the doctor ordered."

I roll my eyes at the acting job. If I didn't know her, I would believe her. Instead, I want to applaud. She would be perfect for Broadway.

"You should see it in the fall." Ruby's voice comes out whimsical, as I'm sure she's remembering some of her favorite things. And one of them is the fall here. She likes being able to rock her leather but not be too cold. The crunch of leaves under her boots and an excuse to snuggle under a blanket and drink hot beverages without people calling her psycho for also enjoying it in the blaze of summer.

I smile at Ruby, and we share a moment. Memories of the fall and of us together over the past few years. Some of the best moments of my life. I know we aren't close, but I lived for those moments. Ones where I could just be me and not pretend to be anything else.

A moment that's shattered when my stepsister speaks. "I'd like that. Maybe you could show me."

"Oh, I'm sorry, visiting hours have ended for this morning. You can come back in the afternoon, but we need to get you out so I can do vital scans and help her get showered and fed."

Oh good, a nurse is here to make me look weaker. Something my stepsister lives for.

"Of course. Ruby, want to get a coffee?" Back to her syrupy sweetness that I just want to punch in the face.

Ruby looks at me, and I see it. I see the distrust in me. I get it. Sort of. She was never honest with me. I mean, her

Kooper

dad wasn't dead. I went to the funeral. Talk about lying. And what about everything else she hid from me? She kept me close, but only for herself, not to bring me closer to her family and friends.

Hurt touches my eyes when I realize Ruby doesn't know who to trust.

And it stings more than anything. Even more when she turns and walks out, my stepsister looping one arm through hers as if they're long-lost friends.

They're gone before I can warn Ruby. Before I can warn them all. My sister is not a nice person. She's the devil incarnate. A vampire, sucking everything and everyone dry.

And they just invited her in.

Chapter 45—Psy

"Enter," I bark at the single knock on my door. The boys learned long ago that I don't like when people walk in on me. I'll let you enter when I want. Not a second sooner.

"We found her. We found Ava." My second-in-command doesn't pussyfoot around the intel. Another thing I don't like.

"Where?"

"Colombia."

I grab the gun on the desk and put it in the back of my jeans. "Let's go get her." I'm not going to waste any more time than we already have finding her.

"She's dead." He gives no emotion, no reaction. Just the facts.

I still for a moment as I take in his words and try to process everything that's happened and will happen from this in thirty seconds. Then I narrow my eyes and ask one question.

"Who?"

Who the fuck would dare mess with the Devils Damned property? We aren't nice. We're fucked-up psychotic assholes, some more so than others. We deal in shit others don't touch because we're both stupid and smart at the same time. We know what we need to do to get the job done and not get caught by fucking police pigs. We've got a reputation for ourselves: You don't fuck with me and mine.

And someone did.

"The Hounds."

This means war.

S.J. Rowe

Get a Free Book

Law will be available May 2026

To sign up for the monthly newsletter and get a copy of LAW: Origins, a free novella, go to my website.

Go to www.SJROWE.com **to get started!**

Thanks for Reading

Thank you for reading Kooper: Hounds of the Reaper MC (Book 9). If you enjoyed this book and would like to give back to the author, please consider writing a review! Reviews are a tremendous help for authors. So, if you were moved and enjoyed this book enough to write even one sentence of encouragement, it would be a huge boon.

Go to www.SJROWE.com **to get started!**

Also by S.J. Rowe

Titles in The Cain and Abel Series:

Marked for Seduction

Marked for Deception

Marked for Protection

Titles in The Hounds of the Reaper MC Series:

Chains

Bulldog

Flint

Mad Max

Gator

Bass

Casper

Domino

Kooper

Coming Soon:

Law

About the Author

After traveling the world as a child, S.J. Rowe has found a home in the southwest with her husband and two kids. She continues to visit exotic destinations around the world with her best friends, and when she is home, she splits her time between watching baseball and singing in the car. To unwind, she enjoys a good cup of coffee while curled up watching Star Wars.

Connect with the Author

JOIN THE S.J. ROWE NEWSLETTER —
Get a free book just for signing up Subscribe Now!

BECOME A H.O.T.R. FAN ON FACEBOOK —
Click the "follow" button on my fan page and you'll see some awesome humor and possible sneak peaks before anyone else
https://www.facebook.com/HOTRMC

CHECK OUT MY WEB SITE —
Get the latest information on all books written by S.J. Rowe
www.sjrowe.com

AMAZON —
If you click the follow button here, you'll get an email each time I put out a new book. Talk about a sweet deal
Amazon.com: S.J. Rowe: books, biography, latest update

TICTOK ANYONE? —
Looking for more facetime? Catch me on TikTok and see all the crazy things that I come up with
http://www.tiktok.com/@sjroweauthor

A GOOD OLD-FASHION EMAIL —

When in doubt, email it out. I would love to hear from any and everyone s.j.rowe@outlook.com

Please enjoy the following exert from the first book in the Hounds of the Reaper Series: Chains

Chapter 1 - Maddy

Five weeks have passed since I became a single mom—of sorts—and things are finally getting into a routine. I didn't know how the kids would react to me. And let's be honest here, I was clueless about what I was doing. I still don't know.

Grace has been easy. The girl stole my heart immediately and had no problem letting me in. From her blue eyes looking into my soul with so much hope for a better life to the way her cornfield-blonde hair curled into ringlets that bounced with each step she took. She's a genuine princess to

Kooper

the core, despite that she refuses to be called one, preferring to be known as Supergirl Grace, or Gigi for short. It doesn't make a lick of sense, but when I first called her that, she couldn't stop giggling. Even Teddy showed one of his rare smiles. She's still so young, which helps me on so many levels. I try not to think about how she has no mama anymore, but I don't think she remembers her much.

From the way Teddy speaks occasionally, even though Jennie died less than a year ago, I get the feeling she wasn't around a ton. It makes my heart ache to know they were alone so much. They had their grandma, at least. She might have forgotten things, but at least she was around. That had to count for something.

For today, Grace is all about superheroes. But with the way I keep showing them new things every day, I'm sure my little superhero will change into something else by the end of the month. Heck, she was all about solving mysteries the first two weeks, and we watched nothing but *Scooby-Doo.*

It took some time, but she soon moved from clinging to her brother to me. Not sure what I did to deserve the love of the sweetest superhero ever, but I cherish each hug, each cuddle with my entire heart. It's made for some difficult times when she refuses to be out of my arms, proving more than once she has abandonment issues. On nights that the cling monster comes out, we usually order in, as there's no way I can cook with one hand. I'm not that talented yet. But I'm working on it.

I have no illusion that I can keep Teddy and Grace, but I willingly live in denial that the day won't come soon.

Teddy has been harder to get to warm up to me. He's a tough nut to crack, and I'm in no rush. He's been through hell. Might weigh the size of a peanut, but he seems to carry everything on his shoulders. Or at least he tries to. He watches over his sister more times than not, and he's started even watching over me. I can't tell if it's his concern for me or being wary of me.

Even without getting the dossier on him that Izzy sent over after the third day, there was sadness in his hazel eyes that no little boy should ever have. His hair matches his sister's in color, but he likes to keep it short. In his words, he wants to see what's coming at all times.

I will admit that I don't have a ton of experience on how to handle trauma kids. Google searches have helped a bit, but mostly they've made me think I've been screwing it all up with what I've been doing. Apparently buying everything the little boy wants, or what I think he wants, is a bad thing. Well, too damn bad. The boy needs happiness, and I'm trying to give it to him, even if that means I have to buy a new Lego set every day. The kid is wicked smart and able to build anything I put in front of him.

The routine is simple for us. Kids wake up at the ass crack of dawn, pulling me out of bed to turn on cartoons. They enjoy a few snacks while watching silliness while I try to wake up after drinking a few cups of coffee. Then breakfast, followed by another cartoon or two, depending on the time. By ten, I usually have them outside. I have nothing really awesome in the backyard. The house is a fixer-upper, in and out. Most of the areas inside are decent enough, which is why we focus on the outside for an hour or two. I try to get them into planting flowers and mowing, which usually works for ten minutes, and then they're off exploring the area,

Kooper

which isn't that large but big enough for them based on the smiles they have. It's great watching them play together.

By half past eleven, we head inside to wash up and eat lunch. Gigi goes down for a nap, and Teddy, who constantly says he's too big for one, will look at one of his books before crashing out for at least an hour. I crash then, too, as the kids wear me out all the time. We typically fill the afternoons with Teddy building something. Gigi was off being a superhero that gave tea parties to all her stuffed animals. And yes, if I get Teddy a new Lego, Gigi gets a new stuffy. What can I say? I've already admitted I'm clueless. Who cares if the girl has about forty different stuffies already? If she spots another one, I know I'm going to buy it for her.

Dinner is early—well, for me anyhow. Before the kids showed, I usually worked on the house till well past eight before calling it quits, but I soon realized that one great asset the kids have is they love to sleep. Bedtime is at 7:30 p.m. for both, which is awesome, but makes dinner at six fun, especially since I have to wrap up my stuff at five. Who knew cooking for three took so much time?

I'd like to believe that once the kids go down, I live it up. That I'd focus on the house, get back on schedule to get things done in the timeframe I planned to sell the place in the next few months. But honestly? I usually spend way too much time googling how to cook something, or buying something new I think they would like. Even looking up ways to coax Teddy out of his shell a bit more. He's said little unless he's trying to protect his sister.

That first day was interesting. After our little coffee talk—always making sure I have one in hand to keep the smile on my face—we did breakfast, then went shopping. I asked them a million questions about what they liked, and they didn't answer, so I just chose what I thought looked good. When I piled up the baskets full of clothes at the first store and bought everything without blinking, they soon realized that if they wanted something, it was theirs. I'm not loaded, but a few delayed installments in my renovation were worth the smiles from Gigi. I even got one out of Teddy when I found his love for Legos while we took a turn around the toy aisle. Books were in the basket already, but kids have to have toys. It's a must.

I'm just cleaning up the cereal bowls as the kids finish the latest *Scooby-Doo* when I hear the grumble of bikes. Both kids notice as well and look at me in alarm. This isn't the first time we've heard the noise of a motorcycle going by. A few times we went into town, one would pass. Both kids freaked at the sound. Gigi usually gets over it quickly with a distraction, but Teddy remembers enough to have nightmares about them.

That's another routine we've gotten into. His nightmares are getting less frequent. Not nightly, like when he first showed up, but a few times a week. He wakes up screaming, and I run to his room asking what's wrong. He never tells me, so I just hold him and tell him it'll be okay. That's the only time he lets me hold him. The boy might pretend he's a man, but those nights, he needs a mama, and I'm always happy to oblige, for a little while at least. The only way for him to drift back to sleep is reading him *The Cat in the Hat*. I don't argue if he wants it nightly, or repeated three times before he sleeps. It's what he needs, and with all my Google searching, that's one thing I learned: do what they need to feel safe.

Kooper

A quick glance out the front window shows five motorcycles pulling in. My heart's in my throat as I hear the pounding their engines made.

I smile at the kids, faking it so much my jaw aches. "Do me a favor and let me know who the shark ghost is. I'll be back soon."

Teddy does the cutest chin lift ever, saying he has my back without words.

Buddy boy, I got yours. Don't you worry about it.

Opening the hall closet, I angle my back to the TV so the kids don't see what I'm doing. I reach for the top shelf and pull down my Remington. Loading it quickly, I walk out the front door, pushing the screen door open with the barrel as I smile down at my guests, who parked in front of the porch.

"Good morning. Can I help you with anything?"

Not going to lie, I totally think I'm smug as shit when they all hesitate to get off their bikes.

Yeah, dumbasses, I ain't letting you take my kids.

Wait, "my kids"?

Shit, I'm already claiming them. That's one rule for being a foster parent: don't get too attached.

Too late, looks like I already am.

My smugness dies as the biggest of the bunch—and probably the sexiest man I have ever seen in my life—slides off his seat, as graceful as water rolling off rocks, and stalks toward me.

My mouth's drier than a dryer sheet and tastes fouler. The man has bulk from what I can see, and it's all in a yummy way. His sunglasses are the type that cost more than a reasonable person should pay, but damn, do they look good on him. I only notice he has no helmet, like the rest of them, because I'm drawn to his hair more than I should be. I have no idea if it's 'cause I'm turned on or just jealous as shit that his dirty-blond hair—emphasis more on dirty—is silky and has a wave to it as it drifts just past his shoulder blades. That and his full beard have me wondering if he's more lion than anything. I mean, it's a lot of hair in one area, like a mane. *Is this guy some kind of king of the pack?* He definitely has the alpha male thing going on. As well as the hunting prey part, especially since he doesn't seem to stop or take his eyes off the house for a second, only halting when I cock the shotgun.

"Where are they?"

His growl sends a shiver over me. I hope he sees it as fear. I would rather him think I'm scared than the fact that his deep, husky voice has another effect on me.

"And who might that be?"

"Don't play dumb with me, bitch. I know they're here. I want to see my niece and nephew right goddamn now."

Yeah, fuck the lust. This guy is definitely on my shit list. I can just scroll the internet and find a Thor lookalike to cure whatever draw I had for him for a second. The second before he spoke, that is.

"First off, don't call me bitch. And second, I don't know who you are or who your niece and nephew are."

"Quit with the bull, honey. We know Teddy and Grace are here. If you know what's best for you, you'll let their uncle see them before we stop playing nice," one of the other bikers still on his ride jumps in, speaking for the group.

Kooper

I spare the guy a look, not foolish enough to take my eyes off the man before me for more than a second. He wears the same glasses. Big fucker too. But while the god before me has more hair than I do—which is a fuck-ton—this one has his hair slicked back to show a widow's peak. Just enough 'stache and beard on him to be more than noticeable but less than using some special gels to maintain.

"Nice? Pretty sure I'm the one with the gun. Now tell me who the hell you are."

"Think that will stop him?" From my periphery, I see his head bob to the beast man before me, the one claiming to be the kids' uncle. "Don't think you want to try it."

I should stand my ground, but against my will, my eyes travel up and down the man who hasn't backed down. His fists are tight at his sides. Wonder if he's contemplating using them against me. I might have the gun—well, the only one with it out, anyway. I'm not an idiot. These boys are packing. But despite my show—for really, it's all show, because I can only get off one round, two if rushed—we all know they can overtake me.

"Doesn't matter," the beast growls in response to my question about who he is.

Is he seriously playing this stupid game with me over what his name is? I might be one against half a dozen, but I will shoot first.

From the clench in his jaw, he must realize I'm not backing down without knowing some idea of who he is.

"Chains."

I barely control my eye roll. "Legal name, dumbass."

"What the fuck did you say to me?" He takes a step forward, hands clenched even tighter, and the men get off their bikes as if in a dance sequence.

I don't hesitate. Pulling the trigger, I fire into the dirt at his feet. He pauses and glares up at me as I cock my shotgun again and aim it at his center mass. "Damn right, I want a legal name. Only two people know who I have inside, me and my friend, and you don't have tits. Now stop acting like a pussy and prove to me you're their uncle. We'll start off slow. Your name, asshole. What is it?"

Through clenched teeth, he snarls, "James Randall."

"And what was your sister's middle name?"

"Are you kidding me with this shit?"

I don't hide my sarcasm. "Does it look like I'm kidding you?"

"Fine. It was Janet."

"No, that was what was on paper. What did the family call her?"

Taking off his sunglasses, he tilts his head to the side as he pauses and looks me over slowly. "You knew Jennie?" His voice changes tone for a moment.

"The name." I hold firm. I'm not about to show I'm anything but badass, but come on. The guy did that slow look up and down on a girl. I'm practically a puddle of goo on the ground from that look. Especially from the intensity that his light brown eyes have right now. So light they're almost yellow. Not yellow like the sun, more like a metallic gold, ones I would have no problem looking at for a very long time.

If things were different, of course.

"Dammit. We called her Dammit Janet."

A twitch of a smile touches my lips. "She hated that movie."

"Who didn't?" He doesn't smile, but the intensity isn't rolling off him as much. I almost feel like I can breathe, as his anger had been choking me even with him off the front steps.

"We done?" His eyebrow quirks up. It's a neat trick, one I've always wished I possessed.

"One more. What was her favorite ice cream?"

He shakes his head before he even speaks. "Trick question. She didn't have one."

"Not as kids, but she did. What was it? If you are who you claim you are, then you know this."

I watch as his eyes draw together before he looks down and then back at his friends, who just shrug. I'm not trying to trick him, but I need to know if he's legit. Jennie may have been a lot of things, but getting tied to trouble was her well-known trait. And from what Izzy showed me of how she died, and what we knew of her activities prior to death, the kids weren't safe. That's why they're with me. The people she associated with were known for many things, but none for being a loving parent. More like stealing kids *from* loving parents.

"Vanilla." He pauses, and I almost pull the trigger on him before turning it on his friends. "Two scoops of vanilla that she topped with a can of Diet Coke and five cherries on the stem and called a cherry float. Tasted like shit."

"Don't knock it. We trademarked it when we invented it."

His eyes widen when he realizes who I am. I never met him, but Jennie and I were pretty close for a while. There was no doubt he would have heard about me and I him. I doubt he got my name, but that ice cream shit was something we created during a semester of community college finals when we were tired but needed the sugar to keep us up.

"Great. Now that we did *that* song and dance, let me see my family."

"Not so fast, dumbass. I might agree you are who you say you are, but that doesn't mean I'm letting you see my kids."

"They aren't yours, bi—" My head twitch has him changing his word. "—woman. They're mine. Jennie always wanted her kids to be with family. With Gran dead, that leaves me. So get out of the way."

"Again, not going to happen. And before you piss and moan any more, I'll tell you why. First off, Jennie didn't leave a will."

"What?"

"Exactly, which means they belong to the state. Also, no way in hell will the state give custody of her kids, family or not, to a felon who just got out of jail. How long have you been out, anyway? Like a week or something?"

"Try three hours."

My brows fly up my forehead. "You got out today? Are you fucking insane?"

"No, just want my family. You get it? *Mine.* Not yours. Don't think I didn't hear you claim them. They ain't yours, so get that out of your head. They belong with me and are coming with me."

Oh my God, I can't even believe this guy. He's a one-track-mind asshole. Did he even think this through? He's right that they aren't mine, but I'm not about to let someone, even if they are family, just take them from me without knowing they're safe. I wasn't instantly a queen at this whole parenting thing, but even I know the basics that are needed with kids. Does he? Ten to one, he has no fucking clue.

My anger at the audacity of this guy has me venting more than I probably should about the personality traits I've learned from the last few weeks of being Teddy and Grace's sole provider.

"Sure, and where will they stay, huh? You got a place? Or do you live with these guys? You got somewhere for them to sleep? 'Cause Grace and Teddy can't sleep in the same room. And Grace needs to have lullaby music to fall asleep to that you have to reset twice for her to stay asleep. Teddy, he might not need music, but he does need a nightlight. And when he comes in your room at night, 'cause it will happen with the nightmares, you better not have anyone with you. The last thing that six-year-old boy needs is to see you finally getting your dick sucked by, I'm sure, the willing groupies you have around your place."

With the way his cheeks hollow, he must be biting them to keep from screaming at me, or just at his lack of planning. I know I won the bet. Wish I'd put money on it; could have used the extra cash. Seriously, did the guy really think he was just going to roll out of here with them?

"Besides, how the fuck are they supposed to come with you? Do you have car seats that strap to the backs of those bikes of yours?"

Breathing deep, I lower the gun, not putting it down completely. I'm not that stupid. But I have to see it from his side. They're his family, but he needs to know it all. Well, not all, but a little more, at least till I trust him completely.

"Besides, motorcycles terrify the kids."

"What the fuck?" This comes from the biker who spoke earlier.

I nod to the group, taking my time to look them over. They're in various leather, clean enough but definitely falling under the scruffy definition compared to clean-cut. "I don't know why. We've seen some in town. The noise bugs the shit out of them, but I usually can get them settled after a bit. But seeing one, that really sets them off. Grace ends up clinging to me like a monkey for hours, if not days. And Teddy shuts down completely, and his nightmares are the worst." I shake my head and feel the pangs of sadness just thinking about the night I'm sure Teddy will have after this. "If you care for them, which I'm sure you do if you came here before thinking twice about getting laid first, like most people do after they get out of prison, then think this through. They don't know you—I mean, not really. You're a name, nothing more right now. Teddy recalls you from what Jennie has told him. Grace, well, she has a picture of you as a kid, but that's about it. Their lives have been shitty lately. I'm not saying I'm making it all sunshine and rainbows, but at least with me, they can count on someone who will have their back."

"I'll have their back." His growl is back again, but his glare isn't half as intense as the first time.

Kooper

"I'm sure you will, just not right now. I'm not trying to replace you. I'm just saying think it through."

"She's right, man," the other one mutters.

Chains runs his hand through his hair. Why is that such a turn-on? "Shit. They're the only family I got left." I can hear the exhaustion in his voice. I've known that type of exhaustion. The kind that eats at your soul, making you feel helpless but knowing you have to keep fighting even if it's taking more strength than you ever knew you had.

"And *you* are the only one they have left." Fuck, I need to compromise on this. Not for me but for them. "Look, how about we plan for a dinner in a week? You come back in a truck or something, spend some time getting to know them. We do that for a few months and see where it leads."

He takes a moment to look at the ground before he raises his head and puts his sunglasses back on. Nodding once to me, he walks back to his bike, sliding his leg over it smoothly.

Wow, okay, didn't expect him to agree so easily. Guess this guy can see sense after all. Just have to break it down for the big ox.

"I'll be back tonight."

He starts his engine just as I take a step off the porch. "Wait, what? Tonight? No, a week or something. Give them time." Panic is setting in. I need time to prepare for this guy at my house. I know my body is sending me all the signals that it wouldn't take much for me to hump his leg. He's pretty with a capital *P*. I want him, and my body is saying it's *craving* him in such a short time of knowing him. But my head—thank God—knows it's beyond bad. I need more time in my head to get my body under control before I spend any length of time with this guy.

Even with his sunglasses on, I can feel his eyes lock with mine. "Tonight."

As the group peels out of the drive, I really hope someone heard me scream that we eat at six. Otherwise, the guy's going to be extremely disappointed if he shows up after eight and we're all in bed.

Made in the USA
Coppell, TX
20 January 2026

66367986R00272